WHEN FRIENDS BECOME LOVERS

FIFTEENTH BOOK IN THE BRIGANDSHAW CHRONICLES

PETER RIMMER

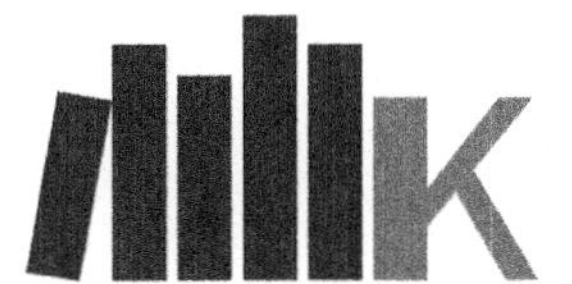

ABOUT PETER RIMMER

~

Peter Rimmer was born in London, England, and grew up in the south of the city where he went to school. After the Second World War, aged eighteen, he joined the Royal Air Force, reaching the rank of Pilot Officer before he was nineteen. At the end of his National Service, he sailed for Africa to grow tobacco in what was then Rhodesia, now Zimbabwe.

The years went by and Peter found himself in Johannesburg where he established an insurance brokering company. Over 2% of the companies listed on the Johannesburg Stock Exchange were clients of Rimmer Associates. He opened branches in the United States of America, Australia and Hong Kong and travelled extensively between them.

Having lived a reclusive life on his beloved smallholding in Knysna, South Africa, for over 25 years, Peter passed away in July 2018. He has left an enormous legacy of unpublished work for his family to release over the coming years, and not only they but also his readers from around the world will sorely miss him. Peter Rimmer was 81 years old.

To read more about Peter's life, please visit his website: https://www.peterrimmer.com/novelist/author/

ALSO BY PETER RIMMER

~

The Brigandshaw Chronicles

The Rise and Fall of the Anglo Saxon Empire

Book 1 - Echoes from the Past

Book 2 - Elephant Walk

Book 3 - Mad Dogs and Englishmen

Book 4 - To the Manor Born

Book 5 - On the Brink of Tears

Book 6 - Treason If You Lose

Book 7 - Horns of Dilemma

Book 8 - Lady Come Home

Book 9 - The Best of Times

Book 10 - Full Circle

Book 11 - Leopards Never Change Their Spots

Book 12 - Look Before You Leap

Book 13 - The Game of Life

Book 14 - Scattered to the Wind

Book 15 - When Friends Become Lovers

~

Standalone Novels

All Our Yesterdays

Cry of the Fish Eagle

Just the Memory of Love

Vultures in the Wind

In the Beginning of the Night

The Asian Sagas

Bend with the Wind (Book 1)

Each to His Own (Book 2)

The Pioneers

Morgandale (Book 1)

Carregan's Catch (Book 2)

Novella

Second Beach

WHEN FRIENDS BECOME LOVERS

First published in Great Britain in December 2022 by

KAMBA PUBLISHING, United Kingdom

10 9 8 7 6 5 4 3 2 1

PART 1

JUNE 1995 – ESCAPISM

1

Six months after leaving Rabbit Farm on the Isle of Man and buying an apartment on the thirty-first floor of his brother Phillip's Manhattan apartment building, Randall Crookshank had still not written a word. Martha had gone back to work a month after the baby was born, leaving Phillip, the stay-at-home venture capitalist, and Ivy, the live-in nanny, to look after the baby. Martha had everything she wanted, exactly as she wanted. It made Randall laugh. Whether his sister-in-law had given Phillip what he wanted was another question. For his brother, the call of the African wilds was always in his head, wealth and life in New York never his passion. Both men were bored. Neither of them had anything to do. They had inherited small fortunes from their maternal grandfather, leaving them financially independent. Randall's passion was writing books; Phillip's, the African bush.

Randall got up from the couch and walked to the big floor-to-ceiling window and stared at New York's skyscrapers. The sun was shining. The noise of the traffic was muted. Meredith had gone to her art class leaving two-year-old Douglas with Ivy on the forty-ninth floor. He was bored. Bored out of his mind. No story in his head. No one talking to him. No story to live in. All he had was the noise and bustle of people, the day-to-day trivia of people. To write, Randall had to go back to Rabbit Farm and upset Meredith. As Phillip had agreed, 'If you want a happy marriage, it's simple: do what your wife wants.'

The phone rang on the small table to the right of the big plate-glass window. Randall picked up the receiver.

"Randall Crookshank speaking."

"How are you today?... Are you talking to me?... It's your publisher, Belinda Chang."

"I know who it is, Belinda. What do you want this time? I'm so sick of book tours and literary festivals I could scream. I thought all a writer had to do was write books. That selling the books was the job of the publisher. Why the publisher gets the lion's share of the money."

"We have to keep you constantly in the eye of the public in order to sell your books."

"I thought they sold themselves. That a good book sold itself."

"Can you come to lunch?"

"I suppose so. I've nothing else to do. I can't write in New York. I can only write in peace and solitude. I want to go back to Rabbit Farm."

"Your poor wife."

"That's the problem. In life, there is always a catch... Who's coming to lunch?"

"A film director. He wants you to write the film script for *Love Song*."

"That's the one book I wish I had never written. It's light and fluffy. Little people, happy in suburban England."

"Why people love the book so much. They relate to your characters. They feel at home in your book."

"I'm not writing the film script. And that's final."

"Please, Randall."

"Why doesn't anyone ever think of what I want? You've made up my mind. I'm going back to Rabbit Farm."

"Are you serious? You just bought yourself an apartment."

"Had to invest my money in something. Tell the man to get a professional scriptwriter. I'm a novelist. Or I was. Sorry, Belinda."

"Why are men always so difficult? Okay. Have a nice day. What are you going to write about if you return to the Isle of Man?"

"Shakespeare. William Shakespeare. A fictional story about the great playwright and how all those plays came from an uneducated, self-taught man who had no connection to the aristocracy, let alone the Kings of England. It's going to be called *Shakespeare's Friend*. I've been doing my research. You know there's always been a question mark over whether Shakespeare wrote those plays."

"Do you think he did?"

"Maybe. Did you know his son could barely read? I think the man who ran a theatre had some help with the writing. Whoever it was had a deep insight into the lives of kings, dukes, princes and fools... How does it sound?"

"You're out of your mind."

"Will Villiers Publishing publish it?"

"Probably."

"Have a beautiful day, beautiful Belinda. I'm going upstairs to get my brother and take him to Harry B's, the best pub in Manhattan."

"Who is Shakespeare's friend?"

"A young English aristocrat who loves writing plays but wants to remain anonymous. A man who likes to be part of the theatre while remaining unknown."

"Are you writing about yourself by any chance?"

"Of course not. I could not have written a single play of Shakespeare's in a million years. He and his friend were far too good. Their minds so clear they could see right through the human psyche in utter revelation of the human condition in all its manifestations. From Macbeth to Romeo and Juliet. From love, to comedy, to tragedy. The two friends saw the inside of history, the inside of the mind, as clearly as I'm looking through my plate-glass window across the sun-washed skyline of New York."

"Didn't the friend want to be famous? Go down in history?"

"He preferred to live a private life and enjoy himself. He already had what he wanted: an ancient title. A castle. All the money a man could ever need. Why would a man like that want to be famous? We only have one life. He wanted to enjoy his life and not be torn apart by an avaricious public. Fulfilling his own dreams was all that mattered. And having some fun with Shakespeare and the other players. He wanted his plays to live forever, not himself."

"What's the friend's name?"

"I don't know. Nobody does. That's the quandary of history. Who was he? Who wrote Shakespeare's plays?... How is Villiers Publishing today?"

"Work. It's all work. Please come to lunch, Randall. You don't have to write the film script. Just talk about the book. Make Norman feel comfortable. People like to see what they are getting. They want to meet the author of the book, Randall. Come over to the office and we'll go and meet him together. You said you got bored. Give you something to do. He's nice. Interesting. Creative like you. Please, Randall."

"How can I resist a beautiful girl?"

"Why can't you write in New York?"

"Too many people churning up my mind. Too many temptations."

"Am I temptation, Randall?"

"Of course you are. Any pretty girl smiling at a thirty-seven-year-old man is a temptation. Away on Rabbit Farm I can live in my books without interruption. You try writing a book with people all around you."

"I wish I could. All I ever wanted to do."

"Then try."

"Will you help me?"

"Temptation, Belinda. I'm a married man with an almost two-year-old son."

"Are you happy?"

"No one in this life is happy. Don't be ridiculous. We like to think we're happy. We say we're happy. Sometimes we are. Why do we want to escape into books? Films? Alcohol? Life's a permanent chase to find what we want. Chasing the phantom. Like Shakespeare and his friend. Shakespeare produced the plays in that wonderful round theatre in London. The Globe Theatre. His friend sat in a room at the top of his family castle writing plays to escape and find his happiness in *Romeo and Juliet*. Or vent his anger in *Macbeth*."

"All I want to be is a good wife and a good mother."

"I'll be in your office at half past twelve."

"Thank you, Randall."

"My pleasure."

"Is the book fact or fiction?"

"What's the difference? What's fact yesterday is fiction tomorrow. I'll make it look like fact. Make the friend real. Give him a life. Apart from his plays, how much do we know about Shakespeare? Writing my book is going to be fun. Making the two friends come alive. Bringing the Shakespeare theatre alive. All those actors. All of them male. All with wives and girlfriends. One big, lovely story. A story, beautiful Belinda. Like all the other stories in history. Some tell us they are fact, like the Bible. Some hide behind fiction. The truth. What is the truth? Does anyone even know the truth about life? I don't think so. If we did, the world wouldn't stay in its permanent mess. One day kings and feudal barons. One day communism. Another time it's capitalism they call democracy. None of them work. They all fall down. And then come all those lovely dictators. Does anyone in this crazy world know what they are doing?"

THE RESTAURANT WAS EXPENSIVE. Randall had showered and changed his clothes to look the part of a successful author. All part of what his publishers expected of him. The man was in his mid-fifties with a strong handshake and a kind smile.

"I've read all your books, Mr Holiday. Please sit down. Belinda told me on the phone you don't write film scripts. Never mind. Tell me more about why you wrote *Love Song*."

"What can I tell you that isn't in the book, Mr Landry?"

"Please call me Norman."

"Of course."

"Most romantic novels have no substance. Yours has a deep understanding of why we need to love another person. You reached deep into the core of the human condition... Do you like to be called Randall Crookshank or Randall Holiday? Does love last, Randall?"

"Probably not. We settle down with each other, the early passion lost to life's daily routine."

"And you won't write me the film script."

"I don't like the way the film opens me to the general public. A book is an intimate exchange between an author and a single reader. One at a time. A conversation between two friends. Why I liked the use of a pseudonym to write my books. Like Shakespeare's friend, I like to stay anonymous."

"Who is Shakespeare's friend you are talking about?"

"The man who wrote his plays."

"Didn't William Shakespeare write his plays?"

"Some think not."

"Do you want me to turn your book into a film?"

"That's not up to me to decide. Villiers Publishing bought my book. The publisher gets to say what happens to it. Why do you want to make a film out of a light and fluffy story set in suburban England? There's no substance to my book. Just the same old story of ordinary people going about their daily lives. Why do you think it will work?"

"You have a deep insight into human nature, Randall. I love your dialogue. Your characters are real to me. You don't mind if I change your leading character's nationality?"

"You've bought the film rights to my book. You can do what you like with it. There's nothing more for me to say or do."

"The story won't change. I bought the story, not just the film rights."

"And my name that has sold millions of books. You bought the name Randall Holiday, Mr Landry."

"That helps. Let's have a drink and get to know each other. What's your tipple today, Belinda? Let the three of us have a lovely lunch together. Villiers Publishing are paying. So, they tell me you were once from Africa. What a shame the British Empire has collapsed. In another time we all had so many places to go to. British colonies. French colonies. Spanish. Dutch. Portuguese. German. To live in colonial comfort. Such a shame it's all over. Now we are in America. Even if you don't do the writing, can I put your name on the script? It's all about making a film written by a famous author with a wide readership. Of course, my film will help sell more of your books. We all scratch each other's backs in a material world... How do you like living in New York?"

"My wife loves it. You've read my book. Do what the woman wants."

"What you going to have, Randall?"

"I'll have a drink. I find a drink brings people together who don't know each other. The reason for this lunch. Everything in the entertainment business is one big promotion. You sign books. You do interviews. Most writers like shouting their mouths off. As if they know the answers to everything. It's so much easier to tell other people what to do if you don't have to do the job yourself. They like to be controversial to gain maximum publicity. Trouble is, most of us writers don't know what we are talking about. We pander to our public. Give them what they want. Say what they want to hear. When communism was the go-to way to run a country, writers wrote about the perfect life with everybody equal and sharing everything. When it failed, like all forms of government, they wrote about the perfect life under a democracy. Now democracy is one big swindle to give the voters what they want by borrowing money the government won't be able to pay back, which gets the smart-arse politicians elected. No one is sure what is going to happen in the future. But it's really quite simple. Under modern democracy the countries one by one will go bankrupt. The savers who lent the money to the banks and the governments will lose their money. The politicians will run away and say it wasn't their fault. And the cycle will start from scratch all over again. And who will suffer most? The poor, of course. The poor sods who were conned by the politicians into thinking that all they had to do was vote for them and be given it all for nothing. No work. No thinking. Just casting their wonderful democratic vote. That's what writers like to shout about to keep themselves in the media and make themselves famous. I prefer to go to the peace and solitude of my smallholding I call Rabbit Farm in the isolation of the Isle of Man and write a book. A book for me and that one reader. A conversation between friends. An escape for both of us. Like Shakespeare's friend, that is how I find my personal satisfaction. Why I don't give a damn about your film, Norman Landry. But don't let me stop you making money and helping beautiful Belinda do her job. If only I could persuade my lovely wife to go to Rabbit Farm and become an artist painting nice pictures, I would be so happy. She tried writing kids' books on Rabbit Farm. Sold the book to Villiers Publishing for fifty thousand dollars. Unfortunately, they did not publish her book and now I'm stuck on the thirty-first floor in Manhattan. Now, about that drink. Make mine a double whisky. As Phillip's friends in Harry B's say quite often: 'Let's get started.' Are you married, Norman? Do you have lovely children? What brought your family to America? Tell me about your life. I much prefer hearing about other people's lives than talking about my own. Other people's lives are the material for my books. I steal their stories. Call me a thief. It's how it works. Or some of it... Am I boring you, Norman?"

"Let's get started."

"Now you're talking... Thank you, Mr Waiter. Mine's a double whisky with a bottle of soda. Whisky and soda... A favourite of my family going back into history when the British ruled a quarter of the world's population. For better or worse. Once upon a time we even ran America until those lovely, popular politicians and generals started a liberation movement and had themselves the American Revolution. Now it's America's turn to run the world through the money markets and the power of Wall Street. Who knows, it may even succeed for a few more years. A few more decades. Who knows, it may even last as long as the British Empire... Thank you, Mr Waiter... Cheers, Norman. Cheers, Belinda. To happiness and world domination. To *Love Song*, the film. To life in general. A beautiful restaurant. A beautiful girl. And a double whisky. What more could a man of thirty-seven ever want?... Now. Where were we? Oh, it's your turn, Mr Landry. If I've been rude, please forgive me. As a writer I'm inclined to forget I'm employed by Villiers Publishing. Without Villiers Publishing my books would never have been published. All those one-on-one conversations with readers would not have happened. We are all inclined to forget what we owe other people."

"Will you proofread the script before we turn on the cameras? Check the dialogue? Make sure your story has the same lovely message of family happiness. I want the people who watch my film to get your message."

"And what's my message, Norman?"

"That it's not all bad. That life is not all bad if people live a simple hard-working life and look after each other."

"And if I don't like your script?"

"You'll have to write it yourself, Randall."

"You're good, Norman."

"I know I am. How's your whisky and soda going down?"

"Perfectly. Where did your family come from originally?"

"France. Paris. My great-grandparents were ordinary folk from the not-so-rich side of Paris. So they sought a new life in America... The fish looks good. They say this is one of the best restaurants for fish in Manhattan."

"Why would an American director want to make a film about suburban England?"

"Because yours is a good book. A good story. Why so many people in America have read your book. Why you have an American publisher... We'll have a nice bottle of white wine to go with the fish and then see what we fancy."

2

By the time they parted company, everyone happy, Randall was nicely tipsy. He caught a cab back to his apartment building. On the thirty-first floor there was no sign of Meredith. For Randall the chance of luck in life was in the reality. His best friend was his brother. His brother, his best friend. In the lift up to the forty-ninth floor he was smiling, the booze still controlling his happy mood. When Phillip opened the door the boredom on his brother's face evaporated.

"You want to go to Harry B's?"

"Why not?"

"Had lunch with Belinda and a new film director. Enough whisky and wine to make me want to go on drinking. Are you alone?"

"Ivy took the kids to the park. Had enough of studying for today. She works hard for her degree. Martha won't be back for hours. She often works until ten o'clock. Don't even have dinner together. The poor woman is usually so tired she wants to go straight to bed. And then she can't sleep. Too many work problems in her head. I have no idea why she does it. We don't need to make money. But she says she loves being a partner in a successful advertising company. I don't understand some people. Let alone my wife. When you've got enough money to live comfortably, why not get the hell out of the way? Relax. Enjoy oneself. Instead, she craves the rush of business. Shall we walk to the pub? I've done absolutely nothing all day. What's a film director got to do with lunch?"

"*Love Song*. My trivial little novel that I wrote out of desperation when I couldn't dream up a big story is going to be made into a Hollywood movie. *Love Song*. It was probably the damn title that caught their attention. Let's catch a cab. If we walk I may drive away my thirst. You know the old game that we started in the Centenary Club. Once we had a few we went on drinking until we were drunk. Do you remember that night on the way back from the club when I drove Dad's truck into the ditch? I was seventeen. You were nineteen. I didn't even have a driving licence. In the bush in Rhodesia in those days driving drunk without a licence didn't matter. All you might kill was a wild animal or yourself."

"Or your poor brother."

"You couldn't even walk straight. How we got that truck back on the dirt road was a miracle. Did you have any lunch, Phillip?"

"Enough. I'll eat a couple of packets of chips. I like Thursdays in Harry B's."

"What the hell are we doing in New York?"

"I have no idea. The women, I suppose. Is Meredith happy?"

"She likes going to her art classes. Having people around her. Is Martha happy?"

"Who knows, old boy? What women say and what they think are two different worlds."

"I'm only happy when writing a book."

"And I'm only happy running my safari camp with Jacques and the others in the African bush."

"We have wives."

"I know we do. You had a first wife, don't forget. Do you ever hear from Amanda?"

"Not a word. She wants me to keep out of James Oliver's life. And maybe she's right. In the past when I've seen my son, he gets confused. He's been brought up by two women. Two lesbians. His life is having two mothers. Not a mother and father. I'm better for him keeping out of his way. When he's old enough to understand what happened and make his own decisions we'll have to see. Wow. These lifts get to the ground quickly. Come on. There's a cab right outside. Let's get rat-arsed drunk and forget the world. You know my big problem, Phillip? I think I've written most of my books. What the hell am I going to do with the next forty years? Without the farm to run, Dad has the same problem. He's got enough money and too much time on his hands. Lucky he bought that block of London flats in the days when you could get money out of Rhodesia. From six thousand acres on World's View to a flat in Chelsea on the River Thames. They say in old age you get used to having nothing to do. Just the old daily routine. Oh, well. And if we didn't have money we'd really be complaining. Life! What's wrong with us, Phillip? What the hell's wrong with me?"

"You achieved all your goals too soon. We all need a challenge. And neither of us have got one anymore... Harry B's, driver. It's round the corner."

"Why didn't you walk?"

"My brother is only half drunk and didn't want to squash the feeling."

"The Carruthers brothers on safari, Phillip!"

"You wish."

"Memories. Life is all about having good memories. These old jokes about the mythical Carruthers in good old colonial India. My, how England has changed in Father's lifetime. We've had a good life. Let's enjoy the rest of it. You never know what's coming next. Is that pretty girl going to be behind the bar? The one who works for a recording studio during the day. She gives me the eye. Flashes her tits. I don't get it. She knows I'm married."

"But you're rich and famous. No one rich and famous stays married to the same person in America. The rich keep trading the older wife for a younger one. The young one wants a rich husband she can soak in a divorce settlement."

"You think they just marry an older man for money?"

"And fame. They like to socialise with celebrities so they can feel important. Many young girls only have their looks to sell. And looks fade. By the time they are thirty the game is over. The hunt for their future is over. In America it's all about money, Randall. Securing a future. Back in the past all the women had to do was find a husband when they were young and pretty, and have lots of babies. Back then, divorce was taboo. Now, it's mayhem. Marry, get divorced and soak the rich bastard in the divorce court... Here we are. Are you still thirsty? That old slippery slide... Give the cab driver a good tip. Got to tip well in America. Welcome to New York."

"I've been here six months."

"Poor bastard."

"If I'm a bastard, brother, so are you... Oh, just look at that. She's behind the bar. I knew it was my lucky day."

"What about your wife?"

"I can look, can't I? No law against looking. She's seen me. She's smiling all over her face. Let's get started."

"On the barmaid or the drink?"

"Both. My boredom is evaporating."

"You're a dirty old man."

"I'm not that old."

"We're both approaching forty."

"You see, a girl like that is a thirty-seven-year old's temptation. Why Meredith should want to go back to Rabbit Farm and keep her husband out of harm's way. What's the girl's name again?"

"Amelia."

"Such a lovely name. From beautiful Belinda to Amelia all in an afternoon. Come on. In we go. Hello, Amelia. How's work at the studio?"

"Slow. Why I'm here. Written any good books lately?"

"That's my problem. Can't write in a city. Make it two malt whiskies. For me a bottle of soda. My brother drinks it neat."

"I know what he drinks. How are you today, Phillip?"

"Fine, thank you. Where's Terry?"

"The owner has taken the evening off. Can you believe it? I'm meant to be running the place. It's chaos. How Terry keeps control of the food and the drinks all at the same time I have no idea. It's going to be fun chasing up and checking the stock. Two whiskies coming up for Terry's best customers."

"Did you see that, Phillip?"

"Why are you whispering?"

"When she bent down she flashed them at me."

"She was just getting your soda bottle out of the fridge. It's under the bar."

"What are you two whispering about? There you go. I'm running one tab for the both of you."

She was smiling sweetly at Randall, her lips slightly pursed, her eyes laughing at him. For the first time all day, his boredom evaporated. Randall tried to make himself feel guilty without success. Anyway, he rationalised with himself, there was nothing wrong with looking. What the game of life was all about.

"They're going to make a film of *Love Song*, Amelia."

"Get out of here! Really?"

"A Hollywood movie."

"Get out of here! I'd love to be part of making a movie. Who's doing it?"

"Norman Landry."

"Get out of here! He's famous. I love his movies. It's fun working in a recording studio producing songs for artists. But filming a Hollywood movie, that's my big ambition... That one went down quickly."

"Give me another one."

"I'd give you anything to get into Hollywood. Norman Landry, wow... You want one too, Phillip?"

"I'm fine for the moment."

"Have a drink, brother... Give us two more. And make them doubles."

A comfortable seat on a barstool up at a bar. A pretty, smiling, tit-flashing barmaid, the company of his best friend. What more could a man want? Randall smiled, enjoying himself. Looking around there was no one he recognised. As people left their offices after work the bar filled up, the pace too much for Amelia. Keeping control of a crowded bar was different.

"You want some help behind the bar? I used to run the bar at the Centenary Club when James had his night off. He was the barman. Now, he knew what he was doing. Never a penny missing from the till. Stock taking was just a formality."

"My brother is drunk. He'd mess it up, Amelia. You'd better phone Terry on his mobile. Why's it so crowded on a Thursday?"

"Terry told everyone I was going to be running his bar while he took a night off."

"Makes sense. They all like you, Amelia."

"They like looking at me, Randall. Do you like looking at me?"

"What a silly question. I'm not too drunk to help you run the bar."

"Come on then. Everyone, the famous author, Randall Holiday is going to help me behind the bar. Give Randall a cheer."

"You're nuts."

"Thank you for your kind words, brother. The girl needs help. Do you think I'll make some good tips? Oh, my goodness. What have I let myself in for? Poor Terry. He'll never balance his books. Here we go. A barman. I always wanted to be a barman. The buggers are clapping. How do I get in?"

"There's a flap at the end of the bar. You lift it up and walk through.

What a giggle. Everyone, Norman Landry is going to make a movie out of Randall's *Love Song*."

"Who the hell's Norman Landry? I want a drink."

"At your service, sir. What will it be?"

"Are you really a book writer?"

"Do you read books?"

"Haven't read a book since I left school. I want a beer."

"Coming up. How the hell does this cash register work?"

"You press the button. Put the beer on my tab."

"And if you walk out without paying?"

"Why on earth would I want to do that? Terry would never let me back again. Harry B's is the best bar in Manhattan. Amelia, the star of the show. Why is everyone in the bar laughing at me? All I want is my beer."

"How does that one look?"

"How did you know which one to give me?"

"Your empty bottle. I'm not that pissed. Tonight's the night, folks, for a celebration. Amelia and I are going to beat Terry's record tonight for the best take in an evening. Drink up. I'll drink with you when the clock strikes midnight. This is fun, Amelia. My boredom has gone. I'm going to apply to Terry for a job. If I can't write a book in New York, at least I can help run a bar."

Phillip was looking at him with a mock pained expression on his face.

"I thought we were going to have a nice evening together. Two brothers chatting about old times. I hate drinking on my own."

Randall smiled sweetly at his brother, put a hand on Amelia's shoulder so he could get round her without brushing her bottom, and went to serve a man waving an empty glass at the other end of the bar.

"That was nice."

"What was, Amelia?"

"Your hand on my shoulder."

He would have to be careful. Instead of just looking at a pretty girl behind a bar, he had touched her. The old two-year itch in a marriage had caught up with him again. He had promised Meredith to be faithful, to love her for the rest of his life. And now here he was playing games with a twenty-four-year-old, thirteen years his junior.

By ten o'clock the bar began to empty. It was a Thursday night, the conscientious knowing they had work to do the next day.

"You can handle it now, Amelia. I'm going back to the other side of the bar and talk to my brother."

"We're not going to break Terry's record."

"I forgot it was work tomorrow."

"Thank you, Randall."

"My pleasure."

"Did you make any tips?"

"They're all in your tip jar. I've poured myself a whisky. Put it on my tab. Wow. That was hard for a while. Writing books is a whole lot easier."

"If you know how to write. And have something to write about... Can you take me to the set when they make *Love Song*?"

"We'll have to see."

"You could put in a good word for me with Norman Landry."

"What about your employer?"

"Life is all about looking forward. Looking for a better opportunity."

"What about loyalty?"

"I'm loyal when I'm working. They get from me what they want. I get my salary. I was the one who introduced Manley and Thombs to Chad Fox and the bag-lady. And what a story that turned out to be. Put my employers firmly on the map. Sure, they thanked me but they didn't increase my salary. Loyalty is a double-edged sword, Randall. I want to succeed in life. To succeed you have to try everything that comes along. Great chances in life are few and far between... Do you love your wife?"

"Of course I do. I have a lovely wife and an almost two-year-old son."

"And where were they tonight?"

"Douglas is with my sister-in-law's nanny. Meredith went to her art class. She'll be home by now."

"But she wasn't home when you and Phillip came into the bar."

"They socialise after class."

"I'll bet they do. How long you been married?"

"We've been together a couple of years."

"Makes sense... Thanks for helping me, Randall."

"You're looking tired."

"Never easy doing two jobs."

Again the sweet smile. The knowing look. And as she bent down away from him to go into the fridge under the bar counter, the tight trousers pressed over her tight bum caught Randall's full attention.

"Stop looking, Randall."

"We'd better go home before I make a fool of myself."

"Only bit of sense all night. Back to our women. How it works, Randall, when you are a married man. Can't have both worlds. Can't have the comfort of home and children and chase other women. For better or worse: you remember that promise? Goodnight Amelia."

They walked home, both of them silent. Both of them, Randall suspected, thinking of Amelia's tight bottom. Both of them feeling guilty.

"She's got a nice arse."

"You can say that again... Martha, darling. How was your day at the office?"

"What's your brother doing here? Have you two been out boozing? I can smell the alcohol on your breath."

"Meredith wasn't home when we stopped on the thirty-first floor. He's come for Douglas."

"The children are both fast asleep in Ivy's bedroom. Let him sleep. Come up again in the morning. I don't know how I'd cope without Ivy. The good news is she passed her latest exam. Studying for an ecology degree through a correspondence course was tough going. So, you went to the pub. Was it Amelia's night on by any chance? That young lady flirts with every rich man who comes in the bar: married or single. You don't have to look guilty, Randall. Men are all the same. Why isn't your wife home at this time of night? She left Douglas with Ivy to attend an art class at lunchtime."

"They socialise after class."

"Do they now? I'm going to bed. I'm tired out. What a day. All go. Didn't stop for a moment. We got another new client. When you do the advertising job properly, word of mouth brings new clients running. Jaz and Franklyn are thrilled."

"Who got the new client?"

"Jack Webber. We made the right decision making him a partner. Bowden, Crookshank, Fairbanks and Webber is flourishing. I love a company when it works. Just wish I had enough time to get a good night's sleep. Are you coming to bed, Phillip?"

"In a minute. I'm going to take a shower."

"You do that. Just don't wake me when you come to bed."

3

When Randall let himself into his apartment he was all alone: his son was sleeping upstairs, his wife nowhere to be seen. He didn't even wish to listen to music, let alone watch television. He sat down plonk on the settee not knowing what to do. Had something gone wrong? Was Meredith all right?

After ten minutes of loneliness Randall's mind began to drift to his other son, the eight-year-old boy named James Oliver after his two old friends, the boy whose view on life would forever be twisted. Would his eldest son have a normal life with a wife and family? Or would he live in a world of homosexuality? When Randall came out of his reverie, he heard a key go into the front door. Randall stayed seated. The door closed quietly. He heard Meredith trip over the small Persian carpet that covered the short corridor from the front door of the apartment to the lounge.

"Damn that bloody carpet."

She was drunk, slurring her words.

"What are you doing, Randall? Why aren't you watching TV?"

"What are you doing, is more important. You're pissed."

"I just so love New York. There's so much to do. The place is so exciting. We all went out drinking. You think I'm drunk, you should have seen the rest of them. Why are you staring at me like that? It was just innocent fun."

Randall watched his wife open the door to the nursery.

"Where's Douglas? He's not in his room."

"Sleeping with Ivy and Carmen upstairs. Martha said leave him there until the morning."

"I'm going to bed."

"I'm sure you are."

"Can't a girl have a bit of fun with her friends every now and again? Anyway, what did you do? Did you go to Harry B's with Phillip to ogle that barmaid?"

"Are we having an argument?"

"I hope not. I hate arguing when I've had too much to drink. My new painting is nearly finished."

"I'll bet it is. What's his name?"

"What are you talking about?"

"You know perfectly well what I'm talking about."

"You're a lot older than me, Randall. And don't forget it. I'm still young. I deserve a night out with friends."

"We should go back to Rabbit Farm."

"Don't be ridiculous. You want a drink?"

"Haven't you had enough?"

"Probably. Have a drink."

"If you insist."

"How was your day?"

"They're making a film of *Love Song*."

"That's wonderful, darling."

"But I can't write. I want to go home to Polar Bear and the cats."

"This is our home. Living in New York we have another of your books being made into a film. Are you writing the script?"

"They want me to."

"That's wonderful. Are you going to pour the drinks? I just tripped over the carpet. Don't want to drop the whisky bottle. Having Ivy upstairs is such a blessing. Takes the pain out of motherhood. How much money are we going to make from the movie? You got to be on top of your publisher and publicist or they forget about you. There's more to being a successful author than just writing the books. When they hear I'm married to Randall Holiday people get so excited. Living in New York you stay in the public eye. Stuck in the remote Isle of Man they'd forget about you. I love New York. Rabbit Farm is boring. I can't sit and paint pictures day after day. There's no social life. No people to enjoy. And how am I going to sell my paintings? Painters, like writers, have to make themselves famous. Why those kids' books of mine didn't work. No one in New York had heard of Meredith. Now, that is nice. Cheers, darling. Don't be upset with me."

"Were all your drinking companions women?"

"Of course they weren't."

"And how old were the men?"

"My age. Maybe a bit younger. They're all learning to paint. I love artists and writers."

"Especially rich and famous writers."

"What are you getting at? I didn't marry you because you were rich and famous. I married you because I was five months pregnant."

"Would you have got yourself pregnant if I wasn't rich and famous? There is such a thing as the pill."

"Or a condom, Randall. My getting pregnant was just as much your fault as mine. We were too busy screwing each other to worry about contraception."

"You're probably right."

"I know I am... How's Phillip?"

"Bored. Why we went to the pub."

"So you did go to Harry B's. Was the girl there?"

"Matter of fact, she was."

"Did you look at her?"

"I suppose so. Did you look at the young men?"

"Of course. They're fellow aspiring artists. Why don't you turn on some music and stop making a mountain out of a molehill."

"You won't go back to Rabbit Farm?"

"Not unless you force me to."

"Then chances are I'll never write another book in my life. The rest of my life will be worthless."

"Every now and again you have to think of other people. People like your wife and your son. Now, let's stop arguing. Tell me more about the new movie. Is it going to be made in Hollywood? Don't you remember I read *Love Song* in handscript in that woodman's cottage in Wales where you'd been writing? Where I found you. The story captivated me. You had just finished the book. It's such a lovely story. Who's going to play the lead? Are we going to Hollywood? Oh, I so love America. Everything is so exciting. Why don't we sit up all night and drink and talk about your new film? I'm so proud of you, Randall. Douglas will be just fine with Ivy. Can

I sit on your lap? Cheers, darling. Down the hatch. Give me a kiss. This is all so exciting."

After the second whisky they were both giggling. Both having fun. Randall smiled inwardly at the simplicity of life: do what they want, and all goes well; everything in the garden of life is rosy. Alcohol. The cure and cause of so many problems. Talking about Norman Landry's movie to Meredith made the project worthwhile. The excitement was palpable on Meredith's face. When they went to bed drunk, Rabbit Farm was as far away as the moon. That place of solitude and comfort where wild bunny rabbits had lived back into antiquity. A place to cherish, a place to write, a place without screaming people with all their selfish evil instincts that made up the wrong side of the human condition: all the lies, all the cheating in every form of cheating, the permanent manipulating to get what people wanted in their endless pursuit of money. Drunk, with a drunk Meredith snoring next to him, Randall questioned the purpose of life, the reason for living, the reason why people existed. To Randall, soused in alcohol, his heart racing, his hangover wailing, it made the passage of life a pursuit without an ending, just an old body to be thrown in a grave to rot, or burned to ashes and scattered to the wind. Money, drink and the pursuit of women. Did she have a new boyfriend? Was he going to do anything about Amelia's bottom? When Randall fell into a drugged sleep, his dream was in turmoil, people everywhere, all arguing with each other, being nasty to each other, making each other's lives miserable. When Randall woke with the dawn his mouth felt like the bottom of a parrot cage. Meredith had stopped snoring, her naked body turned away from him. After trying to go back to sleep against the building noise of New York City, Randall got up and made himself a cup of tea. He felt dreadful.

"I'm never drinking alcohol again in my life."

By the time Meredith came out of her drunken sleep, Randall felt the first wave of his post-alcohol depression.

"There's always a price to pay for everything, you silly old fart."

"Are you talking to me, darling?"

"I was talking to myself. I hate hangovers."

"Join the club... What's on the menu today?"

"Absolutely nothing... You want some tea?"

"Tea and an aspirin. I have a splitting headache... Oh, my goodness. I just remembered. Douglas is upstairs with Martha."

"She'll be at work. We'd better go up and get the little bugger."

"I'll make you all a good breakfast. How do you feel about breakfast?"

"Vomiting. I'm never going to drink again."

"Until the next time."

"The aftermath is so depressing. Why do we drink, Meredith?"

"To have fun. We had a good giggle together that squashed our little argument. Give me a kiss and go make the tea. I'm so excited about the new movie. I've always wanted to visit Hollywood."

The phone rang all morning, Randall finding it difficult to focus. They all wanted something. Nora Stewart, Randall's publicist, had booked an interview for him on the David Letterman show. Henry Stone, Belinda Chang's boss at Villiers Publishing, and Randall's editor, wanted to know if he had started a new book: muddled by his hangover, Randall talked briefly of Shakespeare's friend, receiving no comment from the editor. Manfred Leon, Randall's agent, said he was still arguing with the movie company about the price they would have to pay Villiers Publishing for *Love Song*, ten per cent of which would go to Randall and ten per cent of that to Manfred. Like everything else, it was mostly about the pursuit of money. At lunchtime, when Randall's hangover had reached screaming point, a woman who said her name was Poppy Maddock phoned to discuss her rendition of a film script, having just finished reading *Love Song* for the second time. With his mind in a hungover muddle, Randall was unable to help.

"When are we going to meet?"

"Not today. I feel terrible. Don't I sound terrible?"

"Your voice is gruff. What's the matter?"

"Alcohol. Never drink alcohol. It destroys the mind."

"I'll phone you tomorrow."

"Please don't... How old are you?"

"Twenty-six. What's that got to do with it?"

"Have you written a film script before?"

"I have a degree in English Literature from Oxford University."

"I thought your accent was English. Good luck to you, Poppy. Have a nice day."

Sick of it all, Randall disconnected the phone.

"Poor, darling. What you need is a drink."

"Don't so much as mention the word. I'm going to the gym. Get on the treadmill and work it off. A drink like last night takes three days to get out of the system."

"Why did you pull the phone out?"

"Because I can't stand people. If we were on Rabbit Farm I'd go on a five-mile walk with Polar Bear. I miss my dog. I miss my cats. I miss the two collies we used to have. I really want to go home."

"Our home is here."

"No. Rabbit Farm is, where our pets are."

"Please stop talking about Rabbit Farm."

"How's your hangover?"

"Terrible. Just terrible. Why I want a drink."

"And start the cycle all over again."

"I suppose so... What are we going to do with Douglas?"

"Let him play with the cats."

"We don't have any cats."

"We do on Rabbit Farm. Seven of them. Look after yourselves. I'm off to the gym."

On the way past the kitchen Randall drank two pints of water. The walk to Stigley's gym made him feel better. An hour later, sweat pouring down his face, he felt better. Life was again worth the living. Back at the apartment there was no sign of Meredith or Douglas. Randall sat in the silent lounge listening to the rumble and noise of the outside traffic from down in the street, trying to think of something to do. Controlling himself from getting up and going to Harry B's, he waited for his wife to come home, Shakespeare and his friend unable to find in the hungover muddle of his mind. By six o'clock, Meredith and Douglas were still not home. The phone was still disconnected. After soaking himself in a hot bath he dressed, left the apartment and went upstairs to the forty-ninth floor. When Ivy opened the door Douglas smiled up at him. She was holding his hand.

"Is my wife with you?"

"No. Come in. Martha's at work as usual. Your brother went out. Don't know where he went."

"Did Meredith say where she was going?"

"Something about an art class."

"They don't paint on Fridays. Never have before. Thank you, Ivy. Come, Douglas. Give my love to the family."

"I can take care of Douglas. He's so quiet when I'm studying. Maybe Phillip went down to the pub. He had a hangover. Said it was all your fault. Just joking. I must get back to my books. Nice talking to a fellow African. Do you still miss Zimbabwe? I still miss the sun and space of Africa every day."

"Are you going home after you get your degree?"

"Whoever knows, Randall? Depends which way the wind blows. This job of looking after Carmen and having a room to live in while I study is just perfect. Life's full of luck. Go on. Go look for your brother. This time you can tell him it's his fault. How's the writing going?"

"It's not. Can't write in a city."

Convinced his wife had a lover, Randall walked to Harry B's. Phillip was up at the bar talking to Amelia, the place packed with people. Friday night at the pub. Everybody's favourite.

"What are you doing here, Randall?"

"I was going to ask you the same question. Meredith's gone out again. No idea where she went. We're on our own again. I'm going to drink lemonade."

"Don't be bloody ridiculous... Is there a problem?"

"She's got a lover. One of the lads from her art class. What else can keep her out at night? No note. No word. No nothing."

"Have a beer. You're not writing. What's the difference if you end up with a hangover? And don't jump to conclusions."

"I went on drinking with Meredith when she finally came home last night. Oh, well. Shit happens. What am I going to do with Douglas? I'm just no damn good at marriage. They must get bored with me."

"There's nothing worse than boredom."

"Hello, Amelia. How are you today?"

"Never better now I have both my favourite customers in the bar. A beer or a whisky?"

"A beer... She was right. Not till the next time. Oh, well."

"How's the new film going?"

"They're all on my back. Pulled out the phone. No peace for the wicked. And tonight, getting drunk is your fault, Phillip. What would either of us do without Ivy? I hate life when I'm not writing. It's so empty."

4

While Randall and Phillip were drinking in Harry B's, moaning about their lives, Meredith was putting the last touches to her painting, her teacher standing silently behind her shoulder.

"You can paint, Meredith. We either have it in us or we don't. You are one of the lucky ones who can take what's inside your head and put the images on canvas. I like the rabbit watching the dog. The wind in the trees. The mountain in the background. In one long day you have made a painting that will live on a wall forever. Where is it? I don't see America. The place is so desolate. The rabbit and the white dog are watching each other with palpable intensity. The rabbit full of fear. The dog's full of excitement. The hunter and the hunted... Are you going to try and sell your painting?"

"It's for my husband. He wants to go back to Rabbit Farm. My idea was to bring Rabbit Farm into our New York apartment and make Randall happy."

"Won't the painting make him more nostalgic?"

"I hope not. Thank you for letting me use the studio today. How did the others do? Strange, your Friday class is all women."

"Bored housewives looking for something to amuse themselves. It's more a social gathering than a lesson in the art of painting. None of them will ever be able to paint. But they pay me. A girl has to pay her bills.

Rents are expensive in New York. You're lucky to be married to a rich man. Never found a man I fancied with more than ten dollars in his bank account. The ones I like are artists. Artists never make money. Their paintings only sell for fortunes long after they are dead. The galleries and the auctioneers make the money. Writers are lucky. If they succeed, they get paid big bucks in their lifetime. So where is Rabbit Farm?"

"On the Isle of Man. Between the British mainland and Ireland. It's the most desolate place you could ever imagine. Freezing cold in winter. Rains and rains. No people. Randall loves it. I hate the place... Thanks for your help."

"Do you want me to wrap your painting as a surprise for Randall? I'd love to meet Randall Holiday. You're a lucky girl, Meredith."

"I hope so... What's the time?"

"Eight o'clock."

"I'm so sorry to keep you."

"My pleasure. When you have a party at home you can invite me to meet your husband and all those celebrities. There we are. All wrapped up in brown paper. Have a pleasant evening."

"Is it really any good?"

"I think so."

Not sure if Shelley liked her painting or the idea of meeting Randall Holiday, Meredith went downstairs, caught a cab, and with her painting firmly under her arm walked into the building of her apartment. Upstairs, the apartment was empty.

"Lovely, just lovely."

Upstairs she collected Douglas from Ivy, took him down to their empty apartment and put her son to bed. Alone, she sat down in the lounge.

"Now what?"

The painting, still wrapped in its brown paper, was propped against the end of the settee. Married life. Every girl's dream. He was down in that damn pub again ogling the barmaid, a rich man ready to make his play, if he hadn't done so already. In Meredith's experience men were all the same. They were all looking for something new to screw. After a year or two they satiated themselves and looked for another interest. How the world had stayed populated down the centuries. Life was about procreation. Having children. Keeping life going on the planet. All the talk of doing good, being nice, being faithful, never lying and always being honest was a load of mumbo-jumbo. People, particularly rich men, took what they wanted, when they wanted and to hell with the rest of them. What a world. Getting up, in her frustration she knocked her painting flat on the floor on her way to get a drink. At least she could drink on her own. Douglas, as usual, had gone straight to sleep and would not wake until the morning. She was lucky. At least she had Douglas. And in twenty years, if her marriage broke up, what then would she do? What did a no longer attractive woman do alone for the rest of her life? All the money in the world would never compensate for loneliness. With the whisky bottle on the coffee table in front of her, the painting again propped up against the side of the settee, Meredith turned on the television, switching from channel to channel, finding nothing that amused her, her only consolation the Scotch whisky that tasted rich and powerful. Slowly, the whisky made Meredith relax. She began to feel comfortable. By eleven o'clock there was still no sign of Randall.

"He's screwing the bitch."

When the key went in the lock it was just before midnight. The whisky bottle half finished, and Meredith was seething with jealousy.

"Where the hell have you been? It's midnight!"

"Where were you when I got back from the gym?"

"I went to the studio to finish my painting."

"You don't have classes on a Friday."

"Shelley said I could sit at the back and she'd help me. The class was a bunch of old housewives trying to find something to do with themselves."

"No young men?"

"Not a man in sight. Have you been screwing Amelia?"

"I was in the pub with Phillip."

"Was she flirting with you?"

"Probably. How do I know you were painting?"

"Open that brown paper parcel… What's happened to us, Randall?"

"It's New York. I want to go home."

"Open the parcel. All right. I'll open it for you… How does that look?"

"Blimey. It's Rabbit Farm. I don't bloody believe it. My wife can paint."

"You mean it?"

"Of course I do. Polar Bear and that rabbit are talking to each other… It's wonderful. Can I hang it on the wall?"

"Needs a couple of screws and some wire… You want a whisky?"

"Of course I do."

"So you weren't screwing the barmaid?"

"Ask Phillip. Don't be damn silly. Of course I wasn't. You've painted Snaefell in the background. Now I'm really homesick. Can't we go home, Meredith? You can paint. I can write. We'll be happy again. So will Douglas. We can have another baby. Being a well-known author in New York is a pain in the arse."

"Is the painting really any good?"

"You'd tell me if I was writing crap."

"You said the kids' book was good."

"It was. It is. It's just the publishing business. If they can't see the chance of selling a million copies they are not interested... So, you're not after one of those lads?"

"Of course I'm not. Come and sit down. It'll just take us a little longer to settle down in New York. At least you'll have Rabbit Farm hanging on the wall. We can't bring up Douglas on the Isle of Man. It's desolate. Even creepy. Two people alone with a child. That's not good, Randall."

"Oh, shit. Where am I going to write in peace?"

"We'll soundproof the third bedroom. You've got to think of me and Douglas... How was Phillip?"

"Bored out of his mind. He wants to go back to Zimbabwe."

"Poor Martha. There's no future in Africa."

"How do you know?"

"It's obvious. It'll be one revolution after another. Colonialism kept the place under control. Now it's constant chaos. You can't go back in life, Randall. You have to go forward."

"We'd better go to bed. Too much whisky isn't good for either of us. Where's Douglas?"

"In his bed, fast asleep... So you like my painting?"

"Very much."

"Let's make love, Randall. We haven't made love for a month."

"Is it that long?"

"They say marriage isn't easy. That you have to work at it."

"Let's go work at it."

"You're smiling. We had our wires crossed, Randall."

"I rather think we did. Tomorrow, we'll both go to the gym. Let's make love, my wife. I'm sorry for even thinking you were being unfaithful."

"So am I. We'll have to be more careful. We've got a whole lot of marriage ahead of us."

After making love, it took Meredith an hour to fall asleep. Her last thought: 'Life is never easy.' Douglas woke them in the morning. Both bedroom doors had been left ajar. He was standing next to Meredith on her side of the bed. Picking up her son under his arms, she pulled him into the middle of the bed. They were a family. Within a short while all three of them fell back into sleep. Only when they woke, all of them hungry and ready for breakfast, did the other side of the conundrum penetrate Meredith's mind: it was all very well for her to tell Randall he must think of her and Douglas. Maybe she should think more of Randall. What he wanted. There were two sides to being selfish. By the time she finished cooking them breakfast Randall had hung her painting on the lounge wall, the rabbit, its long ears pinned back in fear staring at the white dog, the dog staring back about to run at the rabbit. With the food on the kitchen table Meredith stood in front of her painting and smiled. Maybe, just maybe, Shelley and Randall were telling her the truth. She could paint.

"Maybe we should be going home. It's still summer. I love those big log fires in the winter. You'll be able to get to know Shakespeare and his friend. Get inside their heads. When I'm here alone all I do is turn on the television. What's the difference? The programmes are the same on the Isle of Man as they are in Manhattan. And I won't have to listen to the constant noise of New York city."

"Do you mean it, darling?"

"I was being selfish."

"Give me a hug. I'm instantly over the moon. If I'm not writing my books there's no point to my life. To hell with the Letterman Late Show. To all the other celebrity crap to just keep my name in the eye of the public. It's about enjoying my book. Not about reading something written by somebody famous. Can we go tomorrow? All we've got to do is turn off the fridge and the lights. Then we go. A flight to Liverpool where we'll say hello to your parents and they can see their grandson, and we'll take the ferry to Douglas. It'll be the summer. We'll bring Polar Bear and the cats home. Douglas loves those cats. By next week I'll be deep in a book again. All the crap of celebrity left behind forever."

"Your publishers won't like it."

"Who cares? Anyway, we're not going to tell them."

"Maybe next Wednesday. Give me time to shop and pack."

"Wednesday it is. Look at us. We're smiling. Douglas is smiling. Let's go eat breakfast. Buy lots of paint, canvases and paint brushes. Meredith, we're going to be happy again."

"I hope so."

"Of course we will be happy. I'll be writing my books. You'll be painting your pictures."

"Can we have another baby?"

"Of course we can."

"What's being happy, Mummy?"

"Eating breakfast together, darling. Having fun."

"I like having fun."

Smiling that her son could talk so early in his life, her hangover from the half bottle of whisky under control, Meredith plated the bacon and eggs while Randall buttered the toast. With Douglas strapped to the back of his highchair at the top of the table, his food cut up for him on a dish sitting on the small tray in front of him, normality returned. They ate in silence, all of them hungry. After wiping the egg yolk off Douglas's face, she cleared the table. Randall turned on the classical music channel on the television, sitting on the settee with a last cup of tea.

"I'll be back in ten minutes. Did you just hear him burp?"

"Where are you going?"

"To thank Martha for letting Ivy look after Douglas. Keep your eye on Douglas. That son of yours might get up to a bit of mischief."

Upstairs on the forty-ninth floor, when Meredith rang the bell, Martha opened the door. She looked irritated.

"What's the matter? I came up to thank you and Ivy for looking after Douglas."

"Men! He came home drunk at midnight!"

"So did Randall. They're brothers, Martha. Old friends. We're going back to Rabbit Farm."

"Are you out of your minds? New York is the best place in the world to live. You just bought your apartment."

"Randall can't write amongst all the noise and interruptions. He can't keep the story in his mind. It's what he wants. I can't be selfish."

"And what are you going to do with Douglas when he wants a friend? Come and sit down. Phillip and I had an argument. He and Ivy have taken Carmen and the pram for a walk in the gardens. Do you think Phillip fancies the nanny? She's not that good looking. That was my idea.

Never employ a good-looking nanny. What a week it's been. Work, work, work. I love it."

"What does Phillip do all day?"

"Oh, he finds things to do. He doesn't have to work. We're rich. Now come and talk to me. You can't go back to that island in the Irish Sea. Randall's got to write a film script for *Love Song*. Be at the production. Promote the damn movie. There's more to books and films than writing them. Everything in the modern world is about promoting the product. You've got to have maximum publicity if you want to be successful. Follow every lead. Use Randall and his fame to make people aware of the movie long before it hits the screen. Randall's out of his mind if he runs away. He's got there. Now he has to stay there. The public has short memories. There's always some other writer knocking on the door."

"He says writing his book is more important than selling it. That we don't need any more money."

"You always need more money."

"Not on little Rabbit Farm. We even grow our own vegetables."

"What are you going to do all day stuck in the middle of nowhere?"

"Paint pictures."

"You tried writing kids' books. That didn't work. Anyway, they won't let Randall leave America. He's too valuable to them as a publicity tool. Even if he doesn't want to make money, you can be sure his publisher and the film producer do. This is America, Meredith. In America it's all about making lots of money. The great American dream of wealth... Do you want a cup of coffee?"

"That would be nice. He says we can have another baby if we go home."

"This is your home. Your baby can be born in America. There's everything a family can ever want in America. Talk some sense into him."

"I want him to be happy. I don't want to be selfish."

"You also don't want to be stupid. I did Phillip the favour of his life bringing him to America."

"Did you?"

"What do you mean?"

"He still has a passion for Africa. For living in the African bush amongst all those wild animals. Where you met him, Martha."

"He was lucky I got myself pregnant the first time. There's no future for the white man in Africa. Those days are over."

"Maybe. Whoever knows?"

"I'll make the coffee. Today is shopping day for Martha. You've got to dress well in the world of advertising. It's all about looking good. Appearances. That's what counts."

"You really think they won't let Randall go?"

"Of course they won't. They're not daft."

"He'll write them another book if we go to Rabbit Farm."

"So will a lot of other people. They want to make their money today. Not tomorrow. They want profits in the next quarter. Not in five years' time. Their careers depend on making money today. In five years, most of them won't be working for the same company."

"It doesn't take five years to write a book."

"Maybe not. But then there's the build-up. The editing. The publishing. All that publicity. No, they want profit from the famous Randall Holiday right now. Their bonuses depend on it... One or two sugars? Here, take the sugar pot."

"Thank you, Martha."

"My pleasure, Meredith. Welcome to America."

For half an hour Meredith listened to Martha talking about her week's business at Bowden, Crookshank, Fairbanks and Webber before making her excuses. She had been through it all before. As a child and a girl, when her father came home from the office all he talked about was his business, the job that paid the mortgage and put her brother Tom through university to give him the chance of a career that would give him money. Both Meredith and her sister Pam had been put through secretarial college. The house had been mortgaged up to the hilt. Like New York, life in Liverpool had been all about making money. Married to a wealthy author had taken the money worry out of Meredith's life.

"How quickly we forget."

"Did you say something, lady?"

"Sorry. I was talking to myself. Here we are. The thirty-first floor. Home."

"You live here? You must be rich! These apartments cost a fortune."

"I suppose they do. We're leaving. Have a nice day."

The moment Meredith opened the door of their apartment she could hear Randall arguing with someone on the other end of the phone.

"I've had enough of arguing. Tell Mr Letterman to shove his Late Show up his arse. No, that's a bit rude. I won't be here, so how can I be on the bloody show? He can find plenty of other celebrities to blow their own trumpets... No, I'm not. Poppy Maddock is going to write the script... Can't you people just get off my back?... I know you helped me to get started, Manfred. But a man needs peace. Everyone wants a piece of me. They use me... You're right, maybe I used them at the beginning. Including Mr Letterman... Let me think about it. Can I at least have a holiday? Please help me, Manfred, I want to write. All I ever want to do is get inside another book. Here in New York my head is filled with so much shit. There's too much noise... No, I never get used to the traffic. I get into my character's head and then bang, a police siren blares at me from down in the street. Writing a story has to be continuous. Not fits and starts... Yes, we've thought of soundproofing but it's not the same as a cottage in the woods of Wales, Rabbit Farm, or World's View where I grew up in Rhodesia. New York is constant panic. And people. I'm sick of people... Not you, Manfred. You're my agent... All right. I'll do the Letterman show. And please don't shout at me... Yes, I'll check Poppy's script... And go to Hollywood... I'm in prison, Manfred. Sometimes I wish I had never published my books. Just written them... No, I had enough money. My paternal grandfather was the famous Hollywood actor Ben Crossley. And he left me and my brother a pile of money. But you know that. His name helped me become famous. My poor dog and cats... Don't be bloody ridiculous. A white Alsatian dog and seven cats cannot live on the thirty-first floor of a Manhattan block of apartments... Yes, I'll come to lunch on Monday. Have a nice weekend. I'm sure you're right. Being a literary agent can't be easy either. Cheers, old boy... It's just an English expression. We called each other old boy at school in Rhodesia... So, the empire has gone but the words linger on... See you for lunch on Monday."

"What was that all about?"

"Shit, I hate people. They always want something."

"Martha says we'd be out of our minds going back to Rabbit Farm."

"She would."

"Are we going?"

"Who the hell knows? It's like having a noose around your neck."

"What's a noose, Daddy?"

"A piece of string... Let's get out of here and go down to the gardens. I want to see a flower and a tree, not a brick wall. And I hate telephones."

"You have a hangover."

"Probably... How's Phillip today?"

"Went for a walk in the gardens."

"Come on. Let's go before I go nuts. Money, money, money. All they think about is money. The whole damn human race is going down the toilet... What did Martha have to say for herself?"

"You don't even want to know... Do you really hate your agent?"

"Of course I don't. I'm being a selfish bastard. Once we get what we want we don't care about other people. It's inherent in the human condition. Manfred's got a wife and kids to look after like everyone else... I really do love that painting. Who taught you to draw so well?"

"A teacher at my primary school in Liverpool. Before you can paint a portrait, you've got to know how to draw. I was always doodling on bits of paper drawing my friends' faces. Gave me something to do. The boys were all into sport. The girls into giggling and making faces. Half my little drawings had the girls with their tongues just sticking out."

"Why didn't you go to art school instead of secretarial college?"

"Dad said artists never made money."

"Did you enjoy being a legal secretary?"

"Not particularly... Who are you having lunch with on Monday? Can't be just Manfred?"

"A woman from the *Herald* who wants to write an inside story about the life of Randall Holiday. They want to pry into my very existence."

"Your readers will enjoy reading about you."

"Probably. But it doesn't help me. I don't even know who they are. I have no idea who reads my books. Why must they know about my private life?"

"It sells books. Martha says it's all about selling. Get the pushchair. Come along, little Douglas. Why did we call him after the port of Douglas?"

"Did we?"

"What's a port, Mummy?"

"The place where you were born."

Outside, the sun was shining, the pavements crowded with people walking in both directions, the road congested with traffic, vendors selling newspapers, policemen on the beat, music blaring from a shop as they pushed Douglas strapped into his chair down the street, the people weaving in and out of each other's paths as they went about their business. To Meredith the constant rush of people was fun. Some smiled, some glared, a few walked casually. Most of the pedestrians were hell-bent in a hurry. When they reached the small park with its benches and well-kept gardens there was no sign of Phillip. They sat down on a bench in front of the grass. Douglas ran around on the lawn quickly finding another child and a small sausage dog to play with. The dog kept barking and wagging its tail. Douglas and his new friend kept laughing. Her son was happy. An old woman was sitting on a bench in front of a flowerbed. A stray cat got up onto her bench, purring and pushing against the old lady's leg. The old lady took a cat-bowl out of her carry-bag and fed the cat. Two boys were playing catch with a tennis ball. A soft breeze rustled the leaves in the tree high above Meredith's head. In the flowerbed in front of her feet was a profusion of brightly coloured daisies. With her hands hidden under her thighs, Meredith crossed her fingers. She loved New York. So did Douglas. The last thing in the world she wished to do was up sticks and move to the isolation of the Isle of Man. The dog and cats would stay happy with their surrogate owners, the neighbours from the next farm that Randall paid to look after the animals.

"He's having so much fun."

"He is, isn't he?"

"And the sun is shining. Isn't that old lady with the stray cat Phillip's friend? He talked about an old lady who feeds stray cats."

"You don't really want to go?"

"Not really. But I will if it's what you want. Just look at them. People aren't all that bad."

"I suppose not. We should have brought a flask of tea."

"Indeed we should. Next time, I'll bring a picnic basket. You want to hold my hand?"

"Of course I do."

"Mum and Dad would love to see Douglas."

"Life is all about choices. The good, the bad and the ugly."

"Like the movie."

"Pretty much."

"I want another little Douglas. Or a little Mary."

"So do I, Meredith. And life goes on, from generation to generation."

"You're lucky you're just a famous author and not a recognisable movie star."

"Now that must be hell on earth."

"I love this garden."

"So do I. Flowers and trees with green leaves. Nature. The essence of good life... You know what I'm going to do?"

"No. What are you going to do, darling?"

"I'm going to fold my arms, close my eyes, and take a nap."

When Randall woke from his dreams, the old lady walked past in front of them, the stray cat staying curled up on the bench. The old lady smiled at Randall as he opened his eyes and yawned.

"I know you from seeing your picture in the papers. You're Phillip Crookshank's brother, Randall Holiday. It's a perfect day in the park. Look at that. Your son is enjoying himself. Have a nice day."

Meredith watched the old girl walk on and out of the park, Randall watching her with a pained expression on his face. Douglas ran across to them and climbed up onto the wooden bench. His friend had gone. None of them spoke for a while, Douglas sitting happily between them.

"It's the price for being a successful author, darling. Don't be upset. She's a friend of your brother. Probably lonely. Lonely people love to talk to strangers. She had a nice smile on her face. Do you want to go?"

"Oh yes. I want to go all right. I want to go to Rabbit Farm."

"That cat's happy."

"It's been fed. We all want to be fed. All that purring and leg rubbing to get what they want and then they fall asleep."

"What are we doing today?"

"Sitting in a park. If only I could find a quiet place to write. I wonder what life in England, in Stratford-upon-Avon was like in the days of William Shakespeare? I want to transport myself into that era. Feel part of it. Then I will get into their heads. Here, I can't even sit on a bench in a park without being interrupted."

"Some people would like it. Most people like attention... How old is Shakespeare's friend? The one you think who wrote his plays. Was he young or old?"

"Oh, he was young. A young aristocrat from a very old English family. Edward de Vere, the Earl of Oxford. How does that sound? Some historians think he had inherited by the time he met Shakespeare. I don't think so."

"How young?"

"Thirty. With nothing to do with the rest of his life except wait for his father to die. The heir in waiting. Some of them wait all their lives before having to run the family estate and finally have some responsibility, something to do. All those years of boredom just waiting. So he wrote plays. Laughed with the actors. Made a life for himself without making himself conspicuous by letting Shakespeare, who managed and owned the theatre in partnership, claim ownership of his plays."

"Wouldn't he like to have taken some credit for his plays? To have recognition, then and in the future."

"He got what he wanted. He wrote the plays. Saw them enacted by Shakespeare and his troupe of actors. That is all the satisfaction a true artist ever wants. To create and be able to see what he created. It must have been terrible for the deaf Beethoven at the end of his life to write that wonderful Ninth Symphony and never hear a note of it played. They say he conducted the première facing the orchestra. He was still conducting when the symphony was finished. A member of the orchestra got up and ran to the podium and turned Beethoven round to look at the audience, who were giving him a standing ovation. Beethoven was as deaf as a post. Only then did he know what he had done."

"Couldn't he hear it in his head?"

"A bit difficult with music, written for a full orchestra... There he goes again. Kids. Nothing better than watching happy kids."

"Friends are so important for Douglas."

"Yes, I suppose they are. I'm going to close my eyes and sit and think. Ah, there they are."

"Who, Randall?"

"Shakespeare and his friend... Your mobile is ringing. At least Shakespeare and his friend didn't have to worry about the bloody telephone."

"I'd better answer it. It may be important. I'll walk down the lawn and leave you in peace."

"Thank you, Meredith. All I want is peace. The most precious commodity on this earth. Peace and solitude. And a book in my head."

"You're nuts."

"Probably."

"Hello, Mum. Where are you? How's Liverpool in summer?... Oh, it's raining... He's fine. Playing with another kid in the park. Toddlers make friends so easily... We're not sure. Soon. Maybe. Who knows in this crazy world?... Randall's fine. A bit bored... Because he says he can't write in New York... Tell me everything... Oh, of course. I'll phone you back. Phone calls are expensive. Let me find a seat and sit down. I can see a vacant bench over there... Randall's taking a nap... I'll call you straight back... Love you too, Mum. Wait. Douglas is crying. The little bugger he was playing with has pushed him over. Sorry. Got to go... As soon as I can."

A park in New York City. A husband napping on a bench. A son plonked and crying on his bottom. A mother miles and miles away in Liverpool waiting for her to call. An empty home on the Isle of Man. It left Meredith shaking her head and wondering what life was all about.

"Are you all right, my baby? Come to Mummy. There. Is that better? Don't cry. That's better. Laughter is always better than crying. What do you want, Douglas?"

"Play with friend."

"Just be careful... Hello, Mum, it's me again... He's fine. Now tell me everything. About Dad, Tom and Pam... He's in love! I don't believe you... Oh, her parents are rich. Good for Tom."

Sitting down on the empty wooden bench, Douglas clearly in her sight, Meredith sat listening to her mother talk and talk, her mind only half concentrating. It was the same old story she had heard all her life. Her mother's daily routine. The life of a suburban housewife with nothing to do. And her mother was lucky. She had married a man who had worked hard for them all his life and provided all their comforts.

"They want him to retire? But what's Dad going to do with himself all day? Yes, you could visit us in America. My poor father. His job at the insurance company was his life... Of course we were his life. But most of his waking day was spent at work... Love you too, Mum. See you soon. Love to Dad."

Not sure if she had enjoyed listening to her mother's conversation with all its complaints, Meredith put the mobile back in her pocket and sat and stared up at the sky. Across at the other bench, Randall had his arms folded in front of him and his eyes shut. A stray cat got up on the bench, purring and pushing its head against her leg.

"Sorry, pussycat. I don't have any food."

The cat went off to look for better pickings. As Meredith got up to go and join Randall, the old lady with the carry-bag who had fed the cat came back into the park. She stopped in front of Randall, whose eyes were still closed. The old lady sat down on the bench next to him and waited. She had taken a book out of her carry-bag. Douglas started running at her as fast as his little legs would carry him. Meredith knelt down on the grass, waiting for her son. They were both laughing. Both happy. When Douglas jumped into her arms they looked close into each other's faces, both of them giggling. Out of her left eye, Meredith could see Randall open his eyes and take the book and the offered pen from the old lady. Sadly, Randall was right. They should go back to the peace and solitude of Rabbit Farm or he'd never write his book.

When Randall had signed the book, the old lady went on her way, a sweet, satisfied look on her face. Randall closed his eyes and folded his arms. Instead of joining him, Meredith sat back on the bench while Douglas ran back onto the well-cut lawn to play with his friend. Meredith could see that Randall had clenched his jaw. It was better to leave him alone for a while. Shakespeare and his friend would have to wait. Life was never simple, however good it seemed. Poor Randall. Behind those closed eyes he would be seething. The two toddlers ran around in front of Meredith, their words mostly unintelligible. As her little son struggled to gain control of language, it was difficult for her to decipher what he was trying to say. The other boy's words were an even bigger jumble. On the other side of the lawn, facing towards Meredith, the other boy's mother was watching them just as carefully. A man with a dog on a leash walked down the path behind Meredith, causing the stray cat to run away. From through the trees came a young man carrying an easel tucked under his right arm. He was smiling directly at Meredith, the smile of a man confident of his effect on women. For a second, Meredith's heart lost a beat. It was Clint, the best looking of the boys in Shelley's art class, the one that always cornered Meredith when the group was socialising after they had finished painting.

"Now that's lucky. If it isn't the beautiful Meredith. Did you finish your painting? Mind if I set up next to you?"

"Weren't you looking for a job?"

"I'm always looking for a job. Luckily, I never find one. I'm an artist. All I want to do is paint. I make just enough waiting tables when they want me. The tips are good. I like the life of a bohemian... How's your rich husband? Did you sign an agreement when you married him?"

"What's that got to do with you, Clint?"

"Oh, you never know. Women marry rich men for their money... Am I bothering you? Oh, that's your son over there."

"And my husband on the bench over there with his eyes closed."

"Why isn't he sleeping on your bench, Meredith? I mean, that's not right. Two people in love, sitting separately."

"He wants to commune with his characters."

"Does he now? That's good. While he's communing with his characters, I can commune with his wife. Do you like my new painting? Painting in the park on a summer's day. What can be more perfect. Is that cat yours?"

"It ran from the dog. A stray cat. Now he's back again. It's not bad.

What would we do without Shelley? No, and don't sit down. I'm a married woman."

"But are you a happily married woman?"

"Of course I am. Please, Clint. Go and paint on the other side of the park."

"Why? Is he jealous? He looks older than you."

"He is. Now bugger off."

"What language. You aren't so nasty when we drink together. Oh, dear. He's seen us. Have a nice day, Meredith. See you in class. You do know you're the best-looking girl in the class. Such a shame you're still married to him, or you and I would have some fun, the ex-wife of a rich and famous author."

"Bugger off, Clint."

"He's coming over."

"You're a pain in the arse, Clint."

"I'd love to give you a feel just in front. I like you better when we're drinking. Off I go. Like a good little boy. Sweet dreams tonight, pretty lady."

When Meredith looked to her left the bench was empty, Randall out on the lawn playing with Douglas. The tall, good-looking Clint was walking the other way with a smirk on his face. Once after class when they had all been drinking he had put his hand on her bare knee sending a surge of excitement through Meredith's body, the same feeling she had felt in the woodsman's cottage in Wales when she first met and made love to Randall. When she looked back at Randall, he and Douglas were walking towards her.

"Who was he, Meredith?"

"A friend from Shelley's art class."

"I rather thought so. We'd better go."

"Did you find them?"

"Only for a little while."

"We should go back to Rabbit Farm."

"We should. And for more than one reason by the look of it. What were you talking about?"

"Nothing much."

"Didn't exactly look casual. He was flirting with you."

"All men flirt, Randall. You flirt with Amelia in Harry B's. I've watched you. What's Douglas trying to say? Sometimes I just can't make out what our son is trying to say. Let's go. Before we have an argument."

"Are we having an argument?"

"Please, Randall. Are you jealous or something?"

"What would I have to be jealous about? And if we go, what are we going to do all day? You've finished your painting and I can't start a book. Might as well muck around in the park. I hate staring out of our window at the skyscrapers of New York. They're always the same."

"Are you bored by any chance?"

"I'm always bored when I have nothing to do."

"I'm going to stop taking the pill."

"That would do the trick. Another baby will give us both something to think about. How was your mother?"

"Much the same as usual. They want Dad to retire from the insurance company."

"What's he going to do then?"

"Nothing, I suppose... There he goes again. One minute they're fighting, and Douglas is crying, the next they're as happy as a couple of crickets."

"So he's not your lover?"

"Of course he's not my lover."

"He's waving at you now he's set up his easel. Funny how the easel has its back to you... Oh, I'm sorry. I'll go back to my own bench and close my eyes."

"What's the matter with you, Randall?"

"I've been telling you. I'm bored with New York and fear the traps we can fall into."

"And that includes Amelia?"

"And that includes Amelia."

"He wanted to know if we signed a prenuptial contract when we got married. Can you believe it?"

"Oh, I can believe it. If I wasn't rich, Amelia wouldn't even look at me."

"What a world."

"You can say that again."

"Which book was it?"

"*Masters of Vanity*. All those lovely greedy rich people, vain as peacocks, who inhabit the executive suites in Manhattan, and people so love to read about. Why is it everyone wants to be rich? To show off? Be the centre of attention? I hate it. All you need in life is a roof over your head and a nice meal on the table and a beautiful, contented wife. The rest is surplus. Unnecessary. Leads to problems. I don't think the super-rich are happy. They're too busy stealing other people's money as they were in the book. One of those French novelists said behind every fortune is a thief. Why can't people be content with enough? Or is it inferiority complexes they think can be overcome with conspicuous consumption? They must live in permanent fear of being found out, plagued by their guilty conscience. What's his name?"

"Clint. I never learned his surname."

"Whatever for? I'm going to sit down next to you and close my eyes and look for my imaginary people. If I fall asleep, all well and good. Where does our son get all that energy? I'm going to buy him a football for his birthday. If I sleep, I'll sleep off my hangover. Hangovers make me bad tempered. I hate hangovers."

And Meredith's day went on. When Phillip wandered into the park on his own he looked like a man with nothing to do, sauntering through the tall trees kicking the occasional tuft of grass. She watched him go from tree to tree, touching the bark of each tree as he passed, oblivious of his brother on the other side of the lawn or his nephew playing with his friend.

"He's wandering around like a lost fart in a haunted shit house."

"What did you say, Randall?"

"You heard me. Now look at that. Surprise, surprise. He's tripped over his nephew. I wonder what he's done with Ivy and Carmen? Sent them back to that paradise on the forty-ninth floor most likely. Wave, Meredith. The bugger has seen us. I'm asleep, don't forget."

"Did you find them?"

"No sign of William Shakespeare or Edward de Vere, Earl of Oxford. People only let you find them when they want to be found. Anyway, there's too much other stuff in my head. All I can think of is my literary agent and what he'll want from me on Monday... My poor brother. He hates the big city life. And Martha can't live without it. The perfect marriage for both of them."

"Why was he touching the trees?"

"For luck. We touched the fence posts on World's View that held up a high, electric fence round the house."

"What was the fence for on a farm?"

"To keep out the terrorists. The bush war started in the seventies and only ended when Mugabe came to power. The house was fired at several times from outside the fence. Luckily, they didn't shoot any of us. What's the matter, Phillip?"

"Nothing. What are you doing in the park? Hello, Meredith."

"Nothing. Like you."

"Who's the artist waving at you? I like his hat. I'd love to have been an artist and paint pictures in a park on a summer's day. How's the new book coming along?"

"It's not. He's Meredith's boyfriend. They're in the same art class. We need a cricket bat and a tennis ball so we can play French cricket like we played as kids when we had nothing to do... Whoops. He's dumped on his little bottom again. They're both dumped on their little bottoms. Oh well, it's better than crawling around on a carpet thirty-one floors up surrounded by walls."

"That's one of Mary's cats. The one she feeds. Can I sit down?"

"Be my guest. What's on today's agenda?"

"Nothing. I thought you might have something."

"Nothing. All I have today is a hangover. Was his painting any good?"

"Not bad. He's painting the trees and the flowerbeds. I looked over his shoulder. I met the homeless violin player in this park. Poor Jonathan. Now he's rich after all my help in claiming his family fortune he doesn't come to the park. All his hobo friends from the soup kitchen are gone. I ruined the life of an old man. What's life all about, Randall?"

"You tell me."

"We could go to Harry B's for a drink."

"And start the slippery slide all over again."

"Can't think of much else to do on a Saturday. Or any day for that matter. For me, all the days are the same. I have absolutely nothing to strive for. When you've got everything material, what's the point? Come here, pussycat, and talk to Phillip. Are you hungry? Of course you are. You can feel as well as hear the cat purr. Don't you miss your cats? Anyway, it's a lovely day. The sun is shining. What the hell was that noise? Sounded like gunfire."

"Relax, old boy. Just a car backfiring. Why didn't you bring a flask of tea?"

"Because nobody asked me to. Did you go to the gym?"

"Not today."

"Neither did I. You know, brother. We're both useless."

"Sit down and I'll tell you a story."

"What about?"

"Once upon a time in Manhattan there were two brothers from Africa, bored out of their minds. So they went to a pub called Harry B's and got themselves drunk."

"That's an old story."

"They're all old stories. There are no new stories in life. Life is just repetition, one generation after another. Until we find extinction."

"You think the human race will ever become extinct?"

"Of course it will."

"How are we going extinct?"

"I don't know. We don't even know how we got here, despite the hope of our religious beliefs. We came from nowhere through our mother's wombs, live three score years and ten if we're lucky, and then we die, nothing the wiser for it."

"They say if we are good our spirits go to heaven."

"And what does a spirit do in heaven for all eternity? What is a spirit? Where does a spirit exist?"

"We'll have to wait and see. Now's for the living. Are you coming with us, Meredith?"

"Why don't you two brothers go on your own? I'll look after Douglas. Before you get drunk, have some lunch."

"I'll leave you to Clint."

"Give my love to Amelia. Come here, Douglas. Just look at them. They're trying to punch each other."

"What was that all about, Randall?"

"The usual. Smile everyone. We're in New York. The most exciting city in the whole wide world."

"What was all that about, Meredith?"

"You tell me. Life in the fast lane. Oh, you mean me and Clint or my lovely son having his first punch-up? It's lovely. Every time they swing, they fall on their bottoms. Good. The other boy's mother has pulled him away. You brothers go and enjoy yourselves. I miss Tom and Pam."

"Your siblings?"

"Yes, my brother and sister, Phillip. There's nothing better in life than growing up close to one's siblings. Some fight like cats and dogs their whole lives, or part company once they grow up."

Meredith watched them go with a feeling of envy, bringing back her loneliness. She had no one to talk to. No one to talk about her problems with. No one with whom to engage, to receive and give sympathy, the thought of being isolated on Rabbit Farm making her feel worse. The brothers were chattering away to each other like monkeys. She needed to get herself pregnant. Give Douglas a brother. With all their money they could afford a big family. One, big happy family. That's what she wanted.

"He's gone. Left the park."

"What do you want, Clint?"

"I want you to come and look at my painting. Tell me if it's any good. An artist never knows if his own paintings are any good. He has to be told."

"The more they pay, the better it is. Everything according to Randall is judged by how much it makes. Everything of any importance has a monetary value. Books. Art. Music. They are just a product to make money out of, according to Randall's agent. He never tells my husband if his books are any good. Manfred is only interested in them if they will sell."

"What's wrong with that? Can I sit down?"

"Won't someone run off with your painting?"

"Not if it's worth nothing. If someone steals it off the easel, I'll know I'm good. Who's his friend?"

"His brother. They grew up close together on an African farm after their mother was killed by a pride of lions. Neither of them really remembers their mother."

"How did she get attacked by lions?"

"She drank too much. Went on a drive by herself and ran out of petrol. Tried to walk back to the farm. She had reached the escarpment of the Zambezi Valley. Phillip's daughter, Carmen, is named after their dead mother. Randall's family farm was deep in the wilds of Africa. Not my idea of fun. Come here, Douglas. This is Uncle Clint."

"I want go home."

"Come then, darling. Have a nice day, Clint. Go back to your painting."

"See you in class."

"Probably."

"I want to be your lover."

"Get lost, Clint. You can't be serious."

"Never know till you try. Bye-bye, beautiful Meredith. What a lovely day."

"What's life all about?"

"You tell me. No, I know. Life's about having fun. Why I'm not going away. Look at that. Your son is toddling back to his friend. How convenient."

WHILE CLINT WAS FLIRTING, Meredith transfixed to her wooden bench unable to move, Randall and Phillip were sitting in a hamburger joint three blocks from the park eating hamburgers.

"Why do people flock to cities, Randall? All crammed into the same crowded space."

"Jobs, probably. If you get fired you get another one. It's one big seething mass of people. You make a mistake, get lost and the next employer has no idea what you've been up to. You can get rich in a city. What people want. People love to use each other for personal gain. It's more difficult in a rural area where everyone knows who you are. Why there are so many thieves in New York, whether criminals or just those lovely investment bankers manipulating the financial markets. Big cities have plush sewers for big rats... That's my lunch finished. Let's go drink. Always better to drink on a full stomach. Let's go fight our way down those lovely sidewalks to Harry B's. What would we do without pubs?"

"You think she'll be there?"

"Who?"

"The girl with the tight bottom. Why we drink in Harry B's. Why Terry employs young, sexy girls to serve his drinks."

"You think it's intentional?"

"It works. Despite all the façades we're all a bunch of sex-maniacs at heart."

"We're getting old, Phillip. That's the trouble. Was man put on earth to be with just one woman? When you fall in love, are you meant to be blind to other women? The church and society try to make us monogamous. Nature encourages us to make as many kids as possible. Let's just walk. It's often better not to think or ask questions. Just look at all these people. When Dad was born there were only two billion on the planet. Now there are six billion. When Douglas gets to our age there'll be twelve billion. All that fornicating. Where are they going to put them all?... Hello, Terry. How's business today? Let's start with a beer. Put all the drinks on my tab... There we go... Cheers, brother. To life. To all those lovely fun and games. Lunchtime on a Saturday and they're all out drinking... Amelia. How are you today?"

"You're early."

"Better than being late."

"When are you taking me to meet all those film producers in Hollywood? Hello, Phillip. Enjoy your beers."

"So here we are again."

"Looks like it, brother. What did you do with Ivy and Carmen?"

"We walked together for half an hour, me pushing Carmen's pushchair. Ivy wanted to go back and study. Her passion is getting that degree and hopefully get a job in America. She thinks the future for the white man is bleak in South Africa. That America will give her a better future."

"We were lucky to enjoy the tail end of the British Empire in Africa. What a life. You remember the Centenary Club? Of course you do, Phillip. An instant smile on your face at the memory. They were mostly English gentlemen. A few Scots. A couple of Irish. Even a Welshman. All well educated at public schools. The great colonial life. Big estates. Servants. Back in the life of the old aristocracy with their English country estates. A six-thousand-acre farm and a gentleman's club with a cricket field, tennis courts, squash courts and a large swimming pool. That was what we were born into. Of course it had to end. Nothing like that could possibly last forever. Enclaves of the super First World rich surrounded by the poverty of the Third World. Dad gave the workers food and housing, a football field, a beer hall, but the disparity in wealth was staggering. All the white farmers will soon be chased off those farms by Mugabe. And I don't blame him. Whether the labour force on World's View is living as comfortably as they did in Dad's day is highly debatable but that's progress. They are ruled by their own people. Who wants to be told what to do by a bunch of foreigners living the life of Riley? Whoever Riley was. But oh those memories. You got drunk in the club and drove home through the bush hoping you wouldn't hit any wild animals in that wonderful wild of Africa. Our fancy apartments halfway up a skyscraper in Manhattan could never compare to the life on World's View. Yes, we were lucky. We got a piece of ultimate living on this crazy planet... Amelia, darling. Give us a couple more. That one went down quickly. I'm feeling better. My bad mood is lifting thanks to the alcohol. Do you think we are addicts, Phillip? Alcoholics?"

"Probably."

"At least in the Centenary Club we played our sport. What a life. Never to be repeated, brother. Oh, well. That's life. Cheers. To the best of life. Forget the worst of life. Make the best of it. Africa. What memories."

"Write a book about it so it will live forever. Go back to the first Englishman to go to Rhodesia. Tell the story. Live it again. Let other people live the story."

"Maybe. I've still got Shakespeare and his friend trying to live in my head. My *The White Saviour* was a futuristic look at Zimbabwe in the twenty-first century. Manfred didn't think much of it. Didn't have a big enough market. *Love Song*'s outsold it twentyfold. You got to give them what they want. Not what you want. That's according to Manfred. *The White Saviour*, a fantasy based on the last white man left in what once had been Dad's Rhodesia. A man they turned to for security in a world of tribal wars and factionalism that had decimated them. I loved writing it. And that is all that matters."

"I enjoyed reading it."

"Good for you, Phillip. After this beer it's whisky. Let's talk about the good old days in Colonial Rhodesia. The ironic part is they are worse off without us. What a world. The growth rate of the Rhodesian economy under Ian Smith was in double digits. We'd have pulled the entire country out of poverty within thirty years. Or maybe. Who knows? It's all so volatile in the global world. All those lovely financial markets. Is your money ever safe and permanent? If you pull a country like China out of poverty, will it stay rich? Or will the predators destroy it?"

"What's a gentleman, Randall?"

"An extinct species who thought they were men of honour, who only told the truth and always did that which was right as opposed to that which was wrong."

"What's right and what's wrong?"

"Ah, that's more difficult. You can read the Bible. Read the philosophers. Talk to people you think have integrity. Chances are at the end you still won't know the difference between right and wrong. One man's right is another man's wrong. Depends on which side of the fence you're on. Oh, I can still see that wonderful cricket field with the big white sight screens at either end of the pitch so the batsman could better see the ball. I can hear the chock of the bat on the ball. Hear the polite 'well done, old boy' and the polite clapping. A field of well-kept grass. I wonder what the blacks will do with that cricket field, that English field in the middle of the African bush?"

"The cows will graze it. The squash courts will be turned into houses. The clubhouse will become the plush home of a senior member of Mugabe's ZANU-PF. They'll turn the tennis courts with their fences into chicken runs. And everyone will live happily ever after. And most of the whites will go back to where they came from, just a blot on the African memory, soon to be forgotten, thrown on the garbage heap of history. Will we leave behind any benefits? Probably. The pluses and the minuses. Will man ever live in peace with himself or his neighbours? I doubt it. The game just goes on in its permanent circles."

"Is life worth the living?"

"Some think so. Most are not so sure. Dad says he finds it difficult to see a purpose in his life, now or in the past, other than bringing up us kids. Now he's handed that baton to us, to bring up Douglas and Carmen. And so it goes on. From life in the African wilds to a concrete jungle in Manhattan. The trick is to be happy, brother. To live in the present. Cheers, old boy."

"Does drinking help?"

"Only during the time you are doing the drinking. It's the hangovers that make our drinking habits futile. But what else do you do on a Saturday in the great city of New York? Or London? It's called suburban living."

"Let's talk about 'raindrops and roses, and whiskers on kittens'."

"That's a much better idea. Who sang that song?"

"You tell me. It's been in my head ever since I was a kid. 'These are a few of my favourite things.' What she said. The rest of life is too complicated and hard, with too many sharp and dangerous edges. The very picture of whiskers on kittens makes me want to smile."

They talked and talked, changing their drink to whisky, oblivious to the others in the bar, only Amelia catching the attention of both of them, with the same tight trousers over a firm bottom and the intentional flash of her young breasts. Randall tried unsuccessfully to keep his eyes off the girl.

"I've got it, Randall. It's been bugging me. Julie Andrews sang that song about 'whiskers and kittens and bright copper kettles'. In the song, she sang they were 'a few of my favourite things'. *The Sound of Music.* Don't you think we should go back to our wives?"

"You remember that one of Dad's? The one his father had passed down to him and who knows how further back it went in our family. 'In the cave of a thousand arseholes, by the sign of the hanging tit, Who Flung Dung was murdered by his brother Who Flung Shit.'"

"We're getting drunk, Randall."

"Probably. Does Martha want to talk to a drunk? Does Meredith?

They don't mind it when you get drunk if they get drunk with you. Never confront them drunk when they are stone-cold sober. They give you that look of disgust. Without a job to do we have too much time on our hands. That's our problem. They have the kids to keep them busy. What are we going to do?"

"How about another drink?"

"Brilliant. Utterly brilliant. Set 'em up again, Terry. What are we going to do with the rest of our lives? We're not even forty. I'm not sure if there are many books in my future, even if I get back to Rabbit Farm so I can write them. And your business is making money as a venture capitalist, looking for all those new ideas you can convert into money. But when you've done everything successfully a couple of times, what's the point? You can only sleep in one bed at a time. Eat one meal at a time, however expensive. I have only so much in my head to write about, and when that's done there's a blank. I think we got what we wanted from life too early. We're like an old, retired couple of men with nothing to do but go to the pub and drink. Thank you, Terry. You're doing well, Terry. The place is full."

"Hard work and concentration. Enjoy your drinks. Coming! You're right, Randall, the place is busy. Amelia, help that guy. Are you two going to eat something?"

"Had a burger on the way."

"Have another one. For your health."

"Thank you. You always look after us."

"Always look after the customers. That's the way it goes. Two hamburgers coming up. I liked that one about the cave. Write it down for me, Randall, so I can tell that one to my late-night customers to make them giggle. Who wrote it?"

"Passed down from father to son over the centuries."

"Someone must have written it."

"It's the story that counts. Not the writer. It's the story that should live on. Not the celebrity of the bloody writer."

"No swearing in Harry B's."

"I'm so sorry, your honour... I'll write it down when I'm sober. You're right. A hamburger will stop us getting fall-down-drunk... Look at them all. Swilling down alcohol. Escapism. Can't be anything else. We all want to get away from the world we live in, to a drunken world where everything is wonderful, where people are fun, where the booze makes us happy. Others do it with illegal drugs. In Muslim countries they don't let you drink alcohol because they know what it does, the damage, not the benefits. And when we get too drunk, we go back to our normal instincts that generate all those wars and start punching each other. Did you ever have a fight in a bar, Phillip?"

"A couple of times. To defend myself. So this is all pure escapism?"

"Why otherwise would a row of people sit by themselves up at a wooden bar, on wooden stools, staring at the bottles stacked behind the bar, hoping that when the man next to us gets drunk enough he'll talk to us? All those drunken conversations with strangers we all so enjoy, because what you say doesn't matter, has no repercussions, both men trying to escape their loneliness in that intimate bar where at the end you go home and forget about it. That old saying 'the worst thing in life is a drinking companion with a memory'. What a bunch of fools we are. But during the lift from the alcohol, everything is fun. Or we think it's fun. The next day, when we suffer the effects of too much drink, we're not sure if any of it was worth the trouble. That we should have done better to stay at home and save our money. But here we are, Phillip. Halfway through a drunk. A drunk with a friend. A drunk worth having... I wonder what they're doing now?"

"Who, Randall?"

"Meredith and Martha. If they're clever, they'll ignore the both of us when we get home. Give us that look of condescension and let us fall into bed. You see, brother, if we had something concrete to do tomorrow we wouldn't do it. But we don't... There we are. A hamburger. Eat up, brother. Soak up some of the alcohol. Am I nuts?"

"Totally. But it's fun talking about old times. You're just being miserable. Our wives are probably happy to get us out of the way. To leave them in peace and solitude. Martha's probably reading a book. Meredith drinking her third cup of tea. This food is good. I'm hungry."

"We're a couple of alcoholics."

"Probably. Both of us must just make sure it doesn't get the better of us. Make sure tomorrow we don't have a pick-me-up in the morning and end up spending another wasted day in the pub."

PART 2

JUNE 1995 – LOVE OR LUST

1

The alarm clock woke Manfred Leon from his trouble-free sleep, his mind focusing immediately on the day's work ahead, the young girl in his double bed no longer important. He remembered the good sex they had had the previous evening but not her full name. They had met, matched and gone home together at a literary function given by Manfred in a downtown Manhattan hotel for his friends in the press, all part of his system to introduce the media to his celebrity clients. Being a literary agent was all about maintaining momentum.

"What's the time?"

"Seven. You want breakfast?"

"Where am I?"

"In Manfred Leon's apartment."

"I better go home. My boyfriend is going to kill me... You will read my book?"

"Of course I will."

"Where is the manuscript?"

"I gave it to my assistant last night to take to the office."

"It's got my name, address and phone number on the last page."

"Do you live with your boyfriend?"

"He'll understand. My life is all about getting published... Did you enjoy yourself?"

"Of course I did."

"How old are you, Manfred?"

"Forty-seven next week. How old are you, Tracey?"

"Oh, good. You remembered my name. I'm twenty-seven."

"Young to have written a book."

"It's the story of a young girl who wants to succeed in life and uses her body to get what she wants. A bit like me. In the book, it works for her beautifully. Of course, she's very sexy. Did you come nicely last night? Of course you did. You went crazy with lust and ejaculation. If you like my book enough to show it to publishers we can do it again... We both have to go to work. It's Monday. I'll go down and get myself a cab. Nice meeting you, Manfred."

"How did you get to my party?"

"Through a friend. We always need help from a friend. In life, you have to make things happen. You don't just write a book and get it published. It's not that easy... You've got such a sweet paunch. I love a big stomach on a man. It's sexy."

"You want coffee?"

"I'm on my way. Don't forget to read *Lust*."

"You just called it *Lust*?"

"I did, Manfred. Have a lovely day. Be hearing from you. There. How do I look in a nice lacy pair of white knickers?... You want to give it a feel? Better not... There we are. Dressed for the street. Don't forget my nice lacy white underwear, Manfred, when you've finished reading my kinky, sexy book."

"Is it pornography?"

"Of course not. It's literature. The way we are. People love to read about their inner thoughts, the thoughts they never dare talk about. I go into the minds of the girls and boys and tell it how it is."

When Manfred opened the door of the yellow cab for Tracey in the street outside his apartment front door, he was not sure if he even liked himself. He was a dirty old man being used by a woman with a purpose. To salve his conscience, he would read her book, instead of flipping a couple of pages.

When Manfred reached his place of work, he asked Faith to bring the book he had given her into his office. She had a sweet, knowing look on her face.

"Don't even think it, Faith. Give me the book. Did you look at it? What's that smirk on your face? I hate Monday mornings. Phone Randall Holiday and Poppy Maddock and remind them we are lunching in the Metropolitan at one o'clock... You're still smirking, Faith."

"If she's as good in bed as the girl in the book, I have every right to smirk. I've worked for you for fifteen years. If she hadn't got at you last night you wouldn't have wanted to look at her book."

"I'm a dirty old man."

"Don't be silly. Of course you're not. If a pretty young girl wants to throw herself at you, what's the problem? You didn't make the move. She was coming on to you the moment she gave you her book. You remember that time fifteen years ago when you'd just started your literary agency and I was your first employee? We both gave each other the look. Fortunately, we agreed to keep it strictly business or I'd just be another of your old, forgotten girlfriends, used and discarded like the rest of them. Why didn't you find a nice girl and marry her? Have children. I'm so happy being married to Charles. Anyway, how old is she?"

"Twenty-seven."

"Then you are a dirty old man, boss."

"What's the book like?"

"Read it and see. *Lust*. Says it all."

"But how does it read? Can she write? Do the words make pictures?"

"Lots and lots of erotic pictures."

"Is there a story? Without a story, it's just porn."

"Read it and see Mr Leon... Now. Down to business. The most important thing today is to make sure Poppy Maddock creates a bond with Randall so he doesn't push off to his island in the middle of the Irish sea. We must never stop promoting our most popular author or he won't be popular anymore. Tell Poppy to do a Tracey on Randall. She's sexy enough from the way I see men look at her. We want Mr Holiday here in Manhattan for the rest of his writing life. I'm having another go at Villiers Publishing to try and get them to publish his wife's children's book. They gave her a fifty thousand advance. Why not publish it? Make her happy. Give them another good reason for staying in New York."

"What would I do without you?"

"Nothing, probably. Oh, and I want you to make me a partner. None of this assistant business. Thank you for reminding me."

"How is Charles?"

"He's gorgeous... Coffee or tea?"

"Tea, thank you."

"Now get on with your work while I make the tea."

"Have you tried writing a book?"

"If I could write, I wouldn't have been your assistant for the last fifteen years. But I know a good one when I see it... The Leon White agency. How does that sound?"

"You want to use your maiden name, Mrs Tyndall?"

"Of course I do."

"Get the printer to do some new letterheads if you're serious. I like it. It's going to be a good day."

"She's put the sparkle back in your eyes."

"Stop laughing."

"I'm smiling, not laughing. We'll go through the day's schedule over our cup of tea."

Not sure if Faith was being serious, or just pulling his leg, as usual, Manfred sat reading his mail, the letters opened by Faith and put on his desk in a pile. Half the mail was letters from aspiring writers looking for an agent. Manfred skimmed the letters and dropped them one by one in the waste-paper basket. The chances of an unknown author finding a publisher were as good as being attacked by a white shark and struck by lightning at the same time. An author had to be famous before a publisher would consider his work. To promote an unknown author was virtually impossible. A good book had nothing to do with it. Good literature was long past. History. All the publishers wanted was a handle to make those sales, climb the bestseller lists, receive all that lovely publicity in the media. Poor Tracey. Even her body wasn't going to help.

When Manfred looked up, Faith was standing in front of his desk.

"Read it now, boss. It's only a little over sixty thousand words. Once you start you won't put it down, you dirty old man."

"Where's my tea? Are you serious about wanting to be a partner? There's a big difference in telling people what to do and being told what to do."

"I'm always telling you what to do."

"Ah, but that's different. You don't have to decide. Tossing good ideas out is one thing. Making the right decisions quite another. If I get it wrong, we could lose a Randall Holiday to another literary agent and with it our income. If you get it wrong, it's not a problem as nothing is done. Give me the book and close the door. If the first chapter doesn't appeal you can bring the tea and we'll have our usual Monday morning discussion. Did you have a pleasant weekend?"

"The kids are driving me crazy. They never stop running around."

"How old are they now?"

"George is ten. Melony turns nine next month. And they are expensive. Luckily Charles makes lots of lovely money. If you don't give me a partnership, how about a raise? That book you're holding is going to sell a million copies. It's just sexy enough to be called a novel, but oh those erotic pictures."

Within a page, Manfred knew the girl who had deliberately seduced him the previous night could write. By the end of the third chapter, he was certain the right advertising would make *Lust* a bestseller. When Faith brought in the tray of tea he was smiling.

"Good books that will sell are as rare as hen's teeth, Faith. And I still don't know her surname."

"Tracey Chapelle. It's on the last page... Who are you going to send it to?"

"I'm not sure. Not one of the big ones. They're too cocky when it comes to new authors. We need a young, new publisher bursting with energy and venture capital to back it."

"Try Godfrey Merchant. He's been going just over a year. Has big money behind him. He uses the new way they call the internet to get at readers."

"Is he young?"

"Young and good looking. And he's single. Tracey will love to have a go at him if she had a go at you."

"Don't be rude, Faith."

"Sorry, boss. The truth always hurts. Put the book on one side and we'll go through our week's agenda. It's quite a Monday morning. And Randall and Poppy have confirmed they'll be at the Metropolitan for lunch. I had a word with her. Told her to come on to Randall. Get his hormones jumping."

"But he's married."

"Doesn't stop them wanting what they shouldn't have. Why on earth did her parents call her Poppy? Rose is bad enough."

"Instead of Faith, they might have called you Charity. Faith, hope and charity."

"When it came to handing out his hard-earned money to charity, my father was as mean as pig-shit. Said charity begins at home. That all those big charities people boast about that call for contributions are just another form of business."

"People benefit from charities."

"Of course they do. I like to take care of my kids and my husband. My father if he needed help. If you make your money legally through hard work and pay your taxes, you don't have to worry about a guilty conscience."

"She was lucky her surname wasn't Tupper."

"Who?"

"Poppy Maddock. We had a girl at my college whose name was Tupper. Pretty as paint. Her father had christened her Poppy. When people, mostly men, asked her her name, the reply sounded like 'pop-it up 'er'. Worked like a charm."

"You think the father did it intentionally? Give me Tracey's manuscript and I'll make a copy. Do you want to take it to Godfrey, or shall I? You can read the rest of it when I've made the copy. I'll give him three days to make up his mind. We want a big advance and a date for publishing. Poppy Tupper. Did she get married? At least she'd have got a name change when she married. People. They never fail to amaze me."

By the time Manfred walked into the restaurant he had almost finished reading *Lust*, a satisfied smile on his face. Instead of leaving Tracey Chapelle in suspense, he had given the girl a ring.

"You can write, Tracey. Your people are alive. You got right into their heads. Once the readers get into the book the characters are part of their lives. But don't let me get your hopes up. Finding you a publisher is going to be difficult. Why would the bookshop chains want to put unknown Tracey Chapelle on their shelves? Why would a passing reader pick your book over hundreds of others whose authors and titles are familiar? It all requires extensive marketing to the general public and that costs big money. For a publisher, you are a gamble, and management in the big publishing houses don't like to take gambles that might jeopardise their careers. Why big publishers pay vast sums in advance to a celebrity who has written a book as millions of people are familiar with the name and the life of the celebrity."

"But why? If my book is good why won't they publish it? Thank you, Manfred. Are you coming round tonight? Of course you're welcome. What are my chances?"

"We are going to do our best. My assistant thinks it will sell. She's delivering a copy of your manuscript to the publisher I have in mind right at this moment. He's young. Full of energy. And best of all, he has venture capital behind him. The kind of backers who like to take gambles in the hope of making exorbitant profits. Tomorrow, I'm arranging lunch with Godfrey Merchant for Thursday so you can turn on your charm. One o'clock at the Metropolitan, my second home for business. See you Thursday."

"How old is he?"

"More your age. Faith, my assistant, was the first to read your book and thinks it will sell a million copies."

"I can't believe it!"

"Do you have another book on the way?"

"There are always books in my head. The stories of people I've never met... Got to get back to my mundane job or my boss will be after me. Get me a good advance and I'll chuck in my job and start another book. Wow, sometimes life works. I'm going to be a famous writer and marry a very rich man, all my money worries over."

"So you don't want to marry me?"

"Are you proposing, Manfred?"

"Not really."

"But we can still have fun, especially if you find me a publisher. I'll wear something really sexy for lunch. It'll have to be quick. My boss gives us an hour. Godfrey Merchant. Got it."

The little giggle before Tracey put down her phone had made Manfred smile, the expectation of what she was going to do to Godfrey Merchant clear as crystal. Not sure if he was running a literary agency or a knock-shop, Manfred looked around the restaurant from his seat at the corner table while he waited for Randall Holiday and Poppy Maddock.

"Bring me a beer while I'm waiting for my guests."

In front of the middle place-setting sat a single gardenia that Manfred had ordered for Poppy, the sweet scent from the white flower intoxicating. Publishing, like most things in life, was one big game, the success of which relied on details. The first to arrive was Randall, closely followed by Poppy. Manfred stood up to greet his guests, the waiter hovering with his tray in the background as Randall picked up and smelt the flower.

"Gardenia! I love the smell of gardenias. My father says it was my late mother's favourite flower. When they dined out at a restaurant there was always a gardenia on the table for Carmen."

"Will you do Poppy the honour of pinning the flower to her dress? May I introduce you to the scriptwriter of *Love Song*? Poppy, meet Randall."

"Hello. I so loved your book. It's so exciting writing a film script for a famous author... Thank you, Randall. That looks and smells so nice. And thank you, Manfred, for pulling out my chair. Such beautiful manners are so rare these days... So Randall Holiday, what are you writing at the moment?"

"Nothing. Can't write surrounded by noise and people."

"Of course you can. It's just a case of getting used to it and blocking the noise and people from your brain. You must have something in your head. All writers have something in their heads."

"There has been a suggestion in history that Shakespeare was not the writer of his plays. That his background was too ordinary to have known so much about the people he wrote about in such vivid detail. I have conjured up the Earl of Oxford as a man who liked to write plays and be part of Shakespeare's theatre without making himself the author so he would stay in the background, a country gentleman in gentlemanly anonymity. Do you know about Shakespeare, Poppy?"

"I told you, I have a degree in English Literature from Oxford University. What do you want to know?"

"Could a ghostwriter have written his plays?"

"There's been that speculation... Oh, Randall, I do hope you're going to help me write your film script."

"The book, if I ever write it, will be called *Shakespeare's Friend*. And no, I don't write film scripts."

"Couldn't we have some nice, cosy discussion at my apartment so I don't do anything you don't like?"

"What are you drinking, Poppy? We'd better order now and not keep the man waiting any longer... You two should get together. You know that old cliché: two heads are better than one."

With the orders placed and the drinks on the way, Manfred relaxed. With Randall pinning the flower to her dress, Poppy Maddock had his full attention.

"What was Shakespeare's theatre called? The round theatre where he produced and directed all his plays? In Rhodesia where I grew up on a farm, Shakespeare wasn't as important as he would have been to a literary student at Oxford University."

"The Globe Theatre."

"And where was it?"

"Southwark. Across from London Bridge."

"I thought it was in Stratford-upon-Avon."

"I can help you with your research, Randall. We can have some fun."

"That would be nice. I'm a writer, but my degree is in finance. Can you believe how our lives can change? So, let's drink to the success of *Love Song* the movie."

By the time lunch was over, Poppy was well on her way. They had agreed to meet at Poppy's apartment the following evening to discuss Shakespeare and for Randall to read through the draft of the first scene of the movie. Whether Randall's wife would be as happy with the arrangement, Manfred wasn't so sure. Manfred, always careful at a business meeting to keep his wits about him, had drunk one glass of wine.

Manfred watched them leave the Metropolitan together, the alcohol firmly in control of both of them. Shaking his head, Manfred went back to his office to get on with his work.

"How did it go, boss? Godfrey has promised to read *Lust* tonight."

"Lots of red wine and a good-looking woman coming on to you. How do you think it went? We men are so stupid when it comes to women."

"If you say so. Life in Manhattan."

"Poor Meredith."

"Maybe she has a boyfriend. You never know. Sex with the same person becomes boring after a while."

"Have you been unfaithful to Charles?"

"Not yet. And I hope I never will be. But I've been tempted. More than once. You have to control your lust, which is more than those characters in *Lust* were able to do."

"One big knock-shop."

"You got it. Everyone screwing everyone. Lying. Cheating. Anything to get their hands on the money. Modern America. No scruples. No conscience. Tracey has it down to a T. In the end, is it much of a life? I don't think so. But it's worked that way since man and woman came out of the sea. Or wherever they evolved from. You can't change what's inherent. Just try and control ourselves if we can. As we did, Manfred, or we wouldn't have had all the fun we've had together building the agency... Wasn't Randall married before?"

"His first wife went off with a woman."

"That's painful."

"His son has been brought up by two women. Randall says he has no contact with James Oliver. That it's better for the boy to be left alone until he grows up and Randall can explain it all to him."

"Randall should write it down in a book. An easier way to explain it to his son."

"He did. It was a good way to vent his bitterness. To get the affair into perspective for everyone. It made a compelling book."

"What was it called?"

"*Nothing Lasts Forever*."

"How did the women take it?"

"I haven't asked. Randall's private life is none of my business."

"Does he ever bring up the first wife in conversation?"

"Sometimes."

"It must have been a very rough time for him. But let's not forget the game on Thursday; Tracey knocking off Godfrey, if she wants to get her book published and make herself money... Here are the phone calls while you were out. You want some coffee?"

"I need time to think."

"We all need time to think. The problem is what we think about. Don't you ever get jealous?"

"Of what?"

"Well, Tracey with whom you've so recently been intimate knocking it off, in your own so descriptive words, with Godfrey Merchant."

"That's her business."

"I'm sure it is. Coffee coming up."

After returning the calls on Faith's list, every call he made having a purpose that would further his business, Manfred sat back in his office chair and thought of what Faith had said to him. Should he be upset at the idea of passing Tracey over to Godfrey? Probably not. The girl wasn't interested in him, only what she could get out of him. The gap in their age only made for a temporary arrangement. Did he want to get married to anyone, settle down and have kids? He didn't think so. In Manfred's experience, every relationship had been sexual and had faded with satiation. Some had broken it off with him, most had just faded into another affair with a new girl looking for a future. He was getting old and if he did not marry soon and have children, his link in the chain of evolution would be gone forever. His life would have no purpose. In Manfred's somewhat bitter analysis of life, the only reason for a person's existence was procreation, the rest a constant chase of phantoms that were meant to give life a worthwhile meaning but never did. In the early stage of his career as a literary agent, he thought finding a great writer was the most important reason for his work. A writer that would go on down through history giving the world something important to read, a work that would better the world by giving people an understanding of what their lives were for. But with all the manuscripts he had read, none had given him that epiphany. Was religion the only manifestation that gave any purpose? And did anyone really know if any religious teaching was true, or just another means of controlling people by putting the fear of God into them and making them behave themselves and not end up for eternity in the fire of hell?

As Manfred sat thinking to himself, the cynic in him began laughing at his naïvety: life was really very simple. To be comfortable you needed food and a roof over your head, and some fun in the process of obtaining comforts. A day-to-day game of petty pursuit, of getting drunk and not caring about the consequences. Like the trap he had set Randall Holiday with Poppy Maddock to obtain the best possible film script for *Love Song*. In the end, Manfred told himself, it was one long manipulation to make money, the money that was meant to buy fun. Manfred knew he was as selfish as the rest of them. Did it worry him? He didn't think so. The life of a literary agent was about finding books that sold and made money, not some great philosophical work that wouldn't change man's bad habits anyway. So if Tracey screwed Godfrey and Godfrey published her book, all three of them would come out of it winners. With just a slight thought of jealousy, Manfred went back to working on the pile of correspondence on the side of his desk. Within a minute he was happily lost in his work, Thursday's luncheon at the Metropolitan forgotten. When Manfred looked up from his work his cup of coffee was stone cold on the desk in front of him. He had not even noticed Faith putting it down on the desk. At eight o'clock, long after Faith had gone home to her husband and children, Manfred went back to his lonely apartment and made himself a plate of sandwiches before turning on the television.

2

When Tracey Chapelle woke on the Thursday, the euphoria brought her instantly awake. She had found an agent. She was going to publish. She was going to be famous. A young woman with a glorious world waiting to fall into her arms. There would be no boss telling her what to do. No men just using her for their sexual pleasures. She was going to be a celebrity that everyone wanted to know.

By the time Tracey showered and ate her breakfast, the good feeling was still with her, making everything around her a pleasure. Only when she arrived at work did reality prevail, the reality of work in an insurance company overwhelming her feeling of happiness, making Tracey tell herself there was still one more hill to climb, one more conquest to be made, one more man to be seduced by her sexual charm. The day went by as she took her boss's dictation and typed his letters. She listened to his bragging, happy she now had an escape. Her whole world was about to change; if Godfrey Merchant published her book, she could tell her self-opinionated boss what she really thought of him. By the time her day in the office sitting at her typewriter was over her confidence had been replaced by a feeling of failure, that Godfrey Merchant would tell her at dinner that he had either not read her book or thought it a load of rubbish. She showered again, plastered herself with perfume and put on a dress that showed off her body and went out of her small, mean apartment where she had written *Lust* and took a cab she could barely afford to the fancy Metropolitan where her last conquest was waiting in the foyer with a man holding her manuscript. Having told Manfred she was only allowed an hour for lunch they had changed the meeting for dinner. When he turned to look at her, Tracey was certain Godfrey Merchant had read her book.

"This is Godfrey, Tracey. He's going to publish your book. Let's all go into the restaurant where Faith reserved us a table. Or shall we take a cocktail up at the bar? We want to talk about how you are going to help us publicise your book. Chat shows. Interviews with the press. Magazine articles. All the usual build-up to the launch of a book."

"How much are you going to pay me for my book, Godfrey? You don't mind my calling you Godfrey?"

"All my writers call me Godfrey. Fifty thousand dollars now and another fifty thousand the day the book is launched. There'll be a big launch party for the press right here in this hotel. Oh, and I want a photograph of you looking your best for the book's back-cover. I'll want you to look your sexiest... There we are. Fifty thousand United States dollars made out to my new protégée, Tracey Chapelle. Lovely to meet you, Tracey. Let's go to the bar and have ourselves a drink to celebrate. Your book had me captivated from the first paragraph and I couldn't put it down until I had finished it. *Lust*. Such a perfect title. You're so young to know so much."

"I started early."

"I'll bet you did. Manfred tells me he only met you recently at one of his drinks parties. Good things happen quickly, Tracey. Don't they, Manfred? Oh, what fun we are going to have. You're the prettiest author on my list. Welcome to Merchant Publishers. Now, tell me about your next book."

"What about the contract, Godfrey?"

"Still being negotiated with Manfred. We've agreed on the advance and the date of publication. He wants fifteen per cent of retail sales as the author's royalty. I usually only give an author's first book ten per cent. If your first book sells as well as we hope it will, your next book will earn you fifteen per cent of retail. When you've proved yourself."

"Take the ten per cent on *Lust*, Manfred. My mother always told me as a child growing up not to be greedy. And film rights? We are going to offer the book to film producers?"

"Leave the detail to your agent."

"Of course. This time last week I didn't have an agent."

Concentrating on Godfrey, avoiding Manfred's knowing smiles, Tracey turned up the volume of her charm. Not only was he her publisher, he was outstandingly good looking, all the women up at the bar who noticed Godfrey Merchant giving him the eye. From Tracey's long years of seducing men and getting what she wanted from them, the young man with her manuscript on the bar in front of him would not find it difficult to choose what he wanted when it came to women. By the time they went into the restaurant she had his full attention, the chat about books and what she was going to be writing a backdrop to their game of seduction. For a brief moment, Tracey even felt sorry for Manfred who, despite the competition, couldn't keep his eyes away from her. At the table in Manfred's favourite corner, the food and wine became secondary.

"I have a late appointment with one of my clients. The bill's paid, Godfrey. You two stay and enjoy yourselves. Send your written contract to my office and we'll put this whole thing to bed."

For a moment, all three of them looked at each other without laughing. They all had what they wanted. Sex for Tracey with Godfrey would be to satiate her sexual craving and have nothing to do with publishing her book. Under the table, she put her hand on Manfred's knee and gave it a squeeze of thankful appreciation. They understood each other. She had given him sex and ten per cent of her royalty payments. He had given her the greatest opportunity in her life. He had given her a publisher.

"Where do you live, Tracey?"

"In a horrible, boring apartment."

"Do you want to come back to my place for a nightcap?"

"Of course I do. Let's just wait for Manfred to leave the building."

"Will Manfred be jealous?"

"I hope not... Who's going to play the part of Fay in the movie?"

"First things first, Tracey."

"You know how it is."

"I rather think I do... Did you sleep with him?"

"Who?"

"You know who I'm talking about. Poor Manfred. He walked out with his tail between his legs."

"He's far too old for me."

"Of course he is. You've got a grin all over your face."

"He's gone by now. Let's go. We don't want to waste time, do we, Godfrey?"

"No we don't."

"Come on then. Happy times are here again."

"And long may they last. One of the things I have learned in life is to enjoy oneself. Never miss an opportunity to be happy."

"We only live once."

"That's what they say... Was *Lust* written from your personal experience or from your imagination?"

"You have to experience things in life before you can write about them despite calling a novel fiction. A good book of fiction is life as it happened, warts and all, without all the excuses that we use to make ourselves look better than we are. We all like to keep up appearances but underneath we are all as bad as each other. We take from life what we want, not caring about the consequences, and lie through our back teeth when the righteous question our habits. *Lust* tells it as it is, so the reader, in the privacy of their mind, can relate to the truth of life through my characters. Fay is a girl who loves men, the more men the better. When she finds a man who is good at it, she tries all the tricks to suck him dry. Threesomes. Gang bangs, or clutter fucks as she calls them. And don't grin, Godfrey. We all like to watch other people having multiple sex. Men like to watch the girls having sex with each other because it turns them on. We'd never admit that out loud to our friends, and certainly not our enemies. We're all a bit kinky, Godfrey... So you think my book will sell?"

"Most writers are afraid to plumb the depths you have gone to. People will buy your book and hide it from their friends out of embarrassment. But, oh wow, will they read it. And you write well. Your words are well chosen. Your sentences are short and easy to read. Those long, convoluted sentences of some writers trying to impress with fancy words most readers don't understand annoy me. The writers are showing off their highfalutin literary skills. Never use a word that isn't easily understood, and if you do, explain its meaning to the reader."

"Does my book need explaining?"

"Not one word of it. We all understand our basic instincts. We're all pretty much animals dressed in smart clothing."

"Will the shops be happy to put my book on their shelves?"

"Some of them won't be to begin with. The snooty bookshops with their noses up in the air. But when your book starts selling in quantity they'll come running. Despite their pride in owning a bookshop with good literature, in the end, it's all about making money, that other primal instinct... Now isn't that nice? A cab right outside the door of the hotel. Are you going to spend the night?"

"I never spend the night or fornicate on the first date. We have lots of time to get to know each other. Maybe we shouldn't sleep together. You know that old saying: 'never mix business with pleasure'. We want our business relationship to last for years so don't let's fuck it out of ourselves. I have a better idea. As one of your writers, I'll introduce you to good-looking girls and you can introduce me to good-looking young men. If we fall in love with each other we'll have to think again. You'd better ask the driver to drop me at my apartment or I won't have the strength of character to keep my word."

"You're keeping me on a string, is that it?"

"I'm just being sensible. First things first. Let's get my book into as many bookshops as possible before we ruin anything."

"Can I have a little kiss?"

"Of course you can. On both cheeks."

"You're incorrigible."

"I know I am. You see, you and I, Godfrey, are going to have lots of fun together. Make lots of money together. And we don't want to screw it up, now do we? A kiss on each cheek and a broad grin on the face. What's wrong with that on a first meeting?"

"Are you as good at it as Fay?"

"Of course I am. Or how else would I know how to write it?"

"When they take your photograph for the back cover, give the camera that same look you gave me in the foyer of the hotel. A first look that sucked my lust right up from my balls."

"You read that in my book."

"Indeed I did. How do you know how men feel?"

"Men talk. I listen. Write it down."

"Can't we pretend it's a second date, Tracey?"

"That's an old one."

"It's not in the book."

"Why it isn't. Sleep tight, Godfrey. Sweet dreams. Can you pay for the taxi? Once I've cashed your cheque, my finances will be a whole lot different."

With the car door closed she gave the driver the address of her mean little apartment, smiled through the glass of the window at a frustrated Godfrey, and once more gave him the look. When she looked back he was still standing motionless on the pavement, a look of puzzlement mixed with astonishment on his face. It made Tracey laugh out loud: not too many women had turned down Godfrey Merchant. Sitting comfortably in the back seat of the cab, she took out the cheque and read the amount all over again. For the first time in her life, she had money. Real money. When they reached the old apartment building that was shortly going to be pulled down and rebuilt for the rich, she fumbled in her bag for her keys and emptied out the few coins.

"Thank you, driver. Next time I'll give you a proper tip."

Upstairs, Tracey took off all her clothes other than her tight knickers and got into her bed. Within a minute she was sound asleep, sleeping dreamlessly through the night. Her first cup of coffee in the morning was delicious. In the office, the first thing Tracey did was type out her letter of resignation and take it through to the office of her boss.

"What's this all about Tracey?"

"Please don't make me be rude."

"You can't leave. You're the best secretary I've had in ages."

"Can I leave now or must I work out my notice?"

"What's happened?"

"My book has been accepted."

"You were writing a book?"

"We've worked with each other day after day in adjacent offices and know nothing about each other... Can I go? Or must I stay another month?"

"Written a book. I'll be damned... Go to accounts and get your last salary cheque. Good luck to you, Tracey Chapelle... What's the book called?"

"*Lust*."

"What's it about?"

"Lust. The power of sexual communication. And don't give me that look, Ferdinand, or I'm going to laugh in your face. Thanks for my job when I needed it. Thanks for not demanding I work out my notice."

"You ever liked me?"

"Not particularly. But it takes all sorts to make the world. You do a boring job well in a boring business. All those insurance reports telling a client exactly what he is and isn't insured against. Most insurance companies just give the client the policy and let them work it out for themselves and only find out the problem when they make the claim. You're an honest man, Ferdinand, but don't you find your life boring?

Once you have enough money in life to pay the bills the worst thing that can happen is boredom. My escape has been going home to my cheap apartment to write my book. And now the money from the book has enabled me to escape again. Have a good life, boss. Enjoy yourself. Do you want me to phone the temp agency or will you look for a permanent? As they say in the classics: nice knowing you. Find yourself a wife and have some kids or you'll die of boredom."

"Please don't slam the door."

"I'll try not to."

"Can you at least send me a copy of your book?"

"It will be my pleasure. When you've read it you'll know what you had in the next-door office. You'll know what you missed."

"Can we shake hands?"

"Of course we can, boss. But this time as equals."

"Please phone the agency and ask them to send me a temporary secretary, and tell them that if she's any good I'll make it permanent. So for the two years we've worked together, you despised me? I must be a fool for not having seen what you thought of me. All I was doing was my job to the best of my ability without coming on to you."

"I'm sorry."

"So am I, Tracey. I thought we were friends doing a job together."

"Now I feel the fool."

"Maybe we are all fools, Tracey. All of us fools just trying to make a living."

When Tracey reached the door to Ferdinand's office and turned to look back, his head was down, absorbed in his work, the contretemps forgotten. Quietly, Tracey closed the door for the last time and went to her desk to phone the agency before going to the accounts department to collect her last salary cheque. An hour later, when she left the building, she was feeling sad, as if she had left a part of herself behind.

"Two years in the same place is a long time. And now it's all over."

Looking up at the sky through the high-rise buildings, Tracey walked to her bank to deposit Merchant Publisher's cheque, not sure what to do with the rest of her day. Back in her apartment she sat at the table with the typewriter she had used to write *Lust*, put in a clean sheet of paper and stared at the blank page. It took an hour before the small demon came out of the back of her head. Then she typed, lost in another world, the satisfaction of writing her story far greater than the pleasure she had received at the bank when she had deposited

Godfrey's cheque. When she finished her day's writing, Tracey knew it was not about the money. In most people's lives, it was always about the money. For her it was writing her book, getting the frustrations and pleasures in life on paper, herself always hovering over the story looking on. If others were going to enjoy her books as much as she enjoyed writing them, they would all be happy. Did Ferdinand get satisfaction out of writing his insurance reports? She hoped so. A job, whatever it was, had to be satisfying. Life. The daily process of getting through life.

"I'm free! Free as a bird."

In the small alcove she called her kitchen, Tracey put the frying pan on the right side of her two-plate and cooked herself bacon and eggs and two pieces of fried bread. She needed a friend. Someone to boast to. To tell them her book had been accepted by a publisher. She thought and thought but there was no one to phone. All her true friends were in her books. All of them imaginary. All of them part of her imagination. Who she wanted was Godfrey. His mind and his body. Reminding herself never to break her own rules, she went next door to talk to her impoverished neighbour, a woman alone in her late thirties without money, family or friends.

"You want to go to a pub and get drunk, Jane? I know you like drinking."

"What are you after, Tracey? You know I don't have money to go drinking."

"But this time I do. I've had my book accepted. I've resigned my job and I'm lonely. To answer your question, I need company. I need a friend. Will you be my friend?"

"A friend in need is a friend indeed."

"Have you ever been in love?"

"Once, as a girl of nineteen."

"What happened?"

"He married the daughter of a rich man. Never looked back at me. And you? A pretty girl like you must have fallen in love many times."

"What is love? Do we fall in love or fall in need? Do we say we love a person when we just need them for one of a multiple of reasons? For money, security or just for sex?"

"Why don't you get us some nice wine and we'll drink it here."

"Will you tell me your lover's story? Writers are always looking for good stories to steal. I'm a writer, Jane. A professional writer. And I can't believe it. No. Let's drink out. See what we can find. Money for me is no longer a problem."

"I'm too old to pick up men."

"Of course you're not. You never know your luck. If nothing happens, we'll bring back a bottle of whisky. Does that sound better? Always have backup, I tell my characters. Tracey and Jane out on the tiles. What's wrong with that idea?"

"Give me half an hour to get myself dressed. Can we go to a bar I once went to in my other life? When I thought my boyfriend loved me and was going to marry me. Spend our lives together. At nineteen, I was so naïve. All he wanted from me was sex."

"We can taxi to your bar. Mind if I look through your bookshelf while you get changed? They say you can tell the real person from the books they read... Shakespeare! I don't believe it. Tolstoy. Hemingway. What happened? You'd better not read my book."

"I like all sorts of books. My one escape. I have a degree in English Literature but it didn't do me any good. I can read but I can't write."

"You could be an editor. A journalist. I don't even know what you do."

"I work in a laundry."

"With a degree in English?"

"Once, I had another life. And then I started drinking. Alcohol warps a person's mind."

"Did you have men in your life?"

"Plenty of them. None of them I remember. How I ended up down the drain in a laundry with just enough income to survive. What I'm going to do when they knock down this place with its cheap rent doesn't bear thinking about. Enjoy my books, Tracey... A good drink. I haven't had a good drink in ages."

"What's the name of the pub?"

"Harry B's."

"Never heard of it."

"You should. It was a favourite haunt of authors and artists in my heyday of drinking. It's going to be so nice having company. Many times on my own I've thought of killing myself. I have nothing of importance to do for the rest of my life. All it can do is get worse."

"You never know, Jane. You never know. Maybe tonight is your night. Hurry and change while I read Hemingway's *A Farewell to Arms*. What's it like?"

"Sad, very sad. At the end, she and the baby die leaving him alone for the rest of his life... You know he shot himself?"

"Who?"

"Ernest Hemingway. All that wonderful writing and still he shot himself."

"Why don't you write the story of when you were nineteen and in love?"

"I've tried. Many times."

"Try again. I'll read what you write. Maybe help. All you need is a good story."

"You're very sweet. Enjoy Hemingway."

When Tracey came out of the First World War in Hemingway's book, the surprise at how Jane looked gave her a happy feeling. The hair was drawn to the back of her head and tied in a short ponytail. The make-up on her face made Jane look five years younger. The dress was out of fashion but made the best of Jane's sex appeal.

"My word, you do look different. Let's go. You'll give the directions to your bar to the driver."

"Did you like Hemingway?"

"He draws you right into his world."

"That's my problem when I try and write. I can't get into the minds and world of my characters. I can use my well-structured English to report on a story. Like a man with a camera looking from a distance. But I can't get inside and bring my reader with me. You know what I'm saying if they have accepted your book. My mind becomes blocked when I try and write about Harvey. And when I begin to see into his mind, I run away... Will you look after me, Tracey, if I get too drunk and make a fool of myself?"

"Of course I will. It's friends' night out."

"Congratulations on publishing your book. You have no idea how jealous I am."

"Maybe you should stop writing about Harvey. Find an imaginary character. Create the man you wanted him to be. Live in your head and describe the life you wanted to have and make yourself happy. Everything we do comes from our mind... When did you last have sex?"

"A long, long time ago... Oh dear, I'm going to get drunk tonight. The one good thing about being poor is not having the money to drink."

"Am I doing something for you I shouldn't?"

"It doesn't matter. I can always kill myself tomorrow. And working the machines in a laundry doesn't require much thinking. It's pretty automatic. You shove it in. And you pull it out... Harry B's. It must have changed. Everything changes, Tracey... You can keep the book. Just give it back when you've finished reading... I wish I was young again. You're so lucky with your whole life ahead of you. My life is finished."

"No, it isn't. And tonight I'm going to prove it."

"What are you going to do?"

"Use my charm and find you a man."

"Then he'll want you, not me."

"Be positive. Some men like a more mature woman. Especially one who reads so widely and has a degree in English Literature. I spend my whole writing life worrying about wrong words and commas."

"Why you have an editor."

"Why didn't you make a career as an editor?"

"I can't even think with a hangover, let alone play around with someone else's hard work when I'm half drunk."

"How did you get the money to drink?"

"Men. Lots and lots of men."

While they were driven through the crowded streets Jane sat fidgeting, looking out of the window, the street lights bright on the crowds of moving people in, to Tracey, the greatest city in the world. When the cab dropped them, Jane led the way. The first person Tracey saw inside was Manfred Leon, her lover from Sunday night. With him was a man of Jane's age that she recognised but couldn't quite place. With them, deep in conversation, was a pretty girl of a similar age to herself. Once up at the bar seated on a stool she could no longer see Manfred. The bar was full even for a Friday night, the music loud, people laughing. The restaurant area away from the bar was half full with seated customers eating their food.

"What are you going to drink, Jane?"

"A beer. I always started with a beer."

"Do you recognise anyone?"

"Not a soul. I think that man over there behind the bar must be the new owner. Bars and restaurants are always changing hands."

"Does it feel familiar?"

"Just a little."

"My agent's at the other end of the bar."

"I told you it was artists and writers. Your agent? How did you get an agent?"

"I screwed him on Sunday night. Deliberately. To make him read my manuscript."

"And he found you a publisher so quickly?"

"Good things happen fast. Or so they say."

"Shouldn't we join him?"

"Yes, you should. Hello, Tracey. I saw you come in. Come and join the party. Who's your lovely friend? I'm drinking with one of my writers and the girl who's writing the script for *Love Song*. Come and meet Randall Holiday and Poppy Maddock. Hello, my name is Manfred. And you are?"

"Jane. Plain Jane."

"Jane has a degree in English Literature. How long were you standing there before you spoke?"

"Come and join the other writers. Do you write, work for a publisher or teach?"

"Not exactly."

"Terry, give my friends a drink. Terry, meet Tracey Chapelle, my about-to-become second most successful author after Randall. What brought you to Harry B's, Tracey?"

"It used to be Jane's watering hole some years ago... I thought I recognised him from his interview with David Letterman on television. Or somewhere. You see so many faces in life they are difficult to place. Is he married?"

"Twice."

"Where's his wife?"

"At home with their young son. He's not staying long."

"I'm sure he's not... Beer for Jane and a glass of red wine for me, Terry. We're going down to the other end of the bar to join Manfred. I like this bar. Got a real buzz. Are you the owner? Who was Harry?"

"No one knows Harry. Harry started the pub just after Prohibition, so the story goes. What the B stood for no one knows... Amelia will bring you your drinks. Welcome to Harry B's."

Each carrying a small handbag, they walked down the long bar to where Manfred placed two more stools in a circle backed by the bar counter. A pretty girl placed the beer and the glass of red wine on the bar, all the time smiling at Randall Holiday, the electricity between them more than barmaid to customer. To Tracey, it looked as if the two were having an affair, the wife left at home to look after the child. In Tracey's experience, men who married more than once never stayed faithful.

"Thank you for the drinks, Manfred."

"How's Godfrey?"

"He's fine."

"I'm sure he is. Did you go off together last night after I left the restaurant?... Never mind. Randall, Poppy meet Tracey and Jane. The two of them have been talking about Shakespeare's friend. The one some think wrote Shakespeare's plays. Do you like Shakespeare, Jane? Jane has a degree in English Literature. A true writers' evening. And the lady behind the bar is Amelia. Say hello to Amelia... My goodness, that one went down fast. You must have been thirsty, Jane. Give the lady another drink."

"Can I have a whisky? That beer was nice."

"Of course you can. A single or a double?"

"Make it a double."

"What brings you back to Harry B's?"

"When I was in my late teens and my twenties I drank regularly at Harry B's. The home of writers and artists. Of course, we all drank too much but it was fun. Once I fell off a barstool and was picked up and taken home by a young man. I still don't remember his name... Now that looks good. Nothing better in life than a good Scotch whisky... Shakespeare's friend. Some say he wrote so much with such diversity it could not have all come from one man. Who knows? What matters are the plays. Don't let me interrupt your discussion, Randall. I enjoyed *Masters of Vanity*. So, Poppy, you are writing the film script for *Love Song*. It must feel so good to be successful. To happy days. A pleasure to meet you all. Thank you for the drinks, Manfred. Was there ever a greater writer than Shakespeare? I don't think so. And I'm back in my favourite watering hole. To Harry B's, everyone."

Smiling to herself, Tracey watched Manfred come on to Jane, payback for her throwing herself at Godfrey in front of Manfred the following evening. When Randall Holiday went home with Poppy Maddock, Tracey made her own excuses. Jane was in full flight, happy to flirt with Manfred. Outside Tracey walked the street until she found a shop selling liquor where she bought a bottle of whisky. Back at her apartment she sat alone with the bottle of whisky and began to drink. It was her turn to get well and truly plastered. She had lied to Manfred to save face on the morning of their one-night-stand about having a live-in boyfriend. But she had an agent and fifty thousand dollars in her bank account.

"Good luck, Jane. I hope you screw the brains out of him. In this lovely modern world, everyone screws everyone. Lust and money. Money and lust. That's what it's all about. Good luck to the lot of them."

Tracey got up from her couch, turned on the music and smiled at herself in the small mirror on her wall. Getting drunk alone was going to be fun. Who needed other people when you had an agent and a publisher, she told herself.

"You can screw Godfrey when he signs the contract. Rules are made to be broken, Tracey Chapelle. Life's about having fun."

Dancing alone to the music, she tripped over the carpet and fell back onto the couch without spilling a drop of her whisky. For the first time in her life, Tracey felt in control. She could do what she wanted when she wanted and not give a damn about anyone.

3

The next morning when Tracey woke with a raging hangover the euphoria had gone, replaced by a bout of panic. Had she done the right thing by resigning her job? Would Godfrey really publish her book and pay her the next fifty thousand? What would happen if the book did not sell? Should she have screwed Godfrey to keep his attention? Instead of being happy her life was hell. She went into the lounge and checked the bottle of whisky. There was an inch left in the bottom of the bottle.

"What the hell? I can't feel any worse."

Instead of pouring the whisky into the glass still sitting on the coffee table, she drank straight from the bottle, making herself choke. The alcohol tasted foul.

"Now what the fuck do I do all day? I can't write. Can't even think."

She was completely alone in a metropolis surrounded by millions of people who didn't know she existed. Life in the fast lane, with nothing to do. She poured what was left of the whisky into the glass and tried again. The small sip went smoothly down her throat. By the time she had finished what was left of the whisky, she was feeling a tad better, making herself think. Many girls of her age had a husband and one or two children, spending their days cleaning their husband's apartment and washing the dishes, their whole lives dictated by other people. Was that what she should have wanted from life? Tracey didn't think so. The very idea of demanding children was unpleasant. And screwing a constant flow of different men was also boring, except when she wrote it down in a book. She made herself a sandwich and ate it sitting on the couch staring at the wall. There had to be more to life but however hard she tried, Tracey could not think of an alternative. By the time the bar down the road had opened, she was walking down the sidewalk. In the bar, she looked around for a man. Or anyone to keep her company. The bar was empty except for the old man who owned the saloon.

"You're a bit early, Tracey. What you want? On your own are you?"

"I'm bored."

"Join the club."

"Make it a beer. I've got a hangover. When do people come in?"

"When they feel like it."

"You got any bright ideas, George?"

"Not really."

"Why is life so boring?"

"Wait till you get to my age... There we go. Do you mind if I read the morning paper? I'm never even sure why I read the news. It's all horrible. Sensational. Another financial crash on the way. A story of some rich celebrity."

"We could talk."

"What about?"

"I have no idea. Go read your paper. I met Randall Holiday last night."

"Who's he?"

"A famous writer."

"Never heard of him."

"I'm about to become a famous author."

"Good luck to you. First, you'd better write a book."

The old man went down to the other end of his bar, sat up on the barman's barstool, flipped open the morning newspaper, put on his reading glasses and began to silently read. Only when Tracey tapped her empty glass on the bar counter did he pay her any attention.

"What's life all about, George?"

"You tell me, Tracey. Luckily, I don't have much time to go."

"How old are you?"

"Seventy. Three score years and ten. Can't be much more. You want another beer? Coming up, lady."

"Would you like to be young again?"

"Not particularly."

"Anything in the paper?"

"Nothing worth reading. Just the same old crap."

"Tell me about your life."

"Whatever for?"

"You must have done something interesting."

"Nothing I can think of. Life is just the process of daily living. The same old day, day after day until the day you die... Enjoy your beer."

"Still no more customers."

"You can only hope. Sit around and hope. Sometimes it works and sometimes it doesn't. The rent is due in less than a week. When they've been paid, it picks up."

"Have you got the rent?"

"Not yet. Some of my old customers owe me money. They'll help. Got to keep your regular customers. You run them a tab and find at the end of the evening they can pay only half the bill. No one keeps count when they're drinking. It's a pain in the arse collecting money for each drink. Anyway, they wouldn't come in. And every regular attracts a couple more customers. How it is, running a bar. People attract people. Why they came in on their own. They can drink at home for a third of the price but most people prefer drinking in company."

"Did you have a wife?"

"Two of them. Both gave up on me when I didn't make enough money to give them the lifestyle they expected."

"Are they both alive?"

"One of them. The first. Divorced her forty years ago. The second died ten years after we separated."

"Any kids?"

"None. When I die I'll have nothing to show for it. A wasted life with no purpose to it. It would be nice to have a kid. To have grandchildren. To know your seed is going to live on after you."

"Couldn't they have kids?"

"I don't know. They both probably thought they had made a mistake soon after they married me."

"Maybe you were infertile."

"I don't think so. I got a girl pregnant after I broke up with Natalie. She wanted an abortion when I wouldn't marry her."

"Why didn't you marry her?"

"I was still married to Natalie. Once Natalie found out Jenny was pregnant with my child she wouldn't go through with the divorce. I'm still not sure if it was nastiness or jealousy. I still think of that child we killed."

"What happened to Jenny?"

"She was ten years younger than me. Went off on her own after I paid for the abortion. No idea what happened to her."

"Was it a boy or a girl?"

"Thankfully, that I never knew. I'm going to end in hell for killing my own child."

"Did you ever hear from Natalie?"

"Nothing. It's a big world. People get lost once you lose contact. We didn't have kids so what was the point? As far as I know, she's still alive."

"Are you certain Jenny's child was yours?"

"A man is never certain. But I paid for her abortion. I helped kill a child. There's no difference."

"Any other family?"

"I'm alone. All alone. You should marry and have kids before it's too late."

"Kids are demanding."

"You'd love your own... Hello, young man. What can I get you to drink on a lovely Saturday morning in the Long Bar?"

"Can I run a tab?"

"Of course you can. Just give me your credit card for safe keeping. It's a new rule. What will it be? This is Tracey. A regular customer of mine. I'm George."

When George gave the man his drink and took his credit card, George went off down the bar to read his newspaper. Instead of staying with Tracey, the young man picked up his drink and walked down the length of the bar to sit opposite George.

"What's the matter with me? Must have lost it. Or maybe the creep's queer. And stop mumbling to yourself."

Twenty minutes later, when Tracey again tapped her empty glass on the bar counter, no one else had come in the bar. The young man had not so much as looked at Tracey. George put down his newspaper, took off his reading glasses and walked up the bar. Standing opposite Tracey he leaned towards her over the bar, asking her to move closer, signalling with his index finger.

"I think he's gay."

"Thank goodness. Thought there was something wrong with me.

There's something rather nice, George, whispering in ears. Did he come on to you?"

"They don't like old men. He wanted to know if the Long Bar was a gay bar. I said I never asked my customers their sexual preferences. Every time I looked up from reading my paper he was staring at me."

"Makes you think, George. Makes you think."

"What would he want to do with an old man? It's creepy. You want another drink, Tracey?"

"Why else did I tap wood?"

"Silly of me. How's work?"

"I resigned. My publisher gave me fifty thousand dollars as an advance."

"Oh, that's wonderful. If I'm in the shit with the rent, can I borrow from you? Just kidding. Somehow or other, I always make the rent."

"Make this my last beer. I'll pay you now. I'm going home for a nap. With luck, I'll wake up without a hangover. Then I can write. I love writing. Gets it all out of you. Thank you, George. Go back and read your paper."

"No ways. I may be old but I still prefer to look at a pretty girl rather than a homosexual. Tell me about this book of yours when I've made myself a cup of coffee... There we go. Change from three beers."

"You shouldn't worry, George. People these days have abortions all the time. Some even think it the right thing to do, to keep down the population and save the planet."

"Since I was born, the world population has trebled. But it doesn't make any difference to my feeling of guilt."

"Have you tried to find out where Natalie is living?"

"No. Why should I?"

"It might be fun if both of you are alone. Old memories shared. The good times remembered. The bad forgotten. You'd have lots to talk about. It's easy to trace people these days. Give it a go. What have you got to lose?"

"So what's it about? Your book?"

"*Lust*. The book's called *Lust*."

"My goodness. Just let me get my cup of coffee. Please don't go away."

They were still whispering, trying not to look down the bar. By the time Tracey had got into the story of her book the young man had gone.

"At least I've still got his credit card. If he wants his card he'll have to come back and pay his bill. Where did he go? I was too absorbed in your story to take notice. No wonder I have trouble paying the rent."

"Your luck's in, George. He's back again."

"You don't have to talk about me behind my back. Where's my credit card?"

"There we are, sir."

"Are you really gay?"

"Don't be stupid, lady. My wife just walked out on me. I hate women."

"I'm so sorry."

"So am I… Did you really write this book you were whispering about? So many people lie about their accomplishments. I don't believe a word people say."

"You really are bitter. Have another drink. Drown your sorrows. Give the man another drink, George. Life's not all bad. Just most of it… Do you have a job?"

"No. I can't work and study."

"Probably why she walked out."

"Your credit card is invalid, young man."

"The bitch has cut off my card!"

"Have a drink on me. I just got a fifty thousand dollar advance from my publisher. My nap can wait."

"That's very kind of you."

"I know it is. We both need company."

"The book, Tracey. You were telling me about the book. I've got my coffee."

"Did you ever find out what happened to Jenny? You could trace her as well as Natalie. We all need company, George. Friends. Good friends. For a moment back there I thought I had lost it. What's your name?"

"Stanislas. My family are Polish. The bitch chopped off my credit card. I can't believe it. And what's your name again? I remember you're George."

"Tracey."

"Of course. Tracey. It's going to be a long day. No home. No money. And nowhere to stay."

"Last night I sat in my apartment on my own and drank a bottle of whisky."

"There is nothing worse than drinking alone… And all the time I thought she loved me."

"Stop crying. There's no point in crying over spilt milk. Give him a double of whatever he's drinking. Today's my day to celebrate. A couple of drinks and now I feel better... Can I call you Stan?"

"You can call me what you like if you're buying the drinks."

"That's better, Stan. Now you're laughing. I'll have a whisky, George. Start another tab. Do you want cash up front?"

"Not for my old customer... And so the world goes round... And look at that. I've got another customer. Three of them. Be with you in a minute. Make yourselves comfortable. Welcome to Long Bar."

"What are you studying, Stan?"

"Information technology at Stanford University through correspondence... Thank you for the drink... The idea was for me to study and get the kind of degree that can earn serious money. The future is in information technology. The technology is difficult to get your head around. I can't have my concentration broken by doing a part-time job. You have to think about what you're studying all the time without breaks in your concentration. You don't need other people's rubbish in your head. If you want to do something properly you have to do one thing at a time. I don't even like Frances interrupting my train of thought. Why we often argue... I'm sorry. I'm talking about myself. There's nothing more boring than a person prattling about their personal problems. She was going to make us a living while I studied so in the end both of us would become rich. Frances works as a teller in a clothing store. She's older than me. I'm twenty-three. She's thirty. I thought it would work. Now she's thrown me out and chopped off my credit... Thank you, George. Now I really need a drink. Thank you, Tracey, for buying me the drink. Sorry, am I interrupting something?"

"You'll have to tell me more about your book some other time. Those three customers are waiting. And here comes another customer."

"Off you go, George. Life in a bar. You just never know what's coming. Wipe your eyes, Stanislas. Today is just starting. Let's forget our problems and enjoy the present."

"Tell me the story of your book being published. It's difficult to get a book published. Where do you live?"

"You can sleep on the couch. Why did you ask George if the Long Bar was a gay bar?"

"I've learned to be careful. I don't go into bars. I'm in such a state my mind is in turmoil. I can't think straight. How am I going to study without my computer? My life is over at twenty-three. The whole idea was for me to get on the bandwagon. Without an education there isn't even a ladder to climb in life. Doing manual work, like Frances, your ability to spend stays the same forever. You never get anywhere. Stuck in a rented property and never building up any capital. To succeed in this competitive world you require a specialised education. I want to invent something and own the patent. Make a company of my own. Can you imagine sitting behind a till for the rest of your life always struggling to pay the bills? I wanted to get rich and enjoy all those wonderful things that money can buy. Make a fortune and retire early. Buy myself a luxury apartment and go to the best restaurants."

"Did you love Frances when you married her?"

"I don't know. I was probably being selfish. Using her. We had the idea when we were drinking in her apartment one night. We were lovers but had never talked of marriage. She said she could help me to study at Stanford. They'd offered me a place but my parents couldn't afford to send me to university."

"How old were you?"

"I'd just turned twenty. Frances was my first lover. How I lost my virginity. She said she preferred young men. We talked about it for a while. It was my only option. I suppose I wanted my degree more than I wanted Frances but what else could I do? Never miss an opportunity, they told me at school. Life slips by quickly. Got to grab it when you can. When you are young. When you first have that thirst for success."

"You want another whisky, Stan? That one went down quickly."

"Please... What am I to do?"

"Why did she throw you out?"

"Says she's bored with me. That we don't have fun. That I'm too absorbed in my studies. That if I got at least a part-time job we'd have money to spend on having some fun. To add to it I think she's having an affair. Someone in the clothing store. Probably the owner. He's always giving her lecherous looks when I go to the store. What am I going to do, Tracey?"

"You could phone your parents."

"They've got enough problems of their own. My dad's business went bust six months ago. When I got my first job after getting my degree I hoped I would be able to help them. You see, if you don't have money behind you in this year of 1995 with all its materialism and expensive living, you get into terrible trouble. I want money. Backup. A life without worry. Not a life of living hand to mouth. Didn't I hear George say that paying his rent every month was a problem? No wonder he wanted to hold my credit card. Can I possibly have another whisky?"

"Tell me more about this IT... George. Same again. Doubles."

"You know what I think. You talk about your book. In the future they won't be reading your book in print form. They'll be reading it on their computers. Listening to them. Can you imagine the new marketing possibilities? They'll know what kind of books you like and be able to recommend the right kind of new book for you to read. The marketing tool of the internet is going to be mind-boggling. Not just for books but for so many other products. My mind rushes off in excitement. Oh, Tracey. What am I going to do?"

"First, we are going to get you drunk to drown your sorrows... Thank you, George."

"And before you both get drunk you are going to tell me and this young man all about your book, Tracey."

"Now. Where was I? You see, her name is Fay..."

By the time Tracey had explained the rudiments of her short novel it was time for another drink. The three men down the bar were calling for another round. Despite the fifty thousand dollars in her bank account the cost of drinking in a bar was three times higher than drinking at home. She had found what she wanted. She had found herself a companion.

"Let's walk back to my place and buy ourselves a bottle of whisky on the way... George. Can I pay? Take what Stan owed you... There we go. Keep the change. Thank you for listening to my story... Here come some more customers."

"Can I really sleep on the couch?"

"You can sleep in my place where you like. I'll buy us a take-away. I hate cooking when I'm drunk. A nice big bucket of fried chicken."

"Do you have a computer?"

"Of course. How I write my books."

"When you're not using it, I can use it for my studies."

"Are you moving in, Stanislas? We've only just met... Now we've got the giggles. Come on. A nice bottle of whisky and a bucket of Kentucky Fried Chicken. When I woke up this morning with a monstrous hangover I felt miserable. Now I'm as bright as a cricket. You can read the original copy of my book and tell me what you think."

"All I've got is what I'm standing up in."

"What you've got is in your body and in your head... Thank you, George. Hope the end of the month turns out fine."

"You two look after yourselves."

"We will. We certainly will. Have a go at tracing Natalie and Jenny. See you next time."

"Good luck with the book."

"Here you go, George. More customers. It's been a lovely morning... You know the problem, Stanislas, now I have money? If I'm not careful I'm going to turn myself into an alcoholic."

"Can you write when you've been drinking?"

"Not a word."

"Then you'll be all right. Your passion for writing will overcome your thirst for alcohol. All you've got to do is carry on writing. Never stop."

"I never will. Writing a book is the most satisfying thing I have ever done in my life. It's going to be my lifetime addiction. But not today. Today I'm still celebrating my book being published... Now, look at that. The streets of New York are full of people."

"They always are... Do you believe in luck?"

"Of course I do. How else did I get published? And find myself a companion when I needed one. Oh, how I love New York. It's teeming with life and excitement."

"What's your surname?"

"Does it matter? Today we are just Stan and Tracey trying to have some fun."

4

Treading lightly, Stanislas followed the woman into the liquor store where she bought two bottles of whisky and gave them to him to carry, and then on to Kentucky Fried Chicken. With a bit of luck, it was all happening again. What older women saw in him was a mystery. It was usually the other way round – rich, old men went for young girls. He would have to turn on the charm. Seduce her as soon as possible and find himself a new home with a computer. The woman had fifty thousand dollars in the bank with more to come. When Frances found out he was staying with another woman, it would make her seething jealous, making her want him back. He needed two more years of being looked after to obtain his master's degree. After that, older women wouldn't matter. He would be able to do what he wanted with Frances without having a guilty conscience. There was always a bright side. Throwing him out when it suited her would let him return the compliment. And if this Tracey found something she liked he could stay without a commitment as he was already married to another woman.

When they arrived the apartment wasn't what he hoped but the computer on the desk was all he needed.

"Food or whisky, Stanislas? Welcome to my humble apartment. They're knocking down the building so I'll have to move away. And when Godfrey gives me the next payment I'm going to upgrade. Find a really nice apartment. So, what will it be?"

"Whisky, if I may. This is very nice... I don't see a couch."

"There isn't one. I'll get the ice. You want some music? What do you like? Put the TV on the music channel... There we go... What's that music you've found?"

"New age. Modern classical... Thank you, Tracey. Cheers. You're being so kind to me."

"Are you crying again?"

"Not really."

"Come here. Give Tracey a hug. Don't be sad. It's all going to turn out fine."

"I hope so. I've never slept on the streets."

"Have a leg of chicken. Make yourself comfortable."

"Where's your book? Let me have a look. I want to read a paragraph."

"Are you sure?"

"Of course I am. I'm so impressed to have met a published author. Never met one before. I've met a few who write books but none of them are good enough to publish, or they would have found a publisher. That's a big advance. They must think they're going to sell hundreds of thousands of copies."

"You think so?"

"I know so."

Stanislas took the book and sat down on an armchair. He put the glass of whisky with the ice Tracey had given him on the coffee table in front of his outstretched feet. He was going to pretend to read and create a pregnant silence... When he smiled at Tracey he could see the fear of rejection in her eyes. The first sentence, 'Fay fucked Christopher an hour after she first met him in the bar', jerked Stanislas out of his plan and took his full attention. By the time his hand went out searching for his whisky, he was glued to the book. The girl could write. He had found himself a lot more than a fifty-thousand-dollar companion. Stanislas slugged down the whisky and moved on to the second chapter.

"You like my book, Stanislas?"

"It's fucking brilliant."

"Then put it down and have another drink. Talk to me. Let's have a giggle... You really like my book? You're not just kidding me? Being polite?"

"It grabbed me by the balls."

"That was the whole idea... Oh, I'm so happy. A writer never knows if she's any good... There we are. Well, isn't this pleasant on a Saturday afternoon? It's so nice not having to work. I wonder if Ferdinand has found himself a new assistant?"

"Who's Ferdinand?"

"My ex-boss. He was so boring. Poor Ferdinand. We're all so selfish."

"Can't I go on reading?"

"No, you can't. Give me my book back, Stan."

"Can I kiss you?"

"What for?"

"To congratulate you, of course... Am I going to sleep on the floor?"

"As I said, you can sleep where you like. There's just one big room and the small bathroom."

"And the double bed."

"And the double bed."

"I like double beds."

"Don't we all?"

The kiss moved from a peck to a mouth swallow washed by the whisky.

"We'd better not, Tracey. We've only just met each other... No, please. I admire you too much to take advantage."

"It's only lust."

"There should be more than lust if you're going to let me stay in your apartment. I respect a person with such a talent."

"You're playing hard to get."

"No, I'm not... Can I have a leg of that fried chicken and change the music channel and listen to some songs?"

"Have another glass of whisky and lose your inhibitions... There we are. The ice in your glass is nicely drowned... Did you really like my book?"

"I think it's wonderful. When can I read the rest?"

"When we're a bit more sober."

"What's your next book about? Would you like me to read it as you write? You think she's changed the locks? I must get my papers and my computer."

"And your clothes."

"Are you asking me to move in?"

"I will if you're any good. Come here, Stanislas. Let's find out if you are any good. Some men are useless. Ten-second wonders. Others last half an hour. You don't have to be shy. She threw you out, don't forget."

"I probably should leave."

"You've nowhere to go. You're right, by now she'll have changed the locks. Didn't my first chapter get you going? Oh, well. Drink your whisky and have a piece of chicken. It's one of those days for me. Swooping highs and plummeting lows. Are you sure you're not gay? Never had a man turn me down before. What a week it's been. First Manfred. Then Godfrey. Now Stanislas."

"Who are Manfred and Godfrey?"

"My agent and my publisher. And this time last week I didn't have either of them. Let alone fifty thousand in my bank account... You're giggling again. That's good. Maybe you're right and we should wait. Until both of us can't stand it anymore. I think I'm getting a little drunk. Nothing wrong with being a little drunk."

"Chapelle."

"How did you know?"

"It's on the front of the manuscript. My surname is Wellensky. Stanislas Wellensky. And in ten years, if I get my degree, that name Wellensky is going to be famous. Do you want to be rich, Tracey?"

"Like you, I want everything money can buy."

By the time she began to talk about her self-righteous parents that always knew better than Tracey, his mind began to wander. She was right. People talking about their personal problems were boring. The trick, if he was going to find himself another home to live in that cost him nothing, was to look interested. Not to look bored. To encourage her to prattle on about herself and look as if he was absorbed in her family story. Behind his smile of sympathy, he was thinking of his own parents, his brother and his sister. They had all got on with each other, unlike Tracey and her siblings. The older brother sounded a self-righteous bore like his parents. The sister, the oldest and married with children, like his domineering kindergarten teacher who never listened to anyone. It made Stanislas even more determined to get the degree that would give him wealth and independence from other people. Going through his mind, as he tried to look as if he was listening to Tracey's every word, was the timing of his seduction. Should he wait and keep her on the hook, or give her a go and make the girl climax until she was exhausted, as he had learned with Frances? Like studying for a degree, sex was all about the climax. Whether he could put up with what he was listening to for two more years was another question, but getting what he wanted from life was never simple. Could he keep up the smile and false interest? Could he hide what he was really up to? Or did Tracey already know she was being used and was using him for her own purposes? A game of mutual manipulation?

"Are you listening to me, Stanislas? Pour yourself another whisky. You have that nice smile on your face but the look in the back of your eyes tells me you are far away. Writers notice these sorts of things. Never mind. I shouldn't talk about myself. Do you have brothers and sisters?"

"A brother and sister. They're quite a bit older than me. My mother said she loved young children and wanted another one. Mothers find it difficult when their children grow up and leave the home. I think she wanted to prolong having a young family for as long as possible, and along came me. Bit of luck for me, or I wouldn't be here drinking your whisky and listening to your lovely stories. My word. Just look at the bottle. Lucky you bought two of them. And the chicken is quite delicious... Songs can be so lovely. Tracey. I'm so lucky to have met you. Please go on with the stories of your family... If she's changed the locks, can't I break in and take back what is mine? That won't be criminal, surely? If she steals my clothes and my papers, aren't I entitled to steal them back again? I'm sorry. I'm interrupting. Go on, Tracey. Please go on. This armchair is so comfortable. I love your little apartment. All a girl and a boy really need."

Relaxed, comfortable and enjoying the effects of his whisky, he tried to concentrate on the task in progress. She had his full attention. By the time a knock came on the door and Tracey opened it to introduce her next-door neighbour, an older woman, the first bottle of whisky was almost empty, the bucket of chicken half empty.

"He's offered me a job. Can you believe it, Tracey? Manfred has offered me the job of his assistant as he wants to make his present assistant a partner. And it's all thanks to you. Hello, I'm Jane. Can I have a glass of whisky to celebrate? I start my new job on Monday. No more dirty clothes. A salary I can afford to live well on. Oh, I'm so excited. When we left Harry B's I thought all he wanted was sex. He wants my mind, not my body. Isn't it wonderful? Of course, I'll have to stop drinking. But now I have a purpose. One quick drink to celebrate and I'm gone. Who's your young man?"

"My name is Stanislas. My family are Polish."

"That's interesting."

"Stan's wife kicked him out this morning. We met in the Long Bar. He's going to be staying with me."

"That's nice. For how long?"

"That depends. Let me find you a glass... There we go, Jane. One minute you're down, the next minute you're up. Life in New York. Full of lovely people and excitement. Here's to the whole damn world. I'm rather drunk but who cares? I'm celebrating. And now we're going to be working together, Jane. Not just next-door neighbours. I do so love life when it goes right. You met Manfred in Harry B's. I met Stanislas in the Long Bar. Cheers to the perfect life. Cheers to the whole damn lot of us. And we still have another bottle of whisky. You can stay for two drinks, Jane. Have a wing of fried chicken. I love the world."

"Well, today is Saturday. Maybe a few drinks, as you say, to celebrate. I've just enough money to go and buy us another bottle of whisky. Don't want to run out, do we? Be back in a flash. Don't go away."

"One bottle should be enough."

"You never know, Tracey. As long as I'm not interrupting anything. You know that old saying. Two's company and three's a crowd."

"Sit down and have a drink. Stanislas, get the chair in front of my desk and bring it over for Jane. If we need more booze, Stan will go to the shop, won't you, Stanislas? I love that name. Very few first names have three syllables. When Stanislas and I are ready to screw each other's brains out, you'll have to up and leave. At the moment we're playing games with each other, aren't we, Stanislas? Life's a game. Always has been, until we all get what we want. So, you've got a job. I thought my agent was after your body. That'll be out when you work for him. One of these days, someone will have to explain to me what life is really all about. Not that it matters. I'm happily drunk... There you go, Jane. A wooden chair and a whisky. Music playing in the background. A bit of company. A day to celebrate. Sit you down. There should be more days like today."

"Do you know the signal, Tracey?"

"What signal, Jane?"

"The little finger wiggle."

"What does it mean?"

"You two want to be left alone."

"Oh, you mean the fuck off signal. Why do we always use swear words when we're drunk?"

WITHIN TEN MINUTES Jane could feel the whisky taking hold. Stanislas, a charmer if ever she saw one, had brought the wooden chair from in front of Tracey's writing desk and offered her his armchair to sit in. Watching the two of them play each other brought back memories. The young, good-looking man was after Tracey's money. Tracey was after his young body. People to Jane were so obvious. With the young man sitting opposite the comfortable armchairs, smiling his charm from one to the other, Jane hoped Tracey knew what she was letting herself in for. Bums, in Jane's experience, were all much the same. They used their charm to get what they wanted. When the second bottle of whisky was almost empty, Tracey gave Stanislas money and told him to walk to the liquor store.

"Can you make it, Stanislas?"

"Of course I can."

"Don't drop the bottles on the way back."

When the door was closed and they were alone, Jane slowly shook her head. For half an hour they talked about nothing in particular, waiting for the young man to return.

"He's going to cost you, Tracey. He hasn't got a cent."

"He's sexy. Don't you like him?"

"He wants to live off you, darling."

"I only want to give him a go."

"I should have left after the second drink. Do you mind my staying?"

"You're going to be working for my agent. Helping promote my book. Of course I don't mind you staying."

"If I'm to work properly for Manfred, tonight must be the last time I get myself drunk. Drink, too much drink, ruins a person's life. Life isn't easy. Take Randall Holiday. Did you know his real name is Randall Crookshank? Manfred thinks Randall has a problem with his young wife. That she's having an affair with a young man called Clint she met at her art class. It's stopped Randall writing. He wanted to go back to his small farm on the Isle of Man but Meredith wants to stay in New York. Randall's taken to drinking when his wife comes home late, which she does every time she goes to her art class. Manfred is worried. Asked me if I could help. A writer who isn't writing costs his agency money. Even when you get what you want in life it can all fall apart. Meredith leaves their son with a nanny when she goes out. Picks the two-year-old up the next morning. A right royal mess."

"Isn't Randall having an affair with that barmaid?"

"Who knows?"

"I hope I never stop writing. Maybe Randall's run out of story. They say all novelists run out in the end. Most write two or three good novels, make a name for themselves, then write a load of rubbish."

"I couldn't even write one good one. Won't this man upset your writing?"

"He'll be studying for his degree. I'm going to get a bigger apartment now I have money."

"Just be careful."

"I'm always careful. And you must be careful. Careful of the booze. It's been quite a week for both of us. Are you going to try and write the story of your Harvey?"

"I'll try again."

"That's my girl. Where's Stanislas? You think he's run off with my money? I gave him a hundred dollars to buy expensive whisky. That would be a giggle. You can't trust anyone in this life, Jane."

"An expensive night's drinking."

"We'll share what's left in the bottle. I wonder where he'll sleep?"

"Maybe with booze in him he's gone back to his wife. With a hundred bucks, she'll be smiling. What happens when you meet strangers in a bar."

"Does Manfred know you have a drinking problem?"

"No, of course he doesn't. And please don't tell him. It's our secret. We're friends. Neighbours. Anyway, I'm going to go on the wagon."

"It's not as easy as we like to think."

"If I don't, I'm finished, Tracey. Then I really will kill myself."

"Maybe it's just as well he's run off with my money. I'm going to get into bed. Get some sleep. Happy you got a job, Jane. You sleep well. A hundred bucks and a bottle of whisky for a bit of company. What has my life come to? And just when I thought I had made it."

"What about the last drop?"

"Leave it in the bottle. Goodnight, Jane."

"Sweet dreams."

"I hope so. I really hope so. Poor Randall Holiday. Sometimes other people's lives want to make me cry."

"Don't cry and don't go to bed. Give me five minutes and I'll be back with a bottle of cheap whisky. I know the people in the liquor store. They'll tell me if Stanislas bought whisky with your money. Better to know, Tracey. Always better to know. Suspense can kill a girl."

"We can have a really good chat."

"That's my girl."

. . .

At the liquor store where Jane spent the last of her money, there had been no sign of a young man buying whisky.

"The man's a thief."

"Who, Jane?"

"Never mind."

Back at Tracey's apartment, Jane put the whisky bottle on the low table in front of the armchairs and smiled at Tracey.

"So?"

"Not a sign of him. What a world. Do you think Manfred will give me an advance on my salary on Monday? The rent's due next week."

"If he doesn't I'll lend you some money. So all that crap about my writing a good book was a con game."

"I see you emptied the whisky bottle."

"I'm a fool, Jane. A naïve fool. And I think I'm so clever. Seducing Manfred to read my book. Trying to keep Godfrey on the hook. And now a lad of twenty-three makes a fool of me. He gave George a credit card that had been stopped. Made me pay for his drinks and then took my hundred dollars. Do you think he really had a wife? The lengths people go to for money."

"If you don't have money you do anything to get it. Lots of people don't have money. The people that have money take it for granted... You got any more ice? I can go next door. Neat whisky on ice. My favourite."

"Pour me a shot and get your ice. Mine's melted... Nothing makes sense to me anymore. You'd think the wife of a successful author and mother of his young son wouldn't play around."

"Manfred says Randall's first wife went off with a woman."

"Oh, shit. That's not good."

"He has a son by her he never has contact with. The boy's being brought up by two lesbians."

"Why do people rip each other apart?"

"For money, usually. It's usually about the money. You marry a man for his money, have his kid and sue him for a pile of alimony and never have to work another day in your life. Or, like my Harvey, you marry a girl whose father is stinking rich, get a job with your father-in-law and end up sitting pretty for the rest of your life... Back in a minute. What's that music?"

"Jazz. I love Dixieland jazz. It's always so happy. And I thought I was going to get myself a screw tonight. I never learn. In the end, I'll land in the trash with the rest of them. Even if I get famous, it won't make any difference. Look at Randall Holiday. Now that man can write books. Have you read *Masters of Vanity* or seen the movie? And still they take advantage of him."

When Jane came back with a bowl full of ice, Tracey was still talking to herself.

"What am I going to do with the rest of my life, Jane? I'm only twenty-seven and I can't seduce a twenty-three-year-old."

"Just imagine what it's going to be like when you get to my age."

"That's a charming thought."

"Write lots of good books and save your money. That's my advice. They say the most difficult thing with money isn't making it, but holding on to it."

"You can say that again. One hundred bucks right out of the window. He was a bit drunk, though. Do you think he fell over?"

"He wasn't that drunk."

"Just a thought to make me feel better. Oh, well. The music is still playing. We still have the best part of a bottle of whisky. And neither of us have to work tomorrow. Tell me more about Harvey. They say that first, young love when you are in your teens is the only real love we ever experience. You were lucky to be in love. Never been in love in my life. All it's been is sex. With multiple partners. The more the merrier. *Lust*, Jane. It's lust. Not love. Or it is with me."

"It was love with Harvey. It's so much easier to understand when you look back from a distance. At the time you think your world is so perfect. But it wasn't. You were being used. Like that young man who used you tonight."

"I was going to use him. I was going to use his body. What a world. We're all horrible."

"No one is perfect."

"No one ever was. Why the world is always in such a mess. One mess after another. Thanks for the company, Jane. I was feeling lonely. Do you ever get lonely?"

"All the time."

"Is there ever a conclusion in life? Or is the only conclusion death?"

"We have moments in life when we think we have got where we want to go. You must have thought that when Godfrey Merchant paid you the full advance for your book. They say we get ecstatic when our child is born. Or that moment as a teenager when a girl and a boy look at each other for the first time and only want to be together for the rest of their lives, the whole world reduced to two people as their souls join together. That sweet moment of true love. That perfect age of innocence when we don't know the horrors of life. We don't know about the nastiness in all of us. The pure selfishness that comes later when we find out what really goes on in the world. That brief, pure period in a life when the body and soul of two people melt into one person. That time of pure, unadulterated happiness we imagine will last forever. Each looking after the other. Only thinking of the other. A world where their children will join them in happiness and live a life without fights or arguments. We had that for a year until Harvey found out making himself a successful career was difficult; success, that in our naïvety we had thought would just come. He realised making a home for a family cost a whole lot of money. And when his eyes opened and he saw reality, along came a girl with rich parents and true love left in that moment of understanding. He fell out of love with me as quickly as he had fallen. Instead of two people joined together, there was one. Just me. Plain Jane on her own. A lost, bewildered Jane that had no idea of what had just happened. My soul died, Tracey. My body has lived on but my soul died. It's still dead. I resorted to alcohol and different men one after the other in an attempt to get away from the person who had come out of perfection into purgatory where I know I will stay until I die. There is no point to life without true love... Why are you crying, Tracey?"

"Because I'm drunk. Because if you are right about the innocence of teenage love never coming true, I too might as well kill myself. Materialism only gives bodily comfort. It never gives us peace of mind and lasting happiness. That perfect feeling of contentment you described, the thought of which has made me cry."

"In that short time when Harvey and I were in love we were so content with each other that nothing else in our surroundings even mattered. We were barely conscious of other people."

"Write it into a story."

"A poem perhaps. A short poem. A short beautiful poem... Let's have another whisky. The only way I escape from the memory of the aftermath when Harvey went off with Lucy... Now I'm crying."

"Let's cry together. But you never know in life. You never know what might turn up. Hope keeps us going."

"Your hundred bucks ain't going to do no turning up. Good. Now you're laughing. Let's try and be happy while we sink the rest of the whisky."

"Not a poem, Jane. You must write the perfect love story from your own experience and tell those of us who never found love what it felt like to be in love. Paint the picture with words. You have that command of English. Instead of lust, write love. I only knew lust. You knew love. A short, sixty-thousand-word novel the size of my book. If you do, Manfred will find you a publisher and that love you found with Harvey will live on in the book forever. You may die emotionally as you say, but your character will live on in love forever. Paint that perfect picture, Jane. Give your story to the world and help us out of our misery. Give us the hope without which there is no point in going on... Is Harvey with Lucy?"

"I don't know if I can... They are still married. Two kids. He's a director of his father-in-law's business. We still have friends from school in common."

"But is he happy?"

"Nice big home. Big car. Money to spend. They say he looks happy."

"And Lucy. Is she happy with a husband beholden to her father?"

"Have another drink, Tracey. Alcohol is my only escape, where I can get out of my mind and not care what happened in my own or Harvey's world."

"A bestseller by Jane Slater made into a movie would get his attention. You would have your revenge."

"Why would I want revenge? A year of pure happiness was better than nothing. I will always treasure that memory."

"Then write it down and share it with people. Don't be selfish. Giving, they say, is better than taking."

"Whisky, Tracey."

"All right. Douse yourself in whisky. That young man really did run off with my money. You think I'll ever see him again?"

"Who cares?"

"I care about my hundred bucks."

"We'd have drunk the money anyway."

"You're right. Thanks for this whisky. All I have to do when we've finished the bottle is fall into that lonely double bed. You only have to get next door... Do older people ever fall in love?"

"Sometimes. Maybe sometimes."

"What a week for two neighbours. I get a publisher. You get a job.

What neither one of us must do is screw it up. Here's to writing your book and finding your soul again."

"Thank you, Tracey. I owe you my job. Probably my life."

"Suicide is the coward's way out."

"If a person has the guts to kill herself she is not a coward."

"What stopped you?"

"The fear of the unknown that may or may not follow death. People say there is another life after this one but no one really knows. Some even say they had previous lives to that of their present. I wasn't sure that killing myself would end the misery. Better to let nature take its course and drink myself to death. Am I rambling, Tracey? We all ramble when we get drunk. It only takes me a few drinks to get into that state of drunkenness. Drunks get drunk quickly. We probably only have one life. So I might as well go through the rest of it to find out if there is any more life worth the living. I'm going to sober up and stay sober. Enjoy my job with Manfred. Try and rise above the mess I've made of my life."

"Write the book, Jane."

"I'll try."

"Good. Then we'll finish our nice new bottle of whisky and have a giggle. There's nothing better than a drunken giggle. Just took my money and left. Makes you think."

"Did you really screw Manfred to get him to read your book?"

"Of course I did. How else was I going to find myself a publisher? We're all horrible. Just how life is. Maybe we shouldn't take life so seriously. To books, Jane. To our books. May they live forever. And screw the lot of them."

PART 3

OCTOBER 1995 – IT'S ALWAYS ABOUT THE MONEY

1

At the end of the summer when the leaves were falling from the trees, a week before the launch of Tracey's book, Meredith walked out on Randall Crookshank, taking two-year-old Douglas with her. For the second time in his life, he had lost a wife and a son. At three months short of his thirty-eighth birthday his life had come to an end. He had success and money, neither of them any use to him. The thought of going back to Rabbit Farm alone to try and start another book no longer had any point to it. She had gone to her art class taking Douglas with her and never came back again. No word. No explanation. No reason so far as Randall was concerned. All through their love affair that had begun in the woodsman's cottage in Wales where he had found peace and solitude to write his book, he had never been unfaithful to Meredith. He could still see in his mind the first time he saw Clint, across the park behind his easel looking back across at Meredith on the wooden bench next to him. That smiley look on his face. Standing at the tall window in the lounge on the thirty-first floor looking out at the skyscrapers of Manhattan, Randall sipped at his glass of whisky, his only solace.

"What the hell, old boy? Go to Harry B's. Get drunk. She'll want money, so give it to her. Who the hell cares? If that's how she behaves, I don't give a damn."

Walking to Harry B's in the sporadic sunshine, the morning whisky having calmed his nerves, he kept wondering what he was going to do with the rest of his life. Even the idea of writing a fictional book about Shakespeare's friend was on the back burner. Did it matter who wrote Shakespeare's plays? They had been written. All that mattered. The play's more important than the writer. Was the seven-year age gap the problem? Was she bored with him? Was making love twice a month enough for a thirty-year-old woman? Had he lost his pull for women as he approached his thirty-ninth year? Had she only gone for him because of his fame and money? Likely, he would never know. In breakups, the truth was never told. Had his constant wanting to go to Rabbit Farm been the problem, a woman and a small boy alone in the wilderness without friend or company just so he could write another of his books in the peace and solitude of his smallholding? Was the breakup his fault? Everything was usually his fault. Amanda had blamed him for making her a lesbian, however on earth that had worked. Had he lost his sexual passion which Meredith had found again in Clint? Apparently Clint had asked Meredith whether she had signed a prenuptial contract and been told that she hadn't. Was the young man going to make Meredith sue him for a staggering amount of maintenance or ask for a massive cash settlement so he could get all the money? In Randall's experience of life, it was always about the money. What a world. As the sick feeling in his stomach built, even the idea of going back to Africa, back to his roots, crossed his mind. Anyway, at least Poppy Maddock had finished the screenplay of *Love Song* to the director's satisfaction. They were casting the movie and thankfully no longer needed his help. He was drinking too much but when he wasn't writing, it didn't matter. Hangovers were not important. Stopping for a moment at the top of the stairs that led into Harry B's, he looked around at the teeming crowd on a Thursday morning in the great metropolis of Manhattan and tried to smile. There was no point in complaining. Life was what it was with all its ups and downs. She had left him. He was on his own. Putting his best foot forward, Randall walked through the doors into the pub. What a life, he kept repeating to himself. What a life.

"You're early, Randall."

"She walked out on me, Terry."

"Who?"

"My wife."

"You want a drink?"

"Of course I do. Why else would I come?"

"Beer or whisky?"

"Let's start with a beer."

"Good to see you."

"Good to see you too, Terry. Just the two of us."

"It'll fill up by lunchtime. Is it raining outside?"

"Not yet... Thank you, Terry. How's business?"

"Never been better. You want me to sit and talk?"

"Why ever not? You always look after your customers. Why your business is so good."

"What are you going to do?"

"Get drunk."

"Find another woman, that's my advice. One goes out the door, another comes in the window."

"I thought we loved each other."

"We always do. We always do. I'm going to break my rules and join you with a beer."

"What would I do without a bar to run to? A friendly owner."

"There's more to running a bar than serving drinks. If my customers, many of whom come here on their own, just wanted to get drunk they would do so on their own. A whole lot cheaper. They come here for company, to talk to people. Talking and getting to know my customers is the cornerstone of my business. You have to like people to run a saloon, Randall. I try to introduce my customers to each other, to make my bar a meeting place... Cheers. Sorry to hear about your wife."

"You never talk about your own private life."

"My customers like to talk about themselves, not hear about me. Unload their problems. If Meredith hadn't walked out, you wouldn't be here. Am I right?"

"Probably... What the hell do you do in life when you've done it? Two wives. Two sons. Bestsellers. Another film coming. More money than I can spend. What do you do with yourself? Is there even any point in trying to write another book?"

"Give you something to do. Something to think about."

"No challenge, Terry. Sorry, I must be boring you with my problems."

"Why I'm here. To listen. You're not boring me. There aren't too many saloons with a famous author for a customer. People like to be seen in the same bar as a celebrity. So they can tell their friends. Today's culture is all about celebrity. The average man or woman's life is insignificant. Brushing shoulders in my bar with a well-known author makes them feel important. Why they want your autograph. Book writers normally only talk to people through their books. Never in person. Why your publishers try and make your books more personal by putting your photograph on the back cover."

"So I help your business?"

"Yes."

"Aren't we friends?"

"Don't get me wrong. Talking to you now isn't just about business. I too get bored. And if I can help you in your problem with your wife, that's what a friend is for."

"This beer tastes good... This morning, standing looking out of my big plate-glass window that runs from the floor to the ceiling, I thought of running back to Africa. To the home we used to call Rhodesia. Go back to the African bush. But it wouldn't help. What am I going to do there on my own? All my school friends have gone. Only ten per cent of the whites that made Rhodesia now live in Zimbabwe under the Mugabe government. They were no longer wanted. He wouldn't want me either."

"Find yourself another girl."

"And what do they want? They won't want me at thirty-eight. They'll want my money. Or as you put it, my celebrity. Might as well visit a whorehouse."

"You could always do that."

"Stop laughing. No, maybe don't. My life's become a laugh. What was life meant to be all about?"

"You tell me, Randall. You're the author. Write what you are going through into a book."

"It would make me sick."

"Then don't write it. Amelia will be happy to hear your wife has left you. You know she fancies you?"

"I'm far too old for the likes of Amelia."

"She doesn't think so... How's your brother?"

"I haven't told him yet. He'll wonder what's the matter with me. Someone said, 'to lose one wife is unfortunate. To lose two is carelessness.' My life's a laugh... There we go. That one went down the hatch. Give this miserable fool a Scotch. A couple of drinks and we'll be laughing at the world. She left. Why must I care? Best I don't give a damn. Who gives a damn about anything anyway... Let's talk about baseball or cricket."

"What's cricket?"

"You're kidding."

"No, I'm not."

"It's a game we played in Rhodesia with a long wooden bat and a ball. Very serious. I played the game at school… Thank you, sir. Cheers again. Thanks for letting me unload my problems. I feel better. Much better… Are you having another one, Terry?"

"Why not? Thursday mornings are quiet. Nothing wrong with breaking the rules every now and again. To help a friend."

"What's going to happen to Douglas? What's going to happen to my son?"

From high to low in a second. The problem would not be the breakup of his marriage. Meredith would go on with her life. Douglas would become an appendage. A liability in Meredith's future relationships. No man was interested in another man's son. Any more than Douglas would be interested in a stepfather. And if Clint and Meredith had children, Douglas would be the odd one out. He would see his real father on holidays and weekends. A constant pull from one parent to the other. Nothing stable. Nothing certain. Never quite sure what to say to one about the other. Life growing up with a stranger only interested in the happiness of his own children. His own blood. His own life going on into the future through the generations that would come from his descendants. The divorce of his birth parents would ruin the boy's life, leaving scars forever. Life was tough enough without not having the comfort of happy parents and a peaceful home where a boy was always welcome. A broken home would leave Douglas with a legacy of bitterness and the dislike of other people that would permeate the rest of his life.

When the second customer came into the bar, Randall found himself alone feeling sorry for himself. There was nothing worse than feeling sorry for himself. Staring at the black wood of the bar counter and Terry's half-drunk beer, not even music playing, his back facing eternity as the ghosts of his past looked down on him, Randall felt a cold shiver of fear. Gripping the front of the wooden bar he tried to control the shudder, his whole body shaking violently. After a while the grip of fear began to leave him, bringing back the physical presence of the bar. For a moment his mind had left his body and gone to another world.

"Are you okay, Randall?"

"I'd better go."

"The drinks are on Harry B's… Are you sure you're all right? Can I get you a cab?... Have some lunch. Did you have breakfast? Happens on an empty stomach. Do you want a doctor?"

"What I want is a life. Don't worry. I'll be fine. Sometimes I think too much."

"Go and talk to your brother."

"He has his own problems. I don't want to burden Phillip with mine. Anyway, what's he going to do? Get them back? When a woman walks out on you there's no point in getting down on your knees. She's gone."

"Finish your whisky and have another one. You're better here than on your own. Your whole body was shaking. I'll bring you a nice ham sandwich with lettuce."

"Please put on some music."

"Any particular music?"

"Anything will do. Just noise to drown the turmoil in my mind... You've got another customer."

"Just don't fall off the barstool."

"I'll try not to."

"Music and a sandwich."

"Thanks, Terry. You really are a friend."

Slowly, the demon of fear, the fear of having no future, left Randall. With his new customers happy on their own, Terry came back to sit opposite Randall, a smile that tried to show encouragement on his face. The music was playing as Terry put the small plate with the sandwich in front of Randall. Neither of them spoke. Randall picked up a triangular piece of the sandwich Terry had cut into four and took a bite of the bread. The music Randall recognised was a song by Whitney Houston, from the soundtrack of *The Bodyguard* movie. He chewed the food and tried to smile.

"Nice fresh bread... What was it like growing up in Brooklyn?"

"Why?"

"I'm sick of talking and thinking about myself. Anyway, writers like to hear other people's stories. How we gather some of our material."

"You had me worried back there... We were poor, like most of the rest of them. No car. My father was a garbage collector. You either walked or caught a bus. Brooklyn is gritty but the people are fun. You don't have to be rich to have fun. I was in a gang. Not a criminal gang. Just a gang of boys who hung out with each other. When it wasn't raining we sat on the steps that led up into the old apartments, making paper darts and throwing them down. Sometimes we hit someone on the sidewalk and had to run. Half-a-dozen kids laughing and having fun. I'm still friends with those boys. We say we will be for the rest of our lives. I loved those years. You were never on your own. Always had friends."

"What did you do with yourselves apart from throwing darts at pedestrians?"

"We messed around. A mix of boys from different cultures. Cubans, African-Americans. Mexicans. The great American melting pot which at that young age we were all unaware of. We were friends. That was all that mattered. My own ancestors are Irish. From County Galway in the south. Why I'm a Catholic. Part of my heritage."

"Have you been to Ireland?"

"Always wanted to go. To look at where we Flanagans came from. Never had the money."

"You have money now. This place of yours does well."

"You can't hand over a bar to an employee to run. My grandmother said the moment the keys to a business were not in your pocket you didn't own it. Maybe one day. When I'm retired. If I've saved enough money. Chances are that kind of holiday money will be spent on my wife and the kids."

"Now we're getting somewhere. How many kids?"

"Two. A boy and a girl. Both in their early teens. They drive us both nuts but we love them to pieces. Kenny wants to go to college. Wants to join the world of business and make himself rich. Lana won't have to worry. She's pretty as paint. Just like her mother."

"When he makes his fortune you can all visit Ireland. They love to see American-Irish in Ireland... Did you cook the ham yourself? It's so juicy. Ham can be dry. You'd better go. Another customer. Putting a boy through university is going to be expensive."

"You're right. You got to make every cent you can when it's there... Coming, lady... Want another sandwich, Randall? She's pretty."

"You're whispering."

"Of course I am. The game can start again anytime. I'm going to tell her who you are. That famous author."

"Don't you dare."

"You'll thank me, Randall."

"I'll have another ham sandwich."

"There we go."

"What did your ancestors do for a living in Ireland?"

"My great-grandfather was a fisherman out of Galway Bay. They say he played his banjo in the local pub. Pubs are in our genes. And yes, we cook our own hams in the kitchen. Just kidding. Comes from the deli down the street."

Trying not to think about Meredith and Douglas and make himself start shuddering all over again, Randall tried to concentrate his mind on listening to the music, every moment agonisingly long. He took sips of his whisky staring down at his hand holding the glass. More people arrived. Groups of people out for lunch. Terry passed back and forth, busy serving his customers. The waiter, who as usual was late for work, was showing the lunch customers to the tables away from the bar. Through the hatch behind the bar, Randall watched the cook begin preparing lunch as she took the written orders from the waiter. Someone sat down on the next barstool after Terry had put another whisky in front of him. The presence and the hum of people made Randall feel more comfortable. The whole morning had been bizarre. One minute he was a married man living as part of a family. The next he was completely on his own.

"*Love Song* was a beautiful book. I hear they are making it into a movie."

"I'm sorry?"

"My name is Rebecca. I thought you somehow looked familiar. Terry told me who you are. I've just finished doing a photo shoot. Got nothing to do until four o'clock when my agent picks me up. All I have to do is smile at the camera. It's boring but they pay me well. A girl has to earn her living these days... I'm sorry. You are Randall Holiday, the author?"

"Actually, I'm Randall Crookshank."

"Then I have the wrong person."

"No, you don't. Holiday is my pen name."

"Ah. So the barman was right."

"He's the owner."

"I've spent most of my life in England. Why I liked your *Love Song* so much."

"It's a trivial piece of nothing. The worst book I ever wrote."

"Is there something wrong?"

"My wife just walked out on me."

"You poor darling. Have you been married long?"

"Not so long. It was my second marriage. The first wife went off with a woman. She told me she was bi-sexual long after we were married. Now she's a full-time lesbian with a full-time live-in lesbian lover."

"Should I go?"

"Probably. I'm not much company today. You want a drink?"

"Thought you'd never ask... Why are you shuddering?"

"Terry, give the lady a drink... Fear, Rebecca. Comes in waves. Part of me is dead. Only the physical body is still alive."

"Did you love her?"

"I thought so. Now I'm not even sure of that. Relationships usually drift together before they become marriage. I don't want to talk about it."

"Of course you don't."

"Why did you come to America?"

"To further my career. My ambition is to be a film actress."

"Have you done any acting?"

"In school. The annual school play. Twice."

"Were you any good?"

"I don't know. I hope so. Have they cast *Love Song*?"

"They're in the process."

"Could you get me an audition? I have the right accent."

"And you look good, Rebecca."

"Thank you for the flattery."

"I can ask Poppy. She wrote the screenplay. Why not?"

"Oh, thank you, Randall. If I get a part, I'll be eternally grateful."

"Careful what you wish for. Succeeding in the world of entertainment isn't all it's cracked up to be. I love writing books, not doing all the promoting that comes with being a successful author. They all want a piece of you."

"No peace for the wicked."

"You think I'm wicked? Thanks, Terry. So, Rebecca. Tell me the rest of your story."

Quietly, Randall shook his head. Like an old, old story grinding away, it was all starting over again. She didn't want to talk to him despite all the smiles. What she wanted was a part in a movie. But it wasn't all bad. She had stopped the shudders. Stopped him fixating on himself. The next trick was to concentrate on what the pretty girl was telling him about herself and look as if he was interested. With his mind wandering far away from the typical story of a girl from England, Randall tried not to think of himself and what, if anything, lay ahead in his future. He could chase women, including Rebecca, having brief, pointless affairs one after the other, his motive sex, their motive his fame and money. Ten years, maybe, of using the bodies of women to overcome his boredom. He could go back to Rabbit Farm and, all on his own, with Polar Bear, his white Alsatian, as his only companion, and try and write, living his life in his book, walking alone, drinking alone and mostly feeling miserable. He could go back to the wilds of Africa and find a spot on the banks of the Zambezi River, sit in a tent, dream up another book and still feel totally miserable.

"You're not listening to me, Randall."

"I'm sorry. I'd better go. Write your full name and phone number on a piece of paper and I'll give it to Poppy."

"You won't forget? Oh, thank you. My life will really begin if I get a part in *Love Song*. You are so sweet to help me. Give me a ring yourself. When you are feeling better. What are you going to do for the rest of the day? Such a pity my agent is picking me up... Now, you won't lose this piece of paper?"

"I lost my wife and son this morning. I'll try not to lose your piece of paper. There we go, Terry. A hundred bucks should cover everything."

"Forty is enough."

"Fine. Whatever. Have a nice day."

Back on the thirty-first floor, Randall went to the drinks cupboard and took out a full bottle of whisky. With a half-a-glass of neat whisky in his right hand and the bottle in the other, he walked over to the big window and stared and stared, his mind mixed with hatred, fear and misery. He drank and drank as the wolves screamed in his head, a howling pack of wolves from the Welsh woods, the same woods where Meredith had come to find him and his wealth. All Randall wanted to do was jump out of the window by smashing the plate-glass with the bottle. As the wolves tore him apart he picked up the bottle and struck the plate-glass window, shattering the bottle and spraying whisky all around the room.

"Well, that didn't work, you silly old bastard."

Not sure he would have jumped if the window had broken, he found another bottle of whisky, put on Mahler's Third Symphony and sat back on the couch. Outside, the light was beginning to fade. All evening Randall tried to get himself drunk without succeeding. He was a failure. An utter failure. Mentally shouting at the wolves in his head, Randall went to bed. When sleep came, the wolves stopped baying from the woods, making him thrash and turn in his sleep. When he woke in the dark of the night he put out his hand for Meredith before the wolves returned to his mind. For the rest of the night, Randall was unable to sleep. He was at the stage in between drunkenness and a hangover. Remembering the gun he carried during the Rhodesian bush war, Randall knew he was lucky. If he'd had that gun now, he would have shot himself. Blown his brains out and killed the howling wolves. When he got up to check the living room he found shards of glass all over the carpet. The room smelled of whisky. To Randall's surprise, there was no crack in the plate-glass window. In the kitchen, he drank down two pints of cold water before putting on the kettle.

"Today is the first day of the rest of your life. Never forget it, old boy. Can't be any worse than yesterday. And look at that. Outside the sun is shining."

Seeing a piece of paper on the coffee table, Randall picked it up, read Rebecca's phone number and picked up his telephone.

"How are you, Randall?"

"If you must know, Poppy, bloody awful. I have a friend I want you to invite to the audition."

"Anything you want. The director loves our final script."

"That's nice."

"See you at the launch of Tracey's book at the Metropolitan."

"You'll have to make my excuses. I'm taking a trip to Africa for a holiday."

"Your wife will love a holiday."

"It's a long story."

"How long are you going to be away?"

"I'm not sure. Good luck with the movie."

"When are you leaving?"

"This afternoon if I can get on a flight. Africa, home of my birth. Beautiful Africa. I need solace, Poppy. Lots and lots of solace. Please don't forget to phone Rebecca."

"What are you going to do in Africa?"

"Again drink the water of the Zambezi River. They say once you have drunk the water of the Zambezi you will always return to Africa."

"You're not making sense."

"Does it matter, Poppy? Does it matter?"

2

On the following Wednesday, while Randall sat in a camp-chair on the riverbank high above the Zambezi away from the crocodiles, writing the first chapter of *Shakespeare's Friend* into the notebook spread on his knees in the shade of the riverine trees, Tracey was reading a piece from her novel to the seated audience in the conference room of the Metropolitan Hotel at the launch of her book. In the front row of chairs sat Godfrey Merchant with a satisfied look on his face, the look of a publisher who had sold three hundred thousand copies of *Lust* prior to its launch. Next to Godfrey sat Manfred Leon, with a similar smile on his face. When Tracey finished reading the erotic paragraph where Fay seduced her rich lover, the second conquest of her day, the audience sat dumbstruck. After a long, pregnant pause, the guests broke into clapping and shouting and banging their feet on the floor, the media cameras turning from Tracey up at the podium to the excited crowd of guests. When Tracey came down off the podium and sat down smugly in the chair next to Godfrey, the waiters now wheeling in the food and drinks, she could barely hear herself think.

"Let the party begin, Tracey. You are now one of the most successful novelists in America. And I have only just begun the barrage of publicity... Can you hear me?"

"Only just. Go and tell the band to start playing."

"They always play when they're ready. Your job tonight is to talk individually to the press and make as many friends as possible. Use your charm, Tracey. Good books are all about maximum publicity. Touch their hands. Kiss them on the cheeks. Make it as personal as possible without going over that inappropriate edge. Just enough to get the men's hormones jumping. Now it's time for a drink. I do so love a plan when it comes together. That comes from a TV series, the name of which I can't for the life of me remember. Not that it matters. Oh, and your final take from the sale of the rights to the movie is two-point-four million dollars."

"You've got to be kidding."

"You can thank Manfred. He's a good negotiator. The movie is going to win an Oscar for best movie of the year."

"You think so?"

"I hope so. With all the publicity we are drawing, the girl playing Fay could well get the Oscar for best actor. She's already a famous actress which helps. Enjoy yourself, young lady. You are now famous, Tracey Chapelle. By the end of December, after the Christmas rush, we will have sold five million copies of *Lust*. You owe me one, Tracey."

"You can have it whenever you like. Don't look so amazed."

"You're serious."

"Of course I am. What would be better than to celebrate? Just the author and her publisher... Now, look at that. Here comes the press."

"Go do your job. And never forget, Tracey, the success of a book comes from good publicity. You can write the best book in the world but if the public is not told about it, they won't read it. It's the hardest part for the author but it has to be done... Ah, there's my friend from the *New York Times*. Work the floor, Tracey. Work the floor. Why we invited them all to the party. There's no such thing as a free drink. Never was. And always ask them their names. People love telling a celebrity their name. Now the band has begun playing as the drink trays go around. The party has just started."

Not sure if she knew what she had got herself into, Tracey did as she was told, talking to one excited journalist after another. For an hour, drink in hand which she barely touched, she smiled and talked to the media, encouraging their questions. On the other side of the room, she could see Manfred Leon surrounded by reporters. Down a little, Faith White, his new partner in Leon and White, was doing the same. Next to Faith, Jane Slater was answering more questions, while Godfrey Merchant moved diligently from person to person. When Manfred caught up with her two hours after her book reading they had both talked one-to-one to most of the reporters in the room.

"You invited all your authors, Manfred. Where's Randall Holiday? I don't see him."

"Ah, now there's a problem. Even his brother doesn't know where he is. Packed his bags the day his wife walked out on him and went back to Africa. I think his writing days are finished... They are beginning to leave. How many did you speak to? Good. You're smiling. By the time I'm finished, I want every major newspaper in the English-speaking world to know about your book. Then we'll start on the translations. There are a quarter of a million Russians in the world. We're going to tap every market... You want to buy yourself an apartment with your film money? When Randall left, he gave the keys to his apartment to his brother and told him to sell it, lock stock and barrel. It's well furnished. If you buy direct from Phillip there won't be an agent's commission. You got to invest somewhere. Why not a place on the thirty-first floor? I don't think we'll see him again in America. All that work promoting Randall Holiday and then he stops writing. Have you started your new book? You'll love writing with a view right over Manhattan. You'd better go and talk to Jane. She's waving at you."

"It's all happened so quickly."

"That's life, Tracey. And if you hadn't seduced me that first night, none of this would have happened."

"You think so?"

"I know so. In life, you have to catch people's attention. I'm a lucky man. You're a lucky girl. Go and talk to Jane."

"You seduced me, Manfred. I didn't seduce you."

"You've got to be kidding. That grin on your face tells me everything."

"How do I get hold of the brother?"

"Talk to Jane. And thanks. She's a good, hard-working assistant."

Not sure if Manfred's final look was not a look of nostalgia for their one-night stand, Tracey walked across to join Jane.

"How's it gone, Tracey?"

"One of the women asked if it wasn't boring writing about orgasms. When I asked her her name she told me to mind my own business."

"How old was she?"

"In her fifties, probably."

"Jealousy. Women who are not getting it are jealous of those who are."

"What are you drinking?"

"Lime juice and soda. I haven't touched alcohol since I joined the Leon and White literary agency. I'm not going to drink anymore, Tracey. I'm no longer moody and don't get depressed... When are you moving out from next door?"

"I'm going to buy myself a place. Randall Holiday has put his apartment on the market and disappeared into the wilds. I want to get the new book going. A whole series of books, all of them erotic. Do you know how many of those reporters asked for my phone number?"

"Did you give it to them?"

"Of course. We want them to write about me. This has been the most exciting night of my life."

"Aren't you tired? I'm exhausted. Happy with the job done properly but tired."

"I can go on all night."

"Who've you got your eye on?"

"All of them. A bit like Fay in my book. I just love the feeling of success. It permeates the body. Total satisfaction that's going to be with me for the rest of my life."

"Keep success in perspective, Tracey. Hasn't helped Randall. Poor man. Not once. Twice. Both of his wives left him. Manfred says the constant attention brought by his fame drove him to drink. A bad combination. Makes you wonder what life is all about."

"Excuse me. Would you like to dance?"

"I'd love to. Jane, can you hold my glass?"

"Not with alcohol in it. Put it on the waiter's tray."

"My name is Arnold. I read the copy of your book sent with my invitation. It's one of the best books I have ever read. If the readers of my column want a good book to read, this is the one. Oh, my goodness... Tell me more about yourself Tracey, so I can write it in my column. Do you like dancing?"

"I like men."

"Of course you do. They always say you can't write about anything you haven't experienced."

"Are you making a pass at me, Arnold?"

"Why not? Who wouldn't? Every man in this room wants to experience what you write in that book. Give me lots to write about, Tracey Chapelle. There's nothing better than a good article about an author, especially an author like you."

"You've done this before?"

"Of course I have. Life in New York. The most exciting city in the world. Tell me, how did you manage to write such an evocative book? It's so alive. All the characters are real. I can see them as I read. I was in the same room. I've tried to write fiction but I can't make my characters come alive. Some say it's a gift. You don't know how lucky you are. I lived in your book for the five hours it took me to read. As the writer, you'd have been immersed in the story for so much longer. I can't wait to read your next book. Come dance with me, Tracey. Let's dance together. I will always remember dancing with the author of *Lust*. The night is still young. Will you sign my copy of your book? How many books have you signed tonight?... There we go, Tracey. Now it is signed I will never lend your book. When does the book tour begin? I would give my right ear to be a successful novelist. Or did van Gogh chop off his left ear?"

"Next week when the shops have had pyramids of my book in their windows to catch the eye of passers-by. They put up a big sign showing the time and day I will be in the shop for the signing."

With the signed book tucked into the pocket of his tuxedo jacket, and given a pat, they began to dance, Tracey keeping her moves just within propriety as she answered his myriad of questions.

"What's your circulation, Arnold?"

"Something over four million."

"How many read your articles?"

"Most of them. My headline will read 'Erotica'. Catch the eye. Can I have your phone number?"

"I wrote it down next to my signature. It's in your pocket... Look at that. The music has stopped. See you later. It's all go."

"Quite the popular girl."

"That's me. It's my night. My first big night. Look after yourself. I'm looking forward to reading what you say."

"And if I praise you to the sky, you'll give me a date?"

"Something like that. Hope springs eternal. Four million circulation. That's a lot of readers."

SEVEN WEEKS LATER, three weeks before Christmas, the day after Tracey completed her American book tour, Manfred took Tracey to meet Phillip Crookshank on the forty-ninth floor of Phillip's apartment building.

Across the country, the sales of *Lust* had tipped the four million mark, making Tracey a very rich girl.

"Come in. My wife is at work, of course, making more and more of what she calls that lovely money. I don't understand her. What's the point of making more money than a person can spend in her lifetime? Ivy, our wonderful nanny, has taken Carmen to the park to give her the feel of the trees. Carmen turns a year-old next month. I sit here most days twiddling my thumbs. I read your book, Tracey, and can see what all the fuss is about. Come in. Come in. I'll put the kettle on for a cup of coffee. So you want to buy my brother's flat? In Rhodesia, we called an apartment a flat. Rhodesia was very English. The last British colony. Never mind, there's no point in being sentimental. Colonialism quite rightly is now history. In the old days, when we British wished to make our fortune, we went to the Caribbean to grow sugar, Ceylon to plant tea and Rhodesia to grow tobacco. All for the people back home. My father was a tobacco farmer. Anyway, that's all history. This is today. Do you like the view? All those lovely skyscrapers. Oh, well."

"Have you heard from Randall?"

"Not a word, Manfred. He'd been drinking too much even before Meredith walked out on him. Said he couldn't write surrounded by buildings crowded with people. Alcohol's been a problem in our family. Our mother got drunk and drove alone from World's View to the escarpment that looks down from two thousand feet over the Zambezi Valley and ran out of petrol. There had been an argument. When she tried to walk back to the farm she was attacked and killed by a pride of lions. Randall never knew his own mother. Affected the rest of his life. Mood swings. Even talked about killing himself when life wasn't going his way."

"You think he might have killed himself?"

"There were shards of glass on the carpet below the big window in the living room when he called me down to give me the keys and told me to sell his flat. The place smelt of whisky. I think he tried to break the window. My poor brother. Two wives. Two sons. And he's all on his own."

"If I like the place, can I buy it?"

"Our two flats are very similar. We can go down, I suppose. The emptiness makes me feel depressed. Anyway, I don't think we should sell it right away. He's probably somewhere deep in the bush trying to get his mind together. You can live in his place, I suppose, with an option to buy once I've found out where my brother is. Dad's going to go out from

England and look for him. How we find him is another question. The Zimbabwe bushveld is vast. I know. I was a safari operator before Martha came out with a group of singles and we had an affair. Oh dear, there I go again, telling you my story when all you want to do is look at Randall's flat. Coffee first. Then we go down to the thirty-first floor."

"Did you like my book?"

"Not quite my kind of reading. But I see why it will sell. Goodness gracious, can I see why it will sell."

"Do you like living in New York City?"

"That's a difficult question. My wife loves running her advertising business with her three partners. Says she'd be bored out of her mind living in the African bush. And now there is Carmen, so I don't have an option. Carmen was named after our mother, so our mother would live again through my daughter... There we go. The kettle's boiling. Milk and sugar, both of you?"

"I do love the view. It's like being on top of the world. I could write here, Manfred. Oh, could I write. Is the view the same on the thirty-first floor? Can I at least rent the place?"

"You're one of Manfred's authors. I'm sure Randall wouldn't expect you to pay rent."

"Do you have any kind of a job?"

"I'm a venture capitalist sitting up here all day waiting for that next big opportunity."

"Have you been successful?"

"You wouldn't even believe how successful if you measure success in dollars... What are you having?"

"Milk and two sugars."

"Mind you, if it wasn't for colonialism, you wouldn't be looking at that view. On the farm, we grew Virginia tobacco. Makes you think just how the world keeps going round and round. When my father went out to Rhodesia, the British were short of dollars. Wanted to buy their tobacco that generated all that lovely tax money in sterling. Told people like my father that Rhodesia would be a wonderful opportunity for a young man. They knew of course Rhodesia and colonialism were on their last legs. But they didn't care. They didn't have the dollars to buy their tobacco from Virginia. India had gone in 1947. Telling a young man to make his career growing tobacco in Africa was a con. And, like fools, we rushed in, to be handed six thousand acres of Crown Land. There was a five-year apprenticeship on one of the existing farms before the colonial government handed over the land. What Robert Mugabe's argument has been about ever since. The fact the land had never been used didn't come into it. All those new jobs as we English developed the land. When Cecil Rhodes took over the land he called Rhodesia, there were less than half a million people in the entire country. All that unused land. Now, when the country became prosperous and the population grew over ten million, Mr Mugabe wants the land back again. Makes sense. The eternal roundabout, some call politics... Let me find Randall's keys. My poor brother. There we are... Oh, let's first finish our coffee."

"So you don't like living in New York?"

"Not particularly. Once you've found solace in the countryside it's difficult to live among hordes of people. Growing up on World's View was a wonderful childhood even without our birth mother. I still love my stepmother very much. Urban and country people are very different. In the big city, you always have to be doing something. You can't sit back and enjoy the scenery or go for a walk through the trees and listen to the birds. Martha always likes to be doing things. Spending money. Entertaining her clients and friends. Oh well. You can't have everything. We have Carmen and all that lovely money that people find so important... I'll lead the way. Randall bought his place to please Meredith. Marriages never were easy... I hate lifts. They remind me of submarines. All enclosed. Not that I've ever been on a submarine... You just press the button and have to wait... Here we are, Tracey. Now, let's see which key fits the door... There we go. As I said, there isn't much difference between this place and mine. Have a look around. Make yourself at home. My poor brother."

"I'll buy it. I just so love the view through the big plate-glass window, the whole front of the living room from floor to ceiling. Name a price."

"I'll have to ask a couple of estate agents. Or do you call them realtors?"

"Oh, Manfred. For a writer, this place is just perfect."

"Now you've seen what you want, we'd better leave Phillip in peace. And please find Randall for me. He's my most successful author."

"And generator of income for your agency."

"He's also my friend."

"I know he is."

"Let me know the minute you hear from him."

"Of course I will. Leave the door open. I'm going to sit for a while on Randall's couch and think of my brother."

In the lift, as the door slid closed and Manfred pressed the ground-floor button, Tracey felt a wave of sadness flow from her mind down through her entire body. Those two poor brothers. Lost in Manhattan. Pining for their roots in the African bush, for Tracey a place she could not even imagine.

"Where did he get the initial capital to become a successful venture capitalist?"

"From his maternal grandfather. The father of the girl whose bones, what was left of them by the lions, were buried at the top of the Zambezi escarpment. Randall told me about visiting his mother's grave that looked far down to the distant Zambezi River. Have you heard of Ben Crossley?"

"The Hollywood actor?"

"Where the money came from. Left both of them a fortune. They say the trick in life is to choose your parents carefully."

"How do you do that, Manfred?"

"I have absolutely no idea."

"You think I'll get that apartment?"

"You never know, Tracey. You never know. Let's just see what happens. What are you doing tonight?"

"Who knows, Manfred? Who knows? And in two weeks it'll be Christmas. Another year gone by. Oh, it's so nice to be rich. All my problems have gone away. Money. What would we do without money? Why can't people be content with what they have in their lives? Those two brothers have everything and they're both miserable."

"They both want to live the life of the old days in colonial Africa that no longer exists. In the peace of the African bush. Either that or they achieved too early what most of us go on striving for throughout our lives. Do we ever know other people, Tracey? What's in their minds? When you've done everything, what's there to do in life? Randall, if he's still alive, must go on writing. That's what gives him peace of mind. Phillip? He's got a daughter to bring up. Maybe he should get his wife pregnant again. Have half a dozen kids. With six kids he wouldn't have time to be sad... Here we go. Ground floor."

"Thanks for the help, Manfred."

"My pleasure. Better get back to the office. Running a literary agency is hard work. I have ten new books waiting for me to read. People are constantly sending me their work. And you have to read all of them or you miss out on an author like Tracey Chapelle. What a game."

"It's always a game."

"I know it is. Why life's so much fun. Are we leaving it as a one-night stand?"

"Looks like it."

"I'm getting old, Tracey. I rather like Jane. She's more my age. Got a brain in her head has our Jane. Anyway, now she's working for us that is no longer possible."

"Break the rules, Manfred."

"You know she doesn't drink?"

"Glad to hear it."

"Asked her to go for a drink a couple of times and she got quite shirty. Said drinking alcohol was the habit of fools."

3

Tracey moved into Randall's apartment on the Friday, a week or so before Christmas. The following day, in her sexiest clothes, she waited, smiling at the tables laden with the drinks and the food, waiting for the guests to begin arriving for the house-warming party.

"Three solid hours of hard work. Such a pity I can't drink. I used to so love a party."

"Where are you going, Jane?"

"Home. Never look temptation in the mouth. Glad to help you get it all ready. Between us, we contacted the entire media, and everyone else tied to the production of your book. Have fun. I really like your new place. I've got to the end of February to find a new home. Oh, and again congratulations. Five million copies sold. After Christmas, after your party time you've been so looking forward to, you'll have to start on the screenplay."

"I don't know how to begin. I write books, not movies."

"Randall said the same. I'll help you. We'll work on it together. Have a lovely party and don't get yourself into too much mischief."

"Manfred's coming. You should stay."

"I don't trust myself. With alcohol or Manfred. Above everything else I have done in my new life, I have no intention of jeopardising my job. You know what the rent of a new apartment is going to cost me? You can't find old buildings with old rents. When people have cheap rents, they won't move. Unless the building is up for demolition."

"Did you ever get a hat-trick in your good old days of partying? My latest ambition. Three different men in one night... Why are you grinning, Jane?"

"Old memories. Just don't get yourself pregnant. Amazing what we get up to when we are drunk."

"I'm on the pill."

"Doesn't always protect you."

"Of course it does. I've been on the pill for years. I'm going to pour myself a drink. I'm going to miss you as my next-door neighbour. What would we do without friends?"

"Get drunk. Score a hat-trick. And not give a damn. What a world, Tracey. Just be careful. Enjoy yourself. The good years go by so fast. Suddenly they're all gone. I'm not looking forward to being old. Next time, hire a caterer."

"I enjoyed your company."

"So did I, doing things with friends. When I get back to my lonely apartment I'm going to be sad. Just watch the booze, Tracey. Watch the booze. Sometimes I wonder what the point is in living. Poor Randall. I wonder where he is? I hope he's happy. The most difficult thing in life is to stay happy. I'll be thinking of the party. Oh, yes. I'll be thinking of you partying. Enjoy what you can when you have it. Good things have a habit of disappearing before you know it."

When Tracey opened the front door of Randall's apartment to let her out into the corridor she could see Jane was crying. Neither spoke. Tracey watched Jane walk to the lift and press the button. When the lift came she got inside and disappeared, leaving Tracey staring at nothing.

WHEN THE LIFT began to descend, Jane leaned back and slid down the wall onto her bottom.

"Now what am I going to do with the rest of my life?"

A man was standing outside the lift when the door opened on the ground floor.

"Are you all right? Can I help you?"

"If you have a gun you can shoot me."

"You'd better get out of the lift. I'm in a hurry."

Turning onto her knees and clawing her way up the wall to the rail,

Jane pulled herself to her feet, wiped her eyes with the back of her hand, and walked out of the lift. She wanted a drink. Her whole body screamed at her to find a drink. A group of people were walking from the entrance to the lifts making Jane turn her head away for fear of recognition. By the look of them, they had already been drinking. They were enjoying themselves. Laughing. Young people ready to party. Outside, Jane hailed a cab, gave the man the address of her old apartment and sat back in her seat. She was sweating. The fear of alcohol was making her sweat. In two months she was turning thirty-eight. Her life was over, with or without her new job. What did a thirty-eight-year-old single woman do with her life? There was no purpose. No future. Not a single thing to look forward to. As she let herself into her apartment she glanced at the door of Tracey's old apartment. With an intensity that brought back her strength, Jane hoped with all her heart that Tracey was not headed down the same path of destruction. Having turned on the music, she sat in an armchair and began softly crying to herself.

"Harvey, why didn't we get married and have children? We would have made enough money. All the money in the world is worthless unless you're happy. We were happy, Harvey. We would have stayed happy for the rest of our lives together."

With her head back and staring through her tears at the dirty ceiling, Jane let out a scream, a constant scream of agony. Nobody came. Nobody cared. Nobody would ever care what happened to Jane. Like millions of others, she was one lost soul in the concrete jungle, with no hope, no future and nothing to live for. To overcome her desperate desire to go out and find herself alcohol, Jane took the last three of her sleeping pills and went to bed. She was lucky not to have bought more of the pills that were due for replenishment on the following Monday. When the pills took over her mind, Jane fell into a troubled sleep, where she stayed until the morning, waking to another day in her lonely apartment, and even that, the familiar, was about to end. Getting up and making herself breakfast, a wry smile came to her face. She was thinking of Tracey.

"Did you get your hat-trick?"

Smiling, she sat at the small table and ate her breakfast. She had won. She had fought the demon and won. She was sober. Her life would go on. Going to her bookcase, Jane took out her copy of *Lust* and carried it to her writing desk. Carefully, she read the first chapter before turning to her typewriter where she began writing the dialogue for the screenplay. Within a minute she was lost in her writing. She was happy.

Two hours later, with the first scene complete, she made herself a cup of coffee. All she wanted to do was trip the light fandango.

"Thank you, Tracey Chapelle. You've just saved my life."

For seven days, without once leaving her apartment, with the phone disconnected and in perfect solitude, Jane wrote the screenplay to *Lust*.

"All it now needs is a new title. There's more to that book than *Lust* and we've got it right in front of us. You can write, you silly old cow. You just can't write the original."

With the finished work in her briefcase, Jane went outside. Somehow New York looked different. Instead of taking a cab, she took the subway. When she finally reached the door of Tracey's new apartment she stood outside and smiled to herself.

"Are we feeling lucky?"

Then she rang the doorbell."

"Jane! What are you doing here at seven o'clock in the morning? Come in."

"Are you alone?"

"What's this?"

"Your film script. Finished. Not a scene or a word to be changed. Is it really seven o'clock in the morning? Are you alone, Tracey?"

"Luckily. We partied for three days. Couldn't take anymore. You look so happy, Jane."

"Did you get your hat-trick?"

"Matter of fact I think I did but it's all a bit hazy... I've started a new book. Tea or coffee? We'll make a deal. You sit and read what I've written, and I'll read your screenplay... I so love this apartment. Just look out of that big window, even though it's dark outside. It's so beautiful. And they still haven't heard from Randall. Happy Christmas, Jane. It's Christmas Day. We'll spend it together. Just the two of us. I've had enough of partying."

"Happy Christmas, Tracey. Happy Christmas. I'd lost track of time. I came right over when I finished the script. I had no idea it was Christmas Day. The year has almost gone. Another year gone by for man. You sometimes wonder how long it will all go on for. I want you to ask the director to give the film a new title. The word *Lust* caught the public's attention but there's more in your story than just sex."

"Do you have any ideas?"

"Not at the moment. Well, maybe. Why not *Let's Dance the Light Fandango*? Maybe not. I'm no good at titles."

"Too long. They want to keep my title to follow up on all the publicity. Famous actors don't change their names. Sit yourself down. Shouldn't take me more than two hours... There you go. My new book. The follow-up to *Lust*. Always follow a winner, Jane... How long did it take you?"

"A solid week without interruption. You know something? For a whole week, I didn't think once of myself."

"You didn't go to work?"

"I left a message for Manfred before I disconnected my phone. Told him what I was doing. Not exactly part of my job but it will do. Nothing much happens in an office in the week before Christmas. I'll make the coffee. You read the screenplay. Are you sure you had nothing planned for Christmas?"

"Absolutely. Sometimes a girl needs time to herself. I like to give my body a chance to recover after a binge. Let the liver unpickle itself. Do I need my pen as I read your script?"

"Read it through. Afterwards, we'll have a discussion. How many pages have you written?"

"Eleven. The start and end are the most difficult part of writing a novel. This is all so neat. Here we go. *Lust* on the big screen. Hollywood. A whole new world."

When Jane put down the mug of coffee, Tracey did not look up from her reading, making Jane feel comfortable with her own work. After reading the eleven pages she stood in the lounge looking out of Randall's window at the breaking dawn. Down below, the traffic was building up, people going about their business. For a long while, Jane stared out of the big window seeing nothing other than what was inside her head. Behind her on the couch, Tracey was quiet. When it began to rain, water flowed down the outside of the plate-glass window. Below in the street, the umbrellas had come out, the slashing rain bringing Jane back into the present. When the first sentence came she turned and moved to the door.

"Where are you going, Jane? I haven't finished."

"Got to go."

"What about Christmas?"

"Enjoy yourself. I liked the new book. Lucky I brought my umbrella. Happy Christmas to you, Tracey Chapelle. And if I don't see you before, have a prosperous new year. Not that you need any more prosperity."

Without waiting for an argument, Jane let herself out of the apartment. When the cab driver dropped her at her apartment, the first sentence was still singing in her head. Upstairs, instead of going to her typewriter, she picked up her ballpoint pen at her desk, moved back the typewriter, put a small block of clean white sheets of paper in front of her and began to write, a straight communication between herself and the paper unobstructed by the bulk of her typewriter. By lunchtime, Jane had written five hand-script pages of her love story, Harvey so close he was inside her head, inside her room, back in her life. She was happy for the first time in years. Writing the script for *Lust* had broken her writer's block, letting the story of Harvey flow out of her, caressing her mind and bringing her peace. With her writing hand numb, she went to her small kitchen, took the meat out of the fridge and made herself lunch. She was ravenous. Happy and ravenous.

"When did you last eat? My best Christmas in years. Just take it slow, Jane Slater. Write at the weekends and holidays. And working for a literary agent should make finding a publisher a whole lot less difficult."

After lunch, she got into her bed and took a nap, falling asleep in peace, her mind free of turmoil. In her dreams she was happy. When she woke, she put both her hands behind her head and let her mind run with the story, the plot flowing ahead. Like all novels, her story was based on her experience, her interplay with other people. In addition to Harvey, there were traces of Manfred and Tracey in the story. She was young again. Happy again. She got out of bed, dressed in her underwear, and danced the light fandango. She was what she always wanted to be. She was a writer.

"It'll last forever. Our love, Harvey, will last forever, shared with whoever wants to read our beautiful story. Young love, never to die. Never to be destroyed by the filth of money. Two young lovers, young forever. What more can a girl ever want? And, in my book, they are going to have children. A boy and a girl. A lovely boy and a beautiful girl. Live in the country away from life's horrors and temptations. Away from that mass of grabbing, thieving and arguing people. Real peace on earth and goodwill to all men. A happy family, Harvey. In my book, we're going to be a happy family, forever and ever, amen."

Outside, when Jane looked out of her small kitchen window, she could see the sun was shining. She put on her thick coat, a hat and a scarf. Downstairs, she walked out into the street with all its lovely smiling people, everything looking different, the world worth living in. For the first time since she fell in love all those years ago, everything she saw was positive, not a negative thought in her mind. Only when the light began to fade did she go home, the story of her book still racing through her mind. With her arms crossed and hugging herself, Jane walked to the front door of her apartment building.

"Happy Christmas, Jane."

"Happy Christmas, Mrs Fortescue. Lovely day."

"Christmas is always a lovely day. I'm off for Christmas dinner with my daughter and my grandchildren."

"Have a lovely evening."

"We will."

Upstairs, her small home felt welcome. She made herself a cup of coffee and turned on the classical music channel on her television, the happy music of Mozart making her smile. She was no longer alone, the thought of having to move to a new apartment no longer a problem. When her phone rang she picked it up without that pang of worry.

"Come over, Jane. Please. I don't want to be alone. Your screenplay is perfect. Why did you leave in such a hurry?"

"I'm on my way, Tracey. I've started writing my love story. I'm back with Harvey."

"That's so wonderful."

"Don't tell me. I'm going to buy us a Christmas cake on my way over. Not a big one. A nice little cake for two."

"Life isn't so bad, is it?"

"Not anymore it isn't. Such a pity we still don't live next door to each other. Never mind. What are taxi drivers for? Especially with Manfred's nice little salary. Hold your horses, Tracey. I'm coming over."

The small shop that stayed open for Christmas had a line of Christmas cakes on top of the long glass display cabinet, all of them covered with icing. The one Jane chose had little candles peeping on top, a cross between a birthday and a Christmas cake.

"It must be sad having to work on Christmas Day."

"We like to be there for our customers. The customer must come first. Enjoy your cake. My daughter and I bake every one of them ourselves."

With the chime of the doorbell still ringing in her head, the boxed cake held carefully in the palm of her hand, Jane got back into her taxi and rode the streets to the more affluent part of Manhattan, the home of the successful authors.

"Now that's better. Come in, Jane. The turkey is in the oven with all the trimmings. Just as well you don't drink. Give my liver a chance to recover... You've taken a lot of sex out of the screenplay. The words, I mean."

"Body language in a movie speaks louder than words. Films are different to books. You look at their pictures. The writer doesn't have to paint that picture with words. I'm not sure after the tea and cake whether I'll be hungry enough for turkey. The good part of a Christmas turkey is you can enjoy eating it cold."

"Manfred's coming for supper."

"Is he now?"

"I wanted to tell him how much I like your screenplay."

"Are you up to something, Tracey?"

"We're all up to something, Jane. We both owe Manfred a lot. Our future, even our lives. He's agreed there'll be no drinking of alcohol. So, how are you finding writing a book? About time. I've been telling you to write that story of you and Harvey for ages and ages."

"Bliss. Utter Bliss. I'm young again. Innocent. The world doesn't hate me anymore. I'm in love. Living with my lover. The horror has gone. I'm what I want to be."

"Don't write it too quickly. Enjoy the writing for as long as possible. The worst part of writing is finishing a book. Losing all your friends. Living back among reality with all its warts. I've made a list of queries about the film. Once you and I have agreed everything, Manfred will hand the script over to the director and it'll be out of our hands. Then it's up to the director and the actors to add their input. Going from my mind through yours and onto a big screen is going to be like a miracle. So many people involved. All those cameras... Cake. I just love this cake. Instead of looking for a separate apartment, why don't you move into Randall's spare bedroom? We can write together. Keep each other's bad habits in check."

"Are you serious?"

"Why not, Jane? And if Randall Holiday doesn't want his place back, it'll be mine. You can start building up your money to buy your own small apartment. Give yourself financial security, and a home they can't tell you to leave... Have another piece of Christmas cake. Happy Christmas, Jane. Good. There's the doorbell... Manfred! Come in. We're eating cake. Just look at this. Old friends together enjoying Christmas. Food and fun. Make yourself at home in Randall's lovely apartment. I wonder where he's spending his Christmas? I'm going to play us Christmas carols. Get us fully into the Christmas spirit. Nothing better on Christmas Day than 'Jingle Bells'. Poor old Randall. I wonder how his wife is enjoying Christmas with her new lover? Life's a sonofabitch. Cake, Mr Leon, let us eat cake. Wasn't it the Queen of France who told them to eat cake when the people had nothing?... And that poor son. Wasn't his name, Douglas? He must be devastated without his father on Christmas Day. What a world. It all just comes and goes. We never quite know where we are going. Some days a beautiful melody. Others a constant discord of argument and pain... There we are. A Christmas carol. Did you hear the church bells ringing? As a child, I once watched the bellringers pulling down hard on the ropes and letting them go. They made the chimes sound like a symphony. Why do the different religions have to hate each other? Be so certain that their religion is the only way to God?... Now just listen to that. The bells are ringing again. Calling the faithful to evensong. A Christmas carol blending with the chimes of the church bells."

Not sure if Manfred was flirting with her or Tracey, his happy eyes following both of them as he listened to Tracey's flow of words through the music and the bells, Jane licked her fingers clean of the cake and sat back in her comfortable chair, content, Harvey and their story still running through her mind, the idea of sharing the apartment with Tracey equally comforting. They had so much in common, including Manfred Leon.

"Randall's father is in Harare right now looking for his son. All he's found out is Randall hired a four-wheel-drive vehicle and a tent. Where he's gone, nobody knows. Jeremy Crookshank is flying back to London after the New Year. Phillip thinks his father is on a wild-goose chase and that Randall will only come out of the bush when he wants to. It's good news. If he was going to kill himself, he wouldn't have rented a vehicle, certainly not with a tent. The best thing we can all do is leave him alone. Let him sort out his problems. No better place to do it than alone in the African bush."

"What about all those wild animals, Manfred? Aren't they dangerous?"

"Not to a man who grew up on an African farm."

"Did he take a gun?"

"They don't know. Probably. To feed himself. A gun and a fishing rod. Phillip thinks by now he won't come back to the Big Apple."

"It's so weird sitting in a man's chair in a multi-million-dollar apartment when the man's living in a tent in the wilds of Africa. Won't it be hot? It's the southern hemisphere. Our winter is their summer. Oh, well. I'll just have to wait and see if brother Phillip will sell me this place."

"Where's the screenplay?"

"Right here. Every word of it. Jane's good, Manfred. And now she's writing her own book."

"Am I going to lose my assistant?"

"Not if I can help it. I'll maybe write in the early mornings. At the weekends. I'm going to save up and buy myself a little place of my own."

"Would you like to visit Africa, Jane?"

"Too many lions and tigers."

"I don't think they have tigers in Africa."

"You two could go on a holiday together."

"Are you trying to get rid of your new roommate, Tracey? Tracey wants me to move into Randall's spare bedroom, Manfred. Can I help you in the kitchen, Tracey?"

"Just basting the turkey. Hope you're hungry after all that cake! I'll put on the vegetables a little later. Dinner will be served, my lord and my lady, in an hour. You can lay the table."

"At your service."

"It's so strange, throwing a dinner party without alcohol. Never mind. With luck, we'll talk sense instead of a whole lot of rubbish. I talk so much crap when I'm drunk."

"Don't we all, ladies? I'm enjoying myself. And the food will taste better when I'm perfectly sober. Alcohol is only a temporary crutch. When you're finally drunk, you fall over. I always ask myself the next morning if it was worth it. I hate hangovers. The older I get, the longer they seem to last. The things we do in life to try and enjoy ourselves. Tonight we will talk about books. Movies made from books. And when we part after a sumptuous Christmas dinner, we will go home to sleep without that drunken sleep screaming nightmares at us in our dreams. Good food and good company, girls. Two lovely girls all to myself. So, you wrote us the film script, Jane. And now you are writing a book. Creativity. There's nothing better than creating something that with a bit of luck will live forever. Or at least make the author a fortune."

"And the publisher and the literary agent."

"In the end, I suppose, it's all about money, Tracey. Everything in life is about money."

"Money, lust and love. What a world."

"True love has nothing to do with lust or money. Not in my book, anyway."

"That's why we call it fiction, Jane."

"Don't be cynical, Manfred. Tell us the story of your life. Where you come from. Your parents and your grandparents. As far back as you can."

"Well, if you're interested, it's a long, long story, starting in Russia before my family came across to America. If you find I'm boring you, tell me to shut up. Now, let me think, where will I start?"

Smiling inwardly at life's most common happiness, a man talking about himself, Jane sat back in her chair, letting her mind wander. When they sat down at the dinner table with Manfred carving the turkey, he was still talking about himself. Maybe drinking alcohol and losing one's memory wasn't so bad after all.

"Now it's your turn, Jane. Tell us about yourself."

"You've got to be kidding. Where do you want me to start?"

"At the beginning."

"Well, my childhood wasn't all that bad. I shared a bedroom with my younger sister... Are you sure I won't be boring you?"

"Of course not, Jane. What was your sister's name?"

"Constance. Little Conny. She was as naughty as hell... That's enough turkey, Manfred. I ate too much cake... Now, where was I?..."

PART 4

DECEMBER 1995 – THE MUMBLINGS OF OUR MIND

1

While Jane was eating her roast turkey, Randall Crookshank was finishing his midnight feast of Zambezi bream, cooked over the open fire. Having pulled the fish apart with his fingers he smiled up at the crescent moon, the night sky full of brilliant stars. He counted the stars in the Southern Cross, cutting a line that pointed exactly south as he wondered at the heavens. All those millions and millions of stars and planets unknown to a half-drunk man licking his fingers as he stared up through three layers of the Milky Way to the dark unknown. Far away on the other side of the Zambezi River, a lion roared in the dark of the night. Randall got up from his canvas chair and threw more wood on the fire, the flames coming up from the disturbance, sending light high into the riverine trees that lined the bank of the river. In the new light, he could see the Nissan with its empty canopy on the back where he slept on a mattress at night. A light breeze was blowing across the water into Randall's face, giving the hot night a brief respite. All through Christmas Day, in the perfection of his solitude, Randall had sipped at his whisky, enough to keep him smiling but not enough to make him drunk. Behind the comfortable chair stood the square-frame tent with its awning in the front that he sat under during the heat of the day. He had stopped writing a month after making camp high up on a bank above the big river, preferring to drink his whisky and think. He was happy on his own, happy to have escaped from people into a world that was only himself, no one pushing him, no one making him feel miserable. He was alone in the African bush, free from people. Raising his glass for the umpteenth time to the stars, his thirty-eighth birthday just gone, he had no idea what his life had been about. Had there been any purpose? Had he done anything that had any importance? He didn't think so. A book was just a means of entertainment. A degree in economics, a means to making money. His marriages just the process that created the next generation to start the process all over again. Did he want to live another thirty-eight years? Would he like to go back and re-live the previous thirty-eight years? He didn't think so. He had done everything there was to do in a life and still he had failed.

Out in the river, a fish plopped, bringing Randall out of his melancholy. In the back of the truck, lined up along the side of the mattress, were the remnants of twelve cases of whisky. When he had drunk all the whisky he would think again. Smiling at the campfire that kept away the wild animals, Randall thought back to the brief argument in the Harare gun shop when the man wouldn't sell him a rifle without a gun licence.

"That was lucky. When the whisky's gone I'd have shot myself. Go to bed, you silly old bugger. Fish, whisky and solitude. Happy Christmas, old boy."

Climbing with difficulty through the backdoor of the truck, Randall crawled onto the mattress before turning and shutting the door. It was hot and humid inside, despite the small windows covered in mosquito netting. Within a minute, lying on his back, Randall fell asleep, only waking to the dawn chorus of the birds. Getting out of the back of the truck and carefully checking for crocodiles in the river, he went down to the water for his morning swim. To the west, clouds were building. It was going to rain in paradise. After the naked swim, he collected his fishing rod and went back to catch his breakfast. With a hairy mopane worm on the end of his line and a butterfly with open wings the size of the back of his hand sitting halfway down the rod, he waited for a bite. The sun was rising over the trees in front of him. From a brief high from the sound of the morning birds, his mood had swung down to abject misery, all those past years and bad memories rushing over him. Putting down the fishing rod and putting a heavy rock on it he went back to the truck and took out a bottle of whisky. Instead of making him feel better, the whisky made him feel worse. What was the point of anything? Another book? So what? Another marriage? He didn't think so. Life in New York? Life on Rabbit Farm? All of it alone. What would be the purpose?

"Why the hell didn't you sell me that gun, you bastard? I offered you a bribe instead of a gun licence. I'm going to die one day, why not now? I don't want to go on living... They're both laughing at me. Both have my sons. Next, she'll want maintenance. She only wanted my money right from the start when she looked for me in that woodsman's cottage. That brief affair was to get at my money. Having Douglas will give her an income for the rest of her life. The bitch will never have to work a day in her life. They both used me to have their sons. What has fame and fortune done for you other than make you a target? I would have been better off poor. So when a woman said she loved me she would have meant it. I could pull a trigger but I don't have the guts to drown myself... What am I going to do when I run out of whisky? My life is a living hell. The lions did you a favour, my mother. Where are the lions? Shit. Look at that. You've got a fish on the line. Where are the lions? Come and get me. Oh, shit. I'm going to lose my rod. That's a tiger fish, not a bream. And you can't eat tiger fish. Too many bones. Coming. I'll let you loose. You can go. Back to your friends. If you have any, you poor bastard. You want a go at the whisky, Mr Tigerfish? What a bloody life we're both having this morning. We're both on the hook. The bastards have caught both of us. And I'm your bastard, you poor bloody fish. Where are the lions? Do you want to live, Mr Tigerfish? Oh. Here we go. I'm reeling you in. Stop jumping out of the water. You'll hurt your mouth. Hooks hurt. There we are. Stop flapping. There we go. Have a good life, you poor sod. Where the hell did I put that bottle of whisky? Where are the lions? I want the lions. Mother, where are the lions? Now, what do we eat for breakfast? I'm sick of mopane worm. Why didn't that terrorist bullet, through the window in World's View, kill me and not my cat? My poor cat. Poor Lady. Why wasn't it me? The lions killed you, my mother, why won't they kill me?... Ah. There's the whisky bottle. Were you hiding from me, whisky bottle? Ah, whisky. What would I do without alcohol? Instead of eating breakfast, let's get drunk. Really drunk. Fall-down drunk. Pissed as a newt. Shit. It's getting hot again. Back to the awning in the shade under the trees. Come with me, my bottle of whisky. We are friends. You, my only friend. Not Shakespeare's friend. Forget Shakespeare's friend. Randall's friend, you nice bottle of whisky. Leave the rod where it is. No one's going to steal it. Mad dogs and Englishmen go out in the midday sun. Where the hell was that from, you stupid prick? There we are, my tent. Me and my whisky. Welcome home. Just me and one big river and my home in my beautiful tent. What more can a man want? Thank you, whisky. I'm feeling better. Happy Christmas, everyone. Or is it Happy New Year? Who cares? The days go by, my only calendar of time is what's left of my whisky. Then we shall go to hell."

Still mumbling out loud to himself, Randall took the canvas chair to the tent and sat back with his bottle of whisky.

"And stop talking to yourself, you old drunk."

When Randall woke from a nap he could hear the sound of an engine coming down the river. The boat came into sight on the Zambian side of the river, before disappearing around the bend.

"That's a bugger. For a moment I thought it was Phillip. The Carruthers brothers on safari. You rescued me last time. Where are you, you old bugger? Memories. Sweet memories. Cheers, everyone. Cheers, Phillip. Drunk as a skunk. Oh, bugger. That boat's coming back again. Run, Randall, run. Damn. You're too drunk to run. Here it comes. That's not Phillip. It's a bloody National Parks boat coming this way. They're after me again. Anyone want a drink?"

Stuck in the canvas chair, Randall watched a man climb out of the boat carrying his boots and wade to the shore. He was wearing a uniform with green epaulettes on his shoulders. The man put on his boots and walked up the bank of the river, carrying a notebook in his right hand.

"What is your name?"

"Randall Holiday."

"What are you doing here? Do you have a permit? Please show me your permit."

"I don't have one."

"Are you drunk?"

"As a skunk."

"Do you have a gun? You require a hunting licence to carry a gun."

"No gun. Just a fishing rod and twelve cases of whisky."

"Where are you from?"

"Manhattan. Or I was the last time. My brother has a safari camp downriver at Chewore."

"What's his name?"

"Phillip Crookshank."

"You said your name was Holiday. How did you get through the gate?"

"The man let me through. He knew Phillip and his partner, Jacques

Oosthuizen. I write books under the name Randall Holiday. You may have heard of *The Tawny Wilderness*. It was set during the liberation struggle here in Zimbabwe."

"Without a permit, Mr Holiday, or whatever you call yourself, you must leave the park immediately."

"I'm too drunk to drive. I can't even stand up."

"If I find you here tomorrow when we return from our patrol, I will have you arrested."

"Don't you know my brother?"

"I don't believe he's your brother. You said your name is Holiday. I wrote it down."

"What's your name, may I ask?"

"Shumba. Robert Shumba. When I was born, my father gave me the first name of the ZANU-PF president, Mr Robert Mugabe. You people are all the same. You think you own the place. It will give me pleasure tomorrow to have you arrested."

"I was born in this country."

"I know you were. I can hear by your accent. Fortunately, most of you people have left the country. Go back to Manhattan. Wherever that is. And don't come back again. You Rhodesians are not welcome in Zimbabwe. We want our land back. All of it."

"Why are you being so rude?"

"I'm treating you the way you people treated my father."

"I'm sorry."

"They all say they are sorry."

Randall watched the man walk back to the boat without taking his boots off, picking up Randall's fishing rod on the way and throwing it far out into the water.

"There really isn't a place to hide. Now what do I eat? Shit happens, even on the banks of the Zambezi River. People. You can never get away from people. Fried mopane worms and no more whisky. Tomorrow you're driving back to Harare. The game's over. Maybe he's done me a favour. Thank you, Mr Game Ranger. Sometimes, even the people who hate you do you the biggest favours. Now where the hell do I go? Anyway, let's finish the whisky. Tomorrow's another day. The power of the people. Good luck to you, Robert Shumba, or whatever you call yourself. Tomorrow, and tomorrow, and tomorrow creeps in this petty pace from day to day, to the last syllable of recorded time; and all our yesterdays have lighted fools the way to dusty death. Now, you old drunk, was that

William Shakespeare or my friend the Earl of Oxford who wrote those words? Whichever one it was they sure understood our miserable lives. You know what, Crookshank, you like talking to yourself. It's better than talking to other people. Nobody answers back. To hell with them all. If I'm still drunk tomorrow morning they can cart me away. No, you'll have to go. No fresh food and no fishing rod. The game's over. First to Harare and give them back their truck. Then to the airport and back to America. There's nowhere to run, and nowhere to hide. Cheers, old boy. Anyone want a drink? To be or not to be, Will Shakespeare. That is the question. And if you're honest with yourself, Randall old boy, you'd be better off dead."

As the sun rose over the trees the next morning, Randall took down the tent and packed everything in the back of the truck. His mouth tasted like the bottom of a parrot cage. Going down to the water for the last time, he went for a swim. Back at the truck, he started the engine without any problem. By the time he reached the tarred road an hour and a half later, his hangover was under control. When he drove into Harare three hours later he had his life back: the man had done him a favour; made him look at reality; stopped him feeling sorry for himself. Getting drunk on his own for weeks on end was nothing short of pathetic: a fool's escape; no answer to any of his problems. Watching the traffic carefully, Randall made his first stop at the travel agent.

"The first flight we can get you on to New York is next Tuesday, Mr Crookshank. I can put you on the waiting list. Sometimes there are cancellations. It's our busiest time of the year."

"Can you get me into a hotel?"

"We can try. Or you can put that truck in a campsite. Are you feeling well, Mr Crookshank?"

"Just a hangover."

"Have a nice day."

"I'll do my best. Book me on the first available flight and then we'll see about cancellations."

"You don't want me to try and book you into a hotel?"

"I know the people at Meikles Hotel. Maybe they will be able to help."

Still hungry, after having eaten breakfast on the road at the café in the small village of Makuti, Randall parked his truck outside the hotel and went in to have lunch, passing reception on the way to the restaurant.

"Randall! What a nice surprise. I have a message for you."

"What do you mean?"

"Your father is in town looking for you. He's staying in the hotel."

"What's Dad doing in Zimbabwe? Is he in the hotel? My father lives in England. Do you have a room for me, Jennifer?"

"We always have a room for our old customers. Especially when they've become famous authors. Lovely to see you again. Your father is having his lunch in the dining room."

"I'll be buggered. Sorry. Shouldn't swear in front of a lady. Take my credit card and book me in until Tuesday morning. Life is full of surprises. I live in Manhattan. Dad lives in Chelsea. And here we are meeting by accident in Harare."

"I read they're making a movie of *Love Song*. When is it coming out?"

"Soon. I've been out of touch."

"I love your books."

"Thank you, kind lady."

"Did you enjoy yourself down by the river?"

"Very much. Peace and solitude."

"Are you writing another book?"

"I hope so. I really hope so. Did you tell my father I was driving down to the Zambezi?"

"I did. Trouble was, I didn't know which part of the river to tell your father... Are you feeling well?"

"Just a hangover. Take three days to get over this one."

"Naughty boy."

"Nothing more stupid than getting drunk on one's own. Will my truck be all right outside? It's on a meter."

"Why don't you put it in our garage at the back of the hotel after you've made contact with your father?... There you are. Room twenty-nine."

"Thank you for the keys."

"My pleasure."

Not sure what to expect from his father, Randall first moved the truck before going back into the foyer of the hotel.

"Safe as houses, Jennifer. Is Dad still in the restaurant?"

"I hope so. I'll have your suitcase sent up to your room."

"Nothing better than being organised."

At the front desk in the big restaurant, Randall searched the room, looking for his father. Most of the tables were occupied, people feeding themselves lunch. The old man was sitting with his back to Randall at a small table by the far window, all on his own.

"Do you have a table booked, sir? You need to book a table."

"Sorry, I'm joining my father."

Across the room, Randall braced himself and put a smile on his face.

"Hello, Dad. You didn't have to come all this way. I'm fine, despite Meredith walking out on me."

"How did you find me?"

"Luck. Can I sit down?"

"Of course, son. What's the matter? You look terrible."

"A long binge on my own down the big river. First, I tried writing. How are you, Dad? How's my stepmother? How's Bergit?"

"Worried. We were all worried when you disappeared without telling anyone where you were going. Sit down. Are you hungry?"

"Starving. A game ranger confiscated my fishing rod yesterday by throwing it into the river."

"Please don't go down the same path as your mother. It was alcohol that killed your poor mother. Not the lions. She grew so bored on the farm so far from people and started drinking on her own when I was out in the lands. She had servants to look after you and Phillip. She was bored, dear woman. I hadn't thought what it would be like for her living on a farm so far from her roots in England. The morning she drove into the bush on her own and ran out of petrol, we'd had an argument. It's all my fault. Please don't drink, Randall. It's in your genes, I suppose. Be careful or it will destroy you. Forget Meredith if you can. There are plenty of fish in the sea. Once a woman is unfaithful to a man he can never trust her again. The same applies when a man is unfaithful. You must get on with your life... Thank you, Josiah... Try the rump steak. Zimbabwe has the best beef in the world. Sit down, Randall. You're making me nervous. I'm your father. Fathers look after their sons however old they are. From little boys to grown men who have just turned thirty-eight. What parents are for. Bergit sends her love."

"Can I have a beer?"

"No, you can't... One rare rump steak for my son... Now, Randall, where was I?"

"How long are you staying?"

"The idea was to find you and take you back to England. Bergit's idea as much as mine. Phillip said he thought you were going to kill yourself."

"It did cross my mind. Two wives walked out on me, Dad. Not one. What's wrong with me?"

"Too much fame and money."

"Can't I have one beer? I'm booked into the hotel."

"Of course you can. Just control your drinking. We've all been through terrible times. After I buried your mother in her grave at the top of the Zambezi escarpment where she died, I was suicidal for days. If it wasn't for you two poor boys I would have done something stupid."

"So it is in the genes?"

"Good. You're laughing... Have you got that, Josiah? Steak and a cold Castle... Do you remember the old Meikles Hotel, Randall? No. You were too young. I was first served lunch by Josiah in old Meikles. The old hotel was so splendid. This one is modern. More practical. Probably makes more bang for the investment buck. Oh, well. I'm just getting old. I hate change. Who would ever have thought we'd be having lunch together again in Meikles Hotel? Everything has changed in Zimbabwe, and everything has stayed the same. Now, tell your father what's going on."

"I must stop drinking. That's top of my list. Thanks for coming, Dad. You are the one person I really need just now."

"How long have we got together in Harare?"

"I'm booked out next Tuesday. Flights are full."

"Then we've lots of time. We can talk about old times. Have a real good chat. Life never was easy, Randall. Why we need our families to look after us when we have a problem. Do you know little Carmen is one year old next month? Your brother wants her to have the life your mother never had. Why he called his daughter after his mother. Let's relax and enjoy ourselves. I like a bit of luck every now and again. I tried every trick to find you and then you just walked in. You've done so much in your life, right from the time you worked for your uncle Paul at Brigandshaw House and worked at night to get your degree in economics. We were so proud of you. And then came the publication of all those books. There's so much still ahead of you, son. You've half your life still ahead of you. So much to do. So much to write... There you go. One cold beer. Drink it slowly. Please don't let alcohol destroy you... Thanks, Josiah. Bring me a cup of coffee... What have you done with your hired truck?"

"It's in the garage. I'll give it back tomorrow. As a tip, the guys can have what's left of the food supplies and the whisky. Thanks, Dad. You have no idea how much this means to me."

"So, tell me. What were you writing?"

"A fictional story about Will Shakespeare and his friend."

"How's it going?"

"I think it's going to go better thanks to you and Robert Shumba."

"Who's Robert Shumba?"

"The game ranger who threatened to have me arrested if I didn't leave the game reserve."

"We both owe him a favour."

"They hate us, Dad."

"They have every reason to. We took their land. I was so naïve when I came to Rhodesia soon after the war. I didn't realise we were being used by the powers-that-be to grow their tobacco they could pay for in pounds sterling. Once the British foreign currency crisis was over some years later, the British government didn't care about us anymore. We farmers were expendable. Then came our unilateral declaration of independence and Ian Smith took over the country for us whites to run on our own. Fifteen wonderful years, according to Smith, and then the blacks took over with Robert Mugabe and the rest of the collapse of the old British Empire are just history. You should write about it. Tell the rest of the world our story. Their story. So now they hate us. Maybe one day they'll appreciate some of the things we did for them, like modern education, how to compete in the world economy. Write it down, Randall. Don't let it get lost in the dump of history... How's that beer?"

"Perfect. Now, look at that. One big, perfect steak. Thanks, Josiah... I wrote some of it down in *The Tawny Wilderness* and I did think about writing a series of fictional books based on the Brigandshaw family. Sebastian Brigandshaw started it all. But I don't know enough about the family. Only bits of them."

"I know you wrote some of it. But write the rest of it. Do some research. Go back in history to the beginning of the empire. Keep you amused for years. We all need something to do, Randall, however rich and famous we might have become. Beware of boredom. Always give yourself something to strive for... How's that steak? My, you are hungry. Good to see you, son."

"Do you think Zimbabwe will succeed?"

"Of course it will. Just not for everyone. They want back all that Crown Land we were so nonchalantly given by the King of England and they'll get it. Like myself, most of us will end up back in England, freezing our balls off in that terrible British climate and pining for the sun of Africa: every man has his day. Now it's Mugabe's day. Good luck to him. I'd hate to have the responsibility of running a country. Keeping everyone under control. Must be a nightmare, always watching your back. It's been the same in politics right through history. No one has ever worked out how to run a country for the benefit of everyone. People are inherently corrupt, inherently selfish. Despite what we might say, we are only interested in ourselves and our families. The longer I live, the more uncertain I think life is. You think you have a solution by going to war twice with Germany in twenty-five years, and when you've knocked each other to blazes you form a European Union and become best friends. Forget all those dead bodies at the Somme in 1916 and the bombed-out cities in England and Germany in 1945. We never seem to learn. Now you are on your own, where do you want to live? Phillip says you told him to sell your Manhattan apartment."

"Maybe I should come back with you to England. Change my flight. Spend a little time in London with you and Bergit. And, in the spring, go back to Rabbit Farm and become a hermit. I miss my dog. Poor Polar Bear."

"Where is he?"

"With one of the neighbours."

"You always loved cats and dogs. Can you write on your own?"

"I wrote *Love Song* in a Welsh woodsman's cottage on my own. When I'm writing I'm not alone. I live with the people in my story. I live in my head."

"And drink on your own."

"That is a problem. What else must I do? Look for another girlfriend? They're not interested in me as a person. They just want my money."

"Not all of them. Try. Don't give up. You need companionship."

"How are Myra and Craig? Do you see them often?"

"We talk on the phone. They have their own lives to live with their families. Bergit misses the children the most. Women have a lot more to do with bringing up kids than men. From carrying them for nine months to feeding them milk. A woman's main purpose in life is bringing up her children. And then they fly the nest."

"What's she doing now?"

"Sitting at home waiting for me to come back."

"What do you do with yourselves all day?"

"The daily routine. Breakfast, lunch and supper. Watch TV. Listen to music. But most of all, we keep each other company. You can't spend the rest of your life alone, Randall. You'll go out of your mind."

"I'm out of it now. You mind if I take a nap after lunch? Then we can take a stroll and look at the streets and parks of Harare. Remember how it was as Salisbury."

"Finish your steak. I'll try to book you on my flight to London. I'll phone Phillip and tell him I found you."

"Tell him to hold selling the apartment. First, I want to get my head straight."

"Now you're making sense, son... A nice walk in the park. Sounds good to me. You know, all those years ago when I first arrived in Africa seem like yesterday. Stop me if I start boring you. I was young and excited. I'd done my national service in the Royal Navy. The British economy was still suffering from the Great Depression and the Second World War. Africa, and farming tobacco on a great estate, owning a great estate, was every young man's dream. Without even imagining the future of Africa, I jumped in boots and all. I'd never even met a black man before... You'd better have another beer and then you can go and sleep... Looking back nearly fifty years later I laugh at myself. The empire had already gone. India was given independence while I was in the navy. The rest were in the process of getting their independence. We Rhodesians were the tail-end of the empire. The last remnant. Britain's future was in a European Union. Colonialism, quite correctly, was over. Every empire has its day. England's future lies in the financial services industry. With luck, London will become the financial capital of Europe, if not of the world. The new Switzerland. But no one ever knows what lies ahead. I was lucky to have invested my profits from the farm in a Chelsea block of flats at a time when we could get money out of Rhodesia. Maybe life is just a game of luck. Good luck and bad luck. People say the most difficult thing in a man's life is not making his money, it's holding on to it. I've held on to mine. Property prices in upmarket London have skyrocketed. Buying the flats wasn't my idea as much as Livy's. She saw the future for us whites in Africa and knew it was coming to an end. Why she didn't want to come and live in Africa. Anyway, enough of your father's love life. So much of life is chance. Those accidental but life-changing meetings in the ongoing turmoil of life. Why you mustn't give up, Randall. There will be another woman. A good woman. A woman who wants to love and be loved by another person. Is every woman just hunting for a partner with lots of money? If that's the case, then life is just boring. What's the point of spending vast sums of someone else's money? Does that make a person happy? I don't think so. You're not fat or balding. Find a nice young girl and have some more children."

"And lose them?"

"Third time lucky, Randall. Oh, what the hell? Who am I to tell you what to do? Each day, each week, each year is just the process of life. We go through one day at a time. Some days are better than others. Luckily, when we are old and look back, we only remember the good parts in our lives. You won't even remember Meredith and Amanda."

"And what of James Oliver and Douglas?"

"They'll always be part of your life. You'll always be part of their lives. You're their father. That can never change. Once James Oliver is free of those women to make his own decisions in life, the first thing he will want to do is get to know his father."

"Are you sure?"

"I'm as sure as being here right now to look after my son. Blood, Randall. Blood is thicker than water. Now, off you go and sleep. Give me a ring when you're ready for our walk."

WHEN RANDALL WOKE from his dreams the wolves were still howling at him from the trees in a cold and wet woodland. In the dream he had called to the wolves to come and tear him apart, a strange and prehistoric Randall dressed in the fur of a wolf: no shoes, just himself from an ancient past covered from shoulder to knees in the skin of an animal. Leaning up in the bed, still trying to work out where he was, the real world came back to him. He looked at his watch, which didn't help: he had no idea of the time difference between New York and Harare.

It was still light outside the window. Randall picked up the phone.

"Put me through to Mr Jeremy Crookshank... Hello, Dad. Let's go for our walk. I'll meet you downstairs."

"Did you sleep well?"

"If you call nightmares sleeping well. Give me five minutes."

"Luck was on our side again. We're both booked for London tomorrow morning. They say we can collect our tickets at the airport. Lucky we used the same travel agent. Harare, like Salisbury, is still a small town. You can return the truck first thing tomorrow morning... What did you dream about?"

"Howling wolves. If I don't start writing again I'm going to go out of my brain."

"A walk in the park will do you good. I phoned Bergit and Phillip. They both send you their love."

With the wolves still churning in his mind, his only thought was to kill himself. Did people really care if he lived or died? Platitudes. None of them understood. His life had entered the gates of hell. Putting his clothes on and not sure if there was a heaven or a hell other than in life, he left the room and went downstairs, putting on a false smile for his father.

"How long have we got before dark?"

"An hour. You feeling better after a sleep?"

"Much better, Dad. Much better."

Lies. All lies. The way life worked. His father was talking, but Randall found it impossible to concentrate on what the old man was saying. All he could hear was the howling of the wolves. Wolves that would howl at him all the way to England, all the way back to the land of his ancestors where the wolves had lived with impunity, no one to fear but themselves. Was he going mad? Probably, not that it mattered. If he went totally crazy and lost his mind, lost reality, it would be the same as killing himself. The problems were in his mind. If his mind died, his problems would go away.

"Are you listening to me, Randall? What are you muttering about? You've been on your own too long, that's your problem. Bergit is so looking forward to seeing you. Oh, and Phillip has let your apartment free of rent to someone called Tracey. Do you know Tracey?"

"She's an author. We have the same agent. The same agent as Grandfather Crossley. That's good. The place is being used."

Across the road from the hotel, they walked into the small park with the tall trees and wooden benches, the heat of the day beginning to cool. For an hour they walked and talked, his father doing most of the talking. For Randall, nothing mattered. Absolutely nothing. He would follow his father and see where it led him. No place to be or not to be.

"There must have been more than just Will Shakespeare. Some say it was the Earl of Oxford."

"I have no idea what you are talking about, Randall. Even at school, I never took much notice of literature. Read what I was told to read to get through my exams. Saw one Shakespeare play. There were three witches. End of school play in the speech hall. Oh, I forgot. Phillip says they want you in New York at the end of March for the première of *Love Song.*"

"They must be close to finishing the film. That was quick."

"Are you going?"

"I don't think so. I wrote the book. That was my job. The rest is just for publicity and I hate publicity."

"Right, Randall. A good supper and then it's off to bed for you, son."

"So the wolves can howl."

"You'll feel better when we get to England."

"I hope so. It'll be cold on the Isle of Man at this time of the year. My poor cats. Do you think they miss me? Seven cats and a dog. The good part of animals is they don't answer back... Did Phillip have any news from Meredith?"

"She wants to serve you with divorce papers."

"Lovely. She wants some money. And life goes on."

"Lucky you and Phillip kept Ben Crossley's money in trust. She won't be able to get anything from the trust."

"Now that really is gratifying to know."

"She's asking for half of the rest of your money."

"My word. She and Clint the lover haven't wasted much time... Why is life all about money, Dad?"

"It's what makes the world go round."

"When Amanda ran away, it was to Evelina her lover. Evelina had the money then... We'd better go back to the hotel. It's getting dark. Not too many white people around these days."

"A good meal and a good sleep. That's what you need."

"Thanks, Dad. And thank you, Mr Robert Shumba, of the National Parks Board or whatever they call it these days."

He ignored his father's queer look, and they walked back to Meikles Hotel in the fading light of the day, Randall having no idea what to do with the rest of his life. Did he want to go to Rabbit Farm and pull his dog and cats from their new home and days later want to run away again? Alone, drunk, unable to write, the wolves would howl at him day and night.

"Do you mind if I just go to my room? I'll get them to send up a plate of sandwiches. So, she wants half of my money. No mention of Douglas. I'm flying round in circles like a lost fart in a haunted shit house. My books and all that money and fame have torn me apart. I would have been better off never writing. Working for a salary. Buying my house through a mortgage. The publishers and movie people use celebrities, they don't care about them. To begin with, all that attention went to my head. I loved it. I loved seeing my books sell and everyone writing compliments, not realising that most of it was a load of rubbish to help sell their newspapers as everyone climbed up each other's arses. I can just imagine all those interviews in the build-up to *Love Song*'s première. The public, bless their hearts, love it. Let the trumpets blow. Suppose it's better than howling wolves."

"You're talking nonsense again, Randall."

"Am I? I wonder... See you tomorrow."

"Don't drink tonight."

"I'll try not to. I hate hangovers. Especially when I have to travel. Goodnight, Dad. And thank you. Sorry to give you so much trouble."

"Take a sleeping pill. I'll send some to your room. Get some sleep. You'll feel your old self again... Your poor mother."

"Am I reminding you of my mother's behaviour?"

"It's the same old story. Too much alcohol. Go to bed."

"I will. And I'll try to behave myself. How much did she drink?"

"Too much. If you want to get your life back again, Randall, you should stop drinking alcohol altogether. Join Alcoholics Anonymous. Stay sober. Booze isn't worth it."

With an overwhelming urge to go to the truck and take a bottle of whisky up to his room, Randall tried to control himself. Getting drunk again would be unbelievably rude to his father who had come all the way from England to give him help. At the reception desk, he gave Jennifer the keys to the truck.

"The address and phone number of the rental company are attached to the keys. Give them a ring and tell them to collect the Nissan and the tent, Jennifer. They can have everything that's left in the car."

"Glad to see you found your father."

"So am I. I'm going to get an early night. We leave for England in the morning. My father has gone into the restaurant for his supper. Hopefully, all's well that ends well. Goodnight, Jennifer."

"Goodnight, Randall. Sweet dreams."

"I hope so. Can you ask the kitchen to send up a plate of sandwiches?"

"Of course."

"You're so kind."

"It's my job. I'm so looking forward to reading your next book."

His father was right. If he wanted any kind of a life he would have to stay sober. It was in the genes. Everything was in the genes. The good, the bad and the terrible.

Not sure if he cared whether Jennifer read his book or not, Randall went to his room. The sandwiches came up ten minutes later with his father's sleeping pills. Throughout the evening he tried to go to sleep, the thought of all that whisky in the truck haunting him. The next thing he knew it was morning and the phone was ringing.

"I'm downstairs. Time to go to the airport. I always like to be early. They've collected your truck."

"Have I time for a shower?"

"Be quick. Did you sleep?"

"Amazingly. Thanks for the sleeping pills. I'll be down in fifteen minutes."

"The taxi is waiting outside the hotel."

2

Four hours later the British Airways flight took off for London's Gatwick Airport, Randall sitting in the seat next to the small round window. They had eaten breakfast at the airport. For hours, Randall stared out of the window trying not to think. All he could see was the sky above the wing of the aeroplane. Next to him, his father had fallen asleep, his head resting on Randall's shoulder. The engines droned on as the aircraft flew up Africa, the past left behind for both of them. They ate their lunch and it was Randall's turn to take a nap, his head against the inside of the small window. They had spoken little. Ten hours after leaving Harare airport they landed at Gatwick airport. Two hours later they arrived at his father's block of flats in Chelsea, the luggage stacked in the back of the taxi. The door of his father's flat opened as the key went in the door. His stepmother put her arms around him.

"You're safe. You had me frightened out of my wits."

"Hello, Mother. Good to see you. Sorry to give you both so much trouble. How is England treating you at the moment?"

"Fine, but I will never get used to the weather. Thank you, Jeremy, for phoning me from the airport. I have a big late supper in the oven."

"What day is it?"

"Thursday. Three days after Christmas. I've missed you so much, Randall. I miss all of you. Anyway, we're lucky to have a nice home in

England with central heating. It's a different life from the farm, living in a big city. But we get by, don't we Jeremy? You're safe, Randall. That's all that matters. You want a cup of tea? Of course you do. How did you find him so quickly, Jeremy?"

"He walked into the hotel restaurant when I was having lunch."

"Did you have a good flight?"

"Slept most of the way. Randall's staying with us for a few days before he goes to the Isle of Man to check out his house and his animals. After that, he's not sure."

"All's well that ends well. What we always say in the family."

"You can say that again."

"Has it ended, Dad? Life never ends until you go into the grave."

"Don't be morbid. At least the flat is nice and close to the river. Everything close to hand that we need. There shouldn't be much to complain about living in such an old and historic city. Make yourself at home. The usual bedroom for you. You will always be welcome, my son... Randall's going to join Alcoholics Anonymous. He's sworn to me he's never going to drink again. The subject is now closed. Let's put on some classical music. All my children love good music. We're going to take him to the Albert Hall for a concert. He wants to hear a Mahler symphony, don't you, Randall? We'll do the theatres. We're going to have lots of fun. The three of us together. Come into the lounge. There we are. The journey is over. We're home, safe and sound."

"In the old days, we'd have had a drink together."

"The old days are over... What's for supper, Bergit?"

"A nice beef casserole. A favourite of Randall's. How's Phillip doing in America? I do so miss you children. My life is empty. Your father says the same. When you've got everything you need, life comes down to sitting on a couch and watching television. Why is there so much rubbish on television these days? All those sci-fi and horror movies. You rarely find a good story in a film. Then there's the news. Always news. Most of it bad. Churns up my mind. In Rhodesia, where we didn't have television, I loved to sit on the veranda in the evenings after I'd put you all to bed, and listen to the song of the crickets. Hear the owls call to each other. No noise other than the beautiful sound of nature. Here, it's traffic, traffic, traffic. But we're lucky to have a place of our own and the income from the rentals of the other flats that we share with Livy... How was Zimbabwe, Jeremy?"

"From what I heard they are going to expropriate all the white farms they haven't already taken, without a penny in compensation. Expropriation without compensation. Many of our old friends in the Centenary are going to be destitute. All those years of building a profitable tobacco farm out of the virgin bush coming to nothing. All that investment worthless. When you're over fifty it's difficult to start again. We were lucky getting out when we did, Bergit. The lucky ones with right of residence in Britain will come here with their tails between their legs and hope they'll get a British pension or some kind of a job. Their farming skills will be of little use to them. Anyway, the whole family is now out of Africa. Tell Bergit all about Phillip's business as a venture capitalist, Randall. We want to hear about everything."

"Including my pending divorce?"

"The good bits, Randall. Forget the bad. They are having the première of *Love Song* in New York at the end of March, Bergit."

"It must be wonderful to be rich and famous."

"Actually, Mother, it's terrible. The idea of being famous is far better than the reality. What do you do when you've done it all? More bestsellers and more money don't help. Writing the books helps. But not the publishing. No one wants to leave you alone. They all want a piece of you. Meredith can have half of my money. I don't give a damn. I don't have anything to spend it on. What must I do? Make an art collection? Buy a Gauguin or a Van Gogh? Oh, for goodness sake. How long can you stare at a painting? You need enough money in life to be comfortable. After that, it's all showing off. Telling everyone how rich you are. How clever you are. It makes me sick. Good luck to Meredith. She'll get what she always wanted. And that wasn't me. Anyway, that's enough of my problems. What do you do to keep yourselves amused? Do you have any hobbies?"

"Not really. Just the daily routine of life and the lovely company of your father. I don't know what I'd do without you, Jeremy. Relax, Randall. You've had a nasty knock. Happens to all of us. We always get over our knocks in life. Part of human nature... There we go, Randall. Enjoy your cup of tea. Just how you like it."

"Fill me in on Myra and Craig."

"Where shall I start? We talk for hours on the phone. That part of my life is exciting. I never get bored talking to my children. The worst thing in life must be not having children. Right. Here we go..."

Trying not to think of Meredith or a bottle of whisky, Randall tried to listen to his stepmother's conversation, his father sitting back comfortably in an armchair with a faraway smile on his face. Once, in the middle of Myra's story, they caught each other's eye and smiled, Randall mouthing 'thank you'. When every detail of his half-sister was told, Bergit went to her kitchen and took the casserole out of the oven. Content, they sat up at the dining room table and ate their late-night supper. For Randall, there was nothing more comforting than the company of his own family. The wolves had stopped howling in his head.

The banality of the conversation went on for the rest of the evening. His stepmother looked happy. His father talked about his old friends. Everything in their lives had come back to normal. Three days later, when they dressed up and went to the Royal Albert Hall, Randall's luck came back again. After a Mozart overture that made everyone in the concert hall feel happy, the quiet build-up of Mahler's Second Symphony began, the music washing over Randall's troubled brain. As the power of Gustav Mahler's music built, it drove the howling wolves away, Randall's desperate need for alcohol subsiding. He had been sober for a week but it didn't help. For almost two hours the symphony flooded the hall, suspending everything. Up in the front row of the balcony, Randall was back in paradise. At the end of the performance, the audience rose to their feet, the applause as loud as Mahler's music. It made Randall understand the real worth of being an artist. It was not the fame and money given to the artist. It was the pleasure and joy the artist gave to other people. Mahler had done more for Randall than any therapist. There was no point in joining the crowd of other drunks at Alcoholics Anonymous. When the wolves howled he would play music. Try to go back to writing a book. Do what his father had suggested and start an African saga right from the very beginning.

After the concert, they dined out at Quaglino's. Randall picking up the tab, the one time his money meant anything.

Not wanting to run away too quickly and seem rude, he stayed in Chelsea until the end of January. A long month of having to behave himself. The flight to Douglas airport on the Isle of Man was booked for the morning of the first of February. Bergit cried when she said farewell at the airport, Randall turning at the gate to wave them goodbye. An hour later when the plane landed, John Stokes was waiting for him at Douglas Airport.

"How long are you staying, Randall? We so love your animals. Are you taking them to Rabbit Farm? The weather's lousy. Been snowing for a week. Just hope we can get onto our farm. Had to use the tractor to clear the path up to our farmhouse. How are you? Where's Meredith and Douglas?"

"She walked out on me."

"Oh, my goodness. That's hell."

"Life's hell, John. How's Wynne."

"She's fine. I left her doing the shopping in town. Come on. Tonight you're staying with us."

"How's Polar Bear?"

"You'll see for yourself."

"You've been most kind looking after my animals."

"The pleasure is all ours. Anyway, you pay us to look after them which helps Wynne's budget. Not much income from a small farm in winter. Not much income anytime from a smallholding. But we love the peace and quiet of our home. That lovely view of Snaefell. How was America? Wynne would love to live in America. Of course, we could never afford it. It gets a bit quiet just the two of us. We were never able to have children. Something wrong with my sperm. We'll pick up Wynne and the shopping and go to the pub. The Leg of Mutton and Cauliflower is the only place we socialise. Wynne doesn't drink when we have to drive so she'll drive us home. You remember the Leg of Mutton?"

"Never forget it. Shit, it's cold. How am I going to warm up my house before my balls freeze? Good to see you, John."

"Likewise. I miss my drinking companion. Glad you're back. Pity about Meredith. She and Wynne loved to natter. Wasn't it your second marriage? Sorry. That probably hurt. Wynne and I met at school. Been together for twenty-two years."

"How are the cats?"

"In the evenings when we sit round the fire they love to lie all over us. Four cats on me. Three cats on Wynne. Polar Bear spread out on the carpet in front of the fire. You'll see tonight. Wow, that is a lot of luggage."

"Keeps following me. Nowhere to leave it. To the pub, John... Have you ever broken an oath?"

"You mean a promise? Probably."

"I promised my father I would never drink again."

"You got a problem?"

"Oh, yes. I'm a drunk."

"We're all drunks. Join the club. Come on. She'll be waiting in front of the tellers at the supermarket. Hope we can get it all in the car. Come on, Randall Holiday. Let's get started."

Mentally asking for his father's forgiveness, Randall took his first drink in the warmth and comfort of the Leg of Mutton and Cauliflower, next to the coal fire in front of the bar, the small room full of smiling people. They all knew each other, why the pub was called the local. By the fourth beer, Randall's worries were far away, drowned and forgotten in alcohol. John's wife had found an old friend and was sitting on the bench near the end of the bar having a good old natter.

"Better get back to the farm. Wynne allows me four beers. Lucky to have a sober driver on a day like this."

"Do you have any booze at home?"

"Oh, yes. I always drink a whisky or two in the evening. Here she comes."

"Ready to go? I've been counting."

"Of course, you have, darling. Randall's so looking forward to seeing his animals. I love this pub. The best thing in the world is a local. Everyone you know. Catch up with what's going on. They say it's going to snow for the rest of the week."

"Is Randall going to Rabbit Farm?"

"No, he's staying with us until we make the place habitable. Cheers, good friends. Lovely to be among friends. What would we do without friends? All we've got to do when we get home is put a match to the fire and open a bottle of Scotch whisky."

"Why don't we call at the bottle store and let me buy a couple of cases of whisky? If we're going to be snowed in, might as well be comfortable. How's that for a good idea, John?"

"Perfect, Randall. Absolutely perfect. What's for supper, Wynne?"

"Fish. Fresh cod. Nothing better than fresh fish. I bought enough food to last us a month. And I can't wait for a nice whisky when we get home. When we were young, John drove home from the pubs. The police are much more diligent these days. Better to be careful than sorry. Oh, it's so much fun having a guest."

"Home, James, and don't spare the horses."

"We're on our way. Just the one stop. Then we head out into the country. I was lucky my father gave us the little family farm, or both of us would have ended up with desk jobs. Mother hated the farm. Why they went to live in London."

"Are you going to spend the rest of your lives on a smallholding, Wynne?"

"We'll see. Not all of us are famous authors with all that lovely money. But we get by. Be grateful for what you have, I always tell myself. A home, a small living and each other. And now we have an old friend joining us to drink his lovely whisky."

"How much room have we left in the car?"

"Why?"

"I'll buy as many cases of whisky as we can get in the car."

"We can strap them on the roof rack."

"Now you're talking. If we get snowed in for the rest of February we'll be happy. Lots of wood on the fire. The cats and dog. Wynne's marvellous cooking. And a dozen cases of whisky. I'm going to enjoy myself while we keep each other company. While we are having fun, I'll make up my mind as to what I must do with Rabbit Farm. Clear my mind of being married. Work out a future."

"Could we possibly keep the animals?"

"I don't see why not, and I won't cancel the monthly stop order until the last cat dies. How does that sound?"

"If you don't sell the place, we can always keep an eye on Rabbit Farm."

"And use the land to grow you more crops. Keeping my money invested in land will likely be as profitable as selling and putting the money in the stock market. Land is land. Share certificates are paper. Cash in the bank is just paper. Let's see how it goes. There we are. That's my fourth beer down the hatch. Just hope breaking my oath to my father doesn't bring the sky down on my head."

"Why did you make the oath?"

"Because he wanted me to, Wynne. We always do what people want, to please them. We say things to please them. And then we forget when it suits us. How we are made. All in our genes. Everything is in our genes."

A half-hour later, with the cases of whisky tied down with rope on the roof rack, Wynne driving, Randall sitting in front next to her, they drove out of town into the snow-capped countryside. Twenty minutes after catching the first glimpse of a snow-covered Snaefell, the mountain beautiful in the distance as the light faded and the snow kept falling down, Wynne drove them up the driveway of the Stokes's farm. When she opened the front door, Polar Bear rushed at Randall, putting his front paws on Randall's shoulders. The cats began howling louder than any wolves, a chorus of caterwauling that made Randall smile: at least someone loved him.

Inside, with the front door firmly closed against the winter cold, John put a match to the ready-made fire. It had taken John and Randall ten minutes to bring everything in from the car: his luggage, the cases of whisky, Wynne's shopping with all the food. The dry wood in the grate burned quickly, bringing warmth to the lounge. In the kitchen, where Wynne had started preparing supper, the coal stove had been burning slowly all day. With low timber roofs in all the rooms and thick insulation above in the ceiling, the farmhouse was warm and inviting, a place to cherish, a place of welcome. Wynne came from the kitchen carrying a large bucket of ice which she put on the drinks cabinet behind the sofa. Randall cracked open the first bottle of whisky while John filled three glasses to the top with ice.

"When we want to eat, all I have to do is fry the potatoes and put the cod under the grill. Now, where's my drink? Welcome to our little home, Randall."

"It's all just so damn comfortable."

"That's the whole idea. Your stuff's in the spare bedroom. The beds are made. Let's have a party. I do so love a party. Twelve cases of whisky. I can't believe it. Just look at those cats. They're sitting all over you, Randall. And Polar Bear on his favourite spot on the carpet in front of the log fire can't take his eyes off of you. Now, if this isn't living, I don't know anything... Thank you, John. Cheers to both of you. To happy times. Happy times are here again. I'm sure there was a musical called that. *Happy Times*. And cheers to all my ancestors who have lived in our lovely family house for over two centuries. Home sweet home, Randall. That's what I love. Oh, that fire is so comforting. Nothing more pleasant than sitting in front of a log fire with a nice glass of whisky and a lovely guest. It can snow all winter for all I care. You'd better stay with us. You'd be far too lonely on your own. John, you forgot to draw the curtains... There we go. Now everything is perfect. I swear that cat is trying to get off the back of the sofa onto the top of your head, Randall. The thought of all those centuries of peace for my family makes me smile. Why Mother prefers London is beyond my comprehension. I'm so glad I inherited the farm. Just hope we can make enough money to get by. And if I'd had the brother I so wanted the farm would have gone to him. Sometimes, I can feel my ancestors' presence. Feel them watching over me. So sad I don't have any children. When I die, the farm will go to a distant cousin. Don't even know who's next in line. Probably sell the place and squander the money. What most of us do with an inheritance. And then it's all gone.

All those generations husbanding the property and one fool brings it all to nothing.

"What are you going to do on Rabbit Farm all on your own? You'll go screaming mad. Why did Meredith leave you? No, sorry, that's none of my business. Even if you take the animals, the quiet will get to you even if you play the music I know you love so much. Can a writer really disappear into his book? Live in his book? I know you said so. I wouldn't know how to begin writing a book.

"Thank you, darling. Just a little more ice. Just say when you are hungry. Just look at that dog. He's gone to sleep. There is nothing more beautiful than a white Alsatian asleep on a Persian carpet. There she goes. She's got her front paws on the back of your hair. Animals. Nature. The tawny wilderness. And one hundred and forty-four bottles of whisky. Last us months, if we pace ourselves. Which we probably won't. What's it like in New York, Randall, surrounded by millions of people? Don't frown. You must have had fun. People can be fun. One whisky and I'm talking ten to the dozen. And don't grin, John. A night to remember. Snowed in with a world-famous author. We've read all your books, Randall. What's better than being curled up on the sofa in front of the fire with a good book? Now, tell me everything you've been up to since you left the Isle of Man to go to America. And next month you'll have to go back again if you don't want to miss the première of *Love Song*. When it comes on television, we'll watch it right here in front of the fire. Isn't that cat scratching your scalp? They have long claws and love to stretch and claw. Now I'm going to shut up and let you do the talking. Do you know, we haven't seen a wild rabbit since well before Christmas. When it snows they go deep into their burrows. Often wonder what they eat. Maybe they hibernate. And then in the spring, they're all over the place. Lucky we have rabbit-proof fences around our acres of vegetables, or the bunnies would eat our income. You see. There I go. I'm off again. But, oh, is this whisky good. Now it really is your turn, Randall. Wonder why no one else in history called their farm after the bunny rabbits?"

Smiling, content, enjoying his whisky in front of the fire, his legs stretched out and just touching Polar Bear, Randall wondered what all the fuss had been about. The whisky on top of the four beers in the Leg of Mutton and Cauliflower had taken away his stress. As long as Meredith and Douglas were happy with their lives, none of it would matter. Throughout life, people came and went. Days now passed without him even thinking of Amanda and James Oliver. Their first child had been stillborn, not even a name. For a brief moment, Amanda's terrible pain came over Randall as his mind drifted back through his life. And if Evelina looked after his son and loved Amanda, it was fine by him. Life was all about being happy. And now the whisky was making him happy, despite breaking the oath to his father. With the soft light of the one standard lamp in the corner, the flickering light from the fire, and the happy tone of Wynne's voice, for the first time since Meredith broke up their marriage, Randall was content with his life, the howling wolves far away. When the food was cooked, they sat in their armchairs with small trays on their laps and ate their suppers in front of the fire, the cats and dog in the kitchen eating out of their bowls. For two hours after eating their food, they sat drinking whisky before going to bed, the big fire guard left in front of the grate. Under the sheets, the thick eiderdown and four blankets, Randall drifted off into a peaceful sleep. He was woken in the morning by Wynne with a cup of tea. They smiled at each other. Wynne opened the curtains.

"Look at that. It's still snowing. Everything white outside. Enjoy your tea. No hurry. Bacon and eggs for breakfast. There's lots of hot water for a bath. A gentle day for the three of us to enjoy together. Last night we just drank enough. John says he doesn't have a hangover. The fish and chips in the middle of our drinking did the trick. We're snowed in for all intents and purposes. Have your tea and go back to sleep. How are you feeling? The one rule in this house is we don't open the bar until six o'clock in the evening."

"Thank you, Wynne."

"My pleasure. When it stops snowing you and John can take the dog for a walk. Go and look at Rabbit Farm. We've kept an eye on the place. Nothing has changed. We don't have burglaries on smallholdings. The thieves keep to the cities. All we have here are friendly neighbours. A quiet life full of peace."

"The turmoil in my mind has gone."

"You needed a rest. Meredith leaving you must have been a terrible shock. We all get over our shocks. Or so they tell me. My life has been so tranquil. I can't even comprehend what you must have been going through. Just rest, Randall. Let it all out of your system. And at six o'clock you can have another glass of your nice whisky. You're a writer, so tonight, when we are comfortable around the fire, I want you to tell us a story. Make it up as you go along. It's how my family entertained themselves back before radio and television. Itinerant poets and storytellers visited the farms. Told them lovely stories in exchange for a warm bed and good food."

"What a lovely idea. Tonight, then, I'll be one of those itinerant storytellers of old. I've got all day to dream up a story. 'Once upon a time.' Thank you both so much for looking after me. What would we do without friends? Just look at that snow drifting down outside the window."

As Randall lay back in the warmth of his small bed, America and all the squabbles seemed a million miles away. Another life. A past life, part of which he no longer wished to remember. Up on one elbow, Randall drank his tea before it went cold. Outside it was still snowing. Turning over, his face on the soft pillow, Randall went back to sleep.

When Randall woke again it was time for breakfast in the warm kitchen, the small door at the bottom of the boiler left open, the coals glowing red. After soaking in a hot bath, he went back to bed with a book taken from the small family library, some of the bindings so aged the books had to be over a hundred years old, making the idea of his own books lasting so long on a family's bookshelf somehow comforting. Leaving behind something to give people pleasure was better than leaving a fortune. The book was called *My Memories* by an author unknown to Randall. Snuggled down, he left the snow-covered farm and entered the writer's memories of Victorian England. The story made Randall smile. Nothing had changed. People were just the same. The arguments and the relationships. Only the mode of transport was different. A nice horse and carriage instead of an aeroplane. A book to read rather than watching television. Watching a small string orchestra play music in the family mansion, the same joy from Mozart's music as experienced by Randall in the Royal Albert Hall with his stepmother and his father. After two hours of reading, he put down the book and contemplated what he was going to tell them in the evening, something like a half-hour short story that if it rolled, would keep them amused. And then he heard his father's words, 'start from the beginning', and knew where he was going. They ate their lunch up at the dining room table, all of them joining in the conversation. Outside, it had stopped snowing, Polar Bear with his paws on the windowsill looking longingly out of the window.

Leaving Wynne in front of the fire with her sewing, John and Randall put on their thick overcoats, earmuffs down to the scarves round their necks, and took the dog for a walk.

"Just be careful you don't slip on the ice. Just look at that snow-covered mountain. We can try and walk to your farm if the snow doesn't get too thick on the road. Snow drifts can be a bugger. Wynne is so enjoying herself. She says you're going to be our itinerant storyteller tonight. Do you have a story to tell us?"

"Oh, yes. Would you like to hear about the first ivory hunter who went to the place we would later call Rhodesia, back in the last years of the nineteenth century? I got the idea from my father and the book I borrowed from your bookshelf. To base it on one of the first white elephant hunters, Sebastian Brigandshaw, who went to the unknown Rhodesia. Whether I'll be able to tell a story when I'm pissed on whisky is another story, if you'll forgive the pun. If it doesn't work, I'll keep it short. I've never before tried to tell a story out loud... You're right. Not a rabbit in sight. Don't let's go to Rabbit Farm today. I'm not quite ready to face all the memories of Meredith and the birth of Douglas. There we go. At the mention of them, I've taken a stab in my gut. A sharp, sinking feeling of loss. Let's leave it a couple of days... Look, there's a crow. I love the call of a crow. Any bird, for that matter... What are you doing?"

"Looking for a bit of wood in the snow to throw for Polar Bear. He loves running after pieces of wood and bringing them back to me."

"You are so lucky to have Wynne."

"I know. When you have a good marriage, you realise just how lucky you are... There we go. Go get it, Polar Bear."

"Can we walk a bit faster? I'm getting cold."

"Just don't fall over."

"Soft landing in the snow. Now, look at that. Our crow has found another crow. They're calling to each other."

"What's his name?"

"Who?"

"The ivory hunter."

"Templeton-Smythe, Lawrence Templeton-Smythe."

"Lawrence of Arabia."

"Something like that... Strange how today, being a hunter killing elephants for their ivory tusks would be abhorrent in a world of nature conservationists. In those days of Templeton-Smythe, there were more elephants in the wild than people. When the elephants went on their great walks over the open veld, there was mile upon mile of moving elephant. A few shot to make ornaments out of their tusks for the rich back in England was not a problem for anyone. Times change.

Sometimes for the better. Man lived as hunters and gatherers. It was all about survival of the fittest. Did you know, keeping slaves was only made illegal across the Empire in 1833? And that ten per cent of the rich in Britain had something to do with the slave trade? Now it's all about democracy and getting votes to give them power, corruption underneath not much different to the good old days of kings and queens. Power corrupts, so they tell us. Using that power for personal gain while talking a load of do-gooder bullshit that all us fools so love to hear. Is the world a better place with all its democracy and modern technology? There are still wars everywhere. People live behind bars to give themselves security among the thronging masses in our great cities. Or are they great cities or just places to live in surrounded by crime, spending hours every week just getting to our places of work, and living in small rooms between concrete walls with windows through which there is no pleasure in the looking? A life of stress. No, give me the life of the hunter, who actually sees and respects what he is killing. Not the so-called righteous who spout their mouths off about elephant and rhino while they eat their chicken.

"Oh, now look at that. Through the snow-covered trees, I can just see my farm. It looks so cold. So unwelcoming. I feel fear, not a welcome home. And Polar Bear has seen the house. He's off. There he goes. A lovely white dog running through a world covered in snow. Polar Bear! Come back! Let's turn round. I can't face that home I once so happily lived in with Meredith and my newborn son, thinking like a fool that my life would never change. Thinking I had found the perfect woman in a perfect world and that happiness lasted forever. Come back, my dog! Here he comes. Try another piece of your wood. Here we are, lost in the snow in a world of perfect silence.

"I'd love to have been Templeton-Smythe, all alone in the African bush with his servant, both of them equally happy when they sat round the campfire at night roasting a guinea fowl under the hot ashes, feathers and all."

"Didn't they pluck the feathers from the bird?"

"Pulled it all off, skin and all in one fell swoop when the bird was cooked inside and ate the meat, pulling it off the bone with their fingers in the light of the fire, a full moon up in the heavens, the crickets screeching, the eagle owls and nightjars calling in a perfect world totally free of people. Oh, yes. Give me those days and a life worth the living without all the scheming and arguments, the conniving, all that manipulation to make more and more money that is now the only mark of a man's success. We live in a horrible world in the cities, John. Pity I can't come back to Rabbit Farm and live my life through as a hermit. But I can't. I've been brainwashed like everyone else at the end of the twentieth century by city life. Do you know half of the planet now lives in cities? I can't think of living the rest of my life alone. What was life all about, John Stokes? For us, or our ancestors? What was the purpose? What was the reason? Or has it only ever been a case of procreation and creating another generation so they can go through life and suffer the same ups and downs as ourselves? All fools hoping somehow we are going to one day be happy, instead of just thinking we are happy when we drink our whisky."

"It's not all bad."

"Maybe not. Let's hope so. The sight of my old home has made me maudlin... Go for it, Polar Bear. Get the stick."

"He's happy."

"I always thought I'd like to be a dog or a cat... How long is it until six o'clock?"

"Eight hours, twenty-seven minutes and thirty seconds, Randall."

"That long?"

"Drink can be a terrible problem when it becomes addictive. Be careful. In the end, it does more harm than good."

"He wants you to take the stick out of his mouth."

"I know he does... How do you respect an elephant when you are about to kill him?"

"The same way he respects you when he's about to put his big front foot on your head. Maybe one just feels sorry for the other. I'll try and think of a reason when I tell you my story around the fire tonight. Maybe Templeton-Smythe would not have felt respect for the elephant. Just felt sorry for him. The elephant had something he wanted, so he took it. And when another elephant kills Templeton-Smythe the human world and the elephant world will become even. Just the nature of the beast. We're all beasts. Did you know the DNA of a gorilla is ninety-eight per cent identical to ourselves? I've been talking too much. Tell me a joke or sing me a song. Now I'm waxing lyrical."

"Are you going to write when you're with us?"

"No. My mind is too full of my own problems. I won't be able to get into the minds of my characters. I need total peace to write. Solitude."

"Then go and live on Rabbit Farm. When you need company, you can come over for a glass of whisky."

"Maybe. I need to calm down. Make peace with my mind."

"We'll miss the cats and the dog. Wynne and I will help you sort out your house. Clean the place. Bring in the wood. Make it warm and comfortable."

"The memory of Meredith and Douglas would haunt me. I'd wake up screaming in the middle of the night, the wolves howling in my head. I'd want to find a gun and shoot myself."

"Please don't shoot yourself. It's so messy... It's beginning to snow again. We'd better get back. Why don't you go back to America and look for another wife?"

"What my father told me to do. Third time lucky. When you have two failed marriages, you wonder if the problem isn't yourself."

With his mind in neutral, Randall followed his friend back to the farm. They both walked in silence among the gently falling snow and went quietly into the house. John relaid the fire in the lounge while Randall sat reading his book. The sight of his old home had made him feel miserable. Even the cats were no help... The day crawled by until six o'clock when the bar was finally opened.

"Tell us your story, Randall."

And like so many other days in Randall's life, the story started and the tale began to unfold. In his mind, he was in the African bush in the year of Our Lord 1886. He was Lawrence Templeton-Smythe. And when Tonga the servant spoke, he was Tonga, Randall deep in the black man's mind. It took Randall an hour to tell the first episode of his African saga that would travel for a hundred years, book after book, story after story as Randall took his characters through the twentieth century. When he finished, both Wynne and John were happily smiling, a cat asleep on each of their laps, Polar Bear watching Randall from the comfort of the carpet, the only sound in the room, the sound of his own voice.

"You must write it down, Randall."

"I rather think I should. Thank you, Wynne and John. Bless you. I think you've got me started. Given me my escape. Do you know something? While I was talking, I didn't even have a sip of my whisky. And now all the ice has melted in the glass. What I'm going to do tomorrow morning is write down this first episode and tomorrow morning tell you the second episode round the fire, and so on. You might just have saved my life."

"Africa must be so beautiful. You describe it so well. It all comes alive for me. Lawrence and Tonga. The perfect itinerant storyteller, Randall. You've certainly earned your supper."

"Thank you, kind lady. And thank you for filling my glass with ice. Now I can get started on the whisky."

"There's a nice desk in your bedroom."

"I know there is."

"Do you have any paper?"

"I always carry lots of sheets of clean white paper."

"When's he going to shoot his first elephant?"

"I don't know. Maybe he won't shoot anything, other than food for himself and Tonga. It's winter. There's no rain in winter in that part of the world. The rivers still flow from the highlands far down through central Africa and on to Mozambique and the sea. They'll just enjoy the bush. On the other hand, necessity, necessity of the ivory to give himself money to live on when he has to return to England, will make him kill the elephants. He'll have to find and employ many servants to carry the ivory tusks on their shoulders so Templeton-Smythe can trek full loads of wagons down to a South African port. Ten wagonloads will make him rich and he'll have enough money to buy himself a mansion back in England. Maybe Tonga will follow him and continue to be his servant in England. Twenty wagons full of ivory and he'll have enough money to buy himself a knighthood. Sir Lawrence Templeton-Smythe, Lord of the Manor. Marry a rich man's daughter and have nine children and live happily for the rest of his life. We'll just have to see how the story goes. Will his greed overcome his love for wild animals? Will his respect for the African elephant be overpowered by greed and the need to provide for the Templeton-Smythe future and all those nine children, to say nothing of the grandchildren and the rest of his descendants? Will he march through the bush killing elephant like Henry the Fifth at the Battle of Agincourt, who killed people securing the future of good old England at the expense of all those dead French soldiers? We'll just have to see. Maybe he'll meet other white hunters and a bigger story will unfold. Do you know, this whisky is just delicious. Cheers, everyone. To life as an itinerant storyteller. What's for supper, Wynne? What's in your lovely oven? Telling stories makes me hungry."

"A bone-marrow soup, rich in our onions and potatoes with lots of garlic, and a plum pie made from our own bottled Victorian plums. We'll eat round the fire when we're ready... I wonder if my ancestors heard your story and smiled down on us from up in heaven, the good memories of their days on earth brought back to them? Life on Hasslet Farm down two long centuries. There was no turmoil on the farm in those days. Why I feel so comfortable with my own life. Just a pity we never had any children but you can't have everything in life. Maybe peace and being comfortable with ourselves is bred into us. Part of who we are, the sum of our ancestors... Are you going to put some more wood on the fire, John? I'm going to the kitchen to check the food. Pour yourselves another whisky. Such a pleasant day. I do so love a little company."

"Do your parents visit you?"

"At Christmas, Randall. Always a lovely family Christmas. This year they stayed for two weeks. They loved the cats and Polar Bear as much as we do. Food, glorious food. We all love good food, don't we, Polar Bear? Come, my dog. Come, cats. It's time for your suppers."

"What do you think he will do, Wynne?"

"Who?"

"Lawrence Templeton-Smythe."

"Oh, he'll fill the wagons with ivory."

"Are you sure?"

"No doubt of it. He'll want that wealth with the elephants. Aren't I right, Polar Bear? Greed always wins. Passed down to us through our ancestors, however much we like to deny it."

"As I've said to myself many times. It's all in our genes."

"You've got it, Randall. It's all in the genes."

The big pot of soup was put in front of the fire next to the soup bowls and the soup spoons. They carried on drinking, the pot staying warm from the heat of the fire. They were all happily tipsy, the cats and dog still in the kitchen eating their supper. Randall looked around the old room at the silent paintings on the walls and two decorated blue plates of Copenhagen china given to John by his Danish godfather. In the flickering firelight and the one covered standard lamp, the paintings and their stories were barely discernible. The paintings were old, by unknown artists, their signatures in the bottom right corners that Randall had studied earlier unintelligible. But they had done what they loved and Randall felt happy for them. Whoever they were it did not matter, their paintings, their art, had survived long after the painter had died. Wynne most likely knew the painter's name.

When Wynne served up the soup, Randall sat with the bowl on a tray nicely balanced on his lap. The first sip of hot soup was delicious.

"There's something in your soup, Wynne, that gives it a perfect flavour. Ah. I know what it is. Mint."

"Dried mint from last summer. The fresh vegetables came from our heated greenhouse. You've seen the greenhouse with the boiler at the back and the big hot water pipes that lead round the greenhouse keeping out the worst of the winter cold. The farm makes us largely self-sufficient. We feed the cows on last year's turnips and swedes. John does the milking in the cowsheds. The chickens lay us eggs right through the year. A lot of other stuff, like the marrow bones that I made this soup from, are stored in the freezer in the shed. It's nice not having to rely on other people. I bake in the oven including our lovely bread. Butter and cheese from the milk of the cows. Oh yes, we Hasslets have been organised for generations... Going back to your story of Lawrence Templeton-Smythe. How does a man buy himself a knighthood? Would he have to bribe Queen Victoria?"

"Not the Queen, Wynne. Her advisors. The politicians. The people who decide who is going to be decorated."

"Does it happen today?"

"Probably. Politicians only make their money as politicians. When they have power, they use it to accumulate money for a rainy day."

"All of them?"

"Probably not. Some politicians, especially the Conservatives, are born rich and go into politics to give themselves something to do. Some people like to make themselves famous. The Queen isn't corrupt. She's far too much of a lady. She's also, from her inheritance, one of the richest women in Britain. Not everyone is a crook, thank goodness, or the world would have fallen apart long ago... I so love this soup... Here they come. They've finished their suppers. Yes, my pussycat. You can sit on my lap when I've finished my supper. Look at that. Plonked in front of the fire. A happy, well-fed dog."

"He loved the soup bones."

"I'll bet he did."

After three bowls of soup and two slices of Wynne's plum pie, Randall could not eat another thing. Fortunately, the food that had filled his stomach had taken away his thirst for alcohol. In the morning, he would be able to write.

"Are you going to play the piano for us tonight, Wynne?"

"What would you like to hear? A Chopin nocturne?"

"I could think of nothing better."

They watched Wynne walk over to the upright piano in its place under one of the paintings, where she sat on the stool, gently lifted the lid to expose the ivory keys of the keyboard and began to play. For Randall, an evening could not be better. A perfect cook and a piano player. He leaned across to whisper in John's ear, not wanting to disturb the flow of the music.

"You don't know how lucky you are."

"Oh yes, I do. She's everything I ever wanted, Randall. Next time you are going to be just as lucky."

"How do I find her?"

"By looking carefully. Very careful. Now she's playing Bach. Johann Sebastian Bach. Her aunt taught her to play the piano. The aunt never married, poor girl. Wynne was like her own child. All she had, really. She died when she was forty. She loved Wynne like her own. A short, sad life but full of music."

"Nothing wrong with that."

"When is life fulfilled?"

"When you teach your niece to play like that."

When Wynne got up from the piano they both gave her a hug. It was time for bed. Time for a good sleep. A time for Randall to be thankful for his friends. The wolves had gone. A new book was growing in his head. He was going to forget his troubles and concentrate on living in a place without squabbles and constant competition, a place where trying to be better than others no longer mattered. They were marooned on an island covered in snow with good food, good company and a whole lot of whisky, which, thankfully, they were drinking in moderation.

In his small bedroom, Randall touched the surface of the small desk, took a pack of white paper from one of his suitcases, put his ballpoint pen down on the desk next to a small pile of the paper and smiled. Tomorrow, he was going to write.

With the light out, tucked up in bed where Wynne, bless her, had put a hot-water bottle, everything was perfectly silent. All Randall was conscious of was the African bush, Lawrence and Tonga, the call of the African owls, and the soft sound of wind in the msasa trees as he drifted off into his dreams. When he woke in the morning, he found himself happy for the first time since Meredith had left him, the first light of day just showing through the curtains. On the mantelpiece above the fireplace, Wynne had placed a box of matches, the wood-fire made up in the grate. Out of bed in his underpants, Randall went to the fireplace, took a match from the full box and lit the fire before opening the curtains and getting back into the warm bed. When Wynne brought him a cup of tea he was up at his desk writing down the story, concentrating on the correctness of each word, each comma, each paragraph, the experience of writing totally fulfilling. By the time he went for his breakfast two hours later he had filled five sheets of paper with words. Outside the window a winter sun was shining, the world so beautiful it made Randall want to cry with pleasure.

As the day unfolded, with Randall helping Wynne with the housework, going to the shed with John and being taught how to milk a cow, the evening's episode came alive in his mind. Back in the kitchen, he watched Wynne make the butter, all three of them smiling. Hasslet Farm was truly peace on earth, a place Randall knew he would cherish in his memory for the rest of his life. Once again, they walked the dog to within sight of Rabbit Farm, Randall still not wishing to break his peace of mind by going into the house.

That night, after two hours of slow whisky-drinking, they fed from a roast leg of pork, each mouthful flavoured with a small dollop of Wynne's homemade apple sauce. Episode two had flowed as easily as episode one, before they had risen from their comfortable seats round the fire to sit up at the dining room table. Once again, the drinking stopped with the food and Wynne played her piano. In episode two, Lawrence Templeton-Smythe had yet to kill an elephant.

"It's an old piano, Randall. If your man brought this ivory to England, who knows, I may have some of it right here in this room. Or is that taking fiction too far?"

"Fact and fiction are often much the same. Please go on playing. If the ivory keys you are pressing so gently are part of my story it joins the two experiences together into one story, the story of old England with all its strange and wonderful history. Music played with the help of the tusks from an elephant. What a strange world we live in. What strange people we are. I wonder if any of those helpful conservationists complained about the ivory keys on the piano while they were at a concert listening to Beethoven's Fifth Piano Concerto, the music as overwhelming today as it was when Beethoven first wrote it. You see, in life, it all depends on what people want. The righteousness of nature conservation or the music of Ludwig van Beethoven? Or is their righteousness just politics to get themselves noticed? I should not criticise what I do not know... Is the concert over, Wynne? Is it time for our beds? And thank you so much for my hot-water bottle. No one has ever done that for me before in my life. Even the winters in Rhodesia could be cold. But there we are. Another lovely day spent on Hasslet Farm. When you want back your privacy you must both of you tell me. This is your beautiful home not mine. Please don't let me outstay my welcome. I suppose I will have to return to America for the première of *Love Song*, as much as I would prefer to stay here in your lovely home. But I can't be selfish. Other people depend on me. My literary agent, Manfred Leon. The people who work at my publishers and have done so much to promote my name and market my books successfully. They will need me at the première in person to use me to talk to the media and promote the film. They have all done so much for me in the past. Just because I don't need any more money doesn't mean I can be selfish and hurt their careers. At this moment in life, I would like to stay buried in the snow forever with my two friends, my cats, and my dog."

"Treat this as a holiday. You are always welcome."

"That's a good one, a new twist on my writer's pseudonym. A holiday for Holiday... I wish I could play the piano. I wish someone had taught me... Do you know the name of the painter and who he or she was? I can't read the signature. I think the signature is the same on all the paintings. Buried in the bottom corners. Has a vague resemblance to Hasslet but could that be possible?"

"The first Hasslet to own this little farm was Henry Hasslet. My great-great-great grandfather. He was an artist, quite well known in his time. He wanted a place to paint, much as you wanted Rabbit Farm to write. A place where his family could be largely self-sufficient, so it didn't matter if the art galleries only paid him a pittance for his paintings. This was his sanctuary, to do what he wanted in life. The story comes down to us that his wife Mary Jane educated the children, teaching them to read and write so they would not have to go to school too early in life. Like your Templeton-Smythe who is going to have nine children, there were many children in the family. No one is sure quite how many. These paintings on our wall are worth more than the whole farm put together. Ironic, don't you think?"

"He was doing what he wanted."

"Of course he was."

"Where did he get the money for the farm in the first place?"

"From his mother's family. An inheritance."

"You know what they say, Wynne. The most important thing in life is to choose your parents carefully. His wife must have chosen her parents carefully. And stop smiling. Do they choose us any more than we choose them?... I'm so looking forward to my sleep. With no worries, thanks to you both, I'm again sleeping through the night peacefully. Tomorrow the tale will continue, I hope. Sometimes the story doesn't work. When it doesn't, I leave it to the next day. Until my characters start talking to me again."

"Do you dream about your story?"

"In bits. Mostly unconnected. My dreams come in short flashes, forgotten a few moments after I wake. Mostly, the story stays deep in my subconscious. Like the story I'm wanting to write of Shakespeare's friend, it's there waiting, I hope. Templeton-Smythe has smothered Shakespeare's friend for the moment. There are always bits of books in my head. I live in a world of daydreams where strangers float in and out. When I'm lucky, I capture them and write down their stories. Maybe the itinerant storyteller will come to an end. We will just have to see. Middle of next month, six weeks at the latest, I must do my duty and fly back to America. Do you think you can put up with me that long? Thank you. You're both smiling. Are you ever going to sell those paintings?"

"Never. They are our family. Our heritage. More important than money. You can't sell your family."

"They did in the days of slavery. Sold off the kids for a couple of bucks. It's a lovely world. Sweet dreams, both of you. Thank you for another lovely day."

"The sentimental value of my ancestor's paintings is their true worth to both of us. Am I not right, John?"

"All you need in life is enough. Why ever would I ask you to sell them? But you never know. Like your crooked politicians, Randall, it's nice to have something for a rainy day."

3

Ten days after finishing the first chapter of the Templeton-Smythe saga, forty pages of written words stapled together in a neat pile on the side of his desk, Randall conquered his fear and walked through the melting snow to Rabbit Farm. He had told John he was just going out for a stroll. The sun was shining from a clear blue sky. With trepidation, Randall approached his home, put the key in the lock and pushed open the door. Polar Bear barked as he ran inside. Everything looked the same as when they had left the place to go to the city of New York seventeen months earlier, apart from the cobwebs hanging from the ceiling, and the dust on the pieces of furniture that were not covered by dust sheets. The first stab in the gut came when he looked into his son's bedroom and saw the cot with its slide-down front. The tears came when he remembered first picking up his son and holding the gurgling baby up to the ceiling. In their own bedroom he could still smell traces of Meredith's perfume, many of her things still sitting on the dressing table. Quietly, walking from room to room, Randall made up his mind: there were too many memories leaving no way he could move back into the house and live there on his own. Once again, the wolves had begun howling in his head. The place was cold, even desolate. Not only was Randall's body cold, his heart was cold, his mind turning bitter as he thought back.

"What did I do wrong? I fed her. Looked after her. Made love every night. What does Clint have that I haven't? Youth, maybe, but in a marriage is that so important, Polar Bear? I don't understand people, my dog. Let alone women... This place is giving me the creeps. Let's go. In two hours, it's whisky and storytelling time. You'll stay happy with Wynne and John. Come on. Stop running around. I want to go. Out the front door, my boy... There you go."

Without looking round, Randall slammed the front door and walked away from his home, a sense of relief coming over him. Instead of going back to Hasslet Farm, Randall picked up his pace and walked on through the country lane, the snow falling from the hedgerows as it melted. He was not going to tell a story tonight or write on the morrow, too much memory of his family temporarily wiping the actions of Templeton-Smythe from his mind.

When he reached John and Wynne's home in the dusk it was just before six o'clock, the bar about to open. John and Wynne were sitting comfortably round the fire in the lounge, cats all over them.

"That was a long walk. Where did you go? We're about to open the bar."

"No story tonight, I'm afraid. I'm never going back to Rabbit Farm. The sight of Douglas's cot made me weep. I just can't see what I did wrong. In that house we were as happy as pigs in shit, if you'll forgive the expression, Wynne. Tonight I want to get myself drunk. Just don't let me knock over the furniture."

"Ah, now there's something. Tonight is to be binge night. Wynne has the supper under control. We can eat when we like... Now listen to that. The clock on the mantelpiece is striking the hour. It's six o'clock. The bar is open. Let's get started... Why are you giggling, Wynne?"

"You men. You make me laugh. All you need is the slightest excuse for a binge."

"Are you joining us?"

"Of course I am. I'll get the ice. As you so rightly put it, my husband: let's get started."

All three of them were equally aware that drinking to excess never solved anyone's problems. But it was fun as they brought the world down to the cosy room, the fire burning, jazz music playing, no thought of running out of whisky. Instead of his story and eating their supper, they carried on drinking. When John went to the toilet an hour before midnight he tripped over the carpet, giving all of them a fit of the giggles. On his hands and knees John crawled to the door of the toilet, putting up his right hand to the knob and opening the door. When he got up to unzip his trousers he fell over sideways into the empty bathtub. Wynne and Randall went into the toilet and helped him out of the bath.

"Out you go, Wynne. Got to pee. Can you put your hand in my back, Randall, and hold me steady? I'm inclined to fall over backwards... Oh goodness. Does that feel better. We should have eaten our supper."

Randall kept his hands in John's back for what seemed like five minutes. When the urination was over, pulling up the zip became a problem.

"Can you help, Randall?"

"You're slurring your words, John Stokes. Of course I can't help you."

"Oh, that feels such a relief. Now I need another whisky. What an evening. Haven't laughed so much in years."

"Get out of the toilet, darling. It's my turn. And both of you stop laughing. While I'm in the loo, get some more ice out of the fridge. We can eat supper tomorrow. Are we not going to have hangovers. It's all your fault, Randall... Come on. I'm desperate."

"My poor wife. You'll have to get the ice, Randall. I can still barely stand up... There we go. Back on the sofa. Where's my whisky?"

"Coming, my lord."

"What were we talking about before I tripped over the carpet?"

"I have absolutely no idea. Lost track of sense hours ago. Is this a one-day binge?"

"Better be... How are you, Wynne? Are you sitting?"

"Of course I am. I'm on the toilet."

When Wynne and John staggered to bed, each holding on to the other and giggling, Randall had no idea what time it was. The second bottle of whisky was almost empty on the coffee table in front of Randall's knees. With effort, he leaned forward and poured the last of the whisky into his glass. For a while, he looked at the ice bucket next to the empty whisky bottle and gave up. He was too drunk to lean forward again. Thankful he could not think straight or feel sorry for himself, he let the alcohol take over his body and mind. Wynne and John's bedroom was quiet, except for John's irregular drunken snoring. The whole world had been removed by a bottle of whisky. The fire had gone down, the one lamp still on too far for Randall to reach. Wynne had turned off the music earlier when they thought they were going to bed. As Randall gently sipped the last of the whisky he smiled at his soft feeling of content.

When he woke in the middle of the night he was cold: the fire was out; John had stopped snoring; the empty glass of whisky sat on the end of the arm of the sofa; two cats were sitting on his lap, both of them purring when he touched the back of their furry necks; Polar Bear lying on his side in front of the cold fire fast asleep. Quietly, Randall put the cats on the floor and pushed himself up from the sofa and crossed the room to his bedroom without knocking anything over. He had left the lamp on behind him instead of creating a drunken havoc. In bed, he pushed away the cold hot-water bottle and tried to go to sleep. He had left the overhead light on for fear of not being able to find his bed in the dark. As much as he tried turning over and over he was unable to sleep, the bad memories surging back through his mind and making his body shiver with cold. When the wolves began howling his whole body was shaking, his mind in panic. Nothing was working in his life, not even the alcohol. When he slept the wolves still howled in his nightmare, a black world of pain and screams.

When Randall woke in the morning, his hangover was excruciating.

"It's not worth it... What are you looking at, my dog? And what are you doing in my bedroom? Are all the cats on my bed? Oh, I see. I left the light on and the door open. Good morning, my pussycats. At least you animals look content... Oh, shit. Do I hate hangovers. It's just not worth it... Anyone else awake?"

Not a sound. The cats ignored him. The dog had closed his eyes. Randall went back to sleep. When he woke, it was half past one in the afternoon by the small clock on the mantelpiece. The cats and dog had gone. He could hear Wynne moving around in her kitchen. To Randall's surprise, he was fully dressed, only his shoes lying beside the bed. He was hungry. Ravenously hungry. Another day had begun.

In the middle of March, with four chapters of the Templeton-Smythe saga completed, Randall made up his mind: it was time to go back to the real world; time to face reality; the game of being an itinerant storyteller in exchange for his bed and his supper was over; the whisky was finally finished, twelve boxes full of empty bottles in the shed. The sinking feeling at the thought of facing the media and all those hungry people wanting a piece of him had to be overcome. The idea of going into Douglas and filling the car with cases of whisky was not an option. It was time for him to face up to his life. The running away was over. She wanted a divorce so he would give her a divorce and see what the rest of his life would bring to him, hopefully not all of it bad. Quietly, without the others seeing him, Randall packed his bags. He would fly from the Isle of Man to London where he would catch a plane to New York.

"Can you drive me to the airport, John? The whisky is finished. Time for me to leave you two in peace."

"Do you want me to phone the airport and book you on the three-thirty flight? We'll miss you."

"Thank you, old friend. Just look after my animals. Here are all the keys to Rabbit Farm. Use the land. Rent out the house. Whatever you get is yours."

"What about the rest of the story?"

"You can read it, Wynne, when they publish the book. It's been a giggle. I can't thank you both enough for your companionship during the worst time of my life. I'll be back in Manhattan well in time for the première of *Love Song*. Manfred Leon will have plenty of time to arrange my interviews with the press."

"Are you going to see Meredith?"

"I want to see my son, John. I have to face reality. Running away has given me the time to think and get over some of my jealousy. She can shove my money up hers and Clint's bottoms, for all I care."

"And if you can't get on a flight to New York?"

"I'll stay in a hotel. Go to a symphony concert on my own. I don't want to disturb my father any more than I have already done. I have a home in Manhattan with two nice girls living in it who will look after me. There are three bedrooms. I'm going to soundproof my bedroom so I can think in the mornings and continue writing my historical saga of Africa. Give me a hug, both of you. There's a time to come and a time to go. It's now time for me to go."

PART 5

MARCH 1996 – THE THREE MUSKETEERS

1

While Randall was being driven to Douglas airport by John, Tracey Chapelle was sitting at her desk in Randall's Manhattan apartment getting nowhere with her new book. With all the money flowing into her bank account, there was little or no incentive to write another book about the sexual habits of young girls. All the attention and chatter had blocked her creative mind. She could not see her characters in her mind's eye, let alone hear them talk. There was nothing to tell. After half an hour of trying to write the first sentence, all she had was a blank page in her typewriter.

"Dammit. All that money and nothing to do. I've screwed Manfred to get a publisher. Screwed Godfrey to thank him for publishing *Lust*. And even that didn't turn out to be much fun. And here I am. It was all about the quest for money and now that need has gone. Men? They're all much the same once you've screwed them. The sales are over seven million copies, Jane's script of *Lust* has been accepted for another pile of money and I've got damn all to do with the rest of my life."

Not sure if she'd been talking out loud or just talking in her head, Tracey got up and went to look out over Manhattan through the big plate-glass window which covered the front of the living room. Outside it was raining, the water dripping down the outside of the window. She could hear the traffic, the general hubbub, and none of it gave her any pleasure. For what seemed to Tracey like an eternity, she kept staring out of the thirty-first-floor window, her mind a blank. Even the idea of taking a drink was not appealing: for Tracey, there was little worse than drinking alone. When the phone rang it made her jump.

"Hello. Who's calling? You've got the wrong number."

"It's me, Tracey. He's coming home. I'm to pick Randall up at the airport at four o'clock this afternoon."

"Is he going to stay with us?"

"Manfred didn't say."

"Is he all right?"

"We don't know. At least he'll be able to promote the film... How's the book coming?"

"A total blank."

"Been there. Never mind. It'll come. What are you doing?"

"Staring out of the goddamn window. All that new money and I'm bored out of my mind. See you later, alligator."

"In a while, crocodile."

"Why do we always talk so much crap, Jane?"

"Because it's fun. Get some food ready for dinner for three. Check the wine. Tonight, we're having a party."

"Do I order in or cook myself?"

"Do what you like. Are we going to have to move again, Tracey?"

"We'll just have to see. Maybe three writers in the same apartment will be fun. Randall will be able to stop my writer's block. Why am I trying to write a sequel?"

"Because your agent and publisher asked you to. People and life are just one big community. You have to do what you are told to fit in. Please everyone, that's the way to go. Money, Tracey Chapelle. It's all about the money. What Randall always said. A good well-paid job, a nice big cheque for writing the film script to your book and Jane Slater is smiling. Better than working in a laundry with people's smelly clothing. Ugh. The thought makes me want to throw up. And writing *Love in the Spring of Life* and bringing back to me all those wonderful feelings for Harvey makes me so joyful. I can see us both as we were then. The whole world just the two of us looking deep into each other's eyes and seeing happiness and nothing else. My book is about love, Tracey. Yours was about lust, sex and manipulation to get what a girl wants. Or what she thinks she wants until she gets it."

"Don't lecture me, Jane."

"Go back to your window, Tracey."

"And then what?"

"Think of someone you'd like for a boyfriend, and when you've found the person put it in a book. Now here's an idea. How about Randall? He'll soon be single and he's stinking rich."

"A bit odd for my taste but a perfect target for one of my sinful, grabbing, self-centred characters with big tits and a nice firm bottom."

"Off you go. To your desk. Go write a book. Put the white wine in the fridge and make sure the ice trays are full."

"Why do you sound so happy?"

"Because I am, Tracey. What's wrong with feeling happy?"

"Nothing."

"Aren't you happy, girl?"

"I'm just bored. But it's better than being a secretary in an insurance company. Now that was boring. My boss was Ferdinand. Boring, boring, boring."

"Go and write your book and stop moaning. Manfred's calling me. Got to go."

Wondering what she would do without Jane's companionship, Tracey went back to her desk. For a long while, she stared at the silent typewriter before pulling it towards herself across the small desk. Without realising what was happening she began to type, the picture of twenty-seven-year-old Lulu clear in her head, the dialogue flowing, the story racing ahead. By the time she got up from her chair to prepare the food and lay the supper table, there were six typed pages sitting on her desk.

"Hurray, I'm away. My boredom has vanished. Here we go again. Life can be fun. A nice piece of fish. That's what we are going to have for our supper. A lightly grilled piece of fish. Off to the fish shop, my girl."

The thought of seeing Randall made Tracey smile. Maybe an older man in her life would give a relationship more substance. There was always something new to try in life. Both of them had picked wrong lovers in their pasts.

With a big hat on her head covered in a layer of plastic and hooked down against the rain, a warm overcoat over her trim body, and an umbrella, Tracey caught a cab outside the front of the building and went shopping. Lulu was still talking in her head, tomorrow's story nicely building. The whole world was Tracey's oyster. Everything looked good.

"Keep with me while I shop. The cost of the cab doesn't matter."

"Are you rich?"

"Do you like my hat? It's got the cover I use in the shower to keep my hair dry."

"Did you inherit a fortune? Lucky girl. Wish someone would leave me money."

"Made every cent myself writing a sexy book. It's called *Lust*. You should read it. My picture is on the back cover. Every bookshop in New York has my book. Find me a fish shop. Why does it always rain in March? How long have you been driving cabs?"

"Twenty years. Still paying off the house mortgage. My wife works. The kids are expensive... There's a fish shop two blocks from here in the supermarket."

When Tracey let herself into the apartment an hour later she could hear Randall and Jane talking in the lounge. She put the bags down in the kitchen, took out the three bottles of white wine and put them in the fridge before taking off her hat and her overcoat. When Tracey finished getting the supper ready, the kitchen clock read half past seven.

"Randall! How lovely to see you. Give me a hug. Hope you don't mind us using your home. Your brother said you didn't mind. If you want the place to yourself just say so. There's another apartment on the block for sale. We've tipped the seven million mark. Don't have to tell you what that means in terms of money. Now, who wants a drink? Let's have a party. Fish for supper. We can all get drunk and tell each other what we are writing."

"You don't have to move. We can keep each other company. I'm going to soundproof one of the bedrooms and try to write. Jane's been telling me all about writing the film script for *Lust*. The three of us are going to the première of *Love Song* together. The three musketeers. How does that sound? A pretty girl on each arm as I walk up the red carpet, assuming they have a red carpet. How about a whisky?"

"I'll get the ice."

"That's my girl, Jane. I'm back in the world."

Tracey watched Randall get up and walk across to look out of the big window at the lights of New York. Despite the nice words, the man looked sad, no smile on his face, his eyes full of pain. Losing a wife and a son was worse than Tracey could even imagine. She could hear Jane in the kitchen cracking open the ice tray and the sound of ice clattering into the ice bucket. She went to the television and turned it on to the classical music channel knowing Randall liked good music. Instead of hearing the traffic and rumblings of the big city, all Tracey could hear was a symphony orchestra playing a Brahms symphony, the sound soothing to her nerves. Randall stood staring through the window without moving as Tracey settled back into the comfort of the big sofa. Jane brought in the bucket of ice with three glasses and a bottle of Scotch whisky, filling the glasses with ice one by one.

"Are you with us, Randall?"

"Sorry. Miles away. I don't even know where he is."

"Who?"

"My son."

"How old is he now?"

"Two and a half. Talking a lot. It's the time in a boy's life when a father begins that long process of explaining life with all its complications. The first glimmer of enlightenment. The start of a life is so important, the foundation upon which the rest of life will grow. You start wrong and see things the wrong way and have problems the rest of your life. Now I can't tell him anything. The most important two people in our lives are our parents. Our blood. Our past and our future."

"Have a drink. Don't think of them."

"Difficult not to. This was our home. Rabbit Farm was the same. Gave me the heaves. Thank goodness I have company tonight."

"Do you want your old bedroom back tonight?"

"No, Tracey. The spare bedroom is fine. They're all the same size."

"I made up the bed."

"Thank you. And thank you, Jane. Vat 69. My favourite whisky. To happier times, everyone. Let us lift our glasses."

"How was Africa?"

"The white man's days in Africa are over. All those white farmers will be forced off their farms by the new government. I don't blame them. It was their land we occupied without so much as thinking of the black man. Most of them will go back to peasant farming. Not a bad way of life. You don't have to depend on other people. You build your own home with local timber and thatch it with grass. Grow your own food. Everything is so different when you look from the other person's point of view. What was wrong becomes right and vice-versa. Africa was at its best before we got involved. A small population with unlimited land. People only fight with each other when they're short of something. The world's overpopulated. Not enough space. All you have to do is look out of this window. Life was much easier in Europe when Brahms wrote this music."

"Was it?"

"Maybe not, Tracey. You only really know what you experience yourself. I'm just so sad. Twice. Not once. There must be something wrong with me, or something I don't understand. But don't let me bore you with my problems. How are you both? Let me come and sit down and you can tell me everything that's been going on while I was away. How's Manfred? How's New York? What's the world been up to while I was hiding?"

By the time Tracey went into the kitchen to prepare the food, they had drunk half the bottle of whisky, all of them chattering nineteen to the dozen. She put the three pieces of fish under the grill, washed the lettuce, cut the tomatoes and made the salad dressing. Watching carefully so as not to overcook the fish, she took the tossed bowl of salad and a nice loaf of white bread to the dining table with three wine glasses and one of the cold bottles of wine.

"Can you pop the cork for me, Randall? The fish is almost cooked. You can also slice the bread... What did you do with yourself on the Isle of Man? Isn't the Isle of Man near the North Pole? Must be cold at this time of year."

"I turned myself into an itinerant storyteller, drank whisky and told my hosts my story of the first white man arriving in what was to become Rhodesia. The next day I wrote it all down. Six weeks of fun and then I didn't want to outstay my welcome, and here I am."

"The corkscrew is on the table."

Back in the kitchen, Tracey heard the cork pop out of the wine bottle as she tested the fish by poking it gently with a fork.

"Just a touch more."

"What was that, Tracey?"

"The fish is almost cooked. Take your places at the table. My word, this fish does look good. Here we are. How does that look? A plate for you, Jane. And a plate for Randall. Help yourselves to the salad. There's nothing nicer than a slice of fresh bread covered in real butter. The three musketeers. I like it. When's the première of *Love Song*?"

"Saturday week. I'm making the appointments with the press tomorrow morning, Randall. You're going to be right royal busy. They are going to run you off your feet."

"It's the part of writing I so hate, Jane."

"I know it is. But it has to be done. You can't sell a book or a movie, or anything for that matter, without chatting up the press or spending a fortune on advertising. The media feed on celebrity and we feed on them."

"How are you enjoying working for Manfred?"

"He works you hard but it's fun. We all get on with each other. Better than working in a laundry, thanks to Tracey introducing me to Manfred. I must just watch the booze. Too many of us don't understand how destructive alcohol addiction becomes. It almost killed me in those early days. Never mind. Tonight is party night and there is a price to pay for everything... You're right, Tracey, the fish is quite delicious."

With their mouths full they ate without talking. Randall got up and poured the wine, the classical music channel still playing. The curtains were drawn giving the large lounge/dining room a comfortable feeling of privacy, the world outside the big window no longer part of their lives. They were home, just the three of them enjoying their supper.

"Help yourselves to more salad. Tell me, Randall. When you made all that money from your books, what did you do with it, apart from paying your income tax? The money is building up in my bank account and I don't know what to do with it. Why I offered to buy this apartment through your brother, Phillip. When are you going to see him?"

"Tomorrow, if I don't have too much of a hangover. Buying an apartment was a good idea. It's bricks and mortar and if you've paid cash the fluctuations in the price of property don't matter. Your apartment isn't vulnerable without a mortgage. My father says the most difficult thing with money isn't making it so much, it's holding on to it. Cash in the bank depends on the financial security of the bank and the value of currency. I put my money into a global equity fund with a mix of shares, government bonds and cash spread across the major countries of the world. Theoretically, the money should hold its value despite all the market fluctuations. Some people buy gold coins: South African Krugerrands. Hide it under the proverbial bed. Others buy antiques or jewellery. The Jews liked to have something to put in their pockets in case the poor sods were chased out of their own country. The world has always been in turmoil: revolutions; coups; wars; financial meltdowns. Be careful with your money, Tracey, and think of your future. Think of what it could be like to go into old age without money or a pension. Think of your children, even though at the moment you don't have any kids. But you will. My maternal grandfather left me a fortune, bless him. You give your children life but all you can do is leave them money. Security. The security of money that most people crave for. Your bank will advise you where to go. Just don't leave all of it in cash in the one bank. That's my father's advice, and despite the meltdown in Rhodesia where he made his money out of tobacco farming, he's done all right to this day because of an investment in a block of flats in London. We need another bottle of wine. To hell with tomorrow's hangover. Tonight we are all going to get as pissed as newts, whatever that means. Why ever did newts get pissed? I'm beginning to talk rubbish. The wine on top of the whisky is beginning to get to me."

"The wine's in the fridge but leave me out. After this glass, I'm going to bed. You and Tracey don't have to work tomorrow. Be careful with alcohol, Randall. It can kill you. Literally. I've been down that road and I won't be doing it no more. The food was lovely, Tracey. Thank you. There are three magazines that Manfred and I want you to write articles for. On Monday you can come to the office and we'll go through all the details."

"You've been working hard, Jane."

"Nothing good happens without hard work. You two enjoy each other's company. Let me get another bottle and then I'm off to the warmth and comfort of my own bed. Lovely to have you back, Randall. Let's just hope the movie is as good as the book... There we go. That was my supper. Don't get too drunk, the pair of you. And behave yourselves."

"What do you mean?"

"You know what I mean, Tracey. You have that sweet innocent smile on your face."

Watching Jane go to the kitchen, Tracey hoped that what was in her head was not so apparent to Randall. The best way to welcome him home and get his mind off Meredith and Douglas was to get him drunk and screw his brains out. There was nothing better than good sex to change a man's feelings. Tonight, her aim was to lift Randall out of the depression that had driven him on a fruitless trip to Africa and onto his smallholding on the Isle of Man. She was on the pill, so there was no chance of her falling pregnant. She would be doing Manfred and Jane a favour, keeping their biggest writer in America.

"Thanks, Jane. Sleep tight. May your dreams be full of happiness. You didn't have to take the cork out of the bottle. We'll turn down the music. Don't wake me in the morning."

Getting up, Tracey took the wine bottle and her glass down the three steps to the lounge area of the living room, put the bottle on the coffee table, sat on the big sofa and patted the seat next to her.

"Come and sit next to me, Randall. On the way, you can turn down the music. The wine is nice and cold. It's so lovely to have you back in New York, the most exciting place in the world for a girl to live. I love New York. The pulse is always beating. You can feel the energy. There is always something to do. You never get bored in the great city of New York. London must be the same. Bring your glass and I'll fill it up for you. There's still one bottle left in the fridge and then there's the whisky. Couldn't we soundproof the entire apartment and turn it into a writer's den? If we all write in separate rooms we won't hear a sound from each other. And after we've finished work we can have a drink together. That's better. This sofa of yours is so comfortable. There we go. Down the hatch, as I've heard you say. All those quaint colonial expressions from your British heritage. How long is your new book about the old Africa going to be?"

"As many books as it takes to bring Lawrence Templeton-Smythe, his friends and what will be his family through the colonial years. Somewhere, I've got to find him a wife so I'll have to temporarily bring him out of the bush as there aren't any women where he is at the moment. And those days, marrying a local and mixing the races was taboo. Not done by an English gentleman. Any more than he would marry a girl from England out of his class. All that public school nonsense. Can't marry beneath yourself or the genes will be wrong for the next generation. The children of old families in those days married the children of old families, a lot of the marriages arranged. They wanted their money to remain within the aristocracy. All just a way of keeping the family money in the right hands. They all had mistresses, of course. Young girls from the lower classes looking for an easy life. Still goes on, though now in America the aristocracy is the rich and famous. In America, you can get to the top of society just by making lots of money. Only money counts, however you get your hands on it. Doesn't matter if you make your money by fraud, as long as they don't find you out. In the days of Templeton-Smythe, you had to come from the right stock. Load of rubbish, of course. But in my book, I'll have to comply with history."

"Of all the places you've been to, what country is your favourite?"

"Rhodesia. Except Rhodesia doesn't exist. Any more than the British Empire exists. Why I want to write the books. To bring that crazy colonial life back into existence so it will live forever through my books. Or, more important, give me a chance to live with memories in a place and time that, for better or worse, no longer exists."

"I'd prefer to live in modern America."

"Of course you would, Tracey. You're part of the rich and famous. You're in the top class... Are you happy?"

"I'm always happy. I want to make you happy. Don't look so sad. There's a whole new life waiting for you right here."

"Are you making a pass at me, Tracey?"

"Of course I wouldn't."

"No man in his right mind would not want a good-looking girl like you to make a pass at him. Not exactly what I should have said. I'm getting drunk."

"So am I. And it's lovely. That's better. The sadness has gone from your eyes, replaced by a bit of good old lust."

"Can you see it?"

"I know all about lust, Randall. Why my book has sold over seven million copies... Now you're laughing. The perfect evening has begun. Boy meets girl. *Lust*, Randall. There's nothing wrong with old-fashioned lust, provided both people want it."

"Do you want lust, Tracey?"

"Come here and find out."

"We haven't finished the wine."

"Then we'll finish the wine and go to bed together."

"It'll have to be in the spare bedroom."

"Forget Meredith. She's past. Went on her way."

"You think she'll be happier with Clint?"

"Of course not. Once he gets his hands on your money he'll toss Meredith out of the window."

"You think he only wanted the money?"

"Wouldn't have so much as looked at her if he hadn't found out you were married to her in community of property. Fraud, cheating, doesn't matter which. They all want to get their hands on the money."

"Did we write our books just to make money? My joy with writing is being able to leave my body and travel to times and places with people I like. A way of avoiding reality. Of escaping the world. It's my perfect recreation. Same as playing sport. Some like playing the piano. I like writing books. All the attention from publishing the books makes me sick. If the reader enjoys reading my books as much as I enjoy writing them, then we are both happy. I don't want anything else."

"You don't like success? I love it. Come on. Have another glass of wine. Let's get well and truly drunk. Who cares, anyway. The only thing that matters to me is the money. I'll take your father's advice and make sure I hold on to my money. Too many people squander their ill-gotten gains."

"Shakespeare watched his money. Did you know he was a money lender? They even say he cheated his taxes. Four hundred years ago. Nothing in this life ever changes. It's part of human nature. How we are made. Ah, now we have Beethoven's Ninth Symphony. Just listen to it. So beautiful. That's what being an artist should all be about. Writing something beautiful that will last forever, giving generation after generation pleasure. That's what a life is for. And yes, to write good plays or good symphonies you don't want to be worrying about money. Good old Shakespeare. Did he understand life. My word. You can see it in every scene, every sentence. 'To be, or not to be, that is the question.' He painted all of our lives with words, from the bottom class to the aristocracy. From young people to old. From love to hatred. It's difficult to so much as imagine the influence one man's brain has had on so many people. Millions and millions of us, generation after generation. Most of us just come and go in this life, forgotten by all but a handful of people, and when those few people die, forgotten forever; insignificant little lives. In the end, the world we live in will go and then nothing, not even Will Shakespeare will be remembered: a total void, like all those lifeless planets we see far up in the night skies. We came from nothing and will end in nothing, no answer to my one big question: 'Why are we alive?'"

"To have a good time. To fall in love. To have and love children. It's better not to look too far but concentrate on the life in front of us. What happened, what's going to happen, has nothing to do with our lives. We are alive, Randall. Isn't it wonderful to be alive?"

"Are we going to make love, Tracey?"

"Probably not tonight. I had the idea of seducing you in a drunken stupor but now I'm thinking far too straight. I'll blame it all on William Shakespeare. Sometimes it's better not to think."

"'Most people would rather die than think. And many of them do.' I quote from Bertrand Russell, the British philosopher. Most things we say or write are copied from other people."

"Let's just enjoy ourselves together."

"I'm just so thankful to both of you that I'm not alone tonight in my old home."

When the wine was finished, they went to their separate beds, Tracey wondering if she was losing her pull. In bed, alone, she couldn't sleep. Even the future of her writing was giving her problems if all she was going to write about was the sexual frolics of her characters. All her books were going to be frivolous, worthless, despite making so much money... Was he asleep? Maybe. Or was he too, wide awake? In her silk nightdress that barely covered her bottom, Tracey got out of bed and opened the door to her bedroom. There was no sound from Jane or Randall, the only sound, the rumblings of late-night New York that barely penetrated her consciousness. In the dark, she walked to Randall's door which she quietly opened and went inside and climbed into his bed, cuddling up to his naked body. Without a sound, they began to make love. When it was over, Randall lay on top of her, the two of them joined. Randall's breathing changed to the softer sound of sleep. For the first time in Tracey's sexual philanderings, a man had fallen asleep on the job. Gently, Tracey pushed him over to the right-hand side of the bed. Smiling, happy, she lay on her back, hoping that what had just happened was only the beginning. With Randall turned on his side, he had stopped snoring. Turning over, bottom to bottom, Tracey went to sleep into a world of perfect dreams. She was in Africa with Randall, running hand in hand through the long grass followed by a white dog, both of them laughing happily, the dog barking, birds in the blue sky, the scent of wildflowers as they ran down to the big river. At the river, they took off all their clothes and dived into the warm water. When they got out, they made love on the grass bank of the river. They were alone. Perfectly alone. Just the two of them in a moment of perfect existence.

When Tracey woke at the end of her dream, the picture was still vivid. Smiling, she went back to sleep and slept until the morning.

"Where am I?... Tracey! What are you doing in my bed?"

"Don't you remember?"

"I remember going to bed on my own."

"Then you must have made love to me in your sleep and that's ridiculous. But you did fall asleep on the job."

"Now I'm the one who's been unfaithful. How did it happen? You're giggling, Tracey."

"Relax. What's a bit of sex between friends? I seduced you, Randall. Deliberately got you drunk, and when the lights were out, climbed into your bed."

"Can you leave me alone?"

"I'm sorry. I made a mistake. Just trying to lift you out of your depression. I'd better move out and buy my own apartment. We all make mistakes in life and this was a big one. If you're not careful, Randall, you'll die a lonely old man. Don't reject people... Oh, my goodness, now you're crying. A grown man crying. And it's all my fault. I'm so sorry. I'll go. Just pretend this never happened."

"If I had a gun, I'd shoot myself. I don't want to live anymore. I make a mess of people's lives. The last thing you want to do, Tracey Chapelle, is get yourself involved with Randall Crookshank. I'm a failure and always will be."

"The alcohol is destroying you. It almost destroyed Jane."

"And what do you do if you don't drink? How do you socialise with people? Do you just sit on your own? My problem is I've done everything. Did it all too young. There's nothing left for me to do."

"And the new series of books?"

"Do they matter? I don't think so. Do historical novels have any importance? I've written what I know about life and now there's nothing. One big blank future with nothing in it. Too much of the world exists on drink, drugs and sex. We're animals... You don't have to stand there naked in the cold. Get back into bed. I don't want to lose a friend. My mind is in such a mess I hate myself but I mustn't inflict my problems on other people. Your intentions were good. I know they were. What a world. You make all that money and just look at us. When Jane has gone to work we'll get up and go for a walk in the park. Go and see my brother, Phillip. I've got to get a hold on myself."

"You do remember last night, don't you?"

"Of course I do. I felt guilty and went into denial. Ever since Meredith left me, I've been trying to run away from myself. And there's nowhere to run. Yourself always catches up on you along with your problems. What are you going to do with me?"

"Put it in a book. Famous author falls asleep on the job."

"Don't you dare."

"Just kidding."

"I know you were. Just don't let me mess up your life. Find a nice young man who isn't just after your money, marry him and have your children. Lead a normal life."

"They'll never let us. For as long as people are reading our books, they'll be chasing us. It's the price of fame. I always say, enjoy what you have in life and make the best of it. You'll get over Meredith. Just take time. Let's see where we go, Randall. Don't take life so seriously. We all drink too much. Who cares? Tomorrow is always another day. A day to be enjoyed. If I get back into bed, will you give me a cuddle? I love being cuddled. Good, now you're smiling. You had me worried for a moment. The one thing I hate in life is rejection. The fear of every writer... There she goes. That was the front door."

"Does she know you're in my bedroom?"

"I have no idea. Let's relax. We have the day to ourselves. We can go and see Phillip tomorrow. How do people fall in love, Randall?"

"I have absolutely no idea. And I've been married twice."

"Maybe it was lust, not love."

"Maybe. We all like to call it love."

"Jane fell in love with Harvey. She's writing it down in a wonderful book. We can learn something from Jane's story. What it means for two people to be totally in love with each other."

"And what happened?"

"The demon money came along. Money trumped love. He married a rich man's daughter. At least we don't have that problem. We've both got too much money. They were young. Jane thinks we only find genuine love when we're young and not absorbed in materialism."

"I'm looking forward to reading her book."

"You want a cup of tea, Randall?"

"I'd love one. So the slate is clean?"

"The slate is clean."

And the day began. A day that Tracey had no idea where it was going. Sighing, tired and frustrated that her seduction plan had not worked, she thought again of buying her own apartment and putting part of her money in something permanent. Relationships came and went, like money left in the bank. There was always something. Having made a success of her writing she now had to start worrying about what to do with the money. All those accountants, financial advisors, all after making money out of her. And if she married and had children, she would be constantly worrying about their problems, never quite knowing what they were thinking. What Randall thought of her now she had seduced him she had no idea, all those thoughts deep in the turmoil of his mind.

After they dressed themselves in their separate bedrooms, they ate breakfast in the kitchen and went out for a walk in the park, wrapped up in their overcoats against the March cold. People holding dogs on leashes were walking beneath the leafless trees. Tracey could see their breath in the cold of the morning air.

"Not even the cat lady. She became a friend of my brother, Phillip.

Brings food for the stray cats and feeds them while sitting up on a bench. Something to do, I suppose. I'm not the only one with nothing to do. Boredom. The curse of so many people's lives."

"Jane has lots for you to do on Monday."

"But nothing I want to do. I hate being interviewed, especially on television. I hate nebulous articles just to promote my name at the bottom of the article: Randall Holiday, author of *Masters of Vanity*. The magazines just want your name to catch the eye of their readers, they don't care what you write. So what's all that about? More waffle. More making money. I sometimes think our world is just about making money and nothing else."

"You're off again, Randall."

"Sorry. It's boring. I don't have any motivation... Are you on the pill?"

"Of course I am."

"That would have been fun. Women like to get themselves pregnant. Sorry, that came out wrong. I really am an ungrateful bastard. A beautiful girl seducing me, what a pleasure. Doesn't often happen. In my experience, a man has to work hard to seduce a girl. All that wining and dining. All the flattery. The girls don't just fall into your bed."

"Now you're smiling. Let's walk a little quicker. It's cold."

"Drunken sex. I sometimes wonder if I have any more children. Those one-night stands: was the girl taking precautions? All I remember is not taking precautions myself. There was a married girl who said she'd been unsuccessfully trying to get pregnant. We had sex in a hotel bedroom. All those games of life. None of us will know. Not even her husband. I met her in a bar and invited her to dinner."

"You think too much. If she had a child, then you gave them both what they wanted. At least the kid would have good genes."

"And a problem with alcohol. But you're right. The chance of being alive is infinitesimal: all those seductions going back to the start of man's evolution, making us all who we are."

"If alcohol has become a problem, you should stop drinking."

"Not so easy in the world I come from. Our world. Where drink is a key part of our lives. Many of my good friends were met in a bar. Business is done in the bar. Businessmen entertain their clients by taking them to dinner in some fancy restaurant to impress them with expensive bottles of French champagne. Newspaper reporters like to take me drinking, hoping the booze will open me up. In my twenties, drink wasn't a problem."

"It was for Jane. Maybe we should have a new rule. No booze on the thirty-first floor."

"The idea is usually better than the execution. We'd bore each other stiff. The three musketeers all sober? I don't think so... When I'm writing, I don't drink. Only when I take a break to let the story build in my head."

"I can't write with a hangover. What we all need to do is work and only have a drink at the weekends."

Still worrying about their earlier altercation, Tracey walked on through the cold of the park, no one taking notice of anyone: hundreds of people, mostly alone and none of them communicating in the great metropolis. Randall prattled on, Tracey barely listening to his problems. Did she want him as a permanent lover? She wasn't sure. At twenty-seven years of age, she had no real idea what she wanted in life. A normal life? What was a normal life? Was bringing up her children when she had them, her only true purpose in life? And when the kids had grown up, then what happened? Life with an old man that was her husband where the pleasure of sex with him had long faded. Just two middle-aged people trying to be polite to each other in an empty house, both hoping one of the kids would come home for a weekend and give them someone to talk to, instead of the same old mundane routine of daily life, both looking back like Randall knowing everything they had to do in life had already been done. Even their so-called friends would find them boring.

"You're not listening to a word I'm saying, Tracey."

"Sorry. Miles away. I was thinking of marriage."

"Not with me, I hope!"

"Poor Randall. Come on. Let's find somewhere warm and have a cup of coffee."

"You know what I miss most in my life at the moment?"

"Your kids, I hope."

"My dog. I was thinking of Polar Bear. I envy all these people walking their dogs... Coffee and cake. Sounds good. One step at a time, my girl. That's how it goes."

"We're lucky we can both write books and escape from our lives... Over there. The Lucky Jam café... I usually end up in a bar, not a café."

"We could go to Harry B's."

"And start the drinking process all over again? I don't think so. A couple of hours and then all the problems."

"Hangovers and depression."

"Does drinking make you depressed, Randall?"

"Of course it does. Makes me feel ugh and my mouth tastes like the bottom of a parrot cage. The pleasure isn't worth the pain. Coffee and cake. Come on."

"And then what do we do?"

"We'll find out."

Inside the Lucky Jam, it was warm, everyone at the surrounding tables chattering over their cups of tea and coffee. The waitresses with their small aprons over their young bellies moved from table to table, big smiles on their faces. Music played over the chattering, the perfect background to a successful business. Someone had said to Tracey earlier in her life that the secret to success was position, position, position. Just off a central Manhattan park was certainly one of them. When the girl brought their coffee and two big slices of sugary cake, her smile was concentrated on Randall, looking for her tip. Many young girls worked part-time in cafes and bars to put themselves through college, the tips the main source of their income. When Tracey took a bite of the cake it was sweet and delicious.

"You want some more cake, Tracey? This stuff is good."

"And puts on weight... Just look at them all. Everyone looks so damn happy."

"And why shouldn't they be? Tea and symphony. Warmth away from the cold... Where are the dogs? Oh, there's one under that table... How's your hangover?"

"Wearing off, thank goodness."

"There are so many children with their parents."

"Happy families. Makes me jealous."

"You should be careful. Don't leave having kids too late. How old are you?"

"Isn't that a rude question to ask a girl? Maybe you're right. I'm turning twenty-eight in three months' time. Then it's just downhill all the way to thirty. Thirty sounds so old."

"Better than being near to forty. Now that's old. And still, the years go on. Let's have another slice of this lovely cake. If we get fat we can go to the gym and run on the treadmill."

"How's your hangover?"

"Comes and goes, like the devil lurking ready to lure me back to the bottle. But not today. Or tomorrow. I want that alcohol soaking out of my system... There we go, lady. Two more slices of your delicious cake... Now, where was I? Oh, yes. Hangovers. They should make alcohol illegal like drugs. Help a lot of people. But, of course, they tried that one here in America."

Trying not to imagine what she would look like in ten years' time, Tracey began thinking of having a child. She had all the money she needed from the books, so marrying a man for his money was not important. She could employ a nanny the way Martha and Phillip had employed Ivy to look after Carmen. As Randall prattled on, the idea began to build. She would give them all another go: Manfred, her agent; Godfrey her publisher; Randall the best-selling author. If one of them got her pregnant the genes would be right without having all the hassle of putting up with a husband, the same man, night after night. She could carry on looking for new material; having fun without a commitment. She would need an apartment of her own, of course. A child would give her something for the future. A future friend. The lifetime companion people talked about when they were thinking of a husband. If she went on sleeping with lots and lots of men but stayed off the pill she would have no idea which one of the men was the father. There would be no guilt. No one to tell. A child would be far easier to control than a husband.

"I'm going to do it!"

"What are you going to do, Tracey?"

"Enjoy this second piece of cake. And you're right about something, I need to put some of my money into an apartment."

"Are you moving out?"

"Not just yet. And If I buy one in the same building I'll have the best of both worlds: a place for my future, close to my friends. Why don't you come with me to the agent? Give us both something to do and keep our minds off going to Harry B's."

"Are we going to Harry B's later?"

"Probably."

"We're out of control."

"Who cares? We're still young."

"What are you going to do in a big apartment all by yourself?"

"Lots of things, Randall. Lots of things. Eat your cake. When are you going to see Douglas?"

"As soon as possible."

"Why don't we go together? I love kids. That'll put one in her eye. We can behave in front of Meredith like lovers. That'll make her jealous. Give her one back. When are we going? Let's go. You know where they live. Pitch up unannounced. You see, we now have something positive to do with our day."

And the luck was in: in all her excitement at seducing the famous Randall Holiday, she had forgotten to take her morning pill. There was an old saying Tracey remembered: 'there was no time like the present'. When the pretty young girl presented Randall with the bill, Tracey was still smiling. She had a plan. A plan for the rest of her life. The life of a prosperous single mother without all the worries and hassles. Life in the fast lane. There was nothing wrong with it. Men, glorious men. And the more the better. Not sure if she wasn't a whore and being paid by her readers for her philandering, Tracey finished the last of her coffee before smiling sweetly at Randall.

"Let's go and pay a visit to your wife and her lover. How did you get her address?"

"It was in the letter demanding a divorce and half my money. Are you sure?"

"Why not? She wants your money. Offer her enough with you having full access to Douglas. If she goes through lawyers it'll take years. I'll bet that Clint wants to start living off your money as soon as possible. Painters rarely make money out of their art. He must be good at charming girls. Probably a great lover. Sorry, Randall, that must have hurt. Flattery. So many girls fall for flattery. Clint, the perfect flatterer. Make me laugh if Meredith gets your money and dumps the bastard. Sometimes professional flatterers let their guard down. What a lovely world we live in. Would you let her back if she asked you?"

"Not on your life. Once bitten, twice shy. All those old clichés. But how right they are... What are we going to do with Douglas?"

"Take him home. Talk to him. Behave like a father, whatever that is. I don't know. He's your son. You know, Randall, the world is plain crazy."

"Shouldn't I phone first? There was a phone number on the letter."

"Now what's the matter?"

"I have a screaming hangover from last night. I won't be in control of myself. I'll say wrong things to Douglas. What else can we do with ourselves? The last thing I want is making a fool of myself by losing my temper. Maybe let the lawyers sort it out."

"And seeing Douglas?"

"He hasn't seen me in a while... I need a drink."

"I know you do. That's the problem. Drink, drugs and sex. My book in a nutshell. What's the time?"

"Just past one o'clock."

"We can catch a cab to Harry B's."

"Let's go."

"You going to change your mind?"

"Whatever for?"

Smiling, trying not to shake her head, Tracey watched Randall pay the bill with a hefty tip for the pretty girl, and followed him out of the warm café back into the outside cold. When Randall went with Jane on Monday to his appointments, she would begin looking for her own apartment. Men. Glorious men. And like herself, most of them drank too much. Why people changed their minds in mid-sentence was beyond Tracey's comprehension. All he had to say right at the beginning was let's go to Harry B's and drown our hangovers in drink. Men. They were all so simple. Most of Randall's talk was rationalising. Making excuses. When all he wanted was a drink.

2

"Welcome to Harry B's, stranger. Where've you been, Randall? Long time no see. What'll it be? A beer to start with? Your usual. Two famous authors in my bar. Can't be bad for business. What would Tracey Chapelle like to drink? Read your book. Kept me horny for a week. Rebecca is over the moon to be in your movie, Randall. Are you here in New York for the première? Quite something for a girl to meet the author through an introduction by me in my bar."

"I didn't know she got a part. Gave her Poppy Maddock's phone number. Poppy wrote the screenplay for *Love Song*. How are you, Terry? Has she got a big part? Now that's what I call luck. Probably change her life forever. Make mine a beer. You want a beer, Tracey? Two beers. How've you been?"

"Where have you been is more important. You were my best customer."

"Here and there. It's a long story. Have a drink with us."

"Bit early. But let's get started. Tell me what's been going on."

"It's boring. But here we go. Is Amelia on duty later? Now, let me start at the beginning. Cheers, Terry. Good to see you."

"Cheers, Randall. Good to see you too."

"You want to come to the première?"

"Love to. But who would run my bar? Business before pleasure."

While Randall told the owner of Harry B's the story of Meredith,

Tracey stopped listening to the conversation: she had heard it all before. Even the best of writers could be boring. A man at the end of the bar caught her attention with a knowing smile. He was young and good-looking. A future prospect. More material for her next book. After ten minutes of Randall's hard-luck story, Tracey walked down the bar on her way to the lady's toilet.

"Hello. Do I know you?"

"I know you. Read your book. Your picture is on the back cover. My name is Teddy. Can I bring round my copy of your book and have it autographed?"

"A pleasure, Teddy. Good-looking young men are always welcome in my life. You got a pen? There we are. My phone number's on the back of your tab."

"Is he your boyfriend?"

"Not really. So you liked my book?"

"I loved it."

"Along with seven million others... Give me a ring, Teddy."

Not sure if she was looking for a story to put in a book or a distraction from her flawed night with Randall, she looked hard at herself in the mirror. One of the toilets flushed as Tracey touched up her mouth with lipstick. When Tracey turned and looked to her right an old woman was washing her hands in the next basin.

"A bit early for an old girl to be in a bar. You just here for lunch? I get so lonely on my own. There's nothing worse than staring at brick walls. Feel like being in a prison. You don't mind my talking to you?"

"Of course not."

"I was never lonely at your age. Men never stopped chasing after me. Married one of them. Divorced him a couple of years later. Married a second. Three kids. All grown up. Never see them. One's in Canada. Married. Has her own life. The boy's in the army. Useless at getting a steady job in commerce. The Lord only knows what he'll do with his life. Not much, if you ask me. The eldest girl lives with a woman. They're lovers. The woman pays for everything. I've been dumped by the lot of them."

"What happened to your husband?"

"Killed himself. Before he shot himself with a 9mm pistol he said he'd had enough of the lot of us. Thought he was kidding. Blood all over the lounge carpet. The police enquiry went on for weeks. They thought one of us had shot the poor bastard. I was drunk in a bar when I met him, poor sod. Moved in that night. The bad luck was getting myself pregnant. Had to marry him. We trailed all over America trying to put down roots and to behave like a family. Never worked. Each time we thought having another baby would make it all right."

"Come and have a drink with us."

"You here with your husband?"

"A friend. A lover. A one-night stand. Three of us live in his apartment. Got drunk last night and crawled into his bed."

"Sounds familiar. I'm Sophie. Nice to meet you."

"Tracey. Come and meet Randall. He's a friend of the bar owner."

"And what do you do for a living to be in a bar so early in the day?"

"We write books. Both of us. Have you heard of Randall Holiday?"

"Haven't read a book in years."

"Thank heaven. Randall hates people gushing all over him. Hang on while I go to the toilet, Sophie. When you've got to go, you've got to go."

"What kind of books do you write?"

"Very bad ones."

"I'd like to read one."

"I don't think so. It's called *Lust*."

"That one I have heard of. I do watch television. All I do, really. What would an old woman do without that box? I'm lucky I recently inherited my father's money after my mother died. Why I can afford to be in a bar. It's so nice to talk to someone, Tracey."

"Back in a tick."

"Take your time."

Tracey sat quietly digesting the old woman's life, asking herself whether her own was going to be any different. Would a child be a lifelong companion? So many times she had been told that once they had what they wanted from their parents they went on their own in the same old pursuits, only thinking of their parents when they wanted something. Never mind. She was going to get herself pregnant. At least the old girl had some kind of a life to look back on. Now, alone, even with her father's money, she had nothing to do with her life, poor woman. Sad. Life was sad. Flushing the toilet, Tracey opened the door. The old woman was waiting, the back of her bottom propped on one of the basins.

"You must have some good memories, Sophie."

"Drowned in arguments long ago. Must have been my own fault. We always like to blame others when we are at fault."

"Come on. Drink time. After you. Let's forget about books... That's him at the other end of the bar... See you later, Teddy. Can you believe it? Teddy and Terry. Terry owns the bar... Randall. Meet Sophie. She's bored and needs company. Is that your second beer? Buy Sophie a beer. Always start with a beer."

"I thought you'd left through the backdoor."

"We were talking. Time flies when you talk... Now, look at that. One beer for Sophie. Terry really is good at his job. Overhears every conversation when his customers talk about what they want to drink. Cheers, Sophie. Tell us a story, Randall. Randall was recently on the Isle of Man, wherever that is, performing for his supper as an itinerant storyteller. Free food and lodging. Not bad. How's the hangover, Randall?"

"Better. The only quick way to get rid of a hangover is to have a drink. I'm a drunk, Sophie."

"I'm not much better when I have the money. Drink drowns my bad memories. Nice to meet you. Tracey says you both write books for a living. You'll have to leave me out. Haven't read a book since leaving school. And that was a whole lifetime ago. How long are you both going to be in the bar?"

"For as long as it takes. Who's the young man at the other end of the bar, Tracey?"

"Teddy. He's read my book. Recognised me from my photograph on the back cover."

"You just can't get away from them. At first, fame is fun. You'll see, Tracey. In the end, you won't have any peace. They all think they own you. Maybe they do. There's always a flaw in making lots of money. The price of selling lots of books... My wife just walked out on me, Sophie."

"My husband shot himself."

"Oh, dear."

"My son says we're better off without him. His own son! What's life all about?"

"You tell me. I've been trying to work that out for years... What's the matter, Terry? Put it all on my tab."

"She's coming over."

"Who?"

"Rebecca. She asked me to phone her if you came into the bar. Wants to thank you. Thought you'd disappeared into thin air. You don't mind?"

"Why ever should I mind a pretty girl wanting to join me in a bar? You don't mind, Tracey?"

"Of course not. Just the pace of life. Let's have a party. You mind if Teddy joins us?"

"Why not? Terry, ask that smiling man down the other end of your bar to come and join us."

"At your service, my lord. I'll do anything provided it's good for business. Got to make money while you can in this life. People brought together stay longer."

"What are you going to do with all your money, Terry?"

"After paying all those lovely taxes I'll buy myself a small estate in the South where it's warm all the year-round. Retire with my wife."

"You don't have a wife."

"I will if I have a small estate in Louisiana. They don't like marrying bar owners because of the competition. But a nice home with rich neighbours is every poor girl's dream."

Ten minutes after Teddy bought them all a round of drinks to impress her, Tracey was introduced to Rebecca.

"Randall. Thank goodness I found you before next Saturday's première. You can't believe what you've done for me. Changed my life. Norman Landry, the director, said he was delighted by my performance as a young London girl on the make. But of course, you know the story. You wrote the book. My luck was being good at doing accents. Got that low-class London accent taped. And best of all, thanks to your writing, Randall, there was a story to the girl behind the pretty face. Makes acting worthwhile. The girl had ambition to make something of her life, and not just by marrying. Put herself through university and got a degree in marketing. Wish I'd done the same. A girl who knows how to sell a product can always earn a good living. How silly of me. I'm telling you your own story. How are you, Randall? I heard about your marital problems. Anyway, you're famous. You won't have any problems finding a replacement. Thank you for introducing me to your friends. Norman has offered me a bigger part in his new movie. I'm going to be a movie star and it's all thanks to you and Terry. Whoever said it didn't all happen in bars was nuts. The luck of life. And here I am with Tracey Chapelle and Randall Holiday."

"What would you like to drink?"

"A gin and tonic. My character in *Love Song* only drank gin and tonics. So British."

"What's the movie like?"

"You'll find out a week from tomorrow, Randall."

"So will the critics."

"The reviews are going to be brilliant. A good book, a good scriptwriter, good actors and a good director. Has to work... Thank you, Terry. To success. Nothing like success... Now that does taste good. Life is so exciting. When are you going to take me out to celebrate, Randall? Oh, I'm sorry. Have I put my foot in it? I thought you and Teddy were together, Tracey, the way he's looking at you... Silence. Oh, dear. Anyway, the film is going to be a sensation."

By the time the old lady excused herself to go home to her loneliness, Tracey had drunk four glasses of whisky and was chirpy as a cricket. The sadness had gone from Randall's eyes. Not sure whether Rebecca was hitting on Teddy or Randall, Tracey decided she did not care. One man was much the same as another. Slowly but surely the alcohol had taken hold of them. Breaking off from the conversation, Tracey walked across to the old woman who was standing at the door with her back to the bar and all the happy people.

"You don't have to go, Sophie."

"Oh, but I do. It's my age. I don't fit in. You're all happy and I'm miserable. You're all going somewhere with your lives. I've reached the end. I can't sit and drink in a bar and try and pretend to myself I'm back in my twenties. Doesn't work. I've had my life. Even my children find me uninteresting. Thank you for the company, Tracey."

"Come back. Tell you what, you and I will drink alone at the far end of the bar. Let Rebecca, the about-to-be film star, chat up the men. I want you to tell me more about your life."

"It's just boring."

"I'm a writer. A good story, however sad or unhappy, is worth listening to. You will be doing me a favour."

"Why are you being so kind?"

"I'm trying to do what I should do for my own parents. Instead, I only think of myself. And Randall's going to get himself drunk again. Now there's a life in a mess. He has everything that life can give, and yet he has nothing. It's killing him inside of himself. The man's depressed. Said if he had a gun he'd kill himself like your husband... I'm sorry. Now you're crying. Let's go and have a good long chat on our own. If that Rebecca says one more time how good she is at acting, I'll throttle the bitch. You see, like all us women, I hate competition. And Randall's not really interested. He's not much interested in anything."

"What about the good-looking Teddy?"

"He's got my phone number if he wants me. What I'm going to do now is ask you to delve back into your life and tell me the good bits when you were happy."

"Are you happy, Tracey?"

"Of course I am."

"Ah. You're young. Yes, I do remember some of those lovely times. There was a trip to London when I was nineteen years old. We went by boat, can you believe it? All the way across the pond. Ten wonderful days on the ocean waves."

"Let's buy us a whole bottle of white wine and drink it together."

"Why ever not?"

"Did you meet a man on board?"

"Of course I did. His name was Jim Slater. I wonder what happened to Jim? Ten days on board the ship and two weeks together in London. We did the theatres. Even went to the Royal Opera House at Covent Garden."

"What opera did you see?"

"*Carmen*. I think the opera was called *Carmen*. To be honest I was more interested in Jim by that stage. Whatever happened to Jim? When I came home at the end of my holiday when the money ran out – I'd bought a return ticket on the boat – Jim stayed in London. He'd enrolled at the London School of Economics. Never heard or saw of him again. But I often remember Jim. I remember more of him the older I get. We were so young. Everything was so new and exciting."

"Did you make love to him?"

"No. We never made love."

"Did you want to?"

"I'm not sure. I didn't want to break the magic spell. I think both of us were virgins."

"How old was Jim?"

"The same age as me. He was nineteen years old. Jim Slater. Never forgot him."

"My friend's name is Slater. Jane Slater. She wrote the screenplay for my book. The film will be finished within the next six months. I remember Jane saying her father's name was Jim. Her father is an economist. What a strange coincidence."

"Is her father alive?"

"Her mother died when Jane was seventeen. Her father never remarried."

"Can I meet her?"

"Of course you can. She works for my literary agent, and the three of us share Randall's apartment. I'll ask her if her father went to the London School of Economics. Where did you get the money for your trip to England?"

"From my mother's father. My grandfather said a voyage on a ship would give me a new look at life. It was my nineteenth birthday present just before he died. Could your Jane be my Jim's daughter? What an extraordinary coincidence."

"If he is, I'll put the story in a book. The world is so big and yet so small. You're both from New York City by the sound of it... Thank you, Terry. A bottle of your best dry white wine and two glasses. Can I use your phone to call Jane? We want her to join us. Another customer, Terry... Thank you... Jane. It's Tracey. Are you busy on a Friday afternoon? Ask Manfred if you can leave now and join me and Randall in Harry B's. There's someone I want you to meet... Fine. Go home first. Oh, and when you're at home pick up that family photo album you've shown me of you and your family when you were growing up... I'll tell you when you get here... Cheers. See you later, alligator."

With the phone given back to Terry and a smile on her face, Tracey turned back to Sophie.

"Jane was the one who introduced us to Harry B's. She used to drink here in her wild days and before when she was with Harvey. She was nineteen when she went out with Harvey, her only love she tells me. Jane's almost finished a book about her year with Harvey she's called *Love in the Spring of Life*. Those same lovely years of perfect innocence when you met Jim on the boat to England. Where did you land in England?"

"London Docks. New York straight to London. I can see it all as clear as daylight... Does she have photographs of her father when he was young?"

"Of course she does. Cheers, Sophie. How are they doing up the other end of the bar?"

"She's all over Randall and his money."

"They always are. Jane's Harvey dumped her for a rich man's daughter and ended up running his company. A lot easier than starting one on his own. Life, Sophie. It's all about money. It's all in the genes... This wine is really good. Let's have some of Terry's toasted sandwiches to soak up the alcohol. I find if I eat when I'm drinking I don't misbehave and make a fool of myself. Tell me more about the trip to England. I want every detail. When it all comes out in one of my books I won't remember where the story originated. Just the story. Randall says it's all part of being a storyteller."

"Well, after Covent Garden we did a tour of all the famous spots in London. Trafalgar Square and the monument to Admiral Nelson. We even stood outside the gates of Buckingham Palace..."

By the time Jane walked into the bar with the photo album tucked under her arm, they had each eaten two thick toasted sandwiches and drunk most of the bottle of wine, the story of Sophie's time as a nineteen-year-old spinning in Tracey's mind.

"Jane! There you are. I want you to meet Sophie. I have a question for you. Did your father attend the London School of Economics when he was nineteen years old?"

"Yes. Why?"

"Can you show Sophie here a photo of your father when he was young? I have a feeling that you might never have been born had Sophie had her way."

"What are you talking about, Tracey?"

"Let's have a look. There we are. A young man with a dog."

"That's him. That's my Jim. I just don't believe it."

"Can somebody explain what's going on? Anyway, when you phoned I'd made all the appointments for Randall. He's going to be working hard on Monday. You've got to promote your writers, Tracey. If you don't constantly push out their name the public don't buy their books. People like to read the books written by celebrities. You'll be next. Despite the great sales of *Lust* and the upcoming movie, we'll have to constantly keep you in the public eye. There's much more to being a successful writer than just writing a book. Film stars spend most of their time pandering to the media. It's not called the fourth estate without reason. The newspaper and television have more power than the politicians. Media moguls last a lifetime. They're the few that that control the world. A few dictators stay around. Politicians are lucky if they stay around for ten years... Isn't that Rebecca with Randall? How is our Randall? Out of interest, where did you sleep last night, Tracey? I heard noise in the night. Never mind. None of my business. So, Sophie, why was I dragged out of the office?"

"You want a drink?"

"I'm in a bar, Tracey. A beer, Terry. How are you? My word, this bar does bring back memories. The good memories with Harvey. The rest not so good. Drink destroys us. What worries Manfred with Randall. But what can you do? The man's old enough to know what he's doing to himself."

"Did your father ever mention a trip to England by boat?"

"When he went to England to study, he went by boat."

"I was on that boat. Your father and I became close friends."

"How long did your friendship last?"

"Three weeks. Then I came back on another boat while your father stayed in England. We never made contact again. I wonder if he still remembers me?"

"Why don't you ask him? Dad worries me. He never goes out socially. Just goes to work in the morning and goes home alone in the evening. I've asked him to lunch to meet Tracey but he always makes excuses. Apart from his work he's a recluse. After my mother died twenty years ago he withdrew into himself. But that trip to England by boat I do remember him talking about."

"He didn't mention a girl?"

"Not in front of my mother. If my father so much as glanced at another woman he was in trouble. She had him right under her thumb... Now, there we are. A nice cold beer. Happy times, everyone. Who's paying?"

"I am. The drinks are on Tracey."

"Where does your father live?"

"Two blocks from here. Round the corner."

"Why don't you ask him to join us for a drink?"

"He doesn't drink."

"He did when he was nineteen."

"He's lived in the same apartment forever. How I found Harry B's with my Harvey."

"Tell him Sophie Roberts is waiting in the bar. Roberts is my maiden name."

"I can try. This is all quite weird. If you can break his solitary life you'll be doing me and Conny a big favour. Conny is my sister... Terry. Can I use your phone?"

"Here we go again."

"Thank you, Terry... Come on, Dad. Pick up the phone. It's just ringing."

"Maybe he's still at work."

"He leaves the office early on a Friday to avoid being asked to socialise with the staff... Dad! It's Jane. I have a lady by the name of Sophie Roberts in Harry B's. Says she met you on a boat when you first went to England. Please come and join us... You will? I don't believe it. We're at the far end of the bar... I don't damn well believe it. Says he'd love to come and have a drink with us. He sounded chirpy. You two must have sweet memories, Sophie. I'd love to ask you more but it's none of my business. My word, I haven't heard that tone in my father's voice since Mother died. Now I get it, Tracey. If Sophie here had married Dad I wouldn't have been born. Neither would Conny. The chance of life. Oh, my goodness. You two were lovers."

"Not exactly. At nineteen I think we were both virgins."

"I'm sorry. I didn't mean to be rude. If you can get Dad out of the doldrums it will make me real happy. Good old Tracey. What would we all do without our friends? Sorts me out with a job in the best literary agency in New York and now she's going to sort out my father. Tracey and I were neighbours in a rundown apartment block before Tracey published *Lust* and made all her money. She turned my life on its head. I was a drunk who worked in a smelly laundry washing other people's dirty clothes. Now I'm Manfred Leon's assistant and a screenplay writer. And it's all because of Tracey. You mind if I leave you two alone while you're waiting for my father? Randall's waving at me to come over. Got to look after one's clients. Thanks for the beer, Tracey. I owe you one. I'll believe it when I see it. Dad in Harry B's! See you later, alligator."

"In a while, crocodile."

Smiling inwardly, Tracey watched Jane join Randall, Rebecca and the good-looking Teddy at the other end of the bar. There was nothing better in life than helping other people and finding out they appreciated what you had done. The old lady next to her was bubbling over with anticipation, watching the entrance to the bar. When an old man with a bald head walked into Harry B's he stood looking first at his daughter and then around the bar. Jane walked across to him and pointed to Sophie. Slowly, the old man walked towards Sophie.

"Is it really Sophie? After all these years. You have no idea how many times I have thought of you over the years. I so often say to myself, 'What happened to Sophie?' Is it really you? I'm afraid all my hair's gone."

"I'm going to leave you two alone to talk of old times. I'm Tracey. I just met Sophie in the lady's washroom. You may have heard of me. Your daughter and I share an apartment. She wrote the screenplay to my book. What a lovely coincidence for you and Sophie. They say in life there is nothing better than old friends. Enjoy your golden memories together."

"Are you married, Sophie?"

"I was. Twice. My last husband shot himself. Three kids. All off on their own."

"Why don't we find a nice quiet restaurant on our own?"

"I can't think of anything I'd rather do."

"Your voice hasn't changed. That same sweet tone."

Wondering if the pair of them were going to burst into tears, Tracey walked away down the bar to join Jane and the rest of them.

"How's it going, Tracey?"

"He's invited her to dinner."

"Lovely. The luck of life. And all this time they'd been living in the same area, neither of them knowing it. Did they recognise each other?"

"No. Must be over forty years... Friday night. The bar's getting really crowded."

"Rebecca and I are going out to dinner. You want to join us, Tracey?"

"I don't think so, Randall. I'm going to spend my evening in Harry B's. Been quite a day, one way and the other. Life on the roll."

When the old man named Jim and the old woman named Sophie passed them by, the father giving his daughter a kiss on the cheek, Tracey wondered if their lives would have been any different: would he have been under Sophie's thumb? Would he have shot himself? Was there ever in life a 'happy ever after'? Judging from Randall and Jane and many more of her friends, Tracey doubted it. People were people. Did being with that different person make them better people? Would Sophie's kids with Jim have loved her any more than the kids she had had? The cynic in Tracey doubted it. Love, eternal love, was only in the imagination. The constant hope for something better than reality. That hope for heaven on earth as difficult to attain as heaven itself. And was there really a heaven? Tracey liked to think so but she wasn't sure. At the door, Sophie turned and blew Tracey a kiss off the palm of her hand. For the moment, Sophie

Roberts was in heaven. Then the two old people went through the door to what Tracey hoped was an evening of happiness.

"You want another drink, Tracey?"

"Why don't we buy ourselves a bottle of wine and get drunk, Teddy? I feel like getting drunk."

"What then?"

"Let the gods decide."

From being surrounded by all her friends she was alone with Teddy, a man she had just met. It was now the two of them. Would Rebecca screw Randall to thank him for finding her a part in *Love Song*? And did she care? She wasn't sure. Having no idea what life was all about, she turned her attention back to the good-looking Teddy. Live life in the present, she told herself. Maybe one day when she had been through more of life's ups and downs she would write a book that let her characters find the true purpose of life. At least now she could still pull men. Or was it her fame and money?

"What the hell? Terry, old friend, give us another bottle of your lovely wine and two fresh glasses. It's Friday night."

"Coming up. Where have the others gone?"

"I have no idea. You'll have to ask them."

3

By the following Saturday when the three musketeers walked up the red carpet at the première of *Love Song*, Tracey holding Randall's left arm, Jane the right, everyone smiling in their dressed-up clothes, Tracey was back deep in her second book, the writing giving her purpose. With Jane at work and Randall in his room struggling to write *Shakespeare's Friend*, having temporarily given up writing the African saga he had started on the Isle of Man as an itinerant storyteller, the apartment quiet, the rumblings from outside not disturbing Tracey as she lived inside her new story, Tracey was back in her element. She had escaped into another world, a world which she controlled, or thought she controlled until her characters ran away with her story. The writing had made her happy.

Inside the theatre, as they sat together in the front row with all the actors and celebrities, the lights went down and the movie began. Gently, Tracey took Randall's left hand in her right hand; the palm of his hand was sweating. The music came up and Randall's story of love began, the story of hope, the hope that was in all of them. When it came to an end, Tracey was in tears, not sure, like in all of Randall's writing, whether she had seen a happy ending, the audience quiet before all the clapping. From the cinema the guests of Norman Landry and the press followed him to the reception in the hotel next to the theatre, a lavish affair where the director and the actors proceeded to ingratiate themselves with the critics who were there to write their reports for the following morning's Sunday papers.

"It worked beautifully, Randall. A lovely film."

"Do you think so, Tracey?"

"I know so. You gave them a good story. Welcome home."

"Is Manhattan my home?"

"It will be if you make it so. When are they going to soundproof your bedroom?"

"On Monday. Have you bought an apartment?"

"Not yet. Working on it."

"Are you moving out?"

"Who knows? I think the three of us together are rather comfortable. Enjoy your evening talking to the press. Here comes one of them. It's all about publicity, Randall. Publicity makes the money. Provided you have a good product. Wow. Just look at all these happy people."

"How do you know he's a reporter?"

"You can always tell someone looking for a story. It's that look in their eyes... Hello. I'm Tracey Chapelle. This is Randall Holiday."

"Hello, Mr Crookshank."

"How do you know my proper name?"

"We know all about you, Mr Crookshank. Part of our business. Why they call us investigative journalists."

"Did you like the film?"

"For myself? Not particularly."

"Will you give it a bad review?"

"Of course not. The public, the readers of our newspaper, love a sloppy love story. I'll be giving it a rave review. Let the readers read what they want to read is my motto. Sells newspapers. So, your wife left you. Shame. Second time I believe?"

"What else do you want to know about me?"

"You tell me, Randall."

"Are you by any chance a frustrated novelist, Mister...?"

"They call me Everard. Are you trying to be rude?"

"Of course not, Everard. What do you want to ask me? We can go and sit on those chairs in the corner. I love writing books, Everard. Or rather I did. At the moment I'm having problems. For the rest, you can stick it up your bottom."

"You don't like me, do you?"

"Not particularly. The word arrogant springs to mind. Too much power. The power of the media."

"But fame made you all your money."

"Not all of it. My maternal grandfather was Ben Crossley."

"That I did not know."

"And if you found some dirt you'd throw it at me to make a story."

"Why did you write *Love Song*?"

"I was bored. Living on my own in a Welsh valley in a cottage. Where I met Meredith. She heard of me in the local pub and came looking for me. A bit like you, Everard. If I wasn't well known you wouldn't have come anywhere near me."

"You don't like giving interviews?"

"Not after this week. I don't like trying to constantly say the right thing. To impress people. To ingratiate myself in exchange for good publicity. I've reached that stage in life where I would like to shoot myself. Trouble is, I don't have the guts. This morning, I received a demand from Meredith for half my fortune. She took my son, now she and her lover want to take my money. Love! What a joke. All they want is your money, Everard. Do you want all the gory details?"

"Lay it on, Mr Holiday. You've fully got my attention. Is she going to get her money?"

"Every penny. Money is worthless after you have enough to put a roof over your head and feed your stomach. And Jane, don't look at me like that. Jane works for my agent. The three of us share an apartment. Why don't you and Tracey go and have fun while I give Everard what he wants? He wants to write a story. Not just a film review. Now I've made him smile. Let's get a drink. My job is nearly over. What I need is a bottle of whisky to get myself out of my misery. How long do you want, Everard?"

"As long as it takes."

"Don't you ever feel bad inside yourself? Must be a horrible life digging up other people's filth. Does it ever prick your conscience? No. Of course not. You don't have a conscience. You don't care whose lives you destroy as long as it sells newspapers. You must be a horrible person, Everard. Do you even like yourself? Or is it just a job that makes you money?"

"You really are a miserable sod."

"At least I don't hate myself for ruining other people's lives. I wonder which is worse, being a mercenary paid to kill or an investigative newspaper reporter? But let's not argue. You have your job to do and I have mine."

"Why did you write your books if you weren't looking for fame and fortune? That's what everyone wants."

"I write to get out of myself and live in the life of my characters. Publishing was to share my happiness from writing them with other people. Not spend a week being interviewed by the media. Writers, hopefully good writers, are mostly recluses. They live on their own at their desks away from real people, making their own friends and enemies in that glorious world we call fiction."

"Meredith Harding was not fiction."

"You even know her maiden name."

"We know all about your life, Mr Crookshank. The son of one of those colonialists who exploited other people's land and their labour to turn themselves into smug, self-satisfied feudal barons. The last aristocrats. The last great landowners with all those servants to feed their egos. Part of that one per cent of the British people who controlled an empire that once covered a fifth of the world's surface and controlled a quarter of its poor exploited people. You talk about my conscience. Where is yours?"

"We created jobs and took them out of poverty."

"Did you? They didn't ask you to come. You people took their land so they then had to work for you."

"What kind of a story do you want to write about me, Everard?"

"The fall of the rich and famous. How a man like you with all this around you ends up down the toilet without a wife or a family. We're just two fellow writers who use other people to get what we want like everyone else. Don't bullshit about not wanting fame. Tracey over there went to bed with your agent over on the other side of the room to get him to read her book. You think I exploit people? Get real, Randall. It's all about getting a story. You should know that. And yes, I would like to write my own novels."

"So you're jealous."

"Envious, maybe. The life of a novelist is a lot easier than that of a newspaper reporter. Sit you down, Mr Crookshank. Tell me the gory details of your lovely wife's infidelities. Make her earn her money. What's the new man in her life's name?"

"Clint."

"Clint who?"

"That's for you to find out."

"He's younger than your wife. We have pictures. If we work nicely together, Mr Holiday, I can help you through your divorce. Most women dislike mud on their face. If you give me what I want tonight you can tell the charming lady I'll rip her private life apart."

"And my son's. I don't think so. This interview is over. Say what you like. I really don't know how you people live with yourselves."

"It's fun. You'll see it in my article. Go and get drunk, Mr Holiday. And please don't shoot yourself. I'm going to enjoy writing about the fall of Randall Holiday for a nice long time. You'll see. There's a man over there waving at you."

"That's my brother Phillip with his wife."

"The last of the colonialists."

"If you say so."

"But I do."

"Then shove it up your bottom."

"Oh, go and shoot yourself you self-righteous, arrogant bastard."

"Temper, Everard. Temper. Enjoy the party. And write what the hell you like. But one day, in a dark room when you are on your own with no one in the world giving a damn about you, the demons will arrive. The wolves will start howling in your head. You will start to go mad as what you have done to people's lives overwhelms you."

"What people do in their lives is their problem. I just write about it. I'm not the one who has done anything wrong."

"Have I done anything wrong?"

"You should ask your wives. Weren't you having an affair with the lovely Amelia, the barmaid in Harry B's?"

"No I was not."

"But you are sleeping with your roommates and you're still married. It's still adultery."

"She walked out."

"And you walked in to those two lovely girls who are still staring at you from across the room. The last colonial. Go and join your girlfriends, Mr Crookshank, while I enjoy the lavish splendour provided by the film director. Or are you going to join your brother?"

"Which newspaper do you write for?"

"I'm a freelancer. Pays better when you own the stories. You'll find my articles. Oh, and Mr Landry is also waving at you. The price of fame and fortune. Off you go. Nice talking to you. There's nothing more pleasant than a good argument. I just love getting under other people's skin. And with you, my colonial friend, I have only just started. The wolves are in your head, not mine or you would not have thought of them. I see through people. See what's in their jumbled minds. I'm going to really enjoy witing about you so the world can see who you were and who you are. They'll be lining up to buy my story... These snacks are so nice. And like the drink, they're free."

"Piss off."

"And there we go again. I'm going to enjoy every moment I spend ripping you apart... You bastard. How dare you punch me. It's called assault. When I've enjoyed the rest of my free evening I'm going to lay a charge against you. Just look at all these lovely witnesses staring at you. You've just doubled the price of my story. After the police have done their job my lawyers will sue you for breaking my nose. I'm bleeding like a stuck pig in front of all these gawping people."

"You're such a wimp, you don't have the guts to fight back. You have to run to the police. Go on, you pathetic little man. Go on. Take a punch... There we go. Now we can both lay charges at the police station."

From across the room, Tracey watched the altercation, expecting the fight to get worse. Instead, Randall walked away towards his brother smiling from person to person.

"What was that all about, Tracey? That's not good for business."

"Leave him alone. They're all looking at Randall with their mouths open. Manfred looks as though he's going to have kittens. And just look at Rebecca. It's given me the giggles. They're all about to have a fit: Poppy, the screenplay writer, Norman, the director, to say nothing of Nora, Randall's publicist. Poor Randall. He really is in a state. Now I know why you never got married, Jane."

"I would have been happy with Harvey."

"How's your father getting on with Sophie? Have they seen each other again? Never mind. It's their business. When you were broke and working in the laundry, why didn't your father help you financially?"

"He said I'd got myself into the mess and it was my job to get myself out of it. He'd paid for my college education and now it was my turn... Why don't we get out of here? I'm sick of people tonight. The movie is over in more ways than one. The one thing I never expected tonight was a fist fight."

"I'm going to buy that apartment on the fifteenth floor."

"I thought you would. And it's time for me to make my own home. I have the feeling that tonight was the last night of the three musketeers. Time to move on. You can't feel sorry for people. It never helps. What they do with their lives is their own business. You've tried with Randall and it didn't work."

"I want to get pregnant."

"That is something. Who do you have in mind?"

"No one in particular. I want to be a single mum without the hassle of men. Did you see that just now? At his own film première! Punches a reporter. Men! I give up, Jane. Let's get out of here."

"Where do you want to go?"

"We'll find a nice bar where we don't know anyone and see what happens."

"Now you're talking... That looks better. They've surrounded Randall and Phillip. They're all laughing. And Manfred, the always organised Manfred, is talking to that reporter and calming him down. Now just look at that. All's well that ends well. It's so nice to have a real friend, Tracey. For the first time in years my father is happy. What a world. And how was the good-looking Teddy?"

"Nice. Very nice. The perfect one-night stand."

"You're a slut, Tracey Chapelle."

"I told you, I want to get myself pregnant. The only purpose in life is having children. The birds and the bees do just the same thing. They work hard to make their nests to breed. I want to breed. Don't you want to breed, Jane? You don't have to marry. In the old days when only the men made the money, a girl had to find a husband to look after her offspring. Now we make as much money as the men. All we need is brain power, not physical strength. You don't have to wield a heavy sword to kill someone. All a girl has to do is pull the trigger. We're even with men, Jane. We don't have to live under their command, cooking the food and doing the housework. So why bother with a husband? I don't want to spend the rest of my life with a Randall. I screwed him and you know what he did? He fell asleep on the job. His mind is in turmoil. All that fame and fortune and still his wives walked out on him. Tells you something. And sadly, most men are the same. Marriage is for poor girls who can't provide for themselves. Who use their bodies to give themselves financial security. My second book is analysing the purpose of lust. How lust makes the world go round and continue into the future, a future we will never know after our three score years and ten. Sex and procreation are the only part of life that has any importance as they ensure the survival of the species."

"And when our planet explodes or becomes unliveable?"

"They are talking already of going to the planets... Are we going to get a taxi? Taxi drivers know the best bars... Did God make us or did our ancestors come from another planet? No one really knows. Fornicate and breed. What my characters tell my readers... I'm glad to be out of that place. We fulfilled our commitment to Randall. Looked after his apartment while he was on his travels. And walked him up the red carpet."

"Randall has children. Hasn't helped him."

"As a single mum, I'll keep my children. No one to walk off with them. Got it, Jane?"

"And love?"

"You put it nicely in your book. So people believe. Give the fools hope of love and a perfect life. Yes, we all want to be loved. The same way we want there to be a God. To look after us. To protect us. Sadly, life doesn't work that way."

"Are you saying that God does not exist?"

"I didn't say that as I don't know. I just hope with all my heart that God exists. The same way you hope love exists. In real life, most of us find love is fiction, or at the best temporary. We only find out the truth about God when we're dead... Here we are, Jane. Get in. I'm on the hunt again... Punched a newspaper reporter. Can't get over it. Now I'm giggling again. Pity we weren't a bit closer to hear what they were arguing about... We're looking for a nice bar, Mr Cabdriver. Can you take us to one?... There you are, Jane. Always leave it to the experts. Poor Randall. I wonder what he's going to do with the rest of his life? Can't go back to Africa by the sound of it. Doesn't want to live alone on Rabbit Farm. And now he's going to have the apartment to himself. Life. What a life."

"He'll come through. I came through. Now my father's found a little happiness. We all came through in the end."

"I hope so."

PART 6

DECEMBER 1996 – HOPE

1

Nine months to the day, on the twenty-fourth of December, the day before Christmas, Tracey Chapelle gave birth to a daughter. After leaving the nursing home with the picture of Tracey still in her mind cuddling her newborn baby, regret and jealousy playing sadly with her own emotions, Jane Slater went up to the apartment on the thirty-first floor, having been told by Manfred Leon to check on Randall and wish him a happy Christmas from everyone at his literary agency. The man was a recluse, rarely seen, despite Jane and Tracey living on the fifteenth floor of the same apartment block, in what Tracey called her investment for the future, a home for a single mother to bring up her children with the help of a live-in nanny. The doorbell rang and rang before Randall finally opened the door, a tired, weary look on his sad face.

"Sorry, Jane. Can barely hear the bell in my writing room. I was far away in the last century, hunting elephant for their ivory. Lawrence Templeton-Smythe lives an isolated life in the middle of the African bush. He's my only escape. Where I go to get away from myself."

"Can I come in?"

"Of course you can. Haven't seen you for ages. Haven't seen anyone for ages as a matter of fact. Locked myself away from the human race. Tried it in Africa. Tried it at Rabbit Farm. Sort of works here since I soundproofed the apartment. Cost me a fortune. Who cares when you have money?"

"Happy Christmas."

"Is it Christmas?"

"Will be tomorrow."

"I had no idea. And how's my old friend Tracey?"

"She's just had a baby girl."

"Is she married?"

"No. She just wanted a baby... What are you doing?"

"Counting on my fingers. Do you know it's exactly nine months since that disastrous evening at the post-première party for *Love Song*?... Woops. Who's the father? Never mind. It's tea or nothing. Don't drink living on my own. Nine months and a week. Makes you think. What a world. Give Tracey my best. Did she give birth downstairs?"

"No. In a private hospital."

"A little girl. Good for Tracey. With her second book making a fortune she won't have to worry about money. Sorry I didn't come to the film première of *Lust*. But you know recluses. At least I'm divorced. I'll put the kettle on."

"Don't you ever get out?"

"Not really. What for? The only place I like to visit is Africa a hundred years ago. Am I mad, Jane? Probably. You don't have to answer. How's my friend Manfred?"

"Everyone at Leon and White wishes you a merry Christmas and a happy New Year."

"Let's just hope the next one will be better than this one. Once Meredith and Clint got their hands on my money they went to live in England. Bought a fancy house in the country, I'm told. He married her after our divorce. Nicely married in community of property, painting his pictures and living the life of Riley on my money. Who the hell was Riley? How are you, Jane? Sit yourself down. How are the sales of my books going? Not that I really care. Alone, I spend very little money... Nine months and a week. Makes me think. We had one drunken night together when we made love. Fell asleep on the job. Poor Tracey. Does she want to know who the father is? Okay. Your expression is enough. She always was a bit wild. Probably doesn't have a clue who the father is."

"Do you want to know?"

"Not really. Sometimes things like that are better left alone. Just give her my love. Maybe one day I'll see her daughter. There we go. The kettle's boiled. Christmas tomorrow. I don't believe it. Two sons. Without Christmas presents. Not even a Christmas card from their mothers. Not that they care. They want to keep me as far away as possible from their children since neither of them need my money... So, what can you tell an old recluse? I turned thirty-nine this month. My own life is mostly over. Just the books. Lucky I write. Help yourself to milk and sugar. How's your father? What happened to him and that woman he first met when he was nineteen?"

"They're living together."

"And they're happy? That's nice. When it comes to women I'm a complete failure. Lucky man so late in his life. How's your book going? How's the job? How is everyone? Not that people care. So, Tracey is now a mother. Good luck to her. Have you got a lover? Sorry, not a question a man should ask. What's life all about, Jane?"

"Why don't you go and visit Tracey in the hospital?"

"Don't be ridiculous. What does she want to see me for? How's the new apartment? You do share it with Tracey? I don't keep track anymore. Just write, cook my food and sleep in my bed. No social life whatsoever. But what's the point in getting drunk and talking a load of bullshit to impress people? Am I boring you, Jane? You have that look on your face. Not quite sure what it means."

"You must get out and meet people again. You can't cut yourself off forever."

"Why not?"

"Don't you even see your brother?"

"Phillip has given up on me. Tried his best after Meredith buggered off. But he has his own life to live. Why would he want a miserable old fart like me upsetting his family? How's the tea?"

"It's fine. It's you I'm worried about."

"Why would you be? Tell Manfred the new book is coming along fine. Probably why he sent you to check on his author. I live in the mind of Lawrence Templeton-Smythe in a world far from the horrors of city life, in a time when men behaved like gentlemen and ladies stayed married to their husbands, when illegitimate children were taboo. Not that I'm criticising Tracey. She's probably got it right. Have her own kid without anyone interfering. Am I chasing you away? Finish your tea."

"When did you last shave?"

"Nine months ago to the day if I think about it. Not since I punched that reporter. Thanks, I expect, to Manfred, never heard from him again. Nothing by him about me in the papers. I cut my hair with a pair of scissors in front of the mirror. Hate looking at myself. Well anyway, at least I'm no longer upsetting people. You know, I don't even have a country anymore. No family. No country. Just poor old me. But I survive. I have a bath every day so at least I don't smell. Now you're smiling. I needed time alone to write and think. Who knows, Jane? Maybe one day I'll come out of my rabbit hole. So, tomorrow is Christmas Day. I always loved Christmas Day as a child on the farm in Rhodesia. Family time. How the world changes."

"Is there anything I can do for you, Randall?"

"Not really. I'll send you the manuscript when it's finished."

"I'm going to make you supper. At least I know my way around your kitchen. You said you don't drink on your own. You won't be on your own so I'll go down to my apartment and bring us up a nice bottle or two of wine. Be just like the old days. You can let it all out. We'll drink to Tracey and her newborn baby. Have some fun. We're pretty much the same age so we can talk about our past if you don't think there's a future. Play some nice classical music. I told Tracey we should never have left you alone for so long. A nice little dinner party for two. Go and trim your beard in the mirror while I go downstairs."

"You don't have to do this."

"I want to. We're old friends. You used to say there was nothing better in life than the company of old friends. You can talk about Africa. Those old colonial days, whatever they were. Leave the front door on the latch in case you can't hear the bell. Behind those dark, morbid eyes I see the trace of a sparkle. Don't go away, Randall. Back in ten minutes."

"You do not have to do this."

"Oh yes, I do. For both of us. Tracey having a baby has made me jealous and feeling lonely. I hate feeling lonely."

"I thought you'd given up your days of drinking?"

"Not tonight. Tonight, you and I are going to have some fun."

"We're both a couple of alcoholics."

"Who cares?"

Not really sure what she was doing, Jane went down in the lift to Tracey's apartment on the fifteenth floor. The baby was going to be the centre of Tracey's life, more important than her friend. Instead of hurrying, she had a bath and changed her clothes. Despite her thirty-eight years she still had pride in her looks, the looks that still attracted men.

Half an hour after leaving Randall to himself, she touched up her make-up and checked herself in the mirror, the new dress she had bought the week before showing off her breasts. With a basket full of food and three bottles of white wine, Jane went back up in the lift to Randall's apartment. To her surprise, the door opened immediately after she rang the bell. Like herself, Randall had changed his clothes. In the background, she could hear the classical music. In the lounge, on the low table, were two waiting glasses. For ten minutes, Jane prepared the food, putting the chicken in the oven with the potatoes, the greens nicely washed in a colander, the vegetables ready for the pot. Back in the lounge, where Randall was sitting comfortably with a smile on his face, the cork had been removed from one of the wine bottles, the other two still in the fridge. Randall poured wine into the two glasses.

"Cheers, Jane. My first company in nine months. How long is Tracey staying in the nursing home?"

"She'll be home tomorrow."

"Just the two of us."

"Just the two of us, Randall. Is it Mozart?"

"Yes. He makes me feel happy. What would I do on my own without Wolfgang Amadeus Mozart? He did so much for the world. One life affecting so many people. So it's roast chicken tonight? Never roast chicken on my own. Too much food for one. Hate throwing away good food. Saw too many impoverished people in Africa. Not on World's View. Dad looked after the labour force. Wonder what the poor sods are doing now without jobs? According to my father, one of Mugabe's cronies has taken over the farm and stopped growing tobacco. Stopped growing anything. A few cattle. Lives in the big house when he isn't in Harare helping Robert Mugabe run the country down the drain. Oh well, it's all about politics. Getting power. Holding on to power by looking after those who put you into power. They all say they care about the people but I often wonder. Democracy is all about getting elected by making promises. Why most governments wherever they are in what they like to call true democracies only last one term. These days politicians know how to bullshit the public but they don't know how to run a country... You look nice, Jane. You changed your clothes. I love your perfume. Do you want me to help with your book? How far have you got or is it finished? I can read what you have done and give you some tips. Like everything, writing is about technique. Keeping the story flowing."

"I'm stuck towards the end."

"Ah, that makes sense. The most difficult parts of a good book are the beginning and the end. Why this time there is not going to be an ending to my story. Just book after book right through the twentieth century. And here I go again talking about myself."

"How's the wine?"

"Delicious. Good to see you, Jane. Next time you visit, bring me your manuscript. Did the movie of *Lust* make lots of money? You wrote the screenplay."

"Lucky for me and Tracey, the film is still capturing an audience."

"Did it beat *Love Song*?"

"I'm afraid it did."

"Wow. And *Love Song* made a fortune."

"Are you bitter about Africa? You always sound as if you hate Mugabe."

"He did what he did. We did what we did. Morally, not much different. The only real difference is that we colonials were efficient at running a country. We know how to manage the economy for the betterment of everyone. When Mugabe took over they just didn't have the training or experience to run a modern economy. Maybe one day they'll come through the gap. Learn by their mistakes. Who knows? Life is all about hope. A few hours and it will be Christmas. I miss those big Christmas trees on the farm. All the twinkling fairy lights. All the glittering tinsel and little coloured decorations. The piles of presents under the tree waiting to be opened on Christmas morning. Are you spending Christmas with your father?"

"They're coming to lunch."

"Christmas is family time."

"Are you spending it with Phillip?"

"No. I'm a recluse. Or I was until you kindly went into my kitchen and started to cook my supper."

"Do you ever clean the place?"

"Not really. Haven't cleaned the windows since you and Tracey left. Keep the bath clean. That's about it."

"Why don't you bring someone in to do the cleaning?"

"I hate people, especially people under my feet. Anyway, why bother? I'm the only one who sees the dirt. Not that I look."

"Do you hate everyone?"

"Just a way of putting it. Let's just say I prefer not to have the interruption of other people."

"I hope I'm not interrupting."

"We're old friends. I'm the problem. I hate myself, Jane. Everything I ever did or wanted has turned to dust."

"Does the vacuum cleaner still work?"

"I have no idea."

"You're impossible, Randall."

"Just an old fool who's run away from being hurt... This wine is going down very nicely."

"I'm going to get you out of your depression."

"Thank you, Jane. Can I fill up your glass?"

"If we run out there's more downstairs."

"That's comforting. Brings back old memories. You're smiling, Jane."

"I too have flashes of those drunken memories... Does Lawrence Templeton-Smythe have a wife?"

"He has nothing. We're the same person."

"I'd better check the chicken."

"You only put it in the oven five minutes ago. I'm sorry. I've become a bore. I bore myself. Hours and hours of being alone and thinking. Wondering what went wrong. Always blaming myself, my only consolation in my morbidity is the pleasure I have given to so many readers. When I read your manuscript, Jane, it will take me into the world of your characters and let me out of my miserable world locked up here in a concrete skyscraper. Why did man build cities, Jane? Why didn't we all stay in the country? My father said he came to Africa so he wouldn't have to work and live in a city... What are you going to do with the rest of your life? Is working for a literary agent satisfying? Do you and Tracey have fun? She'll change now she has a baby. She'll have to be more responsible. The life of a single mother. Doesn't make sense. I always thought the purpose of life was to bring up a family. Kids need both their parents. Or so I thought... Have some wine. Are we doing the right thing now by drinking? Does drink, or having a baby on your own, solve anything?"

"I want to keep you company. People drink together to keep each other company... Are you going to make a pass at me?"

"Should I? I made a mistake with Tracey and who knows what came out of it? What's she going to call the baby?"

"You've given me the look a few times."

"Do you think so?"

"Oh, yes. A girl knows when a man is looking at her sexually when she gets the rush."

"What's the rush, Jane?"

"Now your eyes really are twinkling. The rush is usually in the lower part of the body, if you get my meaning."

"You mean you get horny?"

"Men get horny, girls have the rush. A friend at school called it the rush when a man looked at her and her feelings reciprocated sexually."

"Naughty girl. How old was she?"

"Fifteen."

"Some start young."

"So they say... I like this wine. Not too dry."

"Was it expensive?"

"Of course. Everything worth having is expensive... Are you hungry?"

"Not at the moment. The wine is beginning to take hold... Would you like to have children?"

"Every woman wants to have children. And no, Tracey hasn't decided what name to give her baby."

"*Love in the Spring of Life* is such a beautiful title. Do we only fall in love when we're young? Do young people stay in love? Is love real? I'm looking forward to reading your thoughts. Your manuscript will give me a true insight into Jane Slater. Writers open themselves up when they silently sit at their desks. They tell the truth. Or the truth as they see it. Do older people ever fall in love the same way as teenagers?"

"It would be nice to do it again."

"And have the same consequence?"

"You never know, Randall. Maybe older love will last. I can smell my chicken. I'm going to baste it. A good roast chicken needs lots of basting. Don't go away."

"I'm not going anywhere."

In the kitchen, Jane took the chicken out of the oven and smiled: the bird had barely started cooking. Ever since she read Randall's *Masters of Vanity* she had wanted to find the man behind the book, a man who craved through his main character for more than wealth and triviality. Basting the bird with the oil from the bottom of the pan, she was frightened at having asked him if he was going to make a pass at her, for the first time bringing sex into their conversation. Was she trying to get off with Randall? She wasn't sure. Would he see into her mind if he read her almost finished book? In older people like herself and Randall, it was more important to love each other's minds than love each other's bodies. The draw of sex between two people faded with familiarity but the love of the minds grew and grew in those wonderful years of companionship. Sadly, in the beginning, it was sex that brought a man and woman together. A girl had to seduce a man to get his attention. Was there chance for two old leftovers? Randall had said many times that his problem was having done everything too early in his life, leaving him nothing to achieve, nothing to look forward to, no quests left in his future. In her drinking heyday, there had been so many sexual partners she could no longer count them, let alone remember their names. The trick now, if there was a trick, was not to make a mistake by using sex as her means of getting to know the Randall she had seen by reading his books.

"What are you doing, Jane?"

"Thinking."

"What about?"

"*Masters of Vanity*"

"What brought that up?"

"Your saying you'd see into me if you read my book. There was much more to that book of yours than rich men getting richer and showing off their vainglory."

"Drink your wine. How does our chicken look? Let's both get drunk for a change and forget the world. I've stopped trying to think what it's all about except when I'm inside Lawrence Templeton-Smythe's head. Wine, Mozart and an old friend. An evening of pleasure I'd almost forgotten. The best part of soundproofing my apartment was keeping the noise of people at bay. So it's you, me and Mozart, a bottle or two of wine, and a nice roast chicken."

"You think three bottles will be enough?"

"Probably not for two professionals. Always be prepared, Jane."

"Hold your horses. I'm going down for some more wine before I begin to get nice and tipsy."

"Don't be long this time."

"Can I give you a kiss on the cheek?"

"Of course. Just a peck... There we go. Do you know, Jane, that's the first time we've so much as touched each other. In my culture as the last of the colonials, a man never shakes hands with a woman. We just smile at them."

Downstairs, Jane went straight to her desk and took out the manuscript, every chapter reread and corrected, making the reading more difficult. Whether Randall would be taken with the flow of her story or stumble over the cross-outs and inserts she was about to find out. Going down for more wine had been the excuse to show Randall her book, and hopefully, give him an insight into a Jane Slater that he would find more interesting. Time was running out if she was to find herself a lasting companion. She could still feel the fur of his beard on her mouth: so much for kissing a man's cheek.

"That was quick. You left the door open I suppose. What's that?"

"My book."

"Put the book on the table. Tonight is our drinking night."

"It's written in my handwriting."

"All good books are written by hand. We can't get into the minds and lives of our characters if we are interrupted by the clack of a typewriter or the sight of four moving fingers on the keyboard of a computer. We have to disappear completely into our story and not be conscious of our physical surroundings. When I need a break in my own book I'll read your story... So, Tracey is now a mother. Had she been sleeping with other men?"

"Lots of them. She didn't want to know who the father was."

"That's interesting. So the pregnancy for Tracey was deliberate. You know that old saying: 'We all know who our mother is but never so sure about our father.' Us poor men. And I thought it was men who took advantage."

"She wanted the child to be hers and nobody else's. She learned from the problems of other people... You've opened the second bottle of wine."

"Of course I have... Dear old Tracey. What a world. What's happened to us, Jane? I always hoped my life would find an even keel so I could live in peace with my own family. Does anyone in this world ever find peace and harmony? Or is it all squabbling? Arguing. Nagging each other. Fighting with each other. Families fighting. Nations fighting. A world of constant turmoil. Never mind. Tonight's a fun night. A gentle escape for both of us. We've both been through the mill. What's the point of having children if you never see them? All you are is one small link in the chain that makes up the future generations. Are we any different to the animals? To Lawrence's elephants, the ones he loves so desperately but still shoots to make his living? Is elephant hunting any different to farming chickens? That chicken in the oven had a life as much as Lawrence's elephants. Never mind. I'm rambling. It's the wine. Let's try and enjoy ourselves instead of worrying."

"Do people love chickens?"

"They do if the chickens make them money."

"No one eats cats and dogs. There has to be something in the love of animals. I think it's terrible to shoot a beautiful elephant just to cut off its tusk for the ivory. At least we eat the chicken and not cut off its beak and throw away the carcase."

"It was a long time ago. In those days when there was no chance of a species going extinct, we thought of the wild animals differently. Once upon a time, all our ancestors were hunters and gatherers. A man has to eat one way or the other, by killing his own meat or making money to buy his food in a shop. Today, we get on our high horses without realising how we got here."

"They want us to stay here by not obliterating the planet."

"Nature takes its course. Always has done. People keep their names in the media by championing good causes. Just another way of making a living. Fame makes them money."

"They're not all hypocrites."

"I hope not. For myself, I like to stay out of the lot of it."

"Why don't you champion the chicken?"

"And never eat a nice roast chicken? You're giggling, Jane. You see, we all think we have the answers. Trouble is, none of us do. There was a time when democracy was the panacea for man's problems. And now look at it. A crowd of useless politicians, all of them arse-creeping to get themselves elected to receive a nice salary and all the perks and fame of office. Kings or queens who knew what they were doing, and ran the country properly, were a lot better than the current lot constantly teetering the economy on the precipice above the hole of destruction, as they buy their popularity by siding with rich people who fund their political parties. Rarely are they elected because they know how to do the job properly. Then the world economy collapses as it did in the thirties and the world goes to war. The communists in their quest to stay in power killed the Tsar and his whole family. And now even the communists call themselves a democracy. How did we get here, Jane?"

"It started with hunting elephants I suppose... What's your classical music channel playing this time?"

"I have no idea except it isn't Mozart. Cheers, Jane. Down the hatch. Tonight we're going down the hatch. Two old drunks. Do you mind being called a drunk?"

"You are what you are. But what the hell? The world goes on. Tracey has started yet another generation. Hopefully, both your sons are happy tonight. We all have to live in the present, whatever happens. Maybe one day you'll get back together with your boys. Especially when they want something."

"You mean money?"

"Not necessarily. We all like to know where we come from. At least they know you are their father. Tracey's daughter will likely never know her real father."

"Are you going to write another book when you've finished that one over there on the table?"

"I hope so if I can think of a story. A good story."

"Instead of young love, you could write one about two people in the middle of their lives looking for companionship and comfort... That chicken's beginning to smell good. Hopefully, when we've eaten, we won't want to go on drinking. I do so hate hangovers."

"Let's just see. Tomorrow is Christmas."

"Christmas with your father. That's nice."

"What are you going to do for your Christmas, Randall?"

"Probably drink what's left of the wine in the fridge and commiserate with myself."

"You could join us. Tracey should be back. You can see the baby."

"What are you up to, Jane?"

"I'm trying to make you happy."

"Then buy me a gun."

"What for?"

"So I can shoot myself."

Staring across the room at her book waiting for Randall on the table, Jane was not sure what to say. Was it the alcohol that made him talk of committing suicide or was it his empty life? So much in life seemed pointless once it was over, the high for Jane from writing a successful film script long gone. Would the success of *Love in the Spring of Life* be an equal anti-climax? Randall said the worst thing in life was finding success too early which left a person with nothing to do. Had they both reached that crossroads where life in the future was pointless? Instead of talking happily, they sat and drank in silence. Shaking her head, Jane got up and went into the kitchen and put on the vegetables.

"Are you hungry, Randall?"

"Not really. Bring another bottle of wine with you."

"We're drinking too fast."

"Probably. Does it matter? Nothing matters to me anymore... There we go. Give me the bottle and I'll pull out the cork."

"The food will be ready in twenty minutes. Smile, Randall. We're meant to be having fun."

"I love the sound of a cork popping out of a bottle. Stop staring at your book. I'll read it, Jane, I promise."

"The book will make you feel better. Everyone in the book is happy."

Holding the cutlery she had taken from the drawer in the kitchen, Jane walked up the three small steps in the big living room to the dining room area where she laid the table, moving her book away from where they were going to eat.

"You touched your manuscript with the palm of your hand. That's a good sign, Jane. Shows you like what you wrote. Bring it down. Let me read the first page."

"Let's have our supper. We've both had too much wine to be serious. But thank you. Even the idea of you reading my book makes me nervous. I never know if my writing is any good until someone else reads it. Please tell me the truth. So many people tell you what you want to hear."

"Only the public tell you the truth."

"You mean the more you sell the better the book?"

"Something like that. You need a story that appeals to a large audience. Like the story of young love that stays with us in our mind forever."

"Did you love your wives?"

"I hoped so. Men are fools. We only find out the truth when it all goes wrong. Only then do we find out what they were after. Mostly, it's quite simple. The young girl is looking for the good life: a successful or potentially successful man. They want the best they can catch. The provider. It's not love. When we say we love each other what we are really saying is we love what we can get from each other."

"There has to be more to life."

"You tell me. What happened to Harvey? He went for the money. Whether any of us end up in a good life is questionable."

"Are you going to stay a recluse for the rest of your life?"

"I will unless someone like you can convince me otherwise. But what do you want, Jane? What do you want from life? Want from me? You're going to hope I praise your book, of that I'm certain. Could we ever be passionate lovers? Who knows? Come back and sit down. Drink your wine. The longer I live and go through this crazy life, the less I understand of it. But let's you and I be careful. Stumbling into bed drunk won't help either of us."

WHEN THE FOOD was eaten an hour later they had drunk three bottles of wine. Randall stumbled down the steps into the lounge area and ran falling headfirst onto the sofa, giving both of them the giggles.

"Do you want to go on drinking? You nearly broke your neck."

"No such luck, Jane. That chicken was good. Nothing better than a girl who can cook. Let's carry on drinking. If we drink a bottle or two more we won't remember what we've done."

"Are you trying to get me drunk, you naughty man?"

"We're trying to get each other drunk, Jane. We're both trying to run away. We've both been through the mill so there's no point in kidding ourselves. We're having a good time. That's what matters. I hate those steps. Drunk, I trip up them as easily as down. Who's going to get the wine? Okay, it's my turn."

"Don't fall over."

"I won't when I'm carrying the wine bottle. Just look at the clock. It's almost Christmas. I'll get two bottles so we can drink right through to Christmas."

"It doesn't seem possible two people can drink so much wine."

"We're professionals. I can drink all night."

"Tell me more about your early life in Rhodesia."

"First the wine, Jane. First the wine."

The story of colonial Africa fascinated Jane, a life that seemed almost impossible to imagine let alone live. All that land and open space. A culture of gentlemen behaving like gentlemen. Clubs where they met and played tennis or a game of cricket, everything so frightfully British, the black manservant on the fringe of the white man's perfect style of living, aristocrats on their six-thousand-acre estates they called their tobacco farms that in the end proved to be the paradise of fools. Was she envious of Randall's early life or did she think it wrong? Were Randall's family exploiting the land and the indigenous people or were they the start of bringing the people of Africa into the modern economy and hopefully doing them a favour?

"Yes, we lived like feudal barons, Jane. Probably wrong. But never miss an opportunity is what they said. The people at home needed tobacco to smoke themselves to death so the few of us went out from our suburban homes and grew the weed that satisfied those millions of smokers. Now here I am in America, rich as a man can be, and I'm stuck halfway up a skyscraper living as a hermit with bugger all to do with myself except drink the poison of alcohol... Wait. There it goes. Listen to the chimes on the TV... It's Christmas! Happy Christmas, Jane. If I could, I'd get up from this sofa and give you a kiss but I'm afraid to fall over. I'm legless, Jane. How are you?"

"You had a wonderful life, growing up in Rhodesia. I'm envious. And I'm as drunk as you."

"Better not try going down in the lift. We'll finish the wine and crawl to bed. You can stay in your old bedroom. The bed's made up. Am I slurring my words?"

"It sounds like you have a mouthful of words struggling to get out. Am I slurring?"

"You're lovely. Pass your glass... A bit further. There you go. Cheers, Jane. Happy Christmas... What time's your father coming round tomorrow? You don't want to not be there... I don't believe it. Mozart. Just listen to that, Janey the Slater. Mozart. His music is always so damn cheerful. He must have been happy all of his life."

"Is your new book cheerful?"

"Bits of it... What you doing, Janey?"

"Coming over for a kiss... There we go."

"Don't fall on top of me!"

"Happy Christmas, my future lover."

"Oh, Janey. We're far too drunk. Back you go. One last bottle then it's off across the carpet on our hands and knees to our beds. Done it before. Opening doors is a bugger. Everything's a bugger when you're drunk... And out popped the cork. Christmas in New York. Now, Janey, tell me about your early life. I'm sick of talking about myself. And if I go to sleep on the sofa don't worry. Lovely to see you, Janey. Really lovely to see you. Now that's what they call slurring. I can barely make out what I'm trying to say."

2

An hour later, alone in her old bedroom, Jane couldn't think straight, her mind saturated by alcohol. Instead of going to Randall's bedroom and doing a Tracey, she began to cry, her tears wetting the soft cover of the pillowcase. She had squandered her life. Thrown it away. What would be the point of another seduction, a brief affair that would end in nothing? Were there ever happy, lasting relationships? Were couples better off than singles? Apart from making a living to have money and getting drunk, what was there ahead of her? Jane began to sob. In a room so carefully soundproofed, she could hear nothing except the sound of her own pain. The agony of a 'past-it', a soiled discard, a girl with nothing to live for, each new day as pointless as the last. Like Randall, Jane began to think of suicide, the final way out from her life. The book ended in happiness for her and Harvey, just the memory of true love enough for both of them, the reality of their subsequent lives a different story. Crying, sobbing, unable to sleep in her alcoholic misery, Jane tossed and turned in the dark of the night. Would Randall say the book's happy ending was wishful thinking and tell her the book was no good? Did it matter? Or would she want to kill herself? And thinking of Randall as the horrible night went on made her realise their lives were no different, that both of them were just two lonely spent people.

In the morning, waking from her nightmares, Jane lay quietly under the covers, looking back on their drunken evening, telling herself sadly it would have been better to have left him alone and not to have hoped something would come out of their muddled relationship. When she heard the tap on her door she sat up in bed, pulling the sheet up to cover her naked breasts.

"Good morning, Jane. A cup of tea. Very colonial British but that's how I am. Did you sleep well? It's Christmas Day. How much rubbish did I talk last night? You shall have your tea in peace and I will cook you breakfast. Don't forget you've got to prepare Christmas lunch downstairs for your father. How's the hangover?"

"I cried all night."

"Poor Jane. Maybe instead of getting drunk next time, we should go somewhere. Do something together. My brother just phoned to wish me a happy Christmas but couldn't make me go to lunch... Milk and two sugars. I hope I got it right. Take your time with the tea. I'll be in the kitchen. Are we going to do anything, Janey?"

"What do you mean?"

"I mean with each other. I enjoyed last night. I enjoyed the company."

"Are you going to write today?"

"Don't be silly. Never write on a hangover."

"We're both a mess."

"You can say that again. But you never know. You never know. Even at the lowest point in my life, I still try to hope. That's what we must do. We must hope. If we don't hope we're really finished... I ate some of the cold chicken. Quite delicious. I've been reading your book. So far so good. You can certainly write a story. The book's made me feel cheerful. Bit like Mozart."

"Are you serious?"

"I'm not comparing you to Mozart. Not yet, anyway. I'm only into the third chapter. Enjoy your tea. Young love. That's what it's all about. And you were lucky the way your characters are lucky. They're nineteen-year-olds in love. In heaven. In perfect happiness. Never felt it myself. Or maybe just a little. Hope, Jane. Let's you and I hope. I'm going to spend Christmas Day reading your book."

After breakfast, leaving Randall on the sofa in the lounge reading her book, Jane quietly let herself out of the apartment, not wanting to interrupt his reading. Surprisingly, her hangover was not as bad as she had expected. When her father and Sophie arrived for Christmas lunch there was no sign of Tracey and the baby.

"Your hands have the shakes, Jane. What have you been up to? You're not back on the booze, I hope? Where's Tracey? Sophie's daughter phoned from Canada. So did Conny. She sends her sister her love and wishes you a merry Christmas. Another year has nearly gone. The years go by so fast when you are old. How's the job going? It's so wonderful you pulled yourself out of that horrible laundry."

"What can you tell me, Dad?"

"That we're happy together. I still miss your mother terribly even if she did boss us all around, but I look back now with a smile, appreciating what we all had together. Sophie has brought me back into the world. In the spring, we're going to do a boat trip on a cruise liner, all the way from America through all the islands of the West Indies and across the pond to England. We're going to do it all again to relive our beautiful memories... What's for lunch?"

"Roast turkey with all the trimmings. Just the three of us by the look of it. Tracey had a daughter yesterday. I'll phone the nursing home. Come and sit down, both of you. How are you, Sophie? What luck it was finding out in Harry B's that you knew my father when you were both nineteen. I've written a book about love in the spring of life. What I've called my book."

"Where is it? I now love reading love stories. Oh, Jane, that evening we met in the bar was the luckiest moment of my life. The kids have their own lives. I was so lonely. Now we're both happy. How does our cruise sound to you?... Where's your book?"

"It's upstairs with Randall Holiday. He's reading it right now. I cooked his supper last night. Now there's a lonely man. He won't have anything to do with anyone since his wife walked out on him."

"Were you two drinking?"

"Just a glass of wine or two, Dad. Poor Randall. He's a mess. Two wives walked out on him."

"Probably his own fault."

"Don't knock him, Dad. You haven't been through what he's going through now."

"I mourned your mother on my own for years."

"At least you had a life to look back on. Randall has nothing."

"Don't be ridiculous. He's one of the most successful modern writers. That last movie *Love Song* must have made him a fortune. All I ever get is a salary. Can't get rich on a salary."

"Money isn't everything."

"Isn't it? You weren't too happy in the laundry living in a run-down apartment. I envy the likes of Randall Holiday. Made all that money while he's still young. Now he's free to do what he likes. Is he coming to lunch?"

"No. Wants to be left alone."

"What's wrong with him?"

"He's suicidal, that's what's wrong with him... I can offer you a glass of wine."

"Are you going to drink?"

"As a matter of fact, I am. First, I'll ring the hospital after I've poured both of you a glass of wine. Happy Christmas. Any news from your son and your daughter, Sophie?"

"Not a word. Never hear from them."

"How sad."

"It's worse, I brought them up. Gave them all my love. And now they ignore their mother. Must be my fault, I suppose. Your kids are what you make them. I'd love a glass of wine. It's Christmas."

Leaving her father and Sophie in the lounge, Jane went to the kitchen to check the food and phone the hospital, a quizzical smile on her face. Were they lovers? They lived together. Did people have sex at sixty-three years old? Or was it a relationship of mutual convenience, companionship for both of them, cheap living for Sophie despite her father's legacy, and someone to cook and clean for her father without having to put up with a cleaner? Anyway, she told herself as she basted the turkey, it was a question she was certainly not going to ask her father. Should she phone her sister in Denver before or after Christmas lunch? Still thinking of Randall reading her book, she put the turkey back in the oven and phoned the hospital.

"Is everything all right?"

"Oh, yes. We just wish to keep an eye on both of them for a little longer. Your friend Tracey is very tired. Happy Christmas."

"Give her my love."

In the lounge, she picked up her glass of wine and raised it to the ceiling.

"Happy Christmas, everyone. Tracey's staying today in the nursing home. How long did you stay in the hospital, Sophie?"

"I had the girls at home. Rodney was more of a problem. Been a problem, my son, all his life. Can you imagine a son saying we were better off without him after his father committed suicide? His own father. I stayed a couple of nights in the hospital. Don't worry about Tracey. She'll come home when she's ready. This wine is very nice, Jane. How's the cooking? I owe all my happiness to you and Tracey. It's so amazing how life can so suddenly change. Isn't it Jim? Well, here we are. I have a family again. Don't forget I want to read your book."

"When we talked of Randall in the pub you said you hadn't read a book since leaving school."

"Everything's changed. Jim reads so I read. I'm sure your book will be lovely to read. This is the first Christmas in years that I'm really happy."

"How much is a cruise to England going to cost you, Dad?"

"Nothing. Sophie insists she uses the money from her father's estate to pay for the trip."

"Did he leave a lot of money? Sorry, Sophie. None of my business."

"Just over one million dollars."

"Wow. That's serious money."

"And what's the point in hoarding it for three kids, two of whom ignore their mother? And Alison is doing more than well. Both she and her husband. Those two will never be short of money."

"Did they have any children?"

"Alison couldn't have kids. No, we're going to have ourselves a good time bringing those wonderful memories alive again. We want to see all the spots we visited. Trafalgar Square. We want to stand outside Buckingham Palace again. It's going to be so much fun travelling first class."

Smiling to herself, Jane drank her wine. Randall had told her life was always about the money. Or were they both just cynical?

After lunch and lots of hugs, her father and Sophie went home. Jane picked up the phone and called her sister.

"Did you know she's got a million dollars stashed away from her father's inheritance? They're going on a cruise and Sophie's paying. Why are you giggling, Conny?"

"I wondered what it was all about. Most things in life are about money."

"You're as bad as Randall Holiday."

"Have you screwed him?"

"Not yet. Happy Christmas, sis. How's Denver?"

"Cold. Now tell me everything. I love our chats. They've all gone for a nap after the Christmas lunch. Cheers, my favourite sister."

"Are you drinking?"

"Of course I am. Aren't you?"

"I'm your only sister."

"Doesn't mean you aren't my favourite. To life, Jane. Let's drink to life. Come on. Tell me all the scandal. Are they really having an affair? Why would any woman want an affair with a bald-headed old man?"

"Don't be rude about poor Father."

"But it's true. He's as bald as a coot. A million bucks. That's serious money."

For ten minutes, they talked and drank together, Jane's friendship with her sister a joy that would last the rest of her life.

"And it all started when we shared a bedroom. You'd better go. I can hear one of the kids calling."

Alone again, Jane sat and looked at the empty bottle of wine, not knowing what to do with herself. Smiling as she rethought the conversation with her sister, she drifted off to sleep. When she woke, someone outside was banging on the front door of the apartment.

"Who the hell's that?... Coming... Well, hello, Randall. You're out of your foxhole. Why are you waving my manuscript about your head? Come in, you idiot."

"Have you got any more wine? We need to celebrate. Three minutes ago, I finished your book. It's wonderful, even without an ending. In the book, you should let the two of them marry and live happily ever after. The book's made me happy like Mozart. Where's the wine? We can have a two-day bender. Your father's gone by the look of it. Where's Tracey? Never mind. Give me a drink. I want to celebrate."

"Calm down. I drank the last of the wine. We'll have to drink whisky."

"What's wrong with whisky?"

"Was my handwriting easy to read?"

"The story was so good it didn't matter."

"How long did it take you to read?"

"About six hours... Lots of ice. The trick with a good whisky is to soak it in ice. Where's the fridge? I'll get the ice. You find the whisky. Oh, Jane. You can write. It's so wonderful. The story comes alive in all three dimensions. I can see the characters as if I were in the same room with them. You paint the perfect picture."

"Have you been drinking?"

"No. We drank all the wine last night. Pissed as fiddlers' farts. You know, these apartments are all the same. Good. Plenty of ice. Happy Christmas. And you don't have to work tomorrow do you?"

"Is it that good? I'm so happy."

"It must be good. It got me out of my foxhole. Of course it's good, Jane Slater. You can write."

"Will it sell?"

"Like hot cakes. Manfred will find you a publisher in ten minutes. Let me open the bottle. Put on the music channel. We've got a good book. We've got a whole bottle of whisky. All we need is Mozart. You're smiling, Jane."

"I've never felt happier in my life. I can write. The great and famous writer Randall Holiday tells me I can write."

"We're both painters. We paint our pictures with words so the reader can see not only the people but the scenery surrounding them. And we both get into our characters' heads. I so enjoy being in Lawrence Templeton-Smythe's head and living his life roaming the African bush, enjoying every birdsong, every sight of the wild animals. Being watched by a leopard is exhilarating as the fear pumps his mind and the wind blows in the trees and the doves call, the great grassland all around them free of people, just Lawrence and the leopard, Lawrence's finger on the trigger of his rifle in case the animal attacks. Happiness for both of them when the tension breaks and they go their separate ways. The picture you bring to my mind of you and Harvey laughing with each other as the love enfolds both of you is just as vivid. And your story runs on and on, drawing me along. I was no longer hungover and alone in my silent apartment, Jane. I was in the same room with you and Harvey, watching the both of you. You changed your name to Vanessa but you kept Harvey's name the same."

"My name didn't matter when I was writing. It was Harvey's name I wanted to keep. But if I make the ending happy, I'll be telling a fib."

"Don't upset your reader by telling the truth. Often in life, we don't want to be told the truth. It's one of the joys of writing fiction. You can make up life to have a happy ending. In those old days of writing, far back in history, the great writers ended their stories of people with the words 'and they lived happily ever after.' Cheers, my fellow author. You are going to give so many people so much pleasure and chase away all the horrible problems that surround our world: wars always somewhere on the television. Always attention-grabbing stories of rape and murder. Stock markets plummeting, and people losing their houses when they can't pay the mortgage. All those horrors of modern life. You'll let your readers escape into a world worth the living as I do with Lawrence around the campfire roasting venison over the flames as he chats to his black friend and gun bearer, the two of them perfectly content in the dark of the African bush, the flickering light from the flames of the fire running up and down the surrounding trees. Cheers, Jane. This whisky is just perfect."

"You want some cold turkey?"

"I'd love some cold turkey... How was your father?"

"Happy. He's no longer alone. Love in the twilight of life. It's just as beautiful as love in the spring."

"Write it down, Jane. Make it into another lovely story... Is she coming back today?"

"Who?"

"Tracey. Tracey and her daughter who could just be my daughter. The real and horrible world for both of us. But again it's probably not mine so it doesn't matter. All those men for Tracey. Take your pick. Where are you going?"

"To the kitchen. To get the turkey. We can eat it with our fingers... There. How does that sound? Beethoven. Ludwig van Beethoven by the sound of it."

"His Ninth Symphony. The last. Let's drink to Beethoven and his beautiful music. Let that horrible world outside stay away while the two of us enjoy ourselves together. Randall, Jane, a full bottle of whisky, cold turkey and a Beethoven symphony, and over there on the dinner table your beautiful book, Jane. Life can't get better. The story of Harvey and Vanessa is going to live forever."

"You're mad, Randall."

"Not today, Jane. Not today."

Hoping like hell Randall wasn't just being nice to her, she let him prattle on as the ice melted in their whisky glasses and the booze went down. And the following day was just another day but she did not have to go to work as she had taken the day off. Across the big living room was her book on the dinner table, a sight for sore eyes, a hope for her future and the joy she found like Randall in the writing. Writing fiction was the perfect escape into a better life than she and the rest of the people in the world hoped and craved for. Maybe, if she made a ton of money, she would buy her own home and soundproof it against the turmoil of people, and give herself peace. As was the case with all of them, Randall was talking about himself, telling the story of his white hunter in a life that no longer existed, the new Africa having brought the modern world to the doorstep of the African wilds, destroying its peace and tranquillity in a world of money-grabbing politics where money, and only money and wealth, were important.

"How did they communicate? He's black and has lived all his life in what you call the bush. How can he understand English? How can they talk round the campfire at the end of a day's hunting?"

"They taught each other their native language. Tonga now speaks understandable English and Lawrence has learned Shona. People have to communicate in whatever language they speak. Am I boring you? Tonight I'm the itinerant storyteller, the way I was when I started my saga with John Stokes and his wife, my neighbours who lived in total peace together on his Hasslet Farm on the Isle of Man, far from the madding crowd. You want some more whisky? All you've got in that glass of yours is melting ice. Have some more cold turkey. Give me the carving knife. You know, Jane, despite what I'm telling in my own story, your book is still in my head. Why I'm so happy tonight. Why I can't stop talking... There we go. A nice piece of cold turkey stuck on the end of the knife. Take it carefully. The blade of the knife is sharp. You got it. You know what I think we should do now we are both successful authors?"

"What's that, Randall?"

"We should become lovers. But not until we have finished this nice bottle of Scotch whisky. After we become lovers, you can finish your book in my soundproofed apartment and have it all typed. Then you give it to Manfred. You won't want to write here with a screaming baby girl. They all scream for attention. Been through it twice. Squalling kids. Can't think and write with squalling kids. Poor Tracey. She has no idea what she's let herself in for... Would you like to go to Africa, Jane? We could go on a long holiday and hire a camper. Tour South Africa and up the Skeleton Coast into what is now Namibia. Camp out in the bush. Get away from the world."

"What about my job as Manfred's assistant?"

"When your book sells a million copies you won't need a job."

"What about Manfred?"

"He'll find a replacement. His commission on a million copies of your book will be more than compensation. All a literary agent wants are successful authors. You'll join me and Tracey. Assistants are two a penny.

Good books are as rare as hen's teeth. There we are. Lots of ice doused in whisky. Cheers, Jane. Happy Christmas."

"I'd love to visit Africa."

"There's my girl."

"You really think it will sell a million copies?"

"Of course it will."

"Oh, my goodness. I'm going to be famous."

"To fame and fortune, Jane. Maybe we could find someone with a yacht to sail us to Cape Town and avoid all those airports."

"You're mad again, Randall."

"What's wrong with being a little nuts every now and again? This cold roast potato is quite delicious."

"Who wrote *Far from the Madding Crowd*?"

"I have no idea. I can't remember the author's name of every book I read. It's the book that counts, not the author. Oh, how I wish I lived in that earlier period without advertising agents and publicists all clacking away at the poor public. In those days it was all word of mouth. Maybe a critique in a literary journal or a newspaper. Authors didn't have to stand on their heads and whistle through their pricks to get attention."

"I don't have a prick, Randall."

"Then they'll have you flash your tits. Mark my words. It's all about getting the media and the public's attention. Selling books has nothing to do with a good book these days. Yes, you need a good book to begin with but after that, it's all in the marketing. Our lovely, brave new world is all about selling product. A nice private yacht to sail to Cape Town. How does it sound? Just the wind in the sail. No engine. No noise made by man. Peace on the ocean waves, the boat leaning with the wind, cutting the water. A couple of days in the pubs of Cape Town enjoying the local wine, then we stock the camper with food and lots of booze and head up the coast. The perfect couple without a care in the world. No worries, as they say in Australia. We won't have to worry about money or other people. Long, beautiful beaches all to ourselves. Fish for our supper. Oysters fresh from the sea. Swims in warm water."

"What about the sharks?"

"We'll have to watch out for the sharks."

"There are always sharks, Randall. Are we going to do any writing?"

"Storytelling, not writing. Around the cooking fire at night."

"And Mozart?"

"Not even Mozart. Just nature. You, me and nature, Jane."

"But we're not even lovers."

"But we will be. How's your whisky? Let me top it up for you. A little more ice in the glass and then lots of whisky. To your book, Jane. We're celebrating. Can you imagine all those millions of people who are going to be reading your book? You're going to tell your story to half the planet."

"How long are we going to spend in Africa?"

"As long as we like. Maybe forever."

"But I want children."

"Then our journey, our adventure, will last until you get pregnant. Cheers, my lover-to-be. Happy Christmas... Why do women always want to have children?"

"So the world can continue. If your mother hadn't had you, and my mother hadn't had me, we wouldn't be going on this wonderful adventure. Cheers, my future lover. Happy Christmas. Have some more turkey. Why do we talk so much crap when we drink?"

"We drink to get the crap out of us."

"So a good book doesn't matter, Randall?"

"Oh, you've got to have a good book or the whole process doesn't start. A good book gets the publisher's attention. Gets Manfred's attention. Got to have a good book, Jane, to get the ball rolling."

"So you're not kidding me about my book?"

"Of course I'm not."

Not sure if Randall was telling the truth or just being nice to her to get something he wanted, the usual game of life, Jane sipped her whisky and listened to the music as Randall went on with his story. And a role in the hay wouldn't be bad for either of them, sex a mutual satisfaction if it went right. She smiled at him, a slight twist in the corner of her mouth, the music of Beethoven flowing over Randall's story that let him dream in his other world.

"Why do they call it the Skeleton Coast? That sounds horrible. What kind of skeletons? People skeletons?"

"Sharks and whales I suppose. The carcasses wash up on the shore where they rot and bleach in the sun."

"Doesn't the sea wash them back into the water? How many skeletons?"

"We'll have to see. On the other side of Africa, they call it the Wild Coast. Some ancient explorer must have given the coastline the names.

We'll go as far as the border with Angola, where I hear they are fighting with each other despite the end of colonial rule."

"Why do people always fight with each other?"

"Human nature. Survival of the fittest, evolution eliminating the weak from the gene pool. Why man dominates the animal world. Why we conquered the rest of the animals by learning how to throw things at each other. Like stones and wooden spears. No other animal learned to throw what later with technology became bullets from guns. We'll keep out of Angola. If we find the perfect spot we can hire a little cottage with a nice double bed... Now, where was I? The story must go on. When we've finished the rest of the bottle of whisky we'll go upstairs to my double bed. We'll take the lift of course. We don't want Tracey to come home early tomorrow morning and find us in bed with each other."

"Why not?"

"She might be jealous. I'm just kidding. By the sound of it, she doesn't care who screws who, doesn't our darling Tracey. Anyway, to Tracey and her baby. Raise your glass, Jane. To life in the future. To man's survival. To the whole damn, crazy world."

"They should have called it the Sunshine Coast."

"But they didn't. Can't change a name once it happens. There must be a Sunshine Coast in the world."

"How are we going to find a private yacht to take us to Cape Town?"

"You go on this new-fangled thing they call the internet and search for boats to hire with a crew."

"It'll cost a fortune."

"Who cares? My books are still selling thanks to all those media interviews at the beginning of the year that chased me into my foxhole. But don't let me think of being interviewed ever again by the press and waffling on about myself."

"You're not doing badly, Randall. Waffling, I mean."

"I love your smile. Right. It's your turn. Your turn to talk about yourself. We'll leave Lawrence and Tonga alone. I want to know all about Jane and stop myself from becoming boring. And don't forget that happy ending you're going to write in your book. Harvey and Vanessa getting married and both living their days together happily for the rest of their lives on this beautiful planet with all those honest, trustworthy people who never lie or cheat or steal. Men and women of unbridled honour who only do that which is right, and never that which is wrong. Utopia, Jane. Let Harvey and Vanessa live in that fictitious world they call utopia. Never arguing with each other. Never nagging. Always happy and never miserable. Paint that picture at the end of your book and the world will put your book on a pedestal. They'll ooh and ah and gush over it as they point to how wonderful we humans really are. Your book will be an icon of the perfect world, the way they talk of great people they 'iconacised' in the past. King Richard the Lionheart, the great King of England who in reality killed anyone in his way who was a Muslim in his great crusade in the name of Christianity. Ten years he made war in the name of God. Making King Richard the Lionheart an icon salved their conscience for supporting the Christian Crusade. Who was right in those terrible years that raged through the Middle East in the twelfth century? And one day it'll happen all over again, wars in the name of religion. Make your book tell the same lies and make us look like perfect people."

"A happy ending for all of us."

"You've got it. Tell lies that make us happy. Shout it out in your interviews with the press. Tout it on the internet. Make us all look like heroes in our belief of living happily ever after instead of locked up in a foxhole avoiding the past and the future."

"But you're out of your foxhole. We're about to become lovers and travel the perfect adventure living in perfect harmony. Give me some more of that whisky and let me float up to that heaven, to your fictitious paradise on earth.... Thank you, my about-to-be lover. I'm getting nicely drunk. Cheers to our future. To my successful book. To my fame and fortune, the fame and fortune you already have. Let's drink to all those past and future iconic heroes, all a pile of horse shit."

"To horse shit, Jane. There's nothing wrong with a bit of horse shit. Two-thirds down. A third to go."

"Are we going to make love when we've drunk this bottle?"

"We may just open another bottle. You and Tracey do have another bottle in the cupboard?"

"More than one, Randall. We buy whisky by the case."

"Good girls. To the three musketeers. All for one, and one for all. To happiness. And a bottle of whisky."

Remembering all those times in her past, Jane knew seduction was all about timing. Picking the moment. Making the move. Telling herself she had nothing to lose, she walked over to the couch and bent over, putting both hands on the back of the couch behind Randall and showing him her boobs, trying to make him horny. All she got was a kiss on the nose and a pat on her bottom. Standing up in front of her about-to-be lover, Jane took off her clothes, knowing that what was underneath was damn near perfect from all the hours she spent keeping fit and never overeating. Naked, her legs apart, she took his hand and rubbed it over her crotch. In an instant their hormones screamed as Randall struggled to remove his trousers, Jane giving him frantic help so as not to lose the moment. When he entered her, Jane shouted 'Oh, yes'. Carefully, skilfully, Jane brought him to his climax, both of them coming together, the ultimate paradise on earth. When it was all over they hugged and started to giggle, both of them physically exhausted. Beethoven was still playing, as naked, side by side on the couch, they digested the reality of becoming lovers. Would it turn to love? For both of them, Jane hoped so. And without her book, she was sure it would never have happened. Quietly, holding on to each other, they fell into a perfect sleep.

When Jane woke feeling cold, the music was still filling the room. Without waking Randall, she went into her bedroom. Back in the lounge she covered Randall with the duvet and snuggled down next to him. They were lovers. Would it last? Only time would tell. She had turned off the music along with the lights on her way back from the bedroom. She could hear the rumbling and noise of the traffic from outside, the pulsing rhythm of New York, the real world with its joys, passions and problems, a world she mostly loved. From now on with Randall all she could do was hope. Hope for both of them they would stay together and be happy. And if Tracey came back early in the morning and found them naked on the couch, she would cross that bridge when she got to it, life with all its warts rarely predictable. Was the baby Randall's? Hopefully, they would never find out. All they needed now was a beautiful yacht to sail them to Cape Town in South Africa to start them on their great adventure. Smiling, content, sexually satisfied, Jane fell back into her dreams, dreams full of waves and a sea as far as the eye could see. A sailing boat alone on the ocean, never reaching its destination, never quite arriving, the man with her unknown, the face no one she had ever seen. Just as the face of the man was becoming clear, Jane woke with a start. Someone was putting a key in the lock of the front door. With no time to put on her clothes, and Randall gently snoring in his sleep, she covered them both with the big duvet and put on a smile. When the front door opened a baby began to cry, the noise filling the apartment.

"Who've you got under the cover, Jane? Why aren't you both in your bed? I nearly dropped her opening the door which is why she's crying. You want to see my baby? She's so cute. The most wonderful thing that has ever happened to me."

"Good morning, Tracey."

"Holy cow, it's Randall. What are you doing here, Randall? Shit, you're both naked. Put your clothes on, there's a baby in the room. Stop giggling, Jane. See what happens when I turn my back for even a moment? How did you do it? Oh, well. Back to normal, Randall. Not all bad. I'll put the kettle on."

"Randall read my book."

"So that's how it started. I'm calling her Allegra, a name that I hope will always bring joy, music and happiness to her life. How was your Christmas, or shouldn't I ask?"

"You're not annoyed with me?"

"Why ever should I be? What did you think of Jane's book, Randall? It's not finished. Doesn't have an ending."

"He came down three minutes after finishing it."

"So you took it up to him? I see. There's always method in your madness, Jane."

"He wants a happy ending."

"Don't we all?... Tea or coffee? I'm hungry."

"There's cold turkey in the fridge. Dad's going on a cruise with Sophie. First class. Sophie's paying. She's inherited a million bucks from her father."

"Now it all makes sense... There we go. Allegra in her new cot. Stop crying, darling. You're home... Put your clothes on, you two. I want you to look at my baby. She's so tiny... Cold turkey. Just what I fancy. I hate hospitals. They're so cold and organised. Anyone want any turkey? How are you, Randall? Haven't seen you in ages. Thought you'd locked yourself away for eternity. What you been doing?"

"Writing a book... Jane's book is going to top the charts. Have you read it?"

"Of course I have. It's just the ending that worries me. How are you going to give those two, you and Harvey, an ending that didn't happen, Jane?"

"Call it fiction... Now let me look at my best friend's little baby... Oh, she's so cute. Put on some clothes, Randall. Come and look. Tea for Randall and coffee for me. Happy Christmas, Tracey."

"A million dollars. That's a lot of money. How was your Christmas lunch? Are they going to get married? They can't be in love at that age. Love is all about sex. You'll see it all in my books. Is your father going to give up his job? He must be near to retirement. Lucky for Sophie I met her in the toilet of Harry B's. The luck of life. You walk into the ladies toilet in a state of misery and talk to a woman washing her hands in the basin next to you and it changes your world. Good for both of them. Your father had no social life whatsoever... How does she look, Randall? Luckily it was an easy birth. Look, she's watching you. Just look at those big eyes. She seems to have eyes only for you. Oh, well."

"Who's the father, Tracey?"

"I don't know. That was the whole idea. She's mine and only mine. You know what I'm talking about after two divorces. I can't be bothered with men's shit. She'll be mine until she flies the nest and starts a life on her own. We're going to have some fun together."

"Doesn't she need a father in her life?"

"Didn't help your two boys. When did you last see Douglas? No, Randall, I want to be my own woman and so does she. She won't be short of money growing up."

"She could be mine, Tracey. Nine months and a week since I fell asleep on the job."

"You don't want to know, Randall. Anyway, what are the chances of getting pregnant on a one-night stand?"

"I'm looking at her. We could have a blood test to prove it one way or the other."

"Don't be ridiculous. I said I don't want to know."

"But I do."

"Did you screw Jane last night? Of course you did. Men! Put it this way: there are half a dozen men with a better chance of being the father."

"How do you mean?"

"The timing of my menstrual cycle, Randall. This beautiful little thing here wasn't a fluke. I wanted it to happen. Why I stopped taking the pill."

"Let's have a blood test if you are so sure it wasn't me. Otherwise, I'll spend the rest of my life wondering if she's mine. Allegra. Never heard anyone called Allegra before. Can I pick her up?"

"You might drop her. By the look of that almost empty bottle of whisky, I'd say you two were drinking before you crashed out on the couch. You might drop her. Leave it all alone, Randall."

"I can't."

"Sorry, no luck. She's mine. There we go, my one-night stand. Tea as I remember you like it, Randall... There we go, Jane. Coffee just as you like it. So, you two are lovers. Interesting. Are you on the pill, Jane? Oh, dear, no you're not. You can see everything in a person's expression. Now I've got the giggles. Have some cold turkey. Now just look at that. My little one has fallen asleep."

"Are you quite sure she isn't mine?"

"You're never sure of anything in this life, Randall. You should know. And being sure won't help anyone. She's alive. Going to have a life. That's all that's important. And if she turned out to be yours, you wouldn't want to marry me any more than I want to marry you. Fact is, I don't want to marry anyone. It was a one-night stand. We got drunk together. Leave it alone."

"You seduced me."

"Takes two to tango, Randall. Otherwise it's just jerking off. What have you been up to on your own? Are you writing? Good, you're smiling again."

"And if she grows up looking like my mother?"

"You don't even remember your mother. Neither does Phillip. I'm sorry, I know that hurts... Now, this is fun again. The three musketeers. Give me a hug. I'll tell you what. After the tea and coffee, why don't we each have ourselves a little whisky? I want to celebrate. Celebrate with me. The musketeers have a baby. The fourth musketeer. We don't just have books in common. We have sex. Lust. And now we have a baby. She'll be ours. How does that sound? She'll belong to all three of us. Except that neither of you will have a say."

"You're avoiding the issue, Tracey."

"Of course I am, Randall. Now, what can you tell me? What's been happening in your life?"

"Absolutely nothing. Until Jane came calling. Now we'll have to see."

"We're going to charter a private yacht and sail to South Africa, hire a camper and go up the Skeleton Coast. We're going on an adventure."

"Do you know, I think I'm a little jealous."

"As I am of your baby. I too want a child."

"You never know your luck."

"You're giggling, Tracey. Why are you giggling?"

"You never know. For me, getting pregnant was one big, happy surprise. Can I have a whisky?"

"Don't be ridiculous. It's ten o'clock in the morning."

"So what? Let's all get drunk together."

"What about the baby?"

"At that age they sleep most of the time. Or so I hope. We're all a bunch of drunks."

"A three-day bender, girls. How about that? We always break the rules. In this crazy life you never know what's going to happen next. And what happens if Jane gets pregnant?"

"The plot grows thicker. Get some ice, Jane. Forget about the coffee. We're going to celebrate. What would we ever have done without Randall Crookshank in our lives? Books and booze."

"And babies."

"We're not going to have a blood test, Randall."

"Are you sure?"

"Absolutely goddamn certain. That child is going to be mine. And no one else's. When are you two going on your yacht, Randall?"

"I have absolutely no idea. You know what? Both of you are as mad as hatters. We're all nuts. Mad as March hares. It's so nice to be back in your company again. And mark my words: Jane, here, is going to join us on the bestseller lists, Tracey. Now, where's that whisky? Let's get started. For the first time since my wife walked out on me I'm happy. There we go. An attack of the giggles. You're right, Tracey. Does it matter for Allegra whose sperm gave her life? She's alive. That's what matters. She's going to have a life of her own. And when you go back in our histories more than three or four generations, none of us have any idea of where we came from. But we're alive. Put on some music, Jane. Turn on the music channel. You never know your luck. It may be Mozart. The big trick in life is to live in the present. And enjoy ourselves. Are we going to enjoy ourselves? Of course we are."

"Why do we always say 'of course we are'?"

"It's like the meaning of the word belief. We're not quite sure. But we want it to happen. We want to believe that if we behave ourselves on this earth we will go to heaven. Faith. Hope. 'Of course we are.' 'I believe I'm going to heaven.' They all have the same background of not quite knowing what is going to be. All we really know is what we see right in front of us. The rest is in our imagination. Imagining what we want in the future. Hoping. And believing it will happen. Now, let's get the glasses and the ice and make it happen. The three musketeers having fun together. Life's a whole lot more simple than we make it out to be. The hope for Allegra is she has good genes. From mother and father.

They always say choosing your parents carefully is the secret of a successful life. It's all in the genes. The good and the bad. And most often we don't want to know what's in our genes. Do you want to know if you have an eighty per cent chance of getting breast cancer and pass it on to that child sleeping in the cot? I don't think so. Or you would never have wished to get yourself pregnant. And that goes for either one of you. How did this all start?"

"I asked why we always say 'of course'."

"Of course you did, Tracey. How stupid of me. A new baby. A new bestseller about to happen. Let's get started. Let's celebrate. I've missed you two girls so much you just have no idea."

"Then why did you lock yourself up in your foxhole?"

"Because I was a pain in the arse. Thanks for pulling me out, Jane. Are you on the pill, by the way?"

"I'm not telling you."

"Girls! They're as bad as men. Now just listen to that. It's a Mozart piano concerto and everything in our lives is going to turn out just fine."

"I've got to work tomorrow. I can't go on drinking."

"Call in sick, Jane. You said you two buy your whisky by the case. By the time we've drunk through the whole day and late into the evening we'll all be as sick as dogs tomorrow. But who cares? Live in the present, girls."

"When I breast feed Allegra drunk, will she get some of the alcohol? I never drank when I was pregnant on doctors' orders."

"Even more reason for nailing the whisky. Now, let's have some fun and let the world take care of itself. Manfred won't mind. He'll understand. Especially when I tell him he has another bestselling novelist in his gun sight. Happy days are here again. That was a song, back in the day. We're happy. Got what we want. Life as it should be. For the first time since Meredith walked out on me I'm not thinking of buying a gun."

"What were you going to do with a gun?"

"Shoot myself, Tracey."

"That's the coward's way out."

"Not always. Sometimes life is so appalling the only way is to take your own life. It's a brave man who kills himself. Or at least I believe so. There I go again. Belief. Hope. Faith. You see, in life we just never know. Always try to make good memories and forget about the bad ones. Today is a day for making a good memory for all of us. Whisky, two lovely women and the music of Mozart. What more can a man hope for the day after Christmas?"

Not sure what was going on, Jane drank her coffee wondering what was going to happen next in her life. She was at that point in her month when getting pregnant was most likely but there was no point in telling Randall. In the days she was drinking heavily and screwing any man who came along, she had never fallen pregnant. Very often, she had no idea if she had taken her contraceptive pill. Was she fertile, or were all those young men infertile? Like not telling Randall, it was better not to know.

Tracey was drinking her coffee while Randall filled the ice bucket from the ice in the fridge, putting the bucket and what was left of last night's whisky bottle on the coffee table in front of her. Back with three glasses, Randall sat down back on the sofa and smiled at them. Tracey used her remote to change the music channel on the decoder. Despite the coffee, Jane's hangover was getting worse, the idea of getting drunk again and suffering another hangover the next day no longer pleasant. Randall had poured whisky into the glass full of ice he had placed in front of her. The new music, harsh and loud, jarred on her jaded nerves. Tracey went to check her sleeping baby, the atmosphere in the room a mix of Tracey's smug satisfaction at having her baby, Randall's look of worry mixed with uncertainty, and Jane's own feeling of being lost, part of her still happy with Randall's reaction to her book and part of her being jealous of not having a baby, making her sense of achievement empty and worthless. Was she ever going to have a child, let alone a marriage? Or was her life to be drinking to avoid the emptiness that was all Jane could see in her future, a woman getting older and older until one day soon men wouldn't so much as bother to look at her? And if her book sold ten million copies it wouldn't make the slightest bit of difference. She would still be Jane Slater, a girl on her own, a woman on her own, an old lady on her own, finally going to her grave with nothing to show for anything.

"Oh, what the hell? Cheers, everyone. I hate this music, Tracey."

"So do I."

"Try again. Copy Randall's famous book and movie and go to the *Love Song* channel. I hate my hangover. So here we are again. The three of us. I'm so happy your baby is healthy. Here's to the glorious future that will come to little Allegra. To the next generation. Here we go again, Randall. Two old drunks trying to have fun."

"We're having fun."

"Are we? And if you say 'of course we are' again I'll wring your goddamn neck."

"What's the matter with you, Jane?"

"I've got a hangover. And last night was all my fault. Where are we all going? What are we really up to? I just don't understand life anymore. They tell you to strive for happiness, love and money. Yes, money may come if you're lucky. Do the others? And if they do, is it only temporary? You're right, Randall. Let's get drunk. Who the hell knows about anything in this crazy life? Drinking whisky at half past ten in the morning. We must be out of our minds. I'll probably get fired. But who cares?"

"Have a baby, Jane. It'll make you more positive. Always look on the bright side."

"More clichés, Tracey. I wish I could. But at my age it's probably too late. I'd be pushing sixty before the child flew the nest."

"With a little help from Randall, you just never know. Go on your yacht. Go on your holiday. Make each other happy. Help each other the way we helped Sophie meet your father again. And now look at them. They're happy together... Anyone know who's singing this song? Never mind. It's nice. Just like my little glass full of ice and whisky. And my baby. I love that child with a passion so deep it almost hurts."

"Where are you going, Tracey?"

"To look out of the big window, Jane. Look at that. It's raining, water dripping down the outside of the plate-glass window. All that bustle down there. On the fifteenth floor we're part of it. From Randall's thirty-first floor the movement was distant. Home, sweet home. Oh, well. She'll have to get used to it. There's always a walk in the park. And when you have lots and lots of lovely money you can go on a holiday. Visit the countryside. Look at the birds and the bees. Just look at New York out there. There's just so much of it. Great buildings after great buildings. And all I have to do is sit in my study and write my books. Chase the media. Keep my name constantly in the public eye. Always do what your publicist tells you to do. Never miss a single chance to get your name in the papers or your smiling face on the television. What do you say, Randall? It's all about publicity, selling books."

"Makes me want to vomit. The wolves will be back howling in my head. Please don't bring back that horror. When the wolves howl I want to kill myself. Come and sit down. Drink your whisky. The wolves. I hate the wolves. Why I shut myself away."

"What wolves, Randall?"

"You'll know when they come to you."

"I love all the publicity. It makes me feel good inside myself, people telling me they love my book. That look on their faces of being near to celebrity. It's not just the money. I love being loved by my readers. There's nothing wrong in life giving millions of people pleasure. It's all part of the great world of entertainment. These days you don't have to go to the theatre or a concert. You can turn on the television. Turn on the music channel, whichever one you want. We are among those who provide the content without which there would be no entertainment."

"You and I are so different, Tracey, you have no idea. I like talking my story to people when they are in the room with me. Know who I am talking to. Have a relationship with them. Not just some movie on the box based on one of my stories. It's like they steal your story. Take it away from you forever. Can you imagine those wonderful days when Mozart sat at the piano in the court of the king and played them his music? Only then did he know if his music was any good. He could see people's reaction in their eyes. He didn't need publicity. All he had to do was compose his beautiful music and feel the pleasure flowing back from his audience. They were all part of the same beautiful experience. Now that's entertainment. Today's entertainment is artificial. Most of it sold to us through advertising. Brainwashing. And most of it's junk. Let's drink and be happy in the company of good friends. Real friends. Old friends. Lovers, even. Or the wolves will return to torment me again. Now, let me tell you a story. It was all those years ago in Africa. In the last century. The sun was shining and Tonga was climbing a msasa tree to look out over the great grasslands and watch the wild animals as they grazed. Below, at the foot of the tree, his back comfortably against the bottom of the trunk, sat Lawrence Templeton-Smythe smoking a pipe. There was peace on earth. For three months they had roamed the bush and seen not another man or woman. They were alone in paradise. And then Tonga, from his perch on top of the tree, shouted 'Elephant', and the hunt began..."

Smiling, Jane listened happily to Randall's story. They were more than lovers. They were friends. Would he change his mind about a trip to Africa? She hoped not. And just maybe she was not infertile. When Tracey went to the kitchen and brought back another bottle of whisky, the music channel was again playing classical music. It was gone twelve o'clock in the afternoon, the rain still dripping down the outside of the big plate-glass window. Their day was unfolding, a day of friends, music and an itinerant storyteller. They were making a memory. Tracey, breast feeding her new baby in front of them as she sat on the couch, was as beautiful a picture of a human being as Jane had ever seen. It made Jane begin to hope with all her heart that Randall would make her pregnant, that her life too would continue through her children, the genes passed down from generation to generation for all eternity. When Randall finished telling the latest chapter in his story, her hangover had gone, replaced by the high of alcohol. All three of them were relaxed, the baby asleep in her cot. Not sure if giving a story to only two other people or letting it out into the world by making it into a book was a less selfish form of entertainment, she went into Tracey's kitchen to make them nice turkey sandwiches to douse the alcohol and let them enjoy their drinking for the rest of the day. From the kitchen she listened to Randall and Tracey talking away.

"I so miss my Africa, girls. What am I doing living in a concrete jungle? I'd so love to be Tonga or Lawrence."

"We're going to Africa, don't forget. Sailing the seas on a yacht. We'll camp out in your lovely bush, just the two of us all alone in the wilds like Tonga and Lawrence. You will write down what you just told us? You must. There are so many people in this overpopulated world crammed into cities who would love to escape into the bush through your story. You can curl up with a good book and go where it takes you, the perfect escape from noise and people. There we go. Have a sandwich. Stops me from getting drunk too quickly. Why don't we go on our trip as soon as I find us someone with a yacht? The chances are good for finding what we want through the internet. How the world has changed in a hundred and ten years from the days of your lovely story. Do we live better lives with all our so-called wealth? All that artificial materialism? I wonder. Anyway, it's better to be inside today. Just look at all that rain."

From the pouring rain, Jane looked at her book on the dining room table, the book that had started her affair with Randall. Inwardly smiling at the hope of being pregnant, of Randall's sperm nicely fertilising one of her eggs, she sat back on the couch next to her new boyfriend and ate one of her sandwiches.

"You keep looking at your book on the table."

"Of course I do, Randall."

"These sandwiches are nice."

"Of course they are."

Laughing at their own joke, Jane and her two friends sat comfortably eating, chatting and drinking whisky, no longer a care in the world. Life was all about hope. Tracey hoping to keep her child to herself. Randall hoping that the wolves would stay out of his mind. And Jane hoping by the strangest touch and luck of life that Randall's fertility would do the same for her as it had done for Amanda, Meredith and maybe even Tracey. Only then would she have a future. Taking Randall's left hand, she brought it up to her mouth and kissed the back of it gently.

"What was that all about?"

"Thank you, Randall. Thank you for everything. Thank you for loving my book. Thank you for becoming my lover. It's been a wonderful Christmas."

"And it's not over, you two lovers. Pass the whisky bottle. I'm getting happily drunk."

"How often do you have to feed your baby?"

"I have no idea. I suppose she'll squall when she's hungry."

"And what happens if you're too drunk to get up?"

"Then she'll have to go on squalling and I'll ask you, Jane, to take her into the bathroom and shut the door. Anyway, she sucked me dry. Let the day go on. We'll have to see."

By the time the light began to fade outside the rain-soaked window, Randall had gone horribly silent, a faraway look of fear making his chin twitch. His eyes were watery, and the hand holding his glass of iced whisky was shaking. He had taken himself off to sit on a dining room chair which he had turned to face them. Tracey had stopped talking. The only sound came from the rumblings of New York City and some rock and roll band on the television's music channel. Jane looked at Tracey and back at Randall, who now had sweat forming on his forehead.

"What's the matter, Randall? You look awful. Are you coming down with something?"

"It's the wolves. It's the wolves. The wolves are back."

"You're shouting."

"I must go. This didn't work. Alcohol never works."

"You're going to fall."

"Who cares? Damn the bloody steps. I hate these apartments."

"Do you want me to come up with you?"

"I want to be alone. The wolves are howling."

"I'll search tomorrow for a yacht."

"Do what you like. It's the end. The wolves. The wolves."

When the front door slammed, Jane began to cry.

"Don't cry, Jane. Men are all the same. Once they screw you they go their own way. You had a one-night stand, Janey. Don't get upset. The poor man is fucked in the head. Men like that end up killing themselves."

"But I want to go to Africa. I want to have a future."

"Now the baby's squalling. Must feed my little one. Don't get too upset, Jane. Maybe when he sobers up and the hangover goes he'll come down again. All that twaddle about faith, hope and belief. All you got, girl. Hope. Do your bit. Search the net and find a yacht before Randall Crookshank finds himself a gun. Hemingway shot himself. Artists are highly strung... There we are, my baby. Mother's milk. Don't cry. The slamming of the door woke you up. Don't upset your Aunty Jane more than she is already. This is the way to go, Jane. A single mother who doesn't have to put up with men."

"He was shaking all over. I must go up to him."

"Don't be stupid. Let him deal with his own demons. Nothing you can do anymore. You tried. Didn't work. How it goes. Be a good girl and open another bottle of whisky. I always say: if you're going to do a job, do it properly. Let's the two of us get drunk. Well and truly drunk."

"For a moment I thought we had something."

"You never know. Hope. You just got to hope."

"You're giggling."

"Of course I am. And there we go again. Get the whisky and fill the ice bucket... This baby can really suck. Lucky she doesn't have teeth."

"So you think it's over with me and Randall?"

"Who knows?"

"I'm going up to him."

"Leave him alone. Tomorrow. The next day. When you've found your yacht. Then go up to him. Finish your book with that highly unlikely happy ending. There are no happy endings in most people's lives. They're all in books. The happy endings are all in the books."

THE SAGA WILL CONTINUE in the sixteenth volume in the Brigandshaw Chronicles, *Lovers for Today*.

PRINCIPAL CHARACTERS

~

The Crookshanks
Douglas Crookshank — Randall and Meredith's baby son
Jeremy and Bergit Crookshank — Phillip and Randall's parents
Phillip Crookshank — Randall's elder brother
Randall Crookshank — central character in *When Friends Become Lovers*

Other Principal Characters
Amelia — barmaid at Harry B's
Belinda Chang — assistant editor at Villiers Publishing
Clint — an artist who Meredith meets at her art club
Faith Tyndall (nee White) — Manfred Leon's assistant
Ferdinand — Tracey's insurance boss before she became a successful author
Godfrey Merchant — proprietor of Merchant Publishers
Henry Stone — editor at Villiers Publishing
Jane Slater — Tracey's neighbour and out of work editor
Jim Slater — Jane's widowed father
John and Wynne Stokes — Randall's neighbours on the Isle of Man
Manfred Leon — Randall's New York literary agent
Mr Everard — a newspaper reporter who Randall has a fight with

Nora Stewart — Randall's American independent publicist appointed by Villiers Publishing
Norman Landry — an American film director
Poppy Maddock — a film script writer who writes the script for *Love Song*
Rebecca — a young aspiring actress Randall meets in Harry B's
Shelley — Meredith's art teacher
Sophie Roberts — an older woman Tracey meets in Harry B's
Stanislas Wellensky — a young Polish man who Tracey meets in a bar
Teddy — a Harry B's customer that Tracey befriends
Terry Flanagan — the owner of Harry B's bar in New York
Tracey Chapelle — a young, aspiring author

DEAR READER

~

Reviews are the most powerful tools in our kitty when it comes to getting attention for Peter's books. This is where you can come in, as by providing an honest review you will help bring them to the attention of other readers.

If you enjoyed reading *When Friends Become Lovers*, and have five minutes to spare, we would really appreciate a review (it can be as short as you like). Your help in spreading the word and keeping Peter's work alive is gratefully received. Please post your review on the retailer site where you purchased this book.

Thank you so much.
Heather Stretch (Peter's daughter)

ACKNOWLEDGEMENTS

~

Our grateful thanks go to our *VIP First Readers* for reading *When Friends Become Lovers* prior to its official launch date. They have been fabulous in picking up errors and typos helping us to ensure that your own reading experience of *When Friends Become Lovers* has been the best possible. Their time and commitment is particularly appreciated.

Agnes Mihalyfy (United Kingdom)
Daphne Rieck (Australia)
Hilary Jenkins (South Africa)

Thank you.
Kamba Publishing

Printed in Great Britain
by Amazon